"Promise me you will not forget."

"Forget?" She lifted her hand, gazing at him with more tenderness than he'd thought could exist in this world. "I shall not forget a minute of this night, not a moment. But before I go—please, kiss me once more. Kiss me . . . as if you were doing it for the last time."

At that moment, he'd have climbed the sky and given her the moon if she'd asked for it.

He took her in his arms and held her slight form against him, wondering how someone so fragile had managed to break down all the high walls he'd ringed around his heart. Nobility warred with lust inside him, and lust won handily. Groaning, he lowered his lips toward hers. . . .

Gambler's Daughter

Gambler's Daughter

Ruth Owen

All the best,
Ruth Owen
5/99

BANTAM BOOKS

NEW YORK TORONTO LONDON SYDNEY AUCKLAND

Gambler's Daughter
A Bantam Book / May 1999

ISBN 0-553-57742-5

Published simultaneously in the United States and Canada

Bantam Books are published by Bantam Books, a division of Random House, Inc. Its trademark, consisting of the words "Bantam Books" and the portrayal of a rooster, is Registered in U.S. Patent and Trademark Office and in other countries. Marca Registrada. Bantam Books, 1540 Broadway, New York, New York 10036.

PRINTED IN THE UNITED STATES OF AMERICA

OPM 10 9 8 7 6 5 4 3 2 1

To Carol and Michael Quinto,
two of the brightest stars in heaven.
I miss you.

Gambler's
Daughter

Chapter
One

"That's his daughter," Lavinia Sneed whispered to
Agnes Peak as she nudged her soundly in the ribs.
"The tall girl standing alone at the grave's edge. That's
Murphy's daughter, sure as frost."

Agnes craned her stubby neck to follow her friend's
gaze over the somber crowd assembled in the small
London graveyard. Her eyes flickered past the priest,
whose words of spiritual comfort jarred with his well-
fed cheeks and haughty countenance, and the various
mourners, whose expressions ranged from boredom and
impatience to gawking curiosity. Daniel Murphy wasn't
the most popular man in Cheapside, or the most well-
respected, but he was easily the most infamous, and precious few had passed up the chance to see the notorious
gambler laid to rest.

A fat man in front of her shifted to the left, and
Agnes spotted a slim, black-garbed woman standing
alone by the granite headstone, her head bent low in
prayer. The falling snow dusted her long eyelashes and
her auburn hair, which was pulled back in a severe bun.
Aggie frowned, feeling vaguely cheated. Daniel Murphy

had been as handsome as the devil, but his daughter was plain as a pikestaff. "You certain that's her, Livy?"

"Course I am. Got his hair, don't she? Nobody gets red hair like that unless they got a bloomin' Irishman for a da."

"Well, she didn't get the rest of his looks," Agnes commented bluntly as she pulled her coat closer against the bitter March wind.

"It's the Almighty's own justice it is," Livy pronounced, then paused as she blew a honking sneeze into a flimsy lace handkerchief that was woefully inadequate for the task. Sniffing loudly, she bent back down to Agnes's ear. "Sabrina Murphy may look all pious and holy, but I've got it on good authority that her soul's as black as the inside of a witch's cupboard."

Agnes gasped. "You don't say."

"I most certainly do say," Livy whispered with a knowing nod. "That girl's got a temper like hell's own fire, God forgive me for speaking so bold. She's nearly nineteen, but they say that no man has ever come to court her, nor likely will, considering her looks and her unfortunate disposition. More than once she's driven her poor stepmother to vapors."

Aggie's gaze traveled to the well-padded matron standing with regimental stiffness at the priest's side. The widow Murphy didn't look like the kind of woman who could be driven to vapors by a mere girl, however ill-tempered, but if Livy said it, it must be true. Besides, everyone knew that Daniel Murphy was a rake and a rascal, and it followed that his daughter would be the same. "Who's that young man standing just behind the widow?"

"Her son, Albert Tremaine. By her first husband Ned, who died fighting in the Peninsula War. They say he were a fine man, and his son takes after 'im. A better, more devoted boy never lived."

Considering Albert's girth, Aggie doubted whether he was devoted to anything beyond his dinner plate, but she kept the sentiment to herself. Instead, her gaze was drawn back to the bleak, snow-dusted figure on the other side of the grave, standing so still that she might have been carved of granite herself. An unexpected twinge of pity tugged at Aggie's heart. Sabrina Murphy had just lost her father, even if that father was only a worthless gambler like Daniel Murphy. It was a hard thing for a young girl to bear, even an ill-tempered one. "What will become of her?"

"A better fate than she deserves, and that's a fact. Mrs. Murphy takes in boarders, and I know she's let her stepdaughter tutor some of the tenants' children. Seems the girl knows something of French and such, though it takes more than book learning to make a silk purse out of a sow's ear, if you take my meaning. Good manners can be taught, but good breeding—"

Livy paused, and used her thumbnail to pick a bit of beef from between her teeth. "Good breeding's in the blood, Aggie, and that girl's blood is rife with sin."

The priest closed his prayer book with a harsh snap. With the weather turning bleaker by the minute, the crowd broke up in a hurry, leaving the memory of notorious Daniel Murphy behind like their muddy boot-prints in the snow. The widow also turned to go, pausing just long enough to order her stepdaughter along. The woman might as well have spoken to the headstone. Sabrina remained standing by the grave, her head bent and her hands clasped in front of her, ignoring both the chilling wind and her stepmother's wishes.

"See, what did I tell you?" Livy hissed as she and

Aggie watched the widow depart the cemetery with Albert in tow. "That wicked girl is trouble sure. Never a thought for the poor, grieving mother. Shameless, I call it. As shameless as her brazen red hair."

"I don't see how we can blame her for the color of her hair," Aggie offered as they turned to go.

Livy brushed aside the comment. "She's got her father's red hair and her father's black heart, and she'll come to a bad end, you mark my words. Blood will tell, Aggie. Blood will . . . ooh, look, there's that Betsy Miller. Now you know I ain't one to carry tales, but I heard tell that she and the butcher's boy . . ."

The sky grew bleaker and the wind blew stronger, in sharp, stabbing gusts through the cemetery. It drove the snowflakes like slithering white snakes across the dark granite slabs, piling them up into the joins and cracks that abounded in the graveyard. A small, frigid blow swirled the snow against the yard's newest headstone, building it into a sudden heap that obscured the occupant's name. In her first move since the funeral ended, Sabrina Murphy knelt down beside the stone and carefully brushed out each one of the carved letters.

Pay it no mind, Rina-lass. Pay it no mind.

Her father's loud, laughing voice echoed in her mind. Daniel Murphy had never given a brass farthing for appearances—the costly headstone had been her stepmother's idea, not his. He'd never pretended to be anything other than what he was, and had shrugged off the jibes and insults of the self-righteous as easily as he'd shrugged off an unlucky roll of the dice. As a young girl Sabrina had striven to do the same, but no matter how hard she tried, she always ended up running into her father's arms in tears. "Ah, Rina-lass," he'd say as he gathered her against him, stroking her hair, "you've your mother's soft heart and that's a fact. It's a powerful blessing, and a powerful responsibility, to feel things so fine and deep. But the small, mean words, said by small, mean people—pay it no mind. It's a sure bet they'll all be singing a different tune when our ship comes in. Pay it no mind."

And she hadn't—or she'd tried not to whenever the other children made fun of her for being a gambler's daughter. As she'd grown older she'd been able to hide her feelings so successfully that in time she seemed to forget how to feel at all. Sometimes she wondered if the cure wasn't worse than the symptom. She hadn't shed a single tear for her father, even though his passing had left an aching hole in the place where other people kept their hearts.

She brushed out the final letter and sat back on her heels. *Here lies Daniel Patrick Murphy, beloved husband of Eugenia Tremaine Murphy*. Anger kindled inside her. She scooped up a handful of snow and smeared it against the granite, obscuring her stepmother's name. "Papa, I know you're with mama and little Shawn now. That woman has no hold over you, whatever the stone says."

A bell tolled. Sabrina's head jerked up as she looked at the clock in the church tower. Heavens, was it *that* late? If she didn't get back to the boardinghouse soon she'd miss her tutoring session—her last, though she was the only one who knew it.

Carefully she reached into her pocket and pulled out a folded letter. "It came this morning, Papa. From the Hampton School for Young Ladies of Quality. They want me to come and work for them as soon as possible. They even sent me the fare. I've got a job, a good one. And if Stepmother doesn't like it, I'll happily tell her to—"

A strand of hair whipped across her cheek, as if to censor her unladylike words. Sabrina tucked the unruly strand behind her ear, a soft smile rising to her lips for the first time in longer than she could remember. "Well, it's your own fault, Daniel Murphy. Stepmother may have tried to make a proper lady of me, but at the end of the day I'm still a gambler's daughter."

"That you are, lassie."

Sabrina glanced up in alarm, and saw a short, wiry fellow with a face like a dried apple. He looked down at her with a mischievous smile, his elbows propped on the sacred marker as if he were bellying up to the taproom bar. His well-worn brown topcoat was suitably somber, but the bright yellow-striped waistcoat he wore underneath looked as if it had been cut from the side of a gaudy carnival tent.

Sabrina leapt to her feet and started to back away, conscious of the fact that she was alone in a graveyard with a total stranger, even if that stranger looked about as dangerous as an organ-grinder's monkey.

Apparently he sensed her alarm. "Lord in heaven, child, I ain't goin' to hurt you. It's you I've come to see, if'n you're Dan'l's girl, that is."

"I am," she replied cautiously as she continued to back away, "though I don't see as that's any of your business, sir."

"Sir," he repeated, his grin widening. "Very pretty. I can see there's a bit of Katie Poole in you."

"You knew my mother?"

"Aye. She was the fairest colleen in all County Cork, though few knew it since her parsimonious father kept her locked up like a porcelain doll." He left the headstone and walked over to her, offering his hand. "The name's Quinn, lassie."

Quinn. She hadn't heard the name in years, not since those golden years when her mother was still alive. Sabrina and her family had lived in a small house in Sussex, but to Rina it had seemed like a palace, because the rooms were always filled with laughter. Her father had a steady job as the head groom at a nearby farm, and her mother had taken in fancy needlework and laundry. During the day her mother would teach her her letters, or take Rina with her as she delivered food and extra clothing to the poorer families in the neighborhood. But at night she'd sit with her father by the fire and listen as he spun fantastic, flamboyant tales of Irish kings and warriors.

She loved his elaborate yarns, but her favorite story by far—the one she'd made him tell her over and over again—was absolutely true. It was the tale of a beautiful lady who'd grown up in a grand but loveless manor house. Her father, Lord Harry Poole, was a greedy man who cared more for land than his daughter's happiness, and had pledged her to marry a fat, wealthy merchant. She'd been resigned to her fate—until she'd looked into the green eyes of her father's bold, red-haired groom, and found love. Laughing merrily, Sabrina's father would tell how he and her mother had outfoxed Lord Poole and eloped, escaping to England only a step ahead of the law. But that escape would not have been possible without the help of Daniel's mate, the man who'd helped him rescue the beautiful Katie and had stood up for him at his wedding. Michael Quinn.

Sabrina reached out her hand, warmly clasping the man's offered one. "Papa told me about you. You used to call him the King of Diamonds."

"Aye, and he called me the Knave," Quinn added, giving his knee a lusty slap. "Together we gave the magistrates a gray hair or two, and that's a fact! Your da was the best mate I ever had, and it's sorry I am that I came too late to be saying the same to himself. Dan'l had his faults but he were a good man. He knew how to live. And to love."

In a few short words Quinn had summed up her father far better than the flowery, pretentious words of the minister's oration. She thought about the crowd gathered around the grave. The people had only known her father as a drunk and a gambler, a disappointed man who'd died long before the consumption took his life. "Thank you," she said softly, gripping Quinn's hand a little tighter. "I'm only sorry you had to come all this way for nothing."

"But it weren't for nothing. Dan'l passing is a fierce disappointment, but it's you I came to see."

"Me?"

"I told him when he left that I'd be on the lookout for a situation, something that would set us up for the rest of our lives. Well, I finally found it. The sweetest deal you ever did see. Practically like taking candy from a babe."

The word *deal* set off Rina's mental alarms. She'd seen the same nefarious gleam in her father's eyes when he was getting ready to tell her about one of his gambling schemes. "Mr. Quinn, is this, um, situation you're talking about legal?"

Quinn dropped his gaze, and self-consciously brushed a bit of snow from his waistcoat. "Of course it's legal. Well, mostly. Look, it don't signify. There's easy money to be made, enough money to keep both you and me comfortable for the rest of our lives. You'd be beholden to no one except your own sweet self."

Beholden to no one. The words spun through Sabrina's mind like a brightly twirling kaleidoscope. To live by her own rules. To have enough money to buy her own house in the country, with a flower garden and well-trimmed hedgerows, and maybe a horse or two. To wake up in the morning to a life where she didn't have to worry about the dishes to be washed, or the bread to be baked, or the lessons to be graded . . . well, she was enough of her father's daughter to be tempted by the notion. But the beautiful dream sputtered out. She had an honest future ahead of her—staid and unremarkable, but honest. She'd seen what a life of empty dreams and wishes had done to her father, and she wanted no part of it. "I'm sorry, Mr. Quinn. I know you mean well, but—"

The church bell chimed again.

"Heavens, I'm late!" She turned back to Quinn. "Forgive me, I cannot stay. My stepmother—"

"Will have your guts for garters if you're late," Quinn supplied colorfully. He pulled off his cap and stroked back what was left of his hair, which was sparse but still bright as a copper penny. "Be off with you, lass. But I'll be staying at the Green Dragon in Greygallows Lane through Sunday, if'n you change your mind."

She leaned over and gave him a swift, impulsive kiss. "Thank you, sir. For everything. I . . . I hope we shall meet each other again."

Quinn watched her hurry toward the iron gate of the churchyard, noting how she moved among the stones with a dancer's grace, and how her thick, auburn hair escaped from her torturous bun and cascaded across her shoulders like a ruddy waterfall.

The Red Queen.

"Oh, we'll meet again, my red-haired lassie," he breathed quietly. "There's more of Dan'l Murphy in you than you know."

•   •   •

"The mistress wants to see ya."

Sabrina laid aside her book, reluctantly giving up the first free moment she'd had during the week since her father's death. Tilly, the second maid, leaned against the doorjamb of her attic room. The ribbon had come free from her sloppily tied mob-cap, and a shank of blond hair hung down across her forehead. A plump, blowzy girl with a lazy disposition, Tilly had nevertheless managed to become one of Widow Murphy's favorites without doing a lick of real work. Personally Sabrina suspected that Tilly's lofty status had more to do with Albert's approval than his mother's, but she kept that opinion to herself. "I'll be done with this in a quarter hour. Please inform my stepmother that I'll be down directly."

"You want me to go all the way down them stairs again?" Tilly complained.

"Yes, I do," Sabrina replied evenly. "Unless you can think of another way to tell her."

Their gazes met in a test of mettle, but Tilly broke the stare first. Looking down, she sniffed loudly and wiped her nose with the back of her hand. "I'll tell mistress," she said with reluctant compliance, then shuffled away, grumbling.

Unbidden, Rina's lips curved up in a slight smile of triumph. She knew it wasn't Christian to feel so pleased at Tilly's expense—her mother had often reminded her that the Lord charged His people to turn the other cheek. But she'd been "turning the other cheek" to Tilly for months—tucking in the sheets on the half-made beds, hanging out the laundry that had been washed but not dried, finishing the leftover supper dishes from the boarders' meals. Her stepmother made a business of hiring lazy help, finding their services could be purchased at a cheaper wage. Rina was expected to take up the slack and she had done so—initially because she was

too young to argue, and later because it kept a semblance
of harmony in the household. But Tilly was the worst of
a bad lot, and Rina doubted that even God would
begrudge her a little satisfaction at putting her out. Still,
she figured it wouldn't hurt to say an extra prayer of
penitence at tomorrow's Sunday morning service.

Sunday . . .

Rina bent back to her book, but instead of words she
saw Quinn's button-bright eyes. Since their meeting in
the graveyard she'd tried her best not to think of her
father's old mate. But it was no use. At odd moments
during the day she'd catch herself recalling his cryptic
offer, and speculating about the unknown *situation* that
he'd claimed would make both their fortunes.

Her sudden tendency to daydream unnerved her.
She was a sensible woman—she'd had to be, with a father
like Daniel Murphy. During the black years after her
mother and baby brother had died, she'd been more
adult than child, cooking and keeping house while her
brokenhearted father drank himself into a stupor. Her
role didn't change much when he married her stepmother, except that the house was larger and the drinking spells were longer. She wasn't given to whims or
fancies, or anything that smacked of chance and Lady
Luck. She was a sober, respectable woman with a sober,
respectable future, albeit unremarkable.

So why did she find herself dreaming of country
houses, with flower gardens, hedgerows, and high-
spirited horses?

She rubbed her tired eyes. She was worn out—yes,
that was it. Her father's death and Mr. Quinn's sudden
arrival had been too much for her. In any case, he was
leaving tomorrow, and that would be an end to it. She
closed her book and placed it on the shelf with the half-
dozen volumes that she'd inherited from her mother.

Like the carefully shelved books, everything had a place in life. And hers was as a spinster teacher in the Hampton School for Young Ladies.

Sabrina's musings had caused her to tarry over the quarter hour, so she hurried out of her room and down the stairs. The town house stairs were narrow and steep, built for function rather than beauty, but some imaginative carpenter had carved characters into the edge of every step. Years of use had worn away much of the detail, but Sabrina could still make out the tail feathers on the flustered parrot, and the carrot in the mouth of the lop-eared rabbit.

When she was twelve and first arrived in the house, she'd made up for her loneliness by naming every character and making up stories about their lives. Six years had passed, but she still smiled when she recalled that the rabbit was named Cotton-top and he had an allergy to carrots, and that the parrot Napoleon had ruby feathers and was as vain as a peacock. In a month she would say farewell to this house and all its unpleasant memories, but her stair characters were one of the few things she'd regret leaving behind.

She was so engrossed in studying the steps beneath her that she didn't see the shadow near the bottom of the stairs until she collided with the substantial bulk of a large man's stomach. Plump, moist hands reached out to steady her, touching her in indelicate places.

"You should watch where you're going, sister Sabrina."

She stiffened as she heard the slur of liquor in her stepbrother's voice, and smelled the stale odor of cigars on his expensive lapel. Fine clothes couldn't hide his self-indulgent, dilettante nature. Disgusted, she pushed herself away from him, and batted down his questing hands. "Stop it, Albert. Let me pass."

"Come, Sister. Is that any way to talk to a man who only wants to . . . assist you?"

The barely disguised proposition brought a hot blush to her cheeks. Albert had *assisted* most of the parlor maids in the boardinghouse, including poor Kitty who had been turned off two months ago without a reference. The widow had hired Kitty for a song because she was so young, but the girl proved to be a hard worker and had earned Rina's respect and friendship. Unfortunately, the sweet, trusting girl had also fallen completely in love with Albert.

On the night Kitty left, she confided to Sabrina the happy news that she was going to have a baby. Rina was the first to know—the girl hadn't even told Albert yet, but Kitty hadn't a doubt in the world that *the Master*, as she called him, would marry her. The young girl had dropped her gaze and blushed like a new bride. "Miss Sabrina, I'd be ever so pleased if you'd be my bridesmaid at our wedding."

Just a few minutes later, Kitty was in her room packing up her few belongings, sobbing miserably. Apparently *the Master* had denied everything, and demanded that the "lying chit" be fired. Rina's last glimpse of Kitty had been of a small, lost figure walking away down the dark cobblestones of a London street, her pale breath rising like curls of smoke in the bitterly cold December night. Albert hadn't even let a week pass before he'd taken up with Tilly.

Now, it seemed, he'd grown tired of the second maid as well.

"You're drunk," Sabrina said, her voice brittle with disgust. "Let me pass."

Albert's smarmy smile deepened. "Well, I don't see why you're so high-and-mighty. That da of yours was always in his cups."

Disgust turned to rage. Her father had indeed come home more often drunk than sober, but even on his worst day he had never treated a woman with anything less than complete respect. She clenched her hands into fists. "Let. Me. Pass."

Albert's cheeks paled at her threatening tone. He might not have respected her person, but he had a healthy regard for her temper. Like most bullies he was a coward at heart, and her well-placed kicks and punches had left him with more than one black eye and bruised knee over the years. He backed down the stairs, and stood aside to allow her to go by him. She hurried down the silent hallway without a backward glance, but just before she turned the corner she heard the slurred whisper of a malicious promise.

"You'll get yours, bitch. By God, you will."

Sabrina walked along the musty downstairs hallway leading to the half-open door of her stepmother's parlor. The hallway had once been stately. Its oak ceiling and moldings had been carved with the same eye for detail as the stairs, but years of neglect had left the walls stained and yellowed, and the once elegant wood trim dull and scarred. Eugenia Tremaine had bought the town house shortly after her first husband had been reported missing in action during a battle on the Peninsula. It was common knowledge in the Cheapside neighborhood that Sergeant Tremaine had left his widow and their son fairly well-to-do, and it was hoped that she would restore the old town house to its former glory.

Instead, the widow had put the barest minimum into the house's upkeep, and had rented out the four extra rooms to any who had the coin to pay. What she did with the money was the subject of much speculation, but it was a safe wager that she did not spend it on the house. With puritan thrift, she'd rented her rooms to God-fearing families, invoking both legal and heavenly wrath if they missed their payments. Only once in all her years as a landlord did she waver in her ironclad standards, and that was when a notorious, smooth-talking gambler with a charming smile inquired about renting a room for himself and his young daughter—

"Sabrina! I hear your footsteps!"

Her stepmother's eyesight may have deteriorated over the years, but her hearing was sharp as a cat's. Squaring her shoulders, Sabrina stepped into the parlor and pulled the heavy door shut behind her. She padded across the threadbare carpet to the fireplace, where an inadequately stoked coal brazier tried its best to heat the room. The room smelled musty and sour from the odor of the cheap lamp oil the widow preferred to use over the cleaner-burning but more costly beeswax candles. Except where Albert was concerned, Rina's stepmother was frugal to the point of being parsimonious . . . in affection as well as money.

The widow looked up from her account ledgers and stared over the rim of her pince-nez. "You're late."

The censuring words weren't much of a greeting, but Rina knew from long experience that they were all she was likely to get. A brief, fleeting vision of Rina's beautiful mother rose up in her mind, her radiant, generous smile at odds with the widow's sour expression. Rina stifled a bitter dose of heartache, and settled stiffly into the straight-backed chair that was placed beside the fire.

"I'm sorry, Mother. I was . . . detained."

"Doesn't surprise me. Tilly said that you had your

nose stuck in one of your silly books," Widow Murphy said curtly, the long "oo" in books betraying the lower-class upbringing she'd tried hard to eradicate.

Rina went rigid. Her books were some of the few things she had left from her mother, and were her most beloved possessions. Her hands, folded demurely in her lap, gripped and twisted the black wool skirt of her dress. *Pay it no mind, Rina-lass. Pay it no mind.*

Taking her silence as compliance, her stepmother's mouth twisted into a satisfied smile. She rose from her desk and came closer to the fire, sitting on the chair directly across from Rina. The faint firelight slid over the dark, slick material of her well-worn mourning dress, and Sabrina found herself wondering if it was the same gown she'd worn after her first husband passed away.

"I'm talking to you, gel! That's your trouble. Always have your head in the clouds when there's practical matters to be settled on."

"Practical matters?"

"Matters of your future. Your father's death was a blow to us all," she said, though her tone betrayed little remorse, "but you must see that it ends my obligation to you. In the eyes of the law I'd be well within my rights to turn you out. Of course, I am far too charitable a person to do that."

And you'd lose your best unpaid servant. Rina thought about the letter from the Hampton School that she'd tucked safely away in her dresser—a letter she hadn't yet had the opportunity to discuss with her stepmother. "That is . . . commendable of you, Mother, but you need not trouble yourself on my accou—"

"You are a headstrong and willful girl. You need to be taken in hand. A firm, God-fearing influence is the only thing that can save you from a lamentable future. That is why I have determined you must marry."

If her stepmother had told her to sprout wings and fly, Rina could not have been more surprised. "But there is no one . . . I mean, I have never . . ."

She stuttered, suddenly feeling eight years old rather than eighteen. There was a time when she'd dreamed of marriage—of a little house full of children and laughter, of a man's warm smile, and . . . other things that brought a hot blush to her cheeks. But dreams were all she could have. "I'm plain," she stated with unvarnished honesty. "You have said so many times yourself. I doubt any man could ever fall in love with me."

Widow Murphy bent down and took up the fireplace poker, thrusting it savagely into the undernourished flame. "Love doesn't have a thing to do with marriage, my girl. It's a glittering bauble, a puff of smoke in the wind. It ain't real and it won't last, not for long it won't. And when it's gone it leaves you hollow, as if someone sucked out every one of your dreams and wishes."

In the ruddy glow of the fire, Rina glimpsed a sorrow in her stepmother's eyes that she'd never seen and never suspected. It was common knowledge throughout Cheapside that Daniel Murphy had wooed and married the widow Tremaine for her money. But now Rina saw that there was at least one person who had not been privy to that knowledge, at least not in the beginning. Rina leaned forward and laid her slim hand over her stepmother's dry, bony fingers. "I'm sorry, Mother. I didn't realize—"

The widow jerked back.

"Don't try that Murphy charm on me, girl. I know your heart, and it's as wicked and dishonest as your shiftless father's. The sooner a God-fearing husband takes you in hand, the better." She replaced the poker, clanging it loudly against the brazier's metal screen. "You'll marry Albert before the month is out."

Chapter Two

"*Albert?*" Sabrina asked, her voice strangled by shock. "You cannot mean my stepbrother?"

"And why not? My Bertie's worth twice as much as any man on this street."

Only if you measure by the pound. Rina stared at her stepmother, wondering if the grief of her father's passing had somehow unhinged her.

"You must know . . . you must comprehend . . ." Swallowing her astonishment, she tried again. "Albert has not the slightest regard for me."

"Nonsense. Bertie just ain't the kind of popinjay to wear his heart on his sleeve. Just the other day he was saying that he'd grown right fond of you."

A cold shiver went down Sabrina's spine. She thought back to her earlier meeting with her inebriated stepbrother. At the time, she'd thought his amorous advances were the result of drink. But now, in light of the widow's announcement, his actions took on a more sinister meaning.

Albert may have been cruel and self-indulgent, but he was not a fool. He knew his mother held the purse strings, and he was quite prepared to do whatever was necessary to entice her to loosen them. If his mother wanted him to marry her, then marry her he would. And she would be trapped in the widow's household until the day she died, sharing Albert's name, Albert's bed. . . .

She bolted to her feet. "I thank you for your consideration, but I cannot marry your son. Not ever."

Her stepmother's eyes narrowed cruelly. "Take a look in the glass, gel. It's not as if anyone else is going to offer for ya."

Rina winced, surprised that after all these years those words still had the power to wound. "I know I am not well-favored," she said slowly, carefully keeping any hint of pain out of her voice. "That is why I've taken steps to secure a future where my plainness will be of no consequence."

"A future as what? A kitchen drudge?" the woman sneered. "Or maybe you're thinkin' of asking your grandfather for a helping hand."

Anger flared in Rina's heart. During one of his drunken spells, her father had unwisely told her stepmother about his first wife's death—how Katie had caught the measles while tending the sick in their country parish. When she'd failed to improve, her father had written to her mother's wealthy father, asking for money to take her to a warmer climate to recover. Her father had written repeatedly, promising to pay back the money, to turn himself in to the Irish authorities—to do anything Lord Poole wanted if he would just help his daughter in her hour of need. But the nobleman had not answered even one of the letters, and in the end Katie had died, taking Rina's stillborn brother with her. Her heart still ached at the memory of that terrible night.

Now the widow was using the memory of her grandfather's indifference to mock her. Rina lifted her chin, meeting her stepmother's eyes with a steady gaze that betrayed none of her turbulent emotions. "I have accepted a teaching position in Sussex," she said bluntly, and had the rare pleasure of seeing the older woman struck dumb with surprise. "I will be leaving within the fortnight."

Mrs. Murphy rose to her feet and gripped the stone mantelpiece, as if to steady herself. "You wicked, ungrateful girl. You'd leave, just like that. After all I've done for you—"

"You've done nothing for me!" Rina cried. "You've used me shamefully, treating me more like a servant than a daughter. Not once did you ever make me feel welcome, or cherished, or loved."

"Have a care, girl," the widow warned, her fingers tightening on the mantelpiece.

Rina's Irish blood quickened in her veins. For years she'd bottled up her feelings, stuffing away her hurt and anger for her father's sake. But her father was dead, and so was this woman's hold over her. "You say Papa's death ended your obligation to me. Well, it ends my obligation to you as well. Find someone else to marry your despicable son. I'll leave this house first thing in the morning!"

Sabrina squared her shoulders and marched confidently from the parlor, feeling better than she had since the day she had arrived at the musty old town house. But after she had gone, her stepmother gripped the poker and began stabbing the helpless fire with a vengeance, while her thin-lipped mouth twisted in thought.

" 'Tis no use!"

Sabrina flung back her heavy bedcovers. The silver moonlight flooding through her tiny garret window showed that it was still the middle of the night, but she'd been tossing and turning for hours. She threw her shawl around her shoulders and padded to the window. "I'll not get any sleep tonight."

After she'd left the widow's parlor she'd gone directly to her room and packed up her few belongings, leaving out only the secondhand psalm book that her parents had given her on her confirmation day. As she'd gotten into bed she'd opened the volume, seeking words of hope and guidance. But the only verses that had leapt out at her were full of despair and dire warning. *They have sharpened their tongues like a serpent; adders' poison is under their lips.*

Shivering, Rina stared out through the frost-etched pane. Outside, the night wind howled like a lost soul. She pulled the woolen shawl close to her throat, feeling a chill creep down her spine that had nothing to do with the winter cold. She didn't believe in signs and portents any more than she believed in Lady Luck, but in the lonely garret room it seemed as if the whole world was conspiring against her, to try to turn her from her new life—

A board creaked. Rina twisted around to look behind her, then silently chided herself when she saw nothing but shadows. It was only the wind blowing through the cracks in the old walls. The widow was going to let the place fall to ruin right on top of her. Picturing the old harpy neck-high in rubble held a certain appeal.

Sighing, Rina pressed her cheek against the frosted pane, relishing the feel of the icy glass against her skin. The widow had been right about one thing—without looks or a fortune to recommend her it was doubtful that any man would willingly seek out her hand. But though her stepmother had been right about her dismal matrimonial prospects, she'd been quite wrong about love being nothing more than a fairy tale. Sabrina knew that it existed—she'd seen it every time her parents had looked at one another.

Rina knew she had about as much chance of finding true love as she did of finding a golden nugget in the London gutters, but she'd vowed never to marry for anything less. She might be plain, but she could still dream. . . .

Creak.

That wasn't the wind. Rina spun around and peered at the room behind her.

" 'Lo, S'brina," an all-too-familiar voice slurred.

Albert—a very drunken Albert by the sound of him—had entered her bedroom and closed the door behind him. He stepped toward the window. Rina saw that he'd discarded the coat he was wearing earlier, and his wrinkled, half-buttoned shirt was only partially tucked into his pants. "Get out of my room this instant!"

"Now, 's'at any way to talk to your betrothed?" he asked, taking another teetering step toward her.

"You are not my betrothed!"

Her fury had little effect on him. "Ma said we're betrothed. And what Ma says goes."

He continued toward her. A needle of fear pricked through Rina's consciousness, but she ignored it. After all, this was *Albert*, and she'd discouraged his unseemly advances a dozen times before. She pulled herself up to her full height, which was almost equal to his, and said in her most scathing tone, "Albert, don't be an idiot. Regardless of what your mother says, you don't want to marry me any more than I want to marry you. Now, leave this bedroom at once, and we'll forget this unpleasantness ever happened."

His low chuckle raised the hairs on the back of her neck. "Don't have to be *unpleasant*. No siree, it don't."

He was close enough now that she could smell the strong spirits on his breath, and see the unnatural brightness in his eyes. His gaze swept over her thin night rail, making her feel sick in a way she'd never experienced before. The fear she'd brushed aside came back with a vengeance. "Albert," she said, speaking slowly and precisely. "Albert, this is foolishness. I want you to turn around and leave this room now. Please."

"Please, is it?" he sneered, his ugly laugh rubbing against her raw nerves. "Well, I will please you darlin'. I'll *please* you fine."

She moved back. "Stop it! I'll scream—"

Albert's arms snaked around her and yanked her against him. She opened her mouth to scream, but found her protest stifled by a wet, liquor-stale kiss.

Rina had never been kissed before. She'd imagined it many times, speculating that it would be sweet and slightly bracing. But this kiss was sloppy and vile and it made her feel dirty clear through. She twisted her mouth away from his, and struggled out of his embrace. She backed away and felt the oak bedpost behind her, gripping it for support. "All right, you've had your fun. Now get out."

"Oh, no, S'brina. Fun's just beginning."

Once again she opened her mouth to scream, but he was too quick for her. He reached out, grabbing her breast in a punishing grip. Her words died in a choked gasp. She felt shock and fury, and—shame. She'd never been with a man and was only vaguely aware of what happened when a man and woman mated, but the small bit she did know paralyzed her with horror. She stared at Albert, seeing him in a new, terrifying light. "I beg you, don't do this. Don't—"

He shoved her backward onto the bed and fell on top of her, crushing the air from her lungs with his heavy body. Desperately she tried to twist away, but his weight pinned her down. His hands were everywhere, his moist, sweating palms pinching and squeezing her breasts and midriff. Gasping for breath she tried to scream, only to have his tongue drive deeply into her mouth, nearly gagging her. The foul kiss seemed to last forever, until he finally drew back and placed his hand over her mouth. She struggled, trying to bite him, but he'd expertly turned his hand in such a way that she couldn't get at him. *He's forced himself on women before, dear God, he's done this befo—*

Her thoughts ended in horror as he yanked her night rail up and gripped her naked backside.

"Well, there's a surprise," he muttered with a foul chuckle. "Your looks ain't much, but you've got an ass like a harlot. This ride won't be half bad, no siree."

He lay on top of her, the front of his pants pressed intimately against her most private area. She felt an unnatural stiffness in his groin, a hardness that made her instinctively try to clamp her legs together. But Albert's knee was already stationed between her legs, forcing her to keep them apart.

"Don't worry," he said, his patronizing tone only adding to her terror. "It'll hurt some, but you'll get to like it."

A band of moonlight fell across him, illuminating his fumblings with his pants. Horror and loathing welled up inside her. For years she'd suffered the slights and offenses he and his mother had thrown at her. But if she let this happen she'd never be able to hide from the pain. She was exhausted and terrified, but she had to fight. She had to.

Forcing the panic aside she made herself look at her stepbrother, schooling her expression into something that approximated pleasure. Then, with an acting talent worthy of the great Sarah Siddons herself, she moaned breathlessly against her stepbrother's hand. "Albert. Oh, Albert."

Her sudden change startled him, but only for a moment. Almost immediately, a broad, self-satisfied grin spread across his face. "Like what you see, do ya? You're all the same. I never met a bit o' muslin what didn't want my—"

His sentence ended in a yelp as she drove her knee into his groin.

"You bitch!" he screamed, doubling over in pain. "I'll get you for this!"

Sabrina barely heard him. The minute his grip slackened she reached behind her for the candlestick on the nightstand. Grasping it tightly, she lifted it high, then brought it down on his head in one stroke.

He went limp. She scooted out from under him and backed away toward the door, still clutching the candlestick in front of her. She wanted to be ready if he came at her again, but he lay unmoving on the bed. Staring at him, Rina rubbed the back of her hand across her swollen mouth, trying to scour away the feel of his kisses.

"That's for me," she breathed, her laboring breath slowly returning to normal. "And for Kitty."

The door opened as Widow Murphy barged into the room, a lamp held high above her head. Sabrina blinked at the sudden illumination, then focused on her stepmother. The widow was still wearing her black cap and mourning gown instead of her night-shift. Bile rose in Sabrina's throat. *She's still dressed and awake, probably waiting for her son to report back to her—*

"Albert!" The woman rushed to the prone figure of her son. "Dear God, what's happened?"

"No more than he deserved. He tried to force himself on me, but I expect you already know th—"

"You wicked, evil girl!"

"Evil?" Sabrina cried. "*He's* the evil one. He tried to rape me."

"You think that matters? After what you've done!"

"What *I've* done?"

The widow stepped aside, allowing Sabrina her first clear view of Albert to the light. She skimmed his half-dressed form, shivering as she realized how close he'd come to completing his foul mission. Then she saw his face, and the trickle of crimson blood sliding down across his brow.

"You've killed him," hissed her stepmother. "You've killed my darling boy!"

The bleak winter night yielded to the promise of a glorious dawn. Threads of light quested up into the mother-of-pearl sky, lacing themselves into a bright quilt that furled itself like a golden banner over the dark silhouettes of the eastern rooftops. Wrens and starlings cried their symphony of welcome into the morning sky, while far below horses clattered as they pulled their ice wagons and milk carts over the cobblestone streets. Morning sunlight streamed in through a hundred bedroom windows. But to one young woman in a lonely garret room, the sunlight brought no smiles, and its gentle warmth couldn't heal the icy dread that gripped her heart.

You've killed my darling boy.

The widow's tragic words played over and over in Sabrina's head. It wasn't entirely true—Albert had still been alive when a couple of the male tenants had carried him out of her garret down to his own room on the floor below—but that had been several hours ago. Since then she'd heard nothing. She'd thought about going below stairs, and had even changed into her dark woolen dress for the purpose, but the widow had made it quite clear that she didn't want Rina anywhere near her beloved son. *You did this to him, you brazen strumpet. And if he dies, it will be on your head!*

"I've killed a man," she whispered as she stared blankly at the brightening sky. The fact that the man was a complete rotter made not a whit of difference. Deserved or not, she'd robbed another human being of God's greatest gift. Albert may not have taken her physical innocence, but he'd most assuredly taken her spiritual one.

The door opened. Sabrina turned around, expecting to see her stepmother, but instead met Tilly's stone-dull gaze. Slouching against the door frame, the second maid looked singularly unremorseful at the fact that her lover was dying one floor below. *She must be in shock*, Rina thought, feeling a new weight settle on her shoulders. "Tilly, I'm so very sorry. I know you cared deeply for Albert, and I—"

"You stupid cow."

"W—what?"

"You 'eard me," Tilly said as she entered the room. "You coulda had it sweet. We *both* coulda. He'd have married you up proper to please his mum, and kept me on the side for the necessary. We'd a been in cakes and cream for the rest of our born days. All you had to do was give him a bit a' what comes natural."

"There was nothing *natural* about it. He was trying to force himself on me. Surely as a woman you understand."

"I *understand* that now I got to find me another gentleman what wants to take care of me. Your priss-and-proper ways have cost me dear, they 'ave. Course, they're gonna cost you a good sight more. . . ."

Smiling unpleasantly, the maid raised her fist level with her ear, and made a sharp, jerking motion upward.

For a moment Sabrina didn't comprehend Tilly's pantomime. Then she gasped, her hand flying unvoluntarily to her throat. "Don't be absurd. They can't hang me. I hit Albert in self-defense."

"Ain't a man on God's green earth who'll see it that way. The magistrates all got wives and mistresses of their own, and they wouldn't want 'em gettin' uppity ideas. They'll say you killed your betrothed for wanting some womanly comfort."

"He wasn't my betrothed. He was trying to *rape* me!"

Tilly shrugged indifferently. "Don't matter much if he were. Women been put on this earth for man's pleasin'. That's the way it's been, the way it always will be. If the master dies, they'll hang you for killing a bloke for only wanting what every man jack of 'em expects. And if anyone sheds a tear at your passing, it soddin' well won't be me."

Hanged!

Sabrina stood staring at the door Tilly had closed behind her. Cold spiders of fear began to climb down her spine. Unconsciously, she began to finger the high lace collar circling her suddenly vulnerable neck.

She'd seen a man hanged. When she was seven she'd gone with her parents to a country fair. While her mother was discussing needlework and her father was studying a neighbor's new hunter, Rina had stolen away to a crowded field at the far end of the fairgrounds, where her parents had expressly forbidden her to go. She'd expected to find a play or puppet show taking place on the raised wooden platform overlooking the field. Instead, she'd seen the trap door open beneath the bound figure of a hooded man, and felt the earth shudder beneath her as the rope snapped taut. She could still remember the jubilant cheers of the crowd as they watched his slowly twisting body jerk out the last of its life.

" 'Tis madness!" she cried aloud. "Surely they won't arrest me for defending myself. They can't!"

Her father had told her once that even a sorry hand can be a winner if you play it right. Well, she'd been dealt a sorry hand indeed, but hiding in her room wasn't going to make it any better. She yanked open the bedroom door and headed for the stairs, determined to face the consequences of her actions without fear or regret.

Her bold resolution, however, proved short-lived. When she reached the floor below, she heard voices nearby. The words were too muffled to make out clearly, but as she peered around the corner and down the narrow hallway, she caught a glimpse of the speakers. One was the bent, black-garbed shape of her stepmother. The other was a stout man she'd never seen before, but he wore the unmistakable dark cape and red waistcoat of the Bow Street Runners.

The widow had not even waited for Albert's passing to set the law on her! The Runner would take her to the hellhole of Newgate Prison, where she'd have to defend her honor in open court. *The magistrates all got wives and mistresses of their own, and they wouldn't want 'em gettin' uppity ideas. They'll say you killed your betrothed for wanting some womanly comfort.*

Well, if her stepmother thought Rina would go like a lamb to the slaughter, she was sadly mistaken. Daring and risk were two words outside of Rina's normal vocabulary, but she'd be damned before she'd hang for defending herself against her despicable stepbrother.

She started up the stairs to retrieve her satchel, but dashed down and around to the back of them as she heard someone coming her way. Her eyes level with

Napoleon the parrot, she watched as her stepmother led the Bow Street Runner toward the upper floor. Apparently Rina hadn't left her room a moment too soon!

She considered making a break for it, but she doubted she'd make it down the entire back hall and stairway without running into one of the boarders. In a few minutes the Runner would realize that she was missing, and start a room-to-room search. It would only be a matter of time before they found her.

Her heart pounding, Rina slipped deeper into the shadows beneath the stairs. For years the area had been used for storage, jumbled with the old furniture and worn-out household items that her miserly stepmother refused to throw out. Rina squeezed between the piles of clutter until she reached the back of the small space. She pressed against the wall, and noted in surprise that the wall contained a small window, whose glass was so thickly coated with soot and grime that it appeared opaque.

A brief glimmer of hope flashed through her mind, but it quickly died. The wooden frame of the window was nailed shut. And even if it hadn't been, she was on the second floor, with nothing to stop a straight fall to the brick alley below. A drop like that could break an arm or a leg. A sensible woman would never consider such a risky undertaking.

You're a gambler's daughter, Rina-lass. Take a chance.

Rina started. The words were so clear in her mind, she felt as if her father was standing beside her. The notion was ridiculous, of course, but nevertheless, the words gave her hope. She *was* a gambler's daughter, and it was time she started acting like one.

Breathing a lusty oath, she reached down and hastily tore a length of fabric from her skirt, and wrapped it securely around her fisted hand. She paused, making sure that the hallway was silent, then she deftly broke the window glass and climbed through the frame onto the outside ledge. Her dress tore on the glass, but she ignored it, keeping her attention squarely on her goal. Then, muttering a quick prayer to Lady Luck, she let go of the window frame and dropped to the alley below.

Someone was pounding on Michael Quinn's door.

He sat up in bed, savagely rubbing the sleep from his eyes. Christ, it was practically the middle of the bloomin' night! "I'm paid up proper through evening. Clear off!"

He dove back under his covers. The pounding continued.

Cursing, he stomped to the door, and found himself staring into the bushy black mustache of the Green Dragon's squeeze-penny landlord.

"Another one," the man stated simply.

"Another what—oh, you mean another *lady*. At this hour?"

"Didn't know the time mattered." The landlord shrugged. "You want to see her?"

No, Quinn's mind stated emphatically. He was in no mood to interview yet another lady who "was guaranteed to fit his bill to a tee." Besides, his sources had assured him that he'd already seen the best talent London had to offer. Still . . .

"Is she young? Is she well-spoken?"

"Can't say and didn't ask," the landlord replied unhelpfully. "But she got red 'air. Yards of it."

Well, that was something. Quinn stroked his chin, trying not to get his hopes up. Red hair was essential to his plans, but it was only one of the cards he was looking for. So far, not one of the ladies he'd seen had come close to having the makings of a winning hand. One had been too fat, another too short, another too common, another too untrustworthy. At the end of a wearisome week he was no better off than when he'd first arrived in London. Years of plotting and planning threatened to fall to ruin around his ears. He wasn't in a position to pass up any possibilities. "Best put the lady in the sitting room next door. I'll be there directly."

In short order Quinn shaved and dressed, working with the efficiency he'd learned during his tenure as a day laborer and the nattiness he'd acquired at his stint as a nobleman's valet. Unbidden, his mind stretched back to a day long past, to a sun-drenched room on a Tuscany hillside, where a smiling young woman with butternut hair was lovingly adjusting his collar. Pain stabbed through his heart. *You'll pay, Trevelyan. If I have to scour the empire for a red-haired lassie to help me, I'll bloody well do it.*

Resolved, he gave the hem of his waistcoat a final straightening tug, then opened the door that led to the suite's sitting room. The front room was larger, but the cracked plaster walls and musty furniture made it look even more dismal than the room he'd just left. The gloomy atmosphere was cheered somewhat by the substantial fire that the landlord had laid in the iron grate. And in a chair near the quickening blaze, warming herself as if she were frozen to the bone, sat the lady.

As the landlord had reported, she had a profusion of red hair. Her face was turned away from him toward the fire, but her slim build suggested that she was young enough to suit his purposes. His hopes rose—but were dashed back to earth as he noticed that her dark dress was torn and stained past the point of repair, and her hair was streaked with soot and dirt.

A mudlark, he thought bleakly. Even if the lassie looked the part, she wouldn't have the breeding he needed to pull off the charade. Sighing, he approached her, reaching in his pocket for a shilling to give the poor creature before he sent her on her way. "I'm sorry, lass. You're not—"

She rose from the chair and took a wavering step toward him. The girl was on the ragged edge of exhaustion. He moved closer to assist her, but froze as he recognized the strong Celtic nose, and the canny emerald eyes she'd inherited from her father. "Miss Murphy? Whatever has happened—"

"Oh, Mr. Quinn. I'm in such dreadful trouble," she confessed shakily, then gave way to weariness and collapsed into his arms.

Chapter
Three

Something smelled wonderful.

Sabrina's eyelids fluttered open. Her gaze skimmed over the small sitting room before lighting on a rasher of plump kippers, a rack of golden toast, and a cup of rich, steaming hot chocolate. Her mouth began to water. *If this is a dream, I hope I don't wake up until after breakfast. . . .*

"Welcome back, lassie."

Casting her gaze to the side, she caught sight of Mr. Quinn winking at her from the other side of the breakfast table. He was humming tunelessly, and spreading what appeared to be an entire pot of marmalade on a muffin. Sabrina pressed her hand to her forehead and tried to gather up the scattered bits of her consciousness. She recalled the inn's glowering mustachioed landlord, recalled the fugitive journey through the back streets to Greygallows Lane, recalled the drop to the freezing snowbank in the back alley, recalled the cluttered storeroom, the Runner—

Rina sucked in her breath, memory returning to her in a giddying rush. She glanced at Mr. Quinn, who'd just taken a hearty bite out of his muffin. She doubted he'd be so calm once he learned he was sharing his table with a murderess. "Mr. Quinn, I will not deceive you. I have come here because—"

"Have a kipper," Quinn said, his words slurred by a mouthful of muffin.

She shook her head, waving aside the offered plate. "Thank you for your kindness, but I can't accept your hospitality, not until I tell you why I had to leave—"

"You can tell me when you've had a kipper, lass," he interrupted, his cheerfulness undaunted. "And do try some of the toast and this right tolerable jam. Now, how about a bit o' this lovely hot chocolate?"

Rina's resolve could stand firm against a bakeryful of muffins and a sea of marmalade—but against hot chocolate? Never. She lifted the cup and took a sip, savoring the sweet taste and the way the warmth curled comfortably in her empty middle. Considering the harrowing events of the night before, she ought not to have much of an appetite for this meal. Instead, she found herself laying into the meat and muffins as if she hadn't eaten in a month.

It appears that risk agrees with me, she thought with a self-deprecating smile as she liberally buttered a square of golden toast. She downed two kippers and half a pot of hot chocolate in a snap, but as her appetite diminished, her guilt returned. She laid down the remains of her toast and cleared her throat. "Mr. Quinn, you are all kindness, but I must tell you that—"

"That you took a candlestick to your stepbrother's thick skull," the man finished calmly as he selected another muffin.

"But how did you—? How could you—?"

"Now don't be frettin' so," Quinn said as he patted her hand comfortingly. "When you arrived in such an agitated state I asked the innkeeper to send his boy to make some 'discreet inquiries.' He's a fair wizard at 'inquiries,' that boy is. Part of the reason a bloke chooses to stay at the Green Dragon. In any event, he ran back fair bursting with a story of Runners and 'pothecaries and all manner of mayhem."

She stared down at the tablecloth, and asked hoarsely, "What about Albert?"

Quinn's smile faded. "I won't lie to you, lass. From what the boy heard, he ain't doing well."

In the warmth and well-fed comfort of the little sitting room, she'd been able to put aside the harrowing trauma of the night before. Now once again the spiders of fear began to creep into her heart as she remembered the fate that awaited her—her, and for anyone who aided her.

"I shouldn't have come," she said, abruptly rising from the chair. "I've put you in danger by coming here. Made you an accomplice . . ."

"Missy, you're not going nowhere till you've got your strength back," he ordered. "And as for being an accomplice—well, it ain't as if I was in the law's good graces."

"But I'm a *murderer*," she cried softly.

Quinn's expression softened, and he lifted his hand to brush her cheek. "Ah, lass, I've lived by my wits for too long not to know a pair of honest eyes when I sees 'em. Them Runners could swear on the Good Book that you'd done in sixty men since last night's supper, and I wou'na believe them. You're Dan'l's girl, with Dan'l's blood in your veins. And if you're a murderer, then I'm the bloody pope!"

For years, Rina's stepmother had worn her down with insinuations about her wicked and brazen character, repeating the lies so often that even she'd begun to believe them. She'd learned to live with the fact that people believed the worst of her, concealing her pain and loneliness behind a mask of indifference. But Quinn believed in her innocence, despite the accusations, and that simple trust meant more to Rina than words could say. Impulsively, she wrapped him in a huge hug.

"Here, here. None of that," the scalawag said gruffly, his face beet-red as he pushed himself out of her embrace. Clearing his throat, he crisply pulled down the hem of his waistcoat, recovering at least the appearance of his stern demeanor. "We've no time for such foolishness. This situation with your stepbrother is a pickle, and no mistake. The Green Dragon's safe for now, but that won't last forever. You can't stay in London. Where is it you're bound for?"

Sabrina hadn't a clue. The position at the Hampton School was lost to her, along with any other respectable occupation. She had no prospects, no money, and no friends in the world except for Quinn. "I . . . don't know. Truthfully, I have nowhere to go."

Quinn scratched his chin. "That's not altogether true. You've a flush hand in front of you, if'n you're willin' to pick it up. It's the one we spoke of at your da's grave a week past. Do ya recall it?"

Recall it? She'd thought about that snowy afternoon a dozen times, unable to get their conversation out of her mind. Now, more than ever, the prospect ignited her interest. But Quinn had made no secret of the fact that his plan wasn't entirely legal. And Lord knew she was in enough trouble with the law as it was. "I remember, but I don't think—"

"Hear me out, that's all I ask." He reached into his waistcoat and pulled out a locket. Inside was the faded miniature of a young, stiff-faced child with hair as red as Rina's own. "This here's a likeness of a bairn named

Prudence Winthrope. She was going on seven when this portrait was painted, just before she and her folks was lost in a fire. Their house burned to the ground, and no bodies were ever found. That was thirteen years ago."

Rina took the locket and cupped it in her hand, feeling a vague sorrow for the little girl who'd died so young. "That's tragic, Mr. Quinn, but I don't see what it has to do with me."

"The girl was an heiress, born into a wealthy and powerful Cornwall family, the House of Trevelyan."

"I still don't—" Rina began, but stopped as she took a second look at the child. Red hair. Died in a fire some thirteen years ago—no bodies were found.

"Mr. Quinn, you aren't suggesting that *I* should pretend to be this girl?"

"Ah, you're as quick as your da and that's a fact!" Quinn whooped. "You've the hair and the age for it, and the breeding that comes from your dear mother. With the proper coin in the right hands, I can get documents that'll prove to God himself that you're the long-lost girl. It's years I've been looking for a lass suited to play the part of Prudence, but the minute I sees you I knows I've found the one. My Red Queen. My Queen of *Diamonds*."

"Stop it!" Rina went to the fire and rested her head against the mantel. "Even if you could get the documents, I could not be party to such a scheme. It is monstrously dishonest and I could never keep up the charade. The girl's relatives would find me out."

"The girl's relatives hardly knew her," Quinn argued as he came up beside her. "She stayed with them a spell when she was six, but mostly she lived with her parents on the Continent. Her pa fancied the wine and women of Italy, while her ma—"

Quinn looked down, a lost, sad frown clouding his

eager face. Sabrina had a curious desire to wrap her arms around him, but before she could, his sorrowful expression vanished as quickly as it had appeared. "I've got it all figured, I have. You'll make 'em believe you're Prudence, but you don't have to keep up the game for long. It's not the inheritance we're after, my girl. It's the Dutchman's Necklace." Quinn dropped his voice and leaned closer, the flames playing across his face. "A diamond necklace, with stones plucked from the heart of an Africa mine. Big as goose eggs, they are, and bright enough to outshine the stars themselves. We get that necklace, and our fortunes is made. We can go anywhere, do anything, be *anyone*. Nab that necklace, my bonnie lass, and you'll not have to worry about your sodding excuse of a stepbrother again!"

Rina could change her name, move to another country, travel the world, live all her dreams, and more. It would be a risk, of course, but if she played it right, she could—

She froze, appalled that at least a part of her mind was figuring out the odds of the illicit venture. She ran her thumb over the small portrait, again feeling the fierce, inexplicable sympathy for the long-dead Prudence. Stealing a fortune in gems was one thing, but to steal another person's life . . .

"No, it isn't right. The poor girl's family might not have known her well, but I'm sure they felt her death as keenly as . . . well, as I felt the deaths of my own parents. I cannot be so deceitful to a loving family."

Quinn threw back his head and gave a whoop of laughter. "*Loving family*, is it? Let me tell you a thing or two about her family. The Trevelyans have never loved anything but money. They made their fortune in tin, on the backs of the miners who risked their lives in dark and dangerous mine shafts. The dowager countess is a proper termagant, who rules the house with an unforgiving hand. Her granddaughter ain't much better. Just out of the schoolroom, the girl spends most of her time posin' and preenin' in front of the mirror, and drives her poor maids to distraction over bows and patches and such. And as for the earl—"

The brightness left Quinn's eyes, leaving them dull and gray as a storm-shrouded sea. "The Trevelyans have never been known for their character, but the present lord is the worst of a sorry lot. The miners call him the Black Earl, though whether they're speaking of his hair or his heart is anyone's guess. If there was ever a devil in a man's body, 'tis the Earl of Trevelyan." Quinn shook himself roundly, as if to oust the image of the infernal nobleman from his mind. "He's a bad 'un, that's sure. But there's one blessing to him. He spends little time at his Cornwall home, Ravenshold. Likes the big cities, he does—the bright lights o' London and Paris. They say he couldn't even be bothered to rouse himself from his, er, pleasurable pursuits for his wife's illness and passing, if'n you catch my meaning."

Rina caught Quinn's meaning all too well. She'd grown up stepping aside for the posh carriages of the foppish, self-absorbed aristocrats who spent their days in the fine houses of Mayfair—and their nights indulging in every kind of vile sin and debauchery. She'd seen such men wager a king's ransom on the turn of a card, then beat a poor street beggar senseless for the crime of asking for a penny. She'd seen the young women they used and tossed aside, discarding them with no more thought than they'd give to a wrinkled cravat or a soiled handkerchief.

No, Rina held no love for the gentry, and she was honest enough to admit that she was sorely tempted by the chance to pay one of the blackguards back for the harm they'd done to the weak and destitute. But such a daring charade was not in her nature. She shook her head, and closed the locket with a sharp, defining snap. "I wish I could help you, Mr. Quinn, I truly do. But . . . it's just not in me to do this. Perhaps you could find another red-haired lady."

"Aye, perhaps," Quinn agreed, but without much conviction. "Perhaps. But I'll tell you true, lass. A Red Queen is hard to come by. You were my best hope. My last, I'm thinkin'." He walked over to where his much-mended topcoat hung on a wall peg. Delving into the folds, he extracted a small purse from its voluminous pocket. "Whether you throw in with me or not, you're Dan'l's girl and I mean to see you safe. This money'll take you to a friend of mine in Dublin. He'll take you in, no questions asked. With a new name, he can set you up at a milliner's or a dressmaker's. And there's always a chance you might be able to square things with your grandfather."

I'd rather hang! Rina cried silently. Her grandfather had turned his back on her mother, causing her death as surely as if he had driven the nails into her coffin.

She balled her hand into a tight fist around the locket. It wasn't fair. She was the one who'd been attacked, yet she was the one who was going to be paying for the crime for the rest of her life. It seemed that the rich and powerful always won in the end. Like the widow. Like her grandfather.

Like Trevelyan.

A fierce, righteous anger rose up inside her. Her sensible side warned her that she was being foolish in the extreme, that she should take the safe future Quinn offered and be glad of it.

If her mother had taken a safe course, she would never have given up all she had to run off with Daniel

Murphy. And if her father had taken the safe path, he'd never have asked Katie Poole to marry him, and had to flee his country for the sake of the woman he loved. The truth was, Rina had gambler's blood from both sides of her heritage. And yet the fact that the odds were stacked in favor of the black-hearted earl and his self-absorbed family only made the chance of beating them all the more enticing.

She held the locket against her. *Forgive me, Prudence. I'll only borrow your life for a little while, I promise.* "Well, if I'm going to have to change my name anyway, I might as well make it Winthrope."

Chapter
Four

"Sea air!" exclaimed Mr. Benjamin Cherry as he leaned out of the coach window and took in a bracing lungful of the cool, salt wind. Below, the ocean off the northwest Cornwall coast was scattered with the glitter of diamond-bright sunshine, and churned into a white froth at the base of the solemn gray cliffs. Seagulls wheeled overhead, crying plaintively as they waited for the fishing boats to return with their daily catch. Mr. Cherry gave a satisfied sigh, then sat down against the cushions, his cheeks as round and red as his surname.

"Is it not exhilarating?" he exclaimed to the two women accompanying him. "I vow, had I not determined to take up the law, I would have cheerfully spent my youth as a midshipman on a king's frigate before the mast. Is that not so, Mother?"

He turned to the lady beside him, a figure so heavily wrapped in blankets and woolen shawls that little could be seen of her except for her small eyes and pinched, wrinkled mouth. "Humph," she sniffed. "You'd have caught your death in the cold and damp. Or drowned sure."

Mr. Cherry's jovial smile momentarily lost its luster,

but it returned in a trice as he spoke to the young woman sitting across from him. "And you? Do you fancy the sea, Miss Winthrope? . . . Miss Winthrope?"

Sabrina started, belatedly realizing the solicitor was addressing her. Weeks of Quinn's tutoring and she was still slow on the mark! "Forgive me, sir. I'm afraid my mind was . . . elsewhere."

"Heavens, of course it was," the solicitor stated, nodding in understanding. "No doubt you were thinking about your impending reunion with your dear great-aunt and your cousins. And after all the trials and tribulations you've endured! I vow, if I were in your self-same circumstances, I doubt I could remember my own name."

"You do not know the half of it," Rina muttered. She glanced down, and plucked nervously at one of the numerous satin bows that adorned her skirt. Quinn had commissioned several new dresses for her, all of which he'd insisted be peppered with "them bows, beads and goo-gas that shows you got money to burn." Personally Rina disliked the silk and satin trappings, but the gaudy dress was the least of her worries.

Barely a month had passed since Quinn had spirited her out of London and installed her in a small cottage in the isolated country near the Welsh border. For weeks he'd stuffed her full of every detail of Prudence's fabricated life, from her dramatic rescue by Irish missionaries passing through Italy on their way to Africa, to her adopted father's death and her adopted mother's subsequent return to Dublin, to her mother's deathbed confession that she was not really her mother at all, and her final charge to her adopted daughter to find her true heritage.

To Rina's mind, Quinn's story was the most preposterous tale she'd ever heard—she told him straight out that she doubted that anyone with an ounce of sense would believe it. But he had answered her with a smile and a canny wink. "You've got to tug on their heartstrings," he'd told her. "It muddles their minds. If they hear you're an orphan who's a missionary's girl to boot, they'll take you to their hearts and no mistake."

Quinn's understanding of human nature proved to be dead on. When "Prudence" had appeared in Mr. Cherry's Truro law offices with letters from her deceased "mother" and various witnesses proving her identity, the Trevelyans' solicitor had spent less than a week confirming their authenticity. Soon after, she'd been summoned to Ravenshold, to meet her long-lost family. The speed of her apparent acceptance both astonished and unnerved Sabrina—and made her feel all the more guilty for the ease of her deception.

Mr. Cherry was a dear and generous man, and he'd been very kind to her—far kinder than his legal duties required. She hated deceiving him, but she was going to have to get used to lying to people. Luckily that wouldn't be a problem where the Trevelyans were concerned. If even a quarter of the things Quinn had told her were true, then Prudence's relatives were the most self-centered, detestable, and useless lot that ever roamed the hills of England.

The weather deteriorated as the day wore on. Threatening clouds rolled in from the northwest, turning the bright morning into a gloomy and ominous afternoon. A dank fog chilled their bones, and obscured much of the view of the road ahead. The waves grew fiercer, battering against the base of the cliffs like a titan's fist. The crash of the waves was so loud that sometimes Sabrina was not sure whether she was hearing thunder or the relentless pounding of the sea. Even the land seemed to mirror the inclement weather, turning from rolling green farmland to rock outcroppings as stark as the cliff below.

Strangely enough, the fierce landscape stirred something deep inside her. She'd spent years in the crowded, fouled streets of London, where the people were packed so closely together that it seemed that not even her thoughts were her own. Now the emptiness of the bleak, wild land made her feel free in a way she'd never felt before. It was desolate and barren, and dangerous in ways she couldn't even begin to imagine, but it was also untamed and unbroken, a land that did not compromise. It did not pretend to be anything other than what it was: hard, unrepentant, and . . . beautiful—

"There it is," the solicitor said, pointing out the carriage window. "Ravenshold."

Rina leaned out the window, heedless of the raw wind whipping at her hair as she peered ahead through the storm's gloom. At first she could make out nothing, then a stab of lightning illuminated the landscape— and Ravenshold. The ancient house sat on a rise above the cliff's edge, as gray and foreboding as the coast it commanded.

There was nothing refined or courtly about the manor—it was made of the same somber stone as the cliffs, and built solid and plain to withstand the brutal onslaught of the sea and land. Modern architects might have seen its austere simplicity as ugly, but Rina saw strength and pride in the ancient building. To her it was finer than the most ornate, treasure-stuffed residences of the fashionable ton.

"It's magnificent," she breathed.

"It's drafty and cold as the grave," Mrs. Cherry remarked with her usual sourness. "You *must* be a Trevelyan. They're the only ones who can abide the place, and they'd live nowhere else. In the blood, they say."

In the blood, Rina thought, feeling a curious ache in her heart. She leaned back against the horsehair cushions and closed her eyes, and allowed herself to believe, just for a moment, that she truly belonged to this wild, windswept land.

Her thoughts ended as the carriage lurched sideways. Sabrina clutched the door as the carriage swayed precariously close to the edge of the road.

"Have no fear," the solicitor hastily reassured her. "It was only a pothole left by our inclement winter."

"Weren't no pothole," his mother stated. "It were a warning. From the ghost."

"Mother—" Mr. Cherry warned.

"They say she walks the halls of Ravenshold, and the sea cliffs beyond. Say she's lookin' for someone to avenge her death."

Sabrina didn't believe in ghosts any more than she believed in Lady Luck, but she was intrigued. "And just who might this unfortunate specter be?"

"The spirit of Lady Isabel. Lord Trevelyan's murdered wife."

Murdered? Rina's eyes widened in surprise and alarm. "But I thought the earl's wife died of influenza."

"That is *precisely* what the poor lady died of." Mr. Cherry gave his mother a long-suffering look. "You must understand, Miss Winthrope, that the Duchy of Cornwall is rife with stories of ghosts, ghouls, and superstitions. It's part of our history—some tales even date back to the time of the Romans. Every manor house worth its salt has its share of haunts and curses, and Ravenshold is no exception. But there's no truth to the rumors about Lord Trevelyan's wife's death. You may rest assured on that point."

"*She* may rest—but poor Lady Isabel isn't so lucky," his mother countered sourly. "She's forced to walk the cliffs at night, moaning out the pain in her unavenged soul." She shook a bony finger at Sabrina. "If there's no truth to them rumors, you tell me why the lady was right as rain not three days before her passing. And why the coffin was shut tighter than a miser's purse at the funeral, so that none could see inside. And why the earl walked away from the grave before the parson was half done with the requiem—"

"The man was overwrought!" Mr. Cherry exclaimed. "Miss Winthrope, you are bound to hear many stories concerning his lordship. While I cannot deny that his reputation is far from spotless, I can state without reservation that he was a devoted husband and is an exemplary father—"

Rina started. "*Father? The earl has a child?*"

"Two, actually. Lady Sarah and Lord David, the Viscount of Swansea." He leaned over and gave her hand a companionable pat. "Forgive me. I forgot that you have been so long separated from your family. There is much about them that you have yet to learn."

"Apparently," Rina murmured as she settled back against the seat, nervously fingering the braided gold cord around her waist. A father! Quinn had described the Black Earl as a monster, the closest thing there was to a devil on earth. She'd relied on that image to justify stealing from him and his family. But to find out that he had children made the demon lord somehow more . . . well, human. It put the whole business in an entirely different light.

Which was probably why Quinn had never saw fit to mention the existence of the younger Trevelyans, she thought with a grim smile. She'd known from the start that stepping into Prudence's life was going to be much more difficult than just showing a lawyer a handful of letters, but she hadn't expected the difficulties to include ghosts, suspicious deaths, and children. *Forced to walk the cliffs at night, moaning out the pain in her unavenged soul.*

A chill snaked down Rina's spine. She gazed out the window at the towering cliffs and the pounding, storm-dark sea, and wondered what else Quinn had neglected to tell her.

"Not here?" Mr. Cherry said, his smile disintegrating. "But I wrote to Lord Trevelyan. Several times. He could not have failed to get my letters, could he?"

"Can't say," replied the dour, lantern-jawed butler who bore the unlikely name of Merriman.

"But this is his long-lost cousin, returned home after thirteen years. Surely he would want to be here to welcome her?"

Merriman gave Sabrina a cursory glance, as if she were no more than a bit of lint on his black coat. He turned his gaze back to the solicitor. "His lordship does as he pleases. Always has. Always will. I suppose you'll be wantin' to see her ladyship, then."

"If it's not too much trouble," Mr. Cherry replied.

In Rina's opinion, Merriman looked as if he thought *everything* was too much trouble. "Well, you'll have to wait. Dr. Williams is with her at the moment."

"The physician?" Cherry asked. "I do hope it is nothing serious."

"Maybe it is, maybe it ain't. You'll have to wait all the same." Merriman shrugged and shuffled across the hall, pausing only the briefest moment to motion them to follow. Taking her son's arm, Mrs. Cherry grudgingly started after him, complaining incessantly about wet clothes, drafts, and catching her death of something or other.

Rina lagged behind, caught up in the austere grandeur of the room. The high arched ceiling was supported with rough-hewn beams, and colorful coats of arms decorated the spaces between. Massive bronze chandeliers hung down on chains as thick as her arm, and the oak walls were covered with displays of swords, shields, and armor that must have dated back hundreds of years. She felt as if she'd stepped into one of the stories her mother used to read her by the fire, about the court of the legendary King Arthur.

The butler and the Cherrys continued down the length of the hall, apparently not missing her. She paused in front of a finely polished suit of armor that stood in an alcove off to the room's side. Her imagination called up an image of a knight seated on a black charger, battling some evil lord for the honor of his lady love. Unable to resist she reached up, and traced the intricate scrollwork that covered the breastplate. *A knight in shining armor*, she thought wistfully, recalling her childhood dreams. It was only her imagination, of course, but she almost believed that she could feel the beat of the knight's heart under her hand, and see the glint of his eyes behind the slits of his ornate helm.

A whining sound jarred Sabrina out of her imaginings. Surprised, she peered into the dark alcove behind the armor. At first she could see nothing, but then her eyes picked out the shapes of a gangly girl and a shorter boy. The boy clasped a wiggling, whining ball of fur to his chest.

"Quiet, Pendragon," he whispered. "We're 'posed to be hiding."

Sabrina grinned. She was about to say hello when an angry call echoed through the hall.

"Where is that *beast*?"

Rina whirled around, and saw a short, rotund woman in a mobcap storming across the flagstones, sputtering like a Roman candle. "Where is it? I won't have that filthy animal in my—"

She caught sight of Sabrina and halted, placing her hands on her ample hips as she queried, "And who might you be?"

"Sa—Prudence."

"Ah. The cousin," the woman replied with a disinterested nod. "Well, I'm Poldhu, miss. The cook. And I'm looking for a mangy, flea-bitten mongrel that just stole a hen that was meant for this evening's supper—a fully dressed hen, I might add, that took me a good hour to prepare. I'll have that dog on a spit before I'm through with it. Have you seen the black-hearted creature?"

Sabrina glanced at the alcove, where three pairs of eyes pleaded for her silence. She turned back to Mrs. Poldhu. "I'm afraid I can't help you."

"More's the pity," intoned the cook as she resumed her frantic pace, and bustled out of the hall without so much as a good-bye.

As soon as the cook disappeared through the far door, Rina turned back to the alcove. "It's safe now. She's—"

She stopped, realizing the alcove was empty. Apparently the children had slipped out the far side while she was talking with Mrs. Poldhu. Sighing, she hurried out of the great hall to find the Cherrys. But Sabrina had not gone a dozen steps beyond the hall before she realized she was lost. The corridor split into three, each branch leading off in a maze of doors and passageways. Merriman and the Cherrys were nowhere in sight. She looked around for Mrs. Poldhu or one of the other servants, but the hallways were empty. She was just about to swallow her pride and call out for help when she heard voices coming from the corridor on her left.

Relieved, Rina followed the sound to a nearby door. It was open barely an inch, but she could hear the murmur of conversation, and saw the flicker of a fire reflected in the highly polished wood surface of the doorjamb. Anxious to leave the chill gloom of the deserted hallway behind, she pushed open the door and stepped into the sitting room.

The Cherrys were not there.

The conversation fell to stunned silence as Rina walked in. The man was tall and wore spectacles but it was the older woman in the wheelchair who captured her attention. Her meticulously styled white hair was wrapped around her head like a crown, and her high cheekbones and striking features bore the stamp of what must have once been a remarkable beauty. Her hand rested on a cane with an ornate silver handle, and strands of perfectly matched pearls circled her graceful throat. Even sitting, she bore herself with the pride and power of a queen. She was haughty, imperial, and impressive. And, for the moment at least, speechless.

The dowager countess. Sabrina had been preparing for this moment for weeks, going over and over how she would present herself to the Trevelyan matriarch. In her mind it had been easy—hoodwinking an imaginary family was far less difficult than facing living, breathing human beings. Her conscience urged her one last time to confess that this had all been a dreadful mistake, and to deal with the consequences as honestly and decently as she could. But since those consequences might very well include a hanging, she did not have much choice. She'd been dealt her hand and she had to play it out.

She lifted her chin and returned the dowager's gaze. "Hello, Grandmother. It has been a long time."

The woman's hand tightened on the cane's handle, but her imperial expression didn't flicker. "Maybe it has, and maybe it hasn't. Come closer, girl."

Rina stepped toward her and held her breath as the countess looked her up and down. Her gaze was sharp, reminding Sabrina of the canny produce merchants in the markets of Cheapside. *Now I know how a sack of potatoes feels.*

"You've the Trevelyan hair," the dowager commented at last. "And you always were a skinny thing, even as a child. But you inherited none of your mother's fashion sense. I have never seen an uglier dress."

"And I have never heard a ruder remark," Sabrina answered quietly.

Lady Penelope's eyes flashed fire. "Ha!" she cried as she raised her cane and rapped it against the floor. "You've got spirit, my girl. That goes more to proving you a Trevelyan than hair or looks ever could. Is that not so, Dr. Williams?"

"If she's half as obstinate as you, milady, I shall never have any peace," the doctor said, though without rancor.

Sabrina glanced up at the man, and realized she'd mistaken at least two things about him. With his thinning, wheat-brown hair and his severe clothing she'd assumed him to be in his mid-thirties, but a closer look revealed that he was only a handful of years older than she. And the blue eyes behind his studious-looking spectacles snapped with a warmth and humor that his stern demeanor could not entirely hide. Impulsively she smiled at the young physician, and was answered by an earnest grin. Rina liked him immediately.

He gave her a slight, stiff bow. "Charles Williams at your service, Miss Winthrope. When I am not trying to convince your grandmother to follow my instruction, I'm the head doctor at the Trevelyan mines."

"You're the *only* doctor at the Trevelyan mines," a voice behind Sabrina commented.

Rina turned around. Rising from a rose-colored divan near the window was a girl who appeared to be Sabrina's age—but that was all they had in common. Her skin was porcelain smooth, and her sun-gold ringlets framed a face an angel would have envied. She wore a blue silk gown with puffed, ribbon-laced sleeves that fell in elegantly simple folds around her diminutive figure. The girl was the embodiment of all the fairy-tale princesses Rina had read about as a child, but there was a bored poutiness to her perfect smile that made her ethereal image less than saintly. No doubt this was the divine Amy—and she looked every bit as pretty and petulant as Quinn had said.

"Amy! For heaven's sake, girl, young Fitzroy will be home tomorrow. Stop mooning over your intended's letter and come and greet your cousin," Lady Penelope commanded.

"He's not—" The beauty's smile faltered. For an instant Rina thought she saw uncertainty beneath the haughty expression, but it was gone so quickly that it may have been a flicker of the firelight. Amy walked up to Rina, and placed a halfhearted kiss on her cheek. "Hello, Cousin Prudence. 'Tis so good to have you back with us."

And why don't you jump off the cliffs while you're at it, Sabrina finished silently. Lady Amy's words may have been welcoming, but her tone was anything but. Probably didn't fancy attention being focused on anyone other than herself.

"Thank you, Cousin Amy. I am sure that I'm as delighted to meet you as you are to meet me." Rina was gratified to see Amy's eyes widen in surprise. Emboldened, she continued. "But I was so looking forward to meeting *all* my relatives. Unfortunately, I understand that Lord Trevelyan is not here."

"Nor likely to be, Miss Winthrope," the physician commented as he packed up his equipment into a brown leather satchel. "I've been here four months, and in all that time I've only seen his lordship once—when he hired me. He spends precious little time at Ravenshold."

Amy's pouting mouth pulled into a surprisingly hard line. "My brother is a busy man. He has many estates to see to."

"I'm sure he has, but that is no excuse to neglect this one. Many of the tenants' cottages are in need of basic repairs, and the engine at Wheal Grace should be replaced immediately."

Amy balled her fists in a very unladylike manner. "Edward has good reasons for staying away."

The countess rapped her cane decisively against the floor. "Stop this bickering! It is ill-mannered—especially in front of your new cousin. What must she be thinking?"

What Rina was thinking was that Amy's passionate defense of her brother was the first honest emotion she'd seen the girl exhibit. "I think . . . that there is a great deal I have yet to learn about the members of my family."

"Well spoken!" Dr. Williams stepped past Lady Amy as if she were a piece of furniture. "I know what it is like to be a newcomer in the district. If I can be of any assistance to you, Miss Winthrope, do not fail to call on me."

Amy glared at Sabrina. "I wouldn't be so free with my assistance, Doctor. We do not even know if she *is* Miss Winthrope."

"Amy!" The dowager paled. Rina saw the pain in the old woman's eyes, and felt the echo of it in her own heart. She'd felt it on the night her mother had passed away. She'd felt it again on the morning when she'd held her father's body in her arms, and prayed through her tears that he'd open his eyes and smile at her one last time. It was the need to believe against all odds that someone she'd loved and lost was still alive. And seeing the emotion in Lady Penelope's eyes shook Rina more deeply than anything had since her father's death.

Suddenly her charade wasn't a game anymore. She was playing with people's hearts here. People's souls. If she confessed her duplicity now, she was sure she could make the old woman understand. After all, Rina had lost someone dear to her, too. "Lady Penelope, there is something I need to tell you—"

Rina's words were cut short by a tremendous crash followed by a shriek. "That bloody hound!"

The door burst open, and in ran one small dog and two small children, followed by one rotund, angry cook. Pendragon raced across the room, his toenails clicking against the floor. He circled the room and darted back toward the door, his path taking him right between Rina and Dr. Williams. He'd have made a clean break for it if he hadn't caught a paw in one of the ribbons edging Rina's skirt. The pup's momentum unbalanced Sabrina, who fell into Charles, who toppled into Amy, who tumbled into the children and Mrs. Poldhu. The lot of them went down in a flailing tangle of arms, legs and curses.

The force of the fall knocked the air from Sabrina's lungs. Dazed, she lifted her head, and saw Dr. Williams with his head buried in Lady Amy's bosom. Both of them were red as beets. Nearby, Sarah and David were disentangling themselves from the voluminous folds of Mrs. Poldhu's apron and skirt, while an apparently contrite Pendragon licked the astonished cook's nose. And looking down on them all was the dowager, who stared open-mouthed as if she could not believe that such an unseemly thing could happen in her drawing room.

Since she'd walked through the door of Mr. Cherry's office, Sabrina had kept her emotions in tight check, measuring every word, every look, every tilt of her head against what she believed Prudence would have done. Now, in the sheer absurdity of the moment, her pent-up emotions burst forth. She started to laugh—not the refined titter of a proper lady, but the rich, life-loving laughter that she'd inherited from her father. Dr. Williams started to grin as well, and quite soon they were all laughing along with her, even the haughty Amy. Rina laughed so hard that tears welled in her eyes. Still laughing, she closed her eyes to wipe those tears away.

Suddenly the laughter died. Opening her eyes, Sabrina found herself nose-to-toe with a pair of mud-spattered Hessian boots. She looked up, and saw thick columns of muscular legs, a rain-drenched greatcoat spanning powerful shoulders, a rugged face and piercing gray eyes that were so full of fury that they made the storm outside seem tame.

"What the *devil* is going on here?"

Chapter Five

Lord Edward Blake, seventh Earl of Trevelyan, Viscount Glendugan, Baron Carlisle, and ancestral lord of Ravenshold, was in a foul mood. He'd been in the middle of some tricky negotiations to expand his holdings in Yorkshire when Cherry's misdirected letter about his "cousin" finally reached him. Abandoning the negotiations had cost him dearly in both pride and purse, but he'd left for Cornwall at once by any coach, cart, or horse that would take him.

When he did arrive, he was greeted at the door by an unusually befuddled Merriman, who kept mumbling something about "the misplaced lady." Exhausted, soaked to the skin, and clear out of patience, Edward had ignored the nattering butler and made straight for the drawing room.

And walked in on bedlam.

"What the *devil* is going on here?" he roared.

For a moment everyone in the room froze. Then the young man whom Edward recognized as the doctor he'd hired for Wheal Grace leapt to his feet, and pulled a slightly breathless Amy up after him. "Uhm, good day, my lord. We weren't expecting you."

"I can see that. I'm away for a few months and I walk in on a scene from a lunatic asylum!"

"Oh, Edward, don't be such a grumpy bear," Amy said as she deftly yanked her dress's shoulder back in place. "There's no harm done."

No harm? He'd just endured four days and nights of ankle-deep mud, inns with sour wine and worse food, hard seats, rutted roads, hellish weather—all to return to a home he'd spent the last three years of his life avoiding. He'd done it to save his family, but from their raucous laughter and wide smiles it appeared that his rescue was both unnecessary and unappreciated. Frustrated and disappointed, he slapped his rain-drenched hat against his thigh, spattering a shower of cold water drops across the floor. Looking around, his gaze was drawn as always to his children. They stood arm in arm, watching him with wary eyes. His stomach clenched as he realized how much they looked like their mother. "Did either of you have a part in this?"

"Don't yell at the children. It was not their fault."

No one had taken that tone with him in years. Surprised, he looked down at his feet, and saw something that resembled a gypsy's gauded-up carnival tent pushing itself to a sitting position. He had a scant second to register the well-disguised curves of a feminine figure and a sadly disheveled mess of red hair before the woman turned her face up toward him.

And he saw a pair of the greenest, angriest, and most breathtaking eyes he'd ever seen.

The countess's voice broke the moment. "Edward, the least you can do is help your cousin to her feet."

His cousin. The impostor. *Good Christ.* He purposely

stepped past the woman. "She can sit there and rot for all I care," he proclaimed as he strode toward the dowager. "Grandmother, how could you let another charlatan into our home?"

"She is *not* a charlatan. Mr. Cherry has letters. And her hair is Trevelyan red."

"Letters can be forged. Hair can be dyed." He leaned down, bracing himself on the chair arms as he stared into the face of the woman who had given him love when no one else had given a damn. "I will not let you put yourself through this again. I know how much you want to believe otherwise, but this woman is an impostor. Prudence Winthrope is dead—"

"Are you so certain?"

The soft, sure words pierced the quiet like a skillfully wielded dagger. The woman had risen to her feet, and was calmly smoothing her skirt as if she'd just snagged it on a rosebush at a garden party. Her dress was every bit as ridiculous as he'd thought and her face was far from beautiful, but there was a canniness in her eyes that he'd never seen in a woman so young. The chit was a cool customer, but it was more than that. There was something about the way she moved, even in the way she smoothed her skirt, that drew his eyes. Deep inside him, something long dead stirred to life. He found himself reluctant to turn away from her, and that reluctance disturbed him.

"Do not cross me," he warned. Few people challenged Lord Trevelyan, and the ones who did invariably lived to regret it. He'd reduced men to tears with little more than a glance. But this woman met his anger head-on, her fierce gaze locked with his own without so much as a flinch. It unnerved him. It impressed him. It had been a long time since anyone had stood up to him. It had been far longer since a woman had stirred him—

He looked away. "Very well. If you *are* Prudence Winthrope, tell me something only she and I would know."

For a moment the only sound in the room was the crackling fire, and Edward thought he'd gotten the better of her. Then, with the slow cadence of someone searching their mind for remembrances, she began to speak.

"It was a warm day . . . summer, I think. The air smelled of lilacs and rhododendrons."

Amy chimed in. "She's right about that, Edward. Our garden is full of both those flowers in the summer."

"So is every other garden in southern England," he replied. He crossed his arms over his chest, his lips edging up in anticipated triumph. "You will have to do better than that."

He'd thought to intimidate her. Instead, she lifted her chin and returned his glare with a smile so excessively sweet he was like to get a toothache. "I'd stolen something from you—your hat, I believe. I climbed up a tree and you climbed up after me. But you never caught me. You lost your footing, and fell crashing through the leaves and branches to the ground. I'm afraid you received a number of cuts and bruises on my account."

"That's true," Amy cried as she turned toward her brother. "I've heard Grandmother tell the story. And you've still got that scar on your—"

"All right," he interrupted hastily. "The story's true. I'll own you've been thorough in your study of our family. But an artfully told tale doesn't explain why you went to my solicitor first instead of coming straight to Ravenshold. And it doesn't address why you never came forward during the past thirteen years."

"I went to Mr. Cherry because I wanted to show I had no fear of anyone investigating my background. And as for not coming forward before this time—" Her lower lip quivered. She pulled out a handkerchief, and began to dab her eyes. "For years my first memory was of a fire. On her deathbed, Mother—that is, Mrs. Plowright—told me that I could barely recall how to speak when they found me, much less remember who I was. It is only recently that I have begun to remember what happened on that horrible night. Even now, the memory of it still makes me weak—"

Slowly, she started to swoon. Instinctively Edward stepped forward, but Charles was closer and reached her first. The physician caught her in his arms and laid her on the nearby divan. Stunned, Edward watched as his grandmother, his sister, his children, and even the unflappable Mrs. Poldhu all hovered around his supposed cousin, patting her hand and encouraging her with words of sympathy and concern. The woman smiled up at them weakly, pressing her handkerchief to her forehead as she struggled to overcome her faint. She appeared to be a picture of distressed femininity, but for a brief instant she caught Edward's eye.

She looked like a fox who had just outsmarted a pack of hounds.

Edward's hands clenched into fists. The woman was dangerous. Even on this short acquaintance he could see that she was far more clever than any of the other "Prudences" who'd come to Ravenshold over the years. Most of the counterfeit cousins had been unmasked in a few days; some had lasted not more than a few hours. Yet whether they'd lasted a week or a minute, the same damage was done. Every time a pretender was unmasked, he'd watched his grandmother's hopes come crashing to the ground.

The last had happened two years ago, when the false Prudence proved to be a barmaid from Brighton. It had taken his grandmother a full month to recover. Now the countess was two years older, two years more frail. There was a real possibility that she might not survive another shock.

Trevelyan had long since given up any hope of personal happiness. He'd learned to expect the worst from people, and had yet to be disappointed. But the one thing he'd never wavered from was his duty to his family. It was his place to protect them, however ill-equipped he was to perform that task.

He walked toward the divan, his jaw pulling taut. "How is . . . Miss Winthrope?"

"She's exhausted," the doctor answered curtly as he laid two fingers against the side of the woman's throat. "But her heartbeat is steady. She needs rest."

She'll rest in Old Bailey if I have anything to say about it, Edward thought as he arched a threatening brow. But the lady wasn't the only one adept at hiding her plans behind a pleasant smile. "Of course she does," he said, schooling his voice to a sympathetic timbre. "I'll have Merriman take her to her room. She can rest up a bit before I resume my questions."

The dowager countess shook her cane at him roundly. "Edward! I'll not have you interrogating her like a common criminal. You've already put the poor girl through enough."

"I wouldn't think of it, Grandmother. I intend to ask her only one more question, one I'm sure she'll have no problem with whatsoever—if she is indeed Prudence Winthrope." He glanced at the woman, giving her a smile every inch as deceitfully innocent as the one she'd so recently given him. "I'm sure Miss Winthrope would have no objection to it. In fact, I'm sure she'll look forward to reacquainting herself with her old friend Ginger."

• • •

Sabrina stared into the hearth fire of her bedchamber. It was a pleasant room, with chintz curtains the color of sunshine and a four-poster with a coverlet embroidered with sunflowers and butterflies. The fire was equally pleasant—a bright, cheery blaze that was a far cry from the niggardly brazier in her stepmother's house. It was the cozy kind of room she'd dreamed about during the years she'd spent in her drafty garret. A place she could call home . . . except that this particular home belonged to Prudence Winthrope, not to her. And she'd best remember it, or she might end up on a hangman's scaffold.

"Where do ya want this, miss?"

Rina looked up. A laborer in a rough coat and wide-brimmed felt hat stood in her doorway, holding her valise. She waved him toward the foot of her bed, then returned to her bleak thoughts. Everything had been going fine until *he'd* shown up. Trevelyan had roared into the room with a voice like thunder and an anger as hot as lightning. He wasn't particularly tall—the doctor had topped him by a good half foot. Nevertheless, the room seemed to shrink when he entered.

Quinn had called him the Black Earl, but only now did she realize how well the name fit. The man had a black heart—she'd seen it in his dark, merciless glance. She might expect some measure of sympathy from the dowager, but from the earl, never. Trevelyan's eyes were as gray and forbidding as the rock cliffs Ravenshold was built on. Cliffs that were, according to Mrs. Cherry, haunted by the spirit of the earl's murdered wife.

Once again the laborer's voice interrupted her thoughts. "Will there be anything else you're wantin', Miss Murphy?"

Rina shook her head. "No, that will be—" She

stopped, realizing what the man had said. She leapt from her chair and faced the man . . . saw a pair of bright, mischievous eyes peeping out from beneath the hat.

"Quinn! What are you doing here?"

"That fossil of a butler couldn't lift his own shoe. I hired on to do the fetchin' and carryin', and to tend to the stables. And to keep an eye out for you, Miss Winthrope." He swept the hat from his head in an exaggerated gesture of homage. "You've foxed 'em good and proper, lass. Your da would be proud."

The mention of her father brought a smile to her lips, but it vanished almost instantly. "But I haven't foxed them, Quinn. At least, not Lord Trevelyan. He knows I'm not Prudence."

"What he *knows* and what he can *prove* are different as pounds and pence," Quinn assured her. He glanced around the room. "Like as not they wouldn't have set you up in such swell digs if they didn't believe you. You're on your way, my lass. If the Black Earl had a card to play against you he'd have used it."

"He already has." She rubbed her arms, as if all the warmth had suddenly left the room. "Prudence had a favorite toy named Ginger. Apparently she left it behind when she and her mother returned to Italy. After Prudence died, the countess locked the toy away as a sort of remembrance. But now the earl intends me to go to the nursery, and pick out Ginger from the rest of the . . ."

She stopped as she realized Quinn was no longer listening to her. His eyes had taken on a faraway look. "There were a toy," he mused, his voice so soft that she wondered if he was speaking to himself or to her. "I remember her crying for it the night I tucked her in. Said it were her protector, and that the monsters cou'na get her if she held it close. Said . . ." He shook his head. "That's what the bloke who sold me the locket said, leastways. Told me there were a toy, but didn't say what. Still, how hard can it be? Just look for something a little girl would fall asleep with—"

"That could be anything." Sabrina walked over and sat heavily on the valise, and cradled her head in her hands. "Quinn, I know you've put your hopes in me, but there's a good chance I might not be able to pull this off—"

"Fiddlesticks! Your da was the best confidence artist I've ever seen, and you're his daughter to the nines. I knowed that the minute I laid eyes on you."

"I'm scared, Quinn—scared of what the earl will do to me if he finds out the truth. He's cruel and utterly without compassion. And there's something about the way he looks at me that makes my wits scatter."

"You keep those wits about you, missy," Quinn warned, his eyes sharp with concern. "That man's dangerous in ways you can't imagine. All of his blood are. No, you concentrate on being Prudence. Then, in a couple of weeks we'll have the Dutchman's Necklace, and you can forget all about this evil place and its Black Earl."

There was a knock on the door, followed by Merriman's bored voice. "Miss, I've been sent to collect you."

Sabrina panicked. "Quinn, what do I—?" She turned just in time to see Quinn's lithe form slip through the dressing room door. Once again she was on her own.

"Coming, Merriman." Squaring her shoulders she went to the door, and followed the laconic butler down the hallway. She thought about Quinn's last words to her, that Trevelyan was dangerous to her in ways she couldn't imagine. She didn't fully understand what he'd meant, but it hardly mattered. The ways she *could* imagine were dangerous enough. If she didn't convince him she was Prudence, she'd hang for sure. But if she did . . . well, then she'd have enough money to make a new start in another country, where no one had ever heard of Albert Tremaine or Sabrina Murphy.

It was a gamble, but one worth taking, even if it meant enduring the cold, soulless stare of the Black Earl of Trevelyan. He could curse and bluster all he wanted, but he could do nothing to her as long as she was able to pick out Prudence's old toy.

As Quinn had said, how difficult could that be?

Far more difficult than she'd imagined.

The nursery was a whimsical room, with cream walls painted with rainbows, flowers, and charmingly rendered nursery rhyme characters. The curtains had been pulled back from a bank of windows, letting in the late afternoon sun that had followed the recent thunderstorm. The room was filled with sunshine, fresh air, and the soothing rumble of the distant sea.

The room was also filled with toys.

Sabrina glanced around, her panic rising. There were hobbyhorses, stuffed animals, miniature soldiers, tea sets, picture books, buttons, bows, Christmas crackers, and porcelain dolls as far as the eye could see. For a moment she prayed that she'd accidentally wandered into a toy shop instead of a nursery. That faint hope was shattered by a familiar baritone voice.

"Your old toy is here, *Cousin*. Why the hesitation?"

Sabrina spun around. Behind her sat the dowager, her hand still perched on her silver-topped cane. Amy and an anxious-looking Mr. Cherry stood behind her. But it was the earl who captured Rina's attention. He had changed from his mud-spattered travel clothes into a royal blue superfine coat that molded to his powerful shoulders like a second skin. His black pants and polished boots were of the first quality, and his snow white cravat was simply tied and fixed with a diamond pin, its austerity adding to the authority of his figure rather than detracting from it. Clearly the Earl of Trevelyan had no need for the corsets, sawdust shoulder pads, and other figure-enhancing flummery she'd seen used by the foppish London gentry. He was solid muscle from head to toe, and the sight of him made her heart beat in a peculiarly erratic fashion. *It's only nerves. I'm just anxious about finding the toy.*

"Well, Miss Winthrope?"

The confidence in his voice renewed her courage; if he expected her to be intimidated by a neatly tied stock and a pair of boots he was sadly mistaken. "It has been a long time, my lord. Surely even you have trouble recalling your past sometimes."

A heartbeat passed before he answered. "No. I recall every moment of my past."

His deep-set eyes were as hard and forbidding as before, but for an instant she sensed a haunting sadness behind the remoteness. She'd experienced the emotion too many times herself to mistake it in others, and the thought that she had anything in common with the Black Earl made her heart hammer so hard she feared it would crack a rib.

The countess's voice ended the moment. "For heaven's sake, Edward, give the girl a chance. It *has* been a long time." She turned to Sabrina, her eyes full of encouragement and hope. "Take your time, my dear. We have been waiting years. We can wait a little longer."

Sabrina smiled at the dowager's kindness. She took a steadying breath and started to walk around the room, studying the assembled toys. Some, like the hobbyhorses and dollhouses, she discounted immediately, along with the books and miniature soldiers—no little girl would snuggle with any of them in bed. She also passed by the stuffed animals assembled on the window seat, for they were all sun-faded—and had therefore not been stored away in the dark for thirteen years.

One by one she mentally checked off the toys, weighing the odds of each one being Prudence's favorite against what she knew of the little girl. Quinn's words came back to her. *I remember her crying for it the night I tucked her in. Said it were her protector . . .*

Sabrina looked at the dolls, all lined in neat rows along the cabinet shelves. They were pretty and perfect, with bright smiles painted on their porcelain faces. But none of them looked like a protector. Instinctively her hand covered the locket she wore beneath her dress, the one that contained Prudence's portrait. She always felt reassured when she held it, as if somehow it brought her closer to the long-dead child. In a strange way she could almost feel Prudence beside her, guiding her decision. She took a deep breath. "It wasn't a doll. I recall distinctly that Ginger was not a doll."

A sharp gasp told Rina that she was correct. She turned to see the dowager smiling broadly, and Amy's lips wavering in a slight but unmistakable grin. Mr. Cherry mopped his brow, looking relieved. "I vow, this is far more exhilarating than I anticipated. I believe we should all adjourn for a moment to catch our breaths—"

"No!" Trevelyan's voice roared through the room. "We are not interested in what Ginger *isn't*, Miss Winthrope. Or whatever your name is."

The dowager's cane rapped the floor. "Edward! You will not speak to your cousin in that tone."

"She is not my cousin. Not until she chooses Ginger." He turned back to Rina, his tone low and lethal as he continued. "My grandmother is old and sick. She

cannot bear another disappointment. The last pretender
nearly cost her her life."

Rina fired back, her voice just as lethal. "*I* am not the
pretender, sir. You pretend to care for your grandmother, but all you truly care about is your own pride
and position."

"Why, you—!" Furious, he reached out and gripped
her wrist, apparently intending to frighten her.

Edward's hand burned through her like living fire,
searing her skin from the inside out. Feelings collided
inside her with the force of billiard balls. She felt hot yet
cold, weak yet strong, frightened yet brilliantly alive. She
desperately wanted him to let go of her. Just as desperately she wanted him to go on holding her forever.

He let go. Still reeling from his touch, Rina lifted
her gaze to his—and met eyes as frigid as a winter night.
He looked at her as a parlor maid might glance at an
errant dust mite. Troublesome. Insignificant. Dirty.
Whatever she'd felt had been entirely one-sided.

The fire in her blood changed to a blush of shame.
She turned away, more determined than ever to succeed
in her deception.

She scanned the room, and saw that there were only
two toys left. They were both propped in a wooden
cradle beside the fireplace. One was a stuffed lion, gold
as the sun with a thick mane of ginger-colored yarn. The
other was a bedraggled stuffed bear, who was missing his
left eye and several patches of his mud brown pelt. Both
were the right size for a little girl to cuddle in bed, but
common sense and the telltale color of its mane pointed
to the lion as a sure bet. Still, she didn't reach out. If she
chose incorrectly, Trevelyan would hand her over to the
authorities, who would inevitably link her with Albert's
death. This decision would affect the rest of her life—not
to mention the *length* of her life.

Help me, Prudence. Help me to make the right choice. In her mind's eye she saw the figure of a little girl running through the corridors of Ravenshold, clutching a stuffed toy against her chest. Whether the picture was a true vision or wishful thinking Rina couldn't say, but she saw the animal in the girl's arms—an animal that was constantly squeezed, scrunched, and loved so hard that pieces of its fur had been worn away. Opening her eyes, she reached out with absolute certainty and picked up the tattered bear. As she lifted it into the sunlight, she saw that its one good eye was the color of ginger.

A loud sob shattered the silence. Sabrina turned around, and saw the dowager with tears streaming down her cheeks. "Forgive me. Until this moment I didn't fully know . . . I didn't entirely believe . . . oh, my dear!"

She opened her arms. Rina fell into them, letting the old woman believe she was her Prudence—and letting herself believe that she had a loving grandmother and a family she belonged to. Wiping away tears of her own, Rina accepted Amy's surprised acknowledgment, and Mr. Cherry's hearty and long-winded congratulations. And out of the corner of her eye, she saw the Black Earl standing in the middle of the nursery, watching the scene in front of him with dismay and fury. A hundred Gingers would not have been enough to prove to Lord Trevelyan that she was his long-lost cousin.

Prudence's toy wasn't the only thing she'd found this afternoon. She'd also gained an enemy.

Chapter
Six

Morning.

Groaning, Sabrina screwed her eyes shut and pulled the quilt over her face. She hated mornings. There was always the wash to do and the bread to bake, and she didn't doubt that Tilly had left her a stack of unwashed dishes from the night before. Mornings meant the beginning of a day where she worked from sunup to sundown without a moment to catch her breath. And she had been having the most marvelous dream . . . She burrowed deeper into the covers, and tried to ignore the sunshine, the songbirds, and the smell of salt air that came wafting through her open window—

Salt air?

Rina's eyes snapped open. She lifted the edge of the covers, and peeked out into a bright, sunshine-filled room that was nothing like her garret. It hadn't been a dream at all—she was no longer Sabrina Murphy, the overworked stepdaughter of Widow Murphy. As of yesterday, she was the Honorable Miss Prudence Winthrope, cousin to the wealthy and powerful Trevelyans of Ravenshold. Purring like a contented cat, she stretched with the slow, luxurious indulgence of the idle rich. She'd convinced everyone that she was the long-lost heiress, and the fact that she'd also succeeded in annoying the disagreeable Lord Trevelyan only added to her triumph.

Grinning, she pushed back the covers—and saw two pairs of eyes staring at her from the foot of her bed.

David turned to his sister and said in a loud whisper, "We woke her up!"

"No," Rina said hastily. She pushed herself to a sitting position. "You didn't wake me. I was just getting up, and I appreciate the company."

The children didn't look entirely convinced, but they didn't run away, either. Sabrina very much wanted them to stay. In all the excitement yesterday, she'd formed only a fleeting impression of the red-haired girl and her towheaded brother. Now, in the full light of morning, she took the opportunity to study the earl's children.

Lady Sarah wore a long-sleeved white frock tied at the waist with a spring green ribbon. She was all knees and elbows, with a spray of freckles across the bridge of her nose, but she had her grandmother's cheekbones and slender build, and Rina had no doubt that one day she'd be a great beauty. The young viscount was shorter and more squarely built, much like his father, but there was a sweetness to his smile that had definitely not been inherited from Trevelyan. All at once Rina found herself wondering about the children's mother, who had passed away under such questionable circumstances. Those thoughts ended abruptly, however, with Sarah's next words.

"My father says you are a liar."

Sabrina had challenged her stepmother too many times not to recognize the child's attempt at adult bravado. Sarah was clearly a fighter who did not give her trust easily, but Rina suspected that once given it was a gift worth having. Rina folded her hands on the covers in front of her, and returned the girl's challenge with the respect it deserved. "You're correct. I *am* a liar. After all, I lied to Mrs. Poldhu about not seeing you hiding behind the suit of armor."

"But that was a *good* lie," David blurted out as he tugged on his sister's sleeve. "We're glad she lied, aren't we, Saree? Otherwise Cook would'a got Pen and chopped him into little—"

"Quiet, Davey."

Sarah bit her lip, her earlier confidence wavering. Rina's answer had stumped her, but she was clearly not yet prepared to trust her new cousin. There was a wariness in her eyes that told Rina the girl had been deeply hurt in the past. Hardly surprising, since Sarah would have been five when her mother passed away. She'd have been old enough to remember, but not to understand. *As if something like that could ever be understood.*

A lump rose in Rina's throat as she glanced from one child to the other. "We have something in common, you and I. We have all lost our mothers."

She expected Sarah's expression to soften. Instead, she winced as if from a physical blow. "It's not true. What you've heard about my mother, it isn't true."

Sabrina blinked in surprise. "I haven't heard anything, Sarah. I just want to be your friend."

Sarah stepped back, dragging her confused younger brother after her. She headed for the door, but turned back before she left the room. "I'll never be your friend, no matter what you say!"

Mrs. Poldhu may have the temperament of a sergeant major, but she set a table that would have done Buckingham Palace proud. In fact, the whole breakfast had been very satisfying. The dowager was warm and welcoming. Lady Amy was preoccupied with her own thoughts, but she had not been overtly unkind. Ill-tempered Mrs. Cherry considered it uncivilized for anyone to rise before one. And the earl had left shortly after dawn with Mr. Cherry to visit the mine. Had it not been for her concern over Sarah's disturbing behavior, Rina might have genuinely enjoyed herself. Yet the little girl's hurt and angry words kept coming back to her. *What you've heard about my mother, it isn't true.*

The dowager paused in her morning ritual of depositing exactly one and one half teaspoons of sugar in her morning tea, and looked across the breakfast table. "Do you ride, Prudence?"

"Yes, I do, Grandmother. My father taught me . . . that is, the Reverend Plowright taught me while we were in Africa."

"Excellent. It promises to be a fine day. Amy shall take you riding and introduce you to the Ravenshold grounds."

The decree jarred a petulant protest from Amy. "Grandmother, I have . . . other plans."

"Those plans will wait. It is important that we reacquaint Prudence with her birthright, and since your brother has apparently ignored this duty, you must step in. And it will give you a chance to get to know each other."

Lady Amy looked as if she would prefer swallowing a bottle of foul-tasting medicine to squiring her cousin, and Rina was just as loath to spend the day with the spoiled miss. Besides, she had plans of her own—such as finding Quinn and discussing the next phase of their deception.

"Of course I would love to spend time with my

cousin," Rina lied, "but I cannot go riding with her. 'Tis been years since I've sat a horse. I do not even own a habit."

The dowager swept aside her argument with a majestic wave of her hand. "Amy ordered several new dresses last month, including a new habit. Her old one will suit you until we can secure the services of a modiste. As for not being on a horse in years, it don't signify. Riding is in a Trevelyan's blood, like Ravenshold and Wheal Grace. No, you two shall spend the afternoon in happy association. I will allow no more discussion on the matter."

The dowager was true to her word: A scant hour later, two displeased-looking ladies riding a bay gelding and a sorrel mare left the stable yard for a tour of the grounds of Ravenshold.

Lady Penelope had been right about it being a lovely day. The endless blue sky was dotted with only a few woolly clouds, and the sunlight winked across the calm sea like a handful of butterflies. Yesterday Sabrina had thought the land bleak and barren, but she'd been wrong. Bright pink blossoms grew right up to the edge of the cliffs—sea thrift, Amy called it—and the woods beyond were overflowing with bluebells, jonquils, and other wildflowers. The smell was intoxicating. Fat larks and chattering magpies skittered through the gnarled branches of old oaks, setting up a chorus as fine as any church choir. Everywhere Rina looked, the land seemed to be bursting with color and life, from the green lawns to the flower-filled woods to the whitewashed cottages of the fishing village in the nearby cove.

"That white tower," Rina said as she shielded her eyes against the noonday sun. "The one rising up beyond the trees. Is that a lighthouse?"

"That's the engine at Wheal Grace," Amy answered. "It houses the steam engine that runs the whim."

"Whim?"

"The winding device that lifts the miners up and down the shaft," she explained irritably, as if Rina should have already known such things. "Are you sure this sun is not too hot for you? You look fatigued."

"I feel fine," Rina assured her. It was the truth. The lusty sea wind blew a hint of salt spray against her cheeks. And the simple hunter's green riding habit Amy had lent her was far more to her liking than the tricked-up gowns Quinn had bought for her. She leaned forward and patted her mount's neck, feeling more content than she had since she'd escaped from her stepmother's. "In fact, I feel quite marvelous. Tell me, what are the red stakes for? The ones driven into the ground near the cliff's edge."

"They mark loose rocks, and the parts of the cliff paths that were weakened by yesterday's rain. And speaking of yesterday, I know yours was rather exhausting. You still look a bit peaked. Perhaps you should return to the house and—"

"I'm *fine*," Sabrina repeated emphatically as she turned her mount away from the cliff's edge.

They followed the rocky path toward the forest. Sabrina momentarily halted her mount as her skirt snagged on a bramble. She worked it free and looked up, and caught sight of Amy perched on the edge of her saddle and peering into the woods' tangled shadows, clearly expecting to see something—or someone. When she saw that Rina was watching her, she sat hastily back in her seat. "Uhm, delightful weather we are having, isn't it?"

Amy was up to something—Rina just didn't know

what. Perhaps it had something to do with the "young Fitzroy" whose letter had so preoccupied her attention in the sitting room. The dense, deserted woods would have been an ideal spot for a lovers' tryst. Pulling her horse to Amy's side, Rina stole a glance at the young woman's profile. She seemed the picture of angelic innocence, but Rina knew just how deceiving looks could be.

A young man erupted from the woods in front of them—but not the kind of young man she'd expected. He was a sandy-haired stable lad of about thirteen, riding an old piebald gelding. He carried a large wicker hamper in front of him and had several fat leather sacks slung over his saddle. After clearing the forest he halted and stood in the path, looking from side to side.

When he caught sight of Amy, he rode toward her with all the speed he could urge out of the plodding old horse. "Here it is, your ladyship. I brought the whole lot, including the tarts, though I had to steal them off of the windowsill while they were like to burn my—"

The lad saw Sabrina. Both his horse and his words came to a dead halt. He glanced to Amy, then back to Rina, his eyes wide with guilt and alarm. "I don't know nothin' about nothin'."

Confused, Sabrina walked her mount toward Amy. "Cousin, what is going on here?"

Amy bit her lip while she fiddled with her reins. Then, sighing, she raised her chin, and met Sabrina's questioning glance with a forthright gaze. "All right, I will tell you. There's no point in hiding it, since you have tumbled on to our secret. Toby was following my orders. I told him to steal the food. A few months ago my maid Clara Hobbs was turned off. Her father drowned in a sudden storm last year, and her family can ill afford the loss of her pay. I take them food when I can to ease their predicament."

Rina furrowed her brow, still not understanding. "But why the secrecy? Giving food to a family in need is simple Christian charity."

"There's nothing simple about it. Clara was turned off because she is going to have child. But . . . she has no husband."

Rina sat back in her sidesaddle, comprehending at last. The maid's act was considered a heinous sin, the kind that deserved the full measure of God's wrath and society's condemnation. If the dowager found out that Amy was aiding her wicked servant she would most certainly put an end to it. The nobility did not involve themselves in such sordid matters—though Rina had seen for herself that they were often the cause of them.

Amy took Rina's silence as censure. "I do not care what you think. Clara is my friend and I will not desert her, especially when everyone else has turned their back on her. And if you tell Grandmother what I am doing, I shall simply find another way to help her!"

Rina's father had once warned her never to judge the card in the hole by the four faceup ones surrounding it. Grimacing, she realized she'd done just that. She'd lumped Amy in with all the other pretty, spoiled socialites she'd seen, and had failed to see the true gold behind her pampered nature. "I have no intention of telling Grandmother. A few months ago a housemaid I knew was thrown out for a similar reason. I wasn't in a position to help Kitty, but I'd like to help your friend if you'll let me."

Amy regarded her cautiously. Then a warm grin crossed her face, melting her affected, icy loveliness and revealing a far more beautiful soul underneath. "If you truly want to help, then take one of Toby's sacks. Old Socrates will be glad for the lightened load."

• • •

Once Amy had decided to trust Rina, there was no stopping her conversation. Confidences poured out like wine in a tavern. In short order Rina learned about the disagreeable Larkin sisters who lived at a nearby estate, the handkerchief scandal at last year's Christmas Ball which involved Lieutenant Randall and "a married lady," the concerns the girl had for the poor state of her grandmother's health, the difficulty in receiving the latest fashion magazines in a timely manner, the names of the flowers, frightening tales of the sea, and the deep, uncompromising affection she bore for Ravenshold and her family.

Sabrina listened to the girl's chatter and made a mental note that she'd be a useful source of information for the future. Instantly, she felt a stab of conscience. Amy was the sort of person who thrived on conversation and companionship, but the remoteness of Ravenshold gave her little opportunity to meet people her own age. She'd given her friendship wholeheartedly to Rina— a friendship Rina intended to use to help steal the Dutchman.

She wished Quinn had been right about Amy—that she had turned out to be spoiled and self-centered. But nothing about Ravenshold was exactly as it appeared to be. Not the land. Not the dowager. Not the children. *Not Trevelyan.*

"Is he not the most insufferable creature that you have ever met?" Amy asked.

For a moment Rina feared the young woman had read her mind. She was surprised to hear Amy speak so badly of the brother she'd staunchly defended yesterday. "I thought you were fond of him."

Amy pulled her horse to a halt. She stared at Sabrina, clearly horrified. "I am not! How can you say that? He is the rudest, most loathsome person alive. If it were not for my grandmother's health, I would refuse to receive Dr. Williams at Ravenshold."

Silently Rina chided herself for not paying more attention to the conversation. "Forgive me. I was mistaken."

"You most certainly were." Amy nodded, urging her mare forward down the wooded path. "I would never be foolish enough to form a tendresse for the likes of him. When I fall in love it will be with someone well-bred, who has impeccable taste and manners. Someone like Mr. Paris Fitzroy."

Thinking back, Sabrina recalled that "young Fitzroy" was the author of the letter Amy had been poring over when Rina entered the sitting room. "Is he not the gentleman your grandmother called your intended?"

"He has asked me to marry him, but I have not made up my mind yet. I have known Paris simply forever, and our lands march together—it would be an advantageous match for both families. But there is no hurry. He's devoted to me, and has said he will wait for my answer whether it takes a month or a lifetime. And 'tis not as if our estates would suffer. After all, his sister Cassie is going to marry my brother."

An unexplainable burning sensation flared near Rina's heart. "I . . . did not realize the earl was engaged."

Amy laughed. "La, he has not even asked her. But they are bound to marry someday. Cassie is as devoted to Edward as Paris is to me. I suspect she only married Sir Cyril because her heart was broken over my brother's marriage to Isabel. Then, when Sir Cyril passed away last fall—he was a good deal older than she was— Edward was at Cassie's side, just as she was at his side after Isabel . . . died."

Amy's hesitation lasted the barest moment, but that was long enough to raise Rina's suspicions. She glanced around, and was glad to see that Toby was a good distance behind, whistling broken snippets of a ribald song. Turning back, she leaned toward Amy and lowered her voice to a clandestine whisper. "How did Lady Isabel die?"

Amy looked down and fiddled with her reins. "Uhm, it was the typhus. A sudden and virulent case—"

"Amy, I am no doctor, but I know that typhus takes a fortnight to run its course, and I've heard that the countess was the picture of health not three days before her death."

Amy hesitated, then slowly nodded. "You are right. You are family now, and you have a right to know. Isabel did not die from an illness—that was just a story we invented to protect the children. She was drowned in a shipwreck off the coast of Calais. A sudden Channel squall capsized the boat. Not a soul survived."

It was a tragic tale—and to Rina's mind a puzzling one. "But why should you want to keep it a secret? Why not just say that she drowned in a shipwreck?"

"Because of the *reason* she was on that ship," Amy replied, her voice growing tight with anger. "Isabel was on her way to France . . . with her lover."

Sabrina's jaw dropped in shock. Growing up in London she'd seen the selfishness of the gentry first-hand, but for a mother to desert her young children—to expose them to the shame and scandal of a public affair—seemed the cruelest act imaginable. "How could she do that to Sarah and David?"

"I don't know. Isabel always seemed to adore the children. And she and Edward seemed the happiest of couples. My brother took it very hard. For weeks after it happened he kept to his room, eating too little and drinking too much. The only one who could come near him at all was Cassie. When he did come out, he was a different man—hard, remote, and in a way I can't explain, hollow. I suppose that does not make sense."

To Rina it made all the sense in the world. She'd seen the look of emptiness in her father's eyes after her mother had died—a pain so great that nothing in the world could ever heal it. She didn't for moment believe the earl was capable of the kind of love that her father had held for her mother, but if he'd loved his wife even a little, her betrayal must have cut his self-respect to ribbons. She found herself in the surprising position of feeling sorry for Lord Trevelyan.

"You must never tell Edward that I told you this."

Sabrina grimaced. "I know how to keep a secret. You may depend on that."

The woods that had seemed so tranquil a moment before now seemed close and confining. Rina was thankful when Amy kicked her mare into a trot, and steered her down the forest path. "We will reach the meadow in a few minutes," she called over her shoulder. "After that we should have no more obstacles."

She spoke too soon. Not five minutes passed before the trees began to thin out. Moments later they emerged into a wide, sun-washed meadow—and came face to face with Dr. Williams and Lord Trevelyan.

Chapter Seven

The day had not gone as Edward planned. After a sleepless night he'd left his bedchamber early, intending to confront his "cousin" before breakfast. Mr. Cherry, however, had risen even earlier, and had found several disturbing discrepancies in the mining accounts. Reluctantly putting aside his personal plans, Edward and the solicitor had gone to Wheal Grace to investigate—and discovered that his estate manager had been skimming funds that were earmarked for new equipment and safety improvements. The earl had sacked him on the spot.

Leaving Cherry to scrutinize the ledgers, Edward had started back to Ravenshold, but was *again* sidetracked. This time by Dr. Williams, who'd given Edward an impassioned speech about the deplorable living conditions of his tenants. Again he'd delayed his original plans and followed the physician to the village of Trevelyan Cove. In short order he learned that the generous sums he'd provided for his tenants' well-being and upkeep had gone the way of his mine improvements.

Now, as he and Dr. Williams traveled the little-used back roads leading to Ravenshold, his thoughts were on his people. He'd always despised absentee landlords who let their estates fall to ruin while they pursued their own interests. True, he'd had his reasons, but this did little to ease his conscience. Ravenshold was his home, and he'd neglected it. *I should not have stayed away so long*, he thought as he remembered the grim faces of his once-cheerful miners and tenants.

The doctor's voice cut through his thoughts. "Good heavens, it's Lady Amy!"

"Nonsense. My sister isn't fool enough to wander the deserted back roads near the mines. She's—" Edward's words died as he saw Amy ride out of the woods into the meadow. In her new blue riding habit she looked as pretty as a bunch of violets. And just as defenseless.

Blast the girl. Not eight months before, a gang of Cousin Jacks from the West Carrick mine had accosted a woman less than sixty yards from this very spot—and Amy knew it. Cursing under his breath he kicked his stallion into a fast trot and headed toward his sister. "What the devil do you think you're doing? You know you shouldn't be out here alone."

Amy lifted her chin defiantly. "I'm not alone. Toby is with us."

"Toby is only a boy. And who is *us*? I don't see anyone el—"

As he spoke, a horse and rider cantered out of the woods behind his sister. At first he didn't recognize the slim woman in the dark green habit, who sat her horse with the grace of a queen. Then he saw that the thick hair twisted into a coil beneath her hat was burnished copper. And when she turned her head to look in his direction, his gaze once again collided with that pair of remarkable emerald eyes.

"Good day, my lord," she said quietly.

Edward stared back, all his carefully rehearsed

speeches falling to ruin. He'd been prepared to challenge a cunning charlatan in a silly dress. Instead, he faced a soft-spoken, dignified woman who rode with an ease that would have set her apart even in the best circles. A thin thread of doubt wove itself through his mind. He was sure she was an impostor. Yet impostors didn't ride horses like aristocrats. And they didn't return his gaze with a wide-eyed candor that impressed him, and a wide-eyed innocence that unsettled him in a way he hadn't been unsettled in years.

Amy's voice ended his imaginings. "I don't care a fig for your opinion, Dr. Williams. Clara is my friend, and her family needs my assistance. I intend to help them."

"I never said you should not. But this is rough country, and you're very young—"

"And foolish, I suppose. Well, I'm not so foolish as to let myself be patronized by a narrow-minded country doctor."

"I'm not patronizing you. And I'm *not* narrow-minded. If you'd listen a minute instead of spouting off like some bluestocking—"

"You think I am a *bluestocking*? Of all the horrid, reprehensible, ungentlemanly things to—"

"Peace!" Edward's roar rang out across the meadow, silencing the argument. Sighing, he ran his hand through his hair. He could ask his sister why she was in this isolated part of the estate, but he knew her temper well enough to suspect she'd turn any explanation into another sparring match with the doctor. He could ask Toby, but the poor boy was literally quaking in his saddle. Reluctantly, he turned to the only person left who could give him a straight answer. "Miss Winthrope. What exactly *is* going on here?"

If she was surprised he'd asked her, she didn't show it. In a few concise sentences she summed up the situation with a composure he couldn't help but admire. At the end she met his gaze with a challenge every bit as bright as the one Amy had leveled at Dr. Williams. "Personally, I think your sister's actions have shown her to be a kind and charitable lady, and I wholeheartedly support her."

Edward glanced at Amy. She'd been five when their parents had died in a carriage accident, and in some ways she was more of a daughter to him than a sister. Now he saw that the spoiled, adorable little girl had become a generous-hearted woman. A unique pride filled his heart. He turned back to Miss Winthrope and acknowledged softly, "It appears we agree on at least one thing."

Her jaw dropped open in surprise. Edward had the brief satisfaction of seeing the usually self-possessed woman suddenly lose her composure. Then she pursed her lips together and the corner of her mouth ticked up. It was an uncertain smile, far different from the lavish, practiced expressions of the more accomplished women he knew. Yet her untutored grin left them all in the dust. She may not have had his sister's kind of beauty, but her lush, sensuous lips were designed to take a man to heaven in a heartbeat. And at the moment those lips were curving into a hesitant, wonderful smile.

But she isn't wonderful, his common sense reminded him. *She's an impostor who is deceiving your family. Now she's well on her way to deceiving you, too, just like—*

Edward yanked his reins. He wheeled his black hunter to face first the stable boy, and then his sister. "Toby, you go back to Ravenshold. Dr. Williams and I will escort the ladies to the village. But just this one time." His brows drew together as he turned toward his sister. "I support your intention, Amy, but not your methods. You are not to attempt this again. Do you understand me?"

"But—"

"Do you *understand?*"

Amy's mouth quivered, but she said nothing. Nodding, she turned her mount toward the village, her shoulders bent in defeat. Edward felt a prick of conscience, but he ignored it. Amy's safety was his responsibility. He intended to protect her from all dangers, including villainous attackers—and villainous charlatans.

Clara's family lived in a small but impeccably neat cottage, with crocheted doilies on the furniture and red and yellow flowers overflowing the window boxes. The cozy place was so like Sabrina's childhood home that it brought a lump to her throat. Clara was a sweet, shy girl, and Rina couldn't help but wonder how any man could be callous enough to desert her. She'd taken Amy aside, and asked whether there was any chance that her young man might offer for her. Amy had shaken her head sadly. "Clara has refused to reveal the man's name, even to me. But there are things she has mentioned that make me believe he's a man of position, and will have naught to do with her."

Throughout the visit, Rina could see that there was a real affection between Amy and her former maid. Rina admired Amy even more for the joy and acceptance she brought to the outcast girl's life. Rina thought she saw a glimmer of that same admiration in Dr. Williams's eyes, but if it *was* there, it didn't last. By the time they started back to Ravenshold, Amy and Charles were already embroiled in another one of their frequent arguments. Sabrina rode a few lengths behind, wanting to stay as far from the fray as possible.

"Those two argue like man and wife," a deep voice beside her commented.

Sabrina stiffened. The earl had remained behind in the village to supervise some repairs. She hadn't expected him to join them again so quickly. Now that he had, she found herself at a loss for words. And breath. Attempting to regain her composure, she said the first thing that came into her head. "You have a poor opinion of marriage, my lord."

Instantly, she bit her tongue. Her comment had been horribly thoughtless considering what Amy had told her. But if Lord Trevelyan read any hidden meaning into her words, he didn't show it. Instead, he pulled his black stallion alongside her own mount, and gave her an arch look. "You will find I have a poor opinion about many things, Miss Winthrope. I—ho, there. Easy, Brutus."

Lord Trevelyan brought his high-spirited horse under control. Sabrina looked at him in surprise. "You named your horse after a Roman traitor?"

"Or a Roman patriot, if you consider Caesar a tyrant," he answered as he leaned forward and gave the hunter's neck a pat. "I see you have knowledge of the classics, Miss Winthrope. I would have thought you more versed in the Bible, considering that you were raised by a missionary."

He was trying to trip her up. "We valued all manner of literature in my home. I assume it is the same at Ravenshold. Or are you the type of man who believes women should not be given the opportunity for an education?"

The earl's sharp glance showed that he was not easily baited either. "On the contrary, I prize education in both sexes. That is why I've arranged for my daughter to be tutored alongside my son. I do not intend for her to grow up shallow and bored. But we were talking of you, Miss Winthrope, and your surprisingly eclectic education. Take, for example, your equestrian talent. You are remarkably skilled at handling a horse."

"Th . . . thank you," she answered, surprised by the unexpected compliment.

"Quite remarkable," he continued smoothly. "Especially when I recall how much you loathed horses when you were young."

Drat. She should have known better than to trust his compliments. "I was foolish to dislike them, wasn't I? Horses are a great deal more forthright than most people I know."

Trevelyan's mouth edged up. "Including me, I suppose?"

"I don't know you well enough to say, my lord. But I have known a great many people in my life, and been through a great many hardships. It was bound to change me."

His dark eyes met hers. Gray as storm clouds, they were still remote, still unforgiving, but for the first time she sensed a hint of compassion behind the harshness. Sighing, he turned his gaze to the wide sun-washed meadow in front of them. "I believe that is the first truthful thing you have said to me since we met."

They rode on in silence. Rina did her best to keep her eyes forward, but her glance was inevitably drawn back to the earl. He wore a dark coat and plain buckskin breeches, but the simplicity of his clothes only added to the power of his presence. His hair was ragged and wild from the wind, and somehow, that wildness suited him. His rugged face was too severe to be called handsome, but there was a compelling strength about him that transcended mere looks.

The black hunter he rode—Brutus—was the most magnificent animal she had ever seen. Another man might have struggled to control the high-strung animal, but the earl mastered the stallion with a seemingly effortless flick of his wrists. She looked at his hands, at his long fingers curled with such easy power around the leather reins. Long ago her father had told her that the difference between a poor rider and a great one was "good hands." Even on this short acquaintance she could see that Trevelyan had exceptionally "good hands," and she wondered why this fact should suddenly make her feel so uncomfortable.

The earl's baritone struck through her thoughts. "You have been truthful with me, so I will be truthful with you. You've done a remarkable job in convincing my family that you are my prodigal cousin returned from the dead. I'll even own that on some level I admire your resourcefulness in pulling it off. But it cannot last. Sooner or later I will find you out—you must know that."

Rina *did* know that. Her deception couldn't last forever, but it didn't have to. It just had to last until she and Quinn pinched the necklace. She squared her shoulders, and kept her voice light as she answered. "La, sir, is it so impossible for you to believe I am your cousin?"

Trevelyan's jaw pulled taut. He glanced ahead to make certain that Amy was out of earshot. Then he sidled Brutus alongside Sabrina's horse, so close that their knees almost touched. "What I *believe* is that Prudence Winthrope died in a fire along with her parents," he said, dropping his voice to a rough whisper. "It was a tragic event, but it happened. And I cannot believe in her miraculous return, any more than I believe in happy endings, fairy tales, pixies, and other flummery. Such nonsense is for children and fools."

"Is your sister a fool? Is your grandmother?"

"My sister and grandmother share a loving heart. They have not seen as much of life as I have. They have not—" He rubbed his brow, a stab of pain crossing his

face. When he lifted his gaze his eyes were hard and con-
demning. "My family means everything to me. I will not
stand by and let you break their hearts. As I said, I'll find
you out sooner or later—but for their sakes I would
rather make it sooner. I want you to leave before my
family becomes more attached to you, and I am prepared
to make it worth your while."

"My *while*?"

Trevelyan's lips curled up in a humorless smile. "I'm
a wealthy man. I'm prepared to offer you five hundred
pounds to leave Ravenshold—no police, and no questions asked."

"Five hundred?" It was more money than Sabrina
could earn in a lifetime. Several lifetimes.

"Yes, but only if you leave today. I can arrange a
quiet exit. Once we arrive back at Ravenshold I'll give
you the money and you can be on your way—provided
you agree to never see my sister or grandmother again."

Sabrina considered the offer, determining the odds.
The Dutchman's Necklace would be worth far more, but
there was no guarantee she would ever lay her hands on
it. Besides, she would have to steal the necklace, while
the earl's offer was free and clear. Somehow she knew
she could trust his word that he would not call in the
authorities. He simply wanted her out of his family's life.
He wanted to prove that she wasn't Prudence, that he
was right when he said there were no miracles or fairy
tales.

He wanted to prove that he was right not to believe
in happy endings.

When Rina was little her mother had read her a
story of a beautiful princess who'd suffered terrible trials
and tribulations before she found happiness. During the
grim years in the widow's household Rina had clung to
that story, holding to the belief that, no matter what suf-

fering she went through, eventually she'd find happiness. Life hadn't exactly turned out as she'd expected, but if she hadn't held fast to the hope that she'd be free, she would have knuckled under to the evil woman years ago. She might have even let Albert—

Albert. She closed her eyes, remembering his bleeding body lying across her bed. Whatever she believed or wanted to believe, she was still a murderer. She needed money to escape the country and the gallows, enough money to disappear for the rest of her life. Five hundred pounds wasn't enough for her and Quinn to do that. It was the necklace or nothing.

Maybe she *would* break Lady Penelope's and Amy's hearts. They'd recover. If the authorities caught up with her, she wouldn't. Regretful but resolved, she turned back to Lord Trevelyan. "I am sorry you do not believe I'm telling the truth, my lord, but I *am* Prudence Winthrope. You might as well accept it. I am not going away. Just because you were disappointed by one woman doesn't mean—"

Too late she realized her mistake. Trevelyan reached out and grabbed her bridle, jerking her horse to a halt.

She tried to pull away. "I . . . I only meant—"

"I know what you meant," he said, his eyes dark with fury. "You meant to offer consolation to a poor fool who couldn't satisfy his wife. Well, I don't need your pity. And even if I did, I certainly wouldn't want it from a chit who's too plain to have a man of her own—"

Sabrina pulled the reins free. She wheeled her horse and kicked, sending the mare into a full gallop. She thundered across the meadow, blinking back hot tears of anger and shame. She *was* plain. But the fact that he'd said it made her feel uglier than she'd ever felt in her life. The widow's stinging words came back to her. *Take*

*a look in the glass, gel. It's not as if anyone is going to offer
for ya.*

She kicked her horse again, as if more speed could
help her outrun the truth. But it couldn't. She was plain.
Ugly. Hideous. At least, *he* thought so. She scrubbed
away bitter, blinding tears, and noticed in the process
that she was fast approaching the forest. Her practical
nature overcame her pain. She yanked back on the reins,
intending to pull her mount to a halt before she got too
close to the roots and overhanging branches.

Only then did she realize that her bridle ribbons had
snapped.

Chapter Eight

Charles steadied his startled horse as Miss Winthrope galloped by him. Alarmed, he started after her, but a deep voice commanded him back.

"Let her go." Lord Trevelyan rode up beside him, his expression as hard as the cliffs below Ravenshold. "Leave her. She can take care of herself."

"She was crying, Edward," Amy argued. "What did you say to her?"

"Nothing but the truth." A hurtful truth. He'd called her plain because he wanted to wound her the same way she'd wounded him. And he'd succeeded. His remark had stripped away her confident facade, leaving her looking lost and defenseless, and desperately, achingly young. She was a cheat and a liar who was cruelly deceiving his family. But her pain had been real.

Charles interrupted his thoughts. "Why doesn't she slow down? She's getting close to the trees."

Edward looked up. She *was* galloping toward the forest at an alarming rate. That is, it would have been alarming if Edward hadn't known that she was such an accomplished horsewoman. She could stop her horse any time she pleased. More deception. He gave a short, caustic laugh. "Don't waste your concern on Miss Winthrope. She's . . . she *is* getting close to the trees. Why the devil doesn't she pull back on the reins and—?"

He stopped as he realized she *was* pulling on the reins. Frantically. But the mare wasn't slowing.

Amy's cry split the air. "Her reins have snapped! Oh, Lord, if her horse doesn't stop—"

Edward didn't hear the rest of her sentence. Cursing, he kicked Brutus into action. The horse leapt into a full gallop, tearing across the field with such force that he threw up clumps of dirt and grass behind him. Edward bent low to his neck, ignoring the wind that ripped at his hair and clothes, fighting for even more speed out of his thundering stallion.

Ahead, the runaway mare still raced for the woods. If she reached it, she'd hit the twisted forest path and dive under the branches. She'd likely be forced to stop a few hundred yards in, but that wouldn't come soon enough for her rider. She would be swept off by the first low-hanging tree branch. Years ago on a hunt Edward had seen a man gored to death that way. He could still remember the smell of the blood . . .

Brutus's powerful stride ate up the ground. They were gaining—but not fast enough. At this rate they'd reach the mare seconds late, seconds that could spell the difference between life and death. She was a cheat and a liar, but she didn't deserve this fate. Edward thought about her eyes—her remarkable green eyes dull and lifeless forever. He leaned forward until he was inches away from the big hunter's ear. "Come on, boy," he whispered.

With Herculean effort the mighty horse lengthened his stride, fighting out a final burst of energy. It wasn't much, but it was enough. The extra speed brought the two horses side by side for an instant—just long enough for Edward to reach out and grab the woman's waistband. He yanked her onto his saddle and turned Brutus aside, missing the tearing branches at the forest's edge by a hairsbreadth. The next second the mare crashed headlong into the underbrush, racing under a thick tree limb that swept over her empty saddle by less than a foot.

Trevelyan's heart pounded madly and he drew his breath in harsh, rattling gasps. Beneath him his exhausted stallion skirted the woods with heavy steps, his mouth coated with foam and his sides sleek with sweat. Edward stroked the horse's damp withers, muttering a promise of a rubdown and an extra bag of oats.

The girl sat sideways across his lap, clinging to his neck, staring at the nearby woods with fear and astonishment, as if she couldn't quite believe she was safe. Despite her brave words, the woman didn't believe in miracles any more than he did. This one had caught them both by surprise. *Caught them both.*

She lifted her chin, and met his gaze. Her expression was artlessly confused, her eyes full of questions and wonder. *Fragile*, he thought, his arms instinctively tightening around her. Her wind-torn clothes were twisted in disarray and her once elegant coiffure hung over one ear in a lopsided tangle. But she was alive, and Edward was surprised at how important that simple fact was to him.

"You . . . saved me," she whispered brokenly.

It had been a long time since he'd been anyone's hero. The heavy silk of her hair, the slight rise and fall of her breasts, the wary gratitude in her eyes—all combined into an unexpectedly heady mix. His arms tightened around her. Her skin smelled like summer. Her slim body fit against his as if she'd been made for him. Her hesitant smile stirred a sweet, wild ache in his center, and her bewitching gaze drew him like the moon draws the tide, making him believe there was still a place in the wreck of his life for impossibilities like hope, and innocence, and maybe even forgiveness—

"Miss Winthrope!"

Edward glanced up, and saw Dr. Williams galloping across the meadow, with Amy close behind.

"Miss Winthrope," Charles cried again as he reached Brutus's side. "Are you all right?"

She nodded shakily. "I am fine . . . thanks to Lord Trevelyan."

"Yes, Edward, you were wonderfully brave," Amy agreed. "I cannot wait to tell Grandmother how you rescued our cousin."

Cousin. The truth shattered his fragile illusion. The woman in his arms wasn't sweet or innocent—she was the most deceiving pretender ever to set foot in Ravenshold. She'd made fools out of his family, and he'd come bloody close to letting her make a fool out of him!

He gripped her wrists and lowered her from his saddle so roughly that her knees nearly buckled when she hit the ground. "You can ride home with my sister," he said gruffly as he steered Brutus toward the woods. "I must see to the mare."

Amy gasped at his rudeness. "Edward, surely the mare can wait—"

"She rides home with you or she bloody well walks!" Ignoring further protests Edward waded his horse into the thick ferns and underbrush, welcoming the green canopy of leaves and silence that closed around him. Hell! One look from those green eyes and his common sense had melted like wax. For an instant he'd actually believed the innocence in her smile, the sweetness of her slim, young body. She was good. Damn good. Even now, after he'd remembered what she was, he still found himself wanting to believe the lies.

He glanced behind him. Through the screen of branches he saw that Dr. Williams had dismounted and was valiantly offering his horse to Miss Winthrope. It's what Edward should have offered, what any gentleman should have offered to a lady. But Edward was no gentleman. And *Miss Winthrope* was certainly no lady. She was a liar and he'd find her out, just as he'd found out every other impostor who'd tried to claim Prudence Winthrope's birthright. And when he did, he intended to see just how much she was willing to offer for her freedom.

Edward turned Brutus deeper into the forest shadows. He was no gentleman, but he was practical. He considered it a damn shame to let a woman with a courtesan's body and a sinner's lips rot away in prison. It was a devil's bargain, but one he looked forward to striking.

He smiled grimly. After all, it wouldn't be the first time.

"I cannot believe Edward could be so unfeeling," Amy stated as she walked her horse along the cliff path. "To suggest that you walk home after what you endured!"

"For once I must agree with Lady Amy," Dr. Williams added as he led Rina's horse around a small rocky outcropping. "He should not have treated you like that. 'Tis strange. He is a conscientious man—far more than I imagined. I saw it this morning when he was with the tinners. He was genuinely concerned for their well-being, particularly when it came to the new casing for the whim engine, and the lack of Davy lamps. He even accompanied them down into the mine to check out the conditions, a risk I have rarely seen an owner take for his men—"

Amy sniffed. "Dr. Williams, my cousin does not

want to hear about a bunch of smelly old miners. Look how pale she has become." She sidled her horse next to Rina's and put a caring hand on her forearm. "Would you like to rest? We can stop if you'd like."

Sabrina shook her head. She did not want to stop. A brisk wind blew off the sea, chilling skin that still felt unusually raw and sensitive. Like her emotions. All she really wanted was to be left alone, to sort through her thoughts. So much had happened this afternoon . . .

"Heavens, she's growing pale as a ghost. Charles, we must stop."

"No, really, I am fine," Rina argued, but even to her ears her voice sounded thin. Dr. Williams led the horse off the road, to a small alcove that was protected from the wind on one side by a rock outcropping and on the other by the forest. Ignoring her protests, he lifted Sabrina off her saddle and deposited her on the grassy knoll between the trees and the rock wall.

"You must rest, Miss Winthrope. Even if it's only for a few minutes," he pronounced in his sternest physician's tone. "Lady Amy and I will wait on the other side of these rocks." Then his brown eyes glinted with a hint of the humor he took such pains to hide. He leaned down and whispered, "Please, I'd appreciate it if at least *one* female here listened to me."

Sabrina answered his smile. She watched her two companions walk off toward the bay, and heard the heated tones of another argument as they disappeared behind a stone outcropping. Sighing, she leaned back on the soft blanket of grass and wildflowers, letting the warm afternoon sun bake its healing magic into her sore muscles. They'd been right—she had needed rest. Her wild ride had rattled every bone in her body. But that wasn't the worst of it. There was a pain deep inside her that was far worse than anything that had happened to her muscles, a pain that tangled her emotions as surely as the ride had tangled her hair.

One second she'd been racing toward almost certain death. The next she'd been in his arms. He'd held her close, close enough to hear the ragged cadence of his breathing, close enough to drink in the rich smell of soap and leather on his skin, close enough to feel the hard planes of his chest pressed so intimately to her own. His hold had been shockingly forward, but she hadn't been able to pull away. She'd been caught fast by his gaze, by the feel of his muscular neck under her fingers, by the large hands that cradled her body with such unexpected tenderness.

A strange, sweet lethargy had stolen her strength. Everything inside her felt as if it was turning inside out. She clung to him, falling into his gaze, feeling the emptiness in his eyes echo in her heart. All her life she'd been sensible—believing in nothing, trusting no one. She'd learned the hard way to depend only on herself. But for an instant she'd let down her guard, believing in the honesty in his eyes, in the gentle strength of his rescuing arms, in the hunger in his soul. For an instant she let herself believe that she was wanted, needed, *beautiful*.

And the next instant he'd dumped her from his saddle like a sack of potatoes.

She turned her head into the fragrant grass, but all she smelled was the musk of his skin. She pressed her palms on the cool ground, but felt the hot strength of his arms and neck. Trevelyan's image filled her senses. She realized what Quinn had meant about the earl being dangerous in ways she couldn't imagine.

She shut her eyes, squeezing back tears she wouldn't allow herself to shed. He was arrogant and cruel, just as Quinn said he was. He deserved to have the Dutchman's Necklace whisked out from under his nose. She'd make a fool of him, just as he'd made a fool of her. And she was going to enjoy it—

"Bless me, if it ain't a wood nymph."

Rina's eyes flew open. A few yards away stood a fine thoroughbred, ridden by a stylishly dressed gentleman. Apparently he'd come upon her by the forest path, but she'd been too absorbed in her thoughts to hear his approach. *Wonderful, Rina. Keep letting your guard down and you'll queer this masquerade in no time.* She got to her feet, painfully aware of her disheveled appearance. "Forgive me," she said as she tried to push her fallen hair back into place. "I did not hear your horse approach."

"Didn't want you to. What's the sport in catching a charming wood nymph if your demmed cattle scares her off?"

He looked to be in his late twenties, and his plum brocade coat and cream breeches were the height of fashion. His chestnut locks were meticulously greased and curled, and his snow white cravat was tied in a ridiculously intricate style. He was a devilishly handsome man, and the superior tilt of his chin told Rina that he was well aware of the fact. *A macaroni.* She'd seen enough of them driving their fine carriages through the London streets to know the breed.

Rina lifted her chin in a tilt as proud as his. "Sorry to disappoint you, sir, but I am no wood nymph."

The dandy put his hand over his heart, sighing dramatically. "Fair spirit, you wound me. You have torn my dreams asunder. However, there are advantages to finding an unattended maiden in the woods instead of a nymph." He bent down, and ran his hand suggestively along her jaw. Something decidedly undandyish slithering in the depths of his eyes. "Perhaps in another time and place, we can review those advantages—"

"Heavens, stop bothering the poor lady with your flummery," a woman's voice interrupted.

Rina saw another thoroughbred coming out of the woods. Its rider was just as stylishly dressed as the dandy, in a sable habit that fitted her figure elegantly, and a wide hat that was trimmed with stunning white ostrich feathers. Her hair color and finely cut features were the echo of her companion's, but that was where the resemblance ended. The lady's chestnut hair fell in soft waves around her face. And her blue eyes held a warmth that was as different from the gentleman's haughty expression as night from day.

The lady clicked a subtle command to her mount and walked it toward Rina. "You must not mind him, my dear. He is . . . but you are in distress! Brother, look at her clothes!"

"Paris!" Lady Amy appeared from the other side of the outcropping. She glanced behind her, as if to make sure that Dr. Williams was following. Then she dashed across the path until she reached the gentleman's side, her face shining with delight. "Oh, I'm so glad you're back. But what happened? You weren't supposed to return from Bath for another week."

"Cassie and I heard about your cousin turning up, so we cut our visit short. Besides," he added as he leaned down from his saddle, and tucked his finger under Amy's chin, "I couldn't stay away from my poppet, could I?"

Nearby, Dr. Williams made a loud noise that almost sounded like a cough. Amy shot a withering glance in his direction, then she returned her gaze to Sabrina. "Prudence, may I present Mr. Paris Fitzroy and his sister, Lady Cassandra Rumley. Cassie and Paris, this is Miss Prudence Winthrope, my long-lost cousin."

Rina remembered that Amy had spoken of them

earlier. They were neighbors and longtime friends of the Trevelyans. Mr. Fitzroy was Amy's unofficial intended. And Lady Rumley was the earl's.

"Not a wood nymph? Alas, my heart is broken," Paris cried, his innocuous demeanor showing no trace of the lewdness Rina had glimpsed earlier.

"Oh, Paris, don't be a ninny."

Lady Rumley stared daggers at her brother. Then she turned her gaze to Sabrina, and looked down at her with a warm, sympathetic expression. Words Amy had spoken earlier that day returned to Rina's mind. *For weeks after it happened he kept to his room. . . . The only one who could come near him at all was Cassie.*

The lady continued. "My brother is a bit of a cake, Miss Winthrope, but he means well. We are both very glad to meet you. But—and forgive my forwardness— but it looks as though you have already been through some adventures since your return."

Amy launched into the tale of the runaway horse. Rina would have preferred a far less colorful description of the afternoon's events, but when she tried to tone down Amy's embellishment, the girl praised her for being both humble and brave. After that, Sabrina endured the rest of the story in silence. And as she listened, she tried not to remember how frightened she'd been when she couldn't stop the mare . . . or how distracted she'd felt in Trevelyan's arms.

"So we stopped for a few minutes, to allow my cousin to rest," Amy finished. "Dr. Williams recommended it. You recall Dr. Williams, don't you? My brother has employed him for the Wheal."

Fitzroy brought out his lace handkerchief and gave his nose a disinterested wipe. "Ah, yes. The apothecary."

Sabrina could almost see Charles's hackles rise. He squared his shoulders, and clasped his hands behind him in an earnest stance. "Actually, sir, I am a fully licensed physician. I took my training at Oxford, and am a fellow of the Royal College of—"

"Yes, yes," Paris drawled. He dismissed the doctor with a flip of his handkerchief, which he stuffed neatly back in his coat. Then he dismounted from his horse and swept off his hat in an eloquent salute. "Dear damsel, my charger is at your disposal."

Sabrina glanced at the doctor, but it was Lady Amy who spoke. "But Prudence was riding Dr. Williams's horse."

Paris shrugged. "Now she is riding mine. A superior woman deserves a superior mount. Besides, I am sure the surgeon has duties he needs to perform."

"Physician," Charles corrected through clenched teeth.

With a stiff nod to the women the doctor mounted his horse and rode off toward the mine, barely acknowledging Rina's words of thanks. She watched him go, feeling a kinship the others couldn't suspect. She'd spent her whole life enduring the insults and cruelty of gentry who believed their money and breeding put them above all others. A grandfather who let her mother die because she fell in love with a base-born gambler. A stepbrother who was prepared to rape her without a twinge of conscience. An earl who held her in his arms as if she were the most precious thing on earth, then dumped her to the ground without a backward glance.

She rode back to Ravenshold with a smile on her face, laughing at Fitzroy's jokes, acknowledging the caring concern in both Lady Amy and Lady Rumley. But she could never allow herself to forget that she was Sabrina Murphy, gambler's daughter. She was here to acquire the Dutchman—not family, not friends, not . . . anything else.

When they finally reached Ravenshold, Fitzroy helped her down from his horse. For a moment she was almost as close to him as she had been to Trevelyan, and again glimpsed the licentious gleam in the dandy's eyes. But she experienced none of the fire or confusion she'd felt in the earl's arms.

It was Trevelyan alone who addled her wits, wits she desperately needed to keep about her if she was to succeed in her masquerade. And that made him more dangerous than ever.

Chapter Nine

During the next few weeks, Sabrina became more and more a part of the Trevelyan household. She acted as a companion to Lady Penelope, and a confidante to Lady Amy. The children, though still cautious, began to spend more time in her company, listening to the same stories Rina's father had spun for her as a child. Dr. Williams stopped by frequently to observe Lady Penelope's progress. Rina grew fonder of the serious young man every time she met him, though she could not seem to convince Amy that he had a single redeeming quality. Rina also learned the names and responsibilities of the servants, and was able to use the skills she'd acquired as the housekeeper in her stepmother's boardinghouse to make the household run more efficiently. Ravenshold needed her care and organizational talents like a well-worn piece of furniture needed a new coat of polish. Both she and the house took on a new shine.

Rina told herself that she was doing all this work simply to gain the dowager's confidence, but in her heart she knew that was only half the truth. For the first time since her mother died, she was a part of a family again—a family that needed her. Her days were filled with work and contentment, and a peace she'd never expected to find in a lonely house set on the sea cliffs of Cornwall. And in the mornings, when she woke up to the cry of the gulls, and saw the dancing reflection of the water on her ceiling, she'd lie back in the soft pillows and allow herself to believe that she really *was* Prudence Winthrope.

Only the earl threatened her plans. His dark glares and open suspicion loomed over her like a storm cloud. He remained resolutely set against her. But the mine kept him away from Ravenshold during the day, and in the evening Rina was always in the drawing room in the company of his grandmother or sister. She gave him no opportunity to see her alone—though, in truth, he seemed little interested in seeking her out. He was so tired after his days at the mine that he frequently bypassed the drawing room and headed straight for his own chambers, leaving Rina feeling both relieved and disappointed.

It was on one such night that she heard a knock on her sitting-room door. Opening it, she was surprised to see the stout figure of Mrs. Poldhu filling her doorway.

"I'll not have it," the cook stated, brandishing her wooden spoon like a general's baton. "Not a bit of it."

Rina frowned. "Not a bit of what?"

"His lordship's attitude, that's what! He's been holed up in that study of his every evening this week, and without a decent meal to his name. I've sent him my sweetest tarts, my most succulent pies. And what does he do? Sends 'em back, he does. Yells at my gels until not a one of 'em will go back. He's like an angry bear what's got his foot caught in a trap," she stated, then proceeded to give Rina a few examples of the earl's bearish behavior.

"That is, uhm, unfortunate, Mrs. Poldhu," Rina said, though her concern was hardly genuine. For all she cared, the foul-tempered earl could stay in his study until Judgment Day.

"It's more than unfortunate, miss. His grandmother is that worried about 'im. The last time his lordship was in such a state was when—"

Mrs. Poldhu's words broke off, but her meaning was unmistakable. No wonder Lady Penelope was upset. "Cannot Lady Amy speak with him?"

"His sister's gone to supper at the Fitzroys'. He needs a meal, miss. In the worst way." She nodded to a covered dinner tray sitting on a nearby hall table. "You must try to make him eat something."

"Me? What makes you think he will not throw me out, too?"

"Because you've a way of getting things done when you set your mind to them. Besides, there's no one else."

Rina did not relish the task, but she could think of no way out of it. In any event, she saw no harm in taking the tray to the earl's door, knocking on it, and being turned away like the rest. She stepped out into the hallway and picked up the tray. "I shall do my best, Mrs. Poldhu."

"Lord love you, miss, I know you will. And if he barks, you tell him there's cream tarts on the tray, the same ones he used to steal from my windowsill when he was a lad."

The earl's rooms were in the west wing of the house, isolated from the rest of the family. *Like the man*, Rina thought, feeling an unexpected twinge of sympathy as she approached the door. Shaking off the thought she lifted her hand to knock, and noticed that the door was ajar. Apparently the last kitchen maid who attempted to breach the sanctuary had been driven away before she could close it. She put her eyes to the crack, and peered inside.

A fire roared in the hearth, reflecting on the polished oak walls with a hellfire brilliance. At the center of the room the earl sat at a huge desk that was stacked with books and papers. He checked one of the ledgers and jotted a note on one of the papers, his dark head bent in concentration. His hair was tousled and his collar undone, and his jaw was shadowed by a day's growth of beard. But his unkempt appearance was contrasted by his commanding demeanor. His movements were smooth and economical, profoundly self-assured, wasting nothing. Confident. Masculine. *Sensual.*

Rina swallowed, feeling as if a dozen butterflies had suddenly taken flight in her stomach. She'd never thought that watching a man work could have such an effect on her—especially a man she didn't like. She wanted to deny it, but the truth was she was aroused—mightily. If she hadn't promised Mrs. Poldhu that she would do her best, she'd have retreated down the hall, as far away from the man as possible. But she had promised, so she laid her shoulder to the door and pushed it open. "My lord, I've brought—"

"Get out," he growled without looking up.

The rudeness of his order, along with his arrogance in not bothering to so much as look at her, rankled her senses. She was, after all, doing the man a favor. Annoyed, she marched to the desk and set down the tray with a force that made the china rattle. "I took pains to bring you supper. You could at least have the courtesy to thank me."

Edward's chin shot up. He'd been studying the plans for the mine's new tunnel, his thoughts buried as deep in the calculations as the tin beneath the earth. His frustration with the tunnel was nothing compared to the frustration he felt at having his counterfeit cousin catch him looking like a gypsy. Automatically he started to retie his stock, then stopped when he realized she was the last person he should be wanting to make himself presentable for. "What the devil are you doing here?"

She did not even flinch at his harsh tone. Instead, she pulled off the tray's cloth and began to neatly uncover the dishes. As usual she wore one of her giddily decorated gowns, but the gaudy dress could do nothing to disguise the way the firelight sparkled in her shining hair, nor hide the subtle, fascinating grace that marked every move of her slim arms, nor quench the edgy hunger that consumed him when he remembered her lush body pressed against his. Hell, she could have worn a suit of armor—

Her proper, schoolmarm voice interrupted his less-than-proper thoughts. "I am here because no one else would bring you supper. You have driven them all off with your deplorable behavior."

"Deplorable?" Edward sat up straighter, genuinely surprised. "That's absurd. Who says I've been deplorable?"

"Violet." She fluffed out his napkin and laid it beside the dishes. "Mrs. Poldhu says that you yelled at her."

"I did not yell. Well, not precisely. I simply told her that I did not care for the soup she'd made and asked her to take it away."

"After saying it wasn't fit for the hounds. And then there was Mary Rose. I believe you threw a dish at her."

" 'Twas a spoon. A *clean* spoon," he grumbled. "She was trying to tidy up my correspondence."

"Imagine that," she commented dryly as she glanced at the tower of papers on his desk. "In any case, she was only trying to help. And you were beastly to her."

"I was not . . . at least, I never intended . . . damn!"

He raked his hand through his hair. "I never meant to be unkind."

The truth in his words shook Rina to her core. Suddenly she caught a part of him that she'd never seen before, a rough, unpolished man whose harsh exterior concealed a warm heart. She turned away, unnerved by the vision. As she did, her gaze fell on a nearby sheet of paper. The bold print fairly shouted out at her, making it impossible not to read it. "Why, this is a list of instructions. Supplies and assistance for—Clara Hobbs?"

"Don't look so shocked, Miss Winthrope. The girl was a good worker, and her father a valued tenant while he was alive. If I'd known the family was in such a poor way I would have offered help sooner." His mouth edged up in a world-weary grin. "Contrary to what you've heard of me, I am not a *complete* monster."

"I haven't—" Rina bit her lip. She *had* heard he was a monster—from Quinn, from Mrs. Cherry, and from all the servants who ran scurrying when he stormed down the hall. Lord Trevelyan was a powerful man, by breeding and station, and that power set him apart from the people around him. He was not an easy man to know, and even less easy to like. By rights Rina should have despised him for that power, because his class so often used it to destroy the less fortunate. But the letter of instructions on his desk proved that at least once he'd used his wealth for charitable purposes. A new feeling welled up inside her, totally unexpected, totally unwelcome. Respect.

She turned away. "I should be going. I have . . . things to do."

"Of course. I'm sure it takes a prodigious amount of plotting to convince an old woman and a young girl that you are someone you are not."

Rina's eyes flashed. "Then you are still convinced that I am not Prudence Winthrope."

"More than ever. The Prudence I remember was a nervous child, afraid of her own shadow, who would never have gone out of her way for anyone."

"I was six, my lord. People change."

"That they do," he said, his eyes narrowing. He pushed out his chair and walked over to her, like a jungle cat pacing its cage. "I used to be a trusting sort, till life taught me different. I put up with your deception because I have no choice, but if you do anything—anything at all—to damage the people I love, I will crush you like a bug under my heel. Do you understand me?"

His breath burned her cheek. His gaze seared like fire. She could feel the heat of his body, smell the musk of his scent, see the stormy passion that seethed beneath his controlled exterior. She swallowed, her throat suddenly dry. "You are . . . mistaken. I am Prudence Winthrope."

Rina had reached the end of her tether. She stepped back and slipped out of the room, hurrying down the hall as fast as her legs could carry her.

She didn't see Edward watching her through the open door, following her with his haunted eyes until she disappeared from sight. Nor did she see him walk slowly over to a cabinet, and pour himself a full glass of scotch that he drained in a single draught.

After that night Rina saw even less of the earl, and was glad of it. His disturbing passion, and her even more disturbing reaction to it, made her doubt whether she could pull off her deception. But as the days passed without incident, Rina's confidence began to return. Sometimes she went almost an entire day without thinking of Trevelyan. Sometimes she went almost an entire night—until she'd wake in a tangle of sheets, her heart hammering and her body burning from a dark, vaguely remembered dream.

Along with Lady Penelope and Amy, Sabrina saw a great deal of Mr. Fitzroy and his sister, who were frequent visitors to Ravenshold. Rina did not trust the clever-tongued dandy as far as she could throw him, but she genuinely looked forward to Lady Rumley's company and conversation.

One day in the garden, Lady Rumley told Rina of her past. When she was barely twelve her mother had become gravely ill, and she and her brother were sent to Fitzroy Hall, their father's ancestral home. "Paris could not abide the desolate country," she confessed as she wove the stems of the flowers into a daisy chain, "but I must confess that I fell in love with this land at first sight."

"I did, too," Rina sighed, remembering her first glimpse of the wild, Cornwall seascape. "So you have been here a long time."

"On and off. Even as young children we traveled extensively with our father. That is why I was not here during your first visit."

"Your father was an adventurer, then?"

"Only in the medical sense. He was forever seeking out doctors and specialists, in the hope of helping my mother . . ." Lady Rumley's voice dwindled to a sorrowful silence, and she wiped away an errant tear. "Paris was more affected than I, for he so closely resembled our dear mother in every way."

Somehow Rina could not envision the gentle Lady Rumley's mother as a slack-jawed dandy, but she kept the thought to herself. Instead she reached out, and bent a fragrant rose to her face, inhaling the intoxicating scent.

"Edward is fond of roses, too. Oh, don't look so shocked," she commented at Sabrina's surprised expression. "He may act all bluff and bluster, but underneath he is decidedly sentimental. And he is fiercely protective of every member of his family. Especially since . . ."

Since his wife deserted him, Rina finished silently. The troubled look that clouded Lady Rumley's features told Sabrina more than her words ever could. Rina knew it was none of her business. Yet there was one question she wanted to ask. "What was Lady Trevelyan like?"

For a full minute the distant cry of the wheeling gulls was the only answer Rina received. Then Lady Rumley rose to her feet, and stroked her elegantly gloved hand along the back of a nearby statue of a stone lion. "She was a golden creature, a bright oasis in this harsh landscape. Edward was besotted with her, and not without reason. She shone like a star in the heavens. How were any of us to know how far that star would fall . . ."

Her hand stilled on the lion's back. "I was her best friend. Amy was away at school, and with Edward away on business, and my own dear Cyril's health beginning to decay, Isabel and I were left alone much of the time. We forged a deep friendship, shared our most intimate confidences. Though, not the most intimate, it seems. I had no warning that she would desert Edward. Even after she disappeared I would not believe her duplicity— until Cyril found the article about the drowned ship in the London *Gazette*. It bore a list of passengers. One of the names belonged to Isabel's old governess, a foreign woman who had been dead for years. Isabel once confided in me that she had used the name as an alias in her youth, when she would slip away from her straitlaced guardian to visit the bazaar or purchase the latest penny novel. But I never dreamed she would use the name for such a despicable purpose."

Sabrina frowned. "But perhaps it was another woman with a similar name. Perhaps it was not Isabel."

Lady Rumley sadly shook her head. "Isabel sent a note. To me—she could not even confess her guilt to Edward. It was mailed from the harbor, on the day before the shipwreck. She told me she was leaving, to make a new life for herself with the man she truly loved, as she had never loved Edward. She bid me to say goodbye to her beloved children . . ." She cleared her throat. "But that is all in the past. Now the earl has the happy circumstance of having you returned to him."

"I am not sure he entirely shares your joy," Rina remarked wryly.

Lady Rumley linked her arm through Rina's. "He will come around, you will see. I wish us to be great friends, so you must leave off calling me by my formal name. Is that all right with you . . . Prudence?"

"Of course—Cassie."

They started to walk along the garden path. "I am pleased we are to be friends. After all, in a short while we are to be related."

Of course. Cassie was going to marry the earl. Rina turned her head away and stared off at the sun-dappled sea, reminding herself that it was none of her business. *In a few weeks I'll be leaving this house. I'll never see him again, and I'll be glad of it.*

But her resolve rang hollow.

Chapter Ten

"What do you mean, you can find nothing?" Edward demanded as he pounded his fist on his desk. "Cherry, your investigations must have uncovered *something*."

Mr. Cherry fumbled with his cravat. "Not a thing, my lord. I double-checked all the witnesses and documents Miss Winthrope presented to me. They are all authentic." He lifted his chin, screwing up his courage as he added, "I did warn you that a second investigation would likely yield nothing amiss."

"Then I'll order a *third* investigation!" Edward roared.

Cherry took out his handkerchief and proceeded to mop his brow. "Of course I shall follow your wishes. But I must ask . . . just to be thorough, you understand . . . why is it that you disbelieve the lady so entirely, when she has brought only happiness to your home?"

Edward pulled on his collar, which had suddenly grown insufferably tight. Cherry was right. Miss Winthrope had brought only happiness to his home. And the knowledge vexed him sorely.

He resented her competency in bringing his

neglected household back to order. He was annoyed that his scatterbrained sister had begun showing signs of good sense since her arrival, and that it was Miss Winthrope who'd brought the roses back to his grandmother's cheeks. He was irritated that the Fitzroys adored her, that Sarah and David hung on her every word, and that even stiff-backed Dr. Williams grinned like a schoolboy whenever she entered a room.

But most of all, he hated that he was so aware of her. During the few evenings he'd allowed himself to spend in her presence, his gaze kept straying back to her slight yet somehow stirring figure. Against all reason he found himself caught up by her unconscious, coltish grace, fascinated by the play of firelight in her auburn hair, intrigued by her intelligent conversation, and hopeful for a glimpse of her rare, wonderful smile.

Miss Winthrope was weaving herself into the fabric of his life. And he resented the hell out of her for it.

"She's an impostor, Cherry—I can see it as plainly as I see you. There must be some way to prove it. There *must* be."

"Yes, well, I shall do my best," the solicitor promised as he stuffed his damp handkerchief back into his pocket. "Uhm, on a different note—have you reviewed the plans for the new tunnel?"

Edward's hard expression relaxed as his mind moved to the safer subject. "I did. The men have made a promising start. In a few weeks we should be well along the coast, and smack in the middle of the new vein of tin." He spread a map of the coast out on his desk, tracing the progress of the tunnel with his index finger. " 'Tis interesting. If we keep on digging as we are, we'll end up tunneling under Fitzroy Hall."

"You have the right. Your father bought the mining rights from Fitzroy's father years ago."

"Along with half Fitzroy's land, and two estates in the north. My father had a head for business." *And precious little else*, Edward thought as he rubbed his tired forehead.

Cherry was squirming in his chair, clearly anxious to be away. Edward sighed, realizing he could use some relaxation himself. "We have been at it all day and much of the evening. Why don't we call it a night?"

His solicitor was only too glad to agree. He leapt out of his chair with surprising alacrity and headed for the door. "I am glad we finished early, my lord. Miss Winthrope is telling one of her stories tonight."

"She's *what?*"

"Telling a story. She tells the most marvelous—" As if recalling who he was speaking to, Cherry's enthusiasm faltered. "I know you do not like the lady, but I must tell you that she has a real gift for tale-spinning. One of the children gives her a sentence, and she creates a wonderful story out of thin air. It is quite remarkable and shouldn't be missed . . . that is, unless you miss it because you do not want to acknowledge Miss Winthrope in any way. In that case, missing her stories is perfectly understandable. I . . . will not attend if you do not wish it."

For a moment Edward said nothing. "Go if you like, Mr. Cherry. Somehow I have no trouble believing that spinning a tale is something she excels at."

Delighted, Cherry sprinted out of the room. Edward returned to his mountain of paperwork, telling himself that he was glad for the time alone. He enjoyed his solitude, and this room was his own private kingdom. But on this particular evening, his kingdom seemed rather dull. His paperwork failed to grasp his interest. He picked up a book, but fared no better. He lit a cigar and poured himself a glass of fine brandy, but even these pleasures failed to interest him. Finally he decided he needed a walk on the cliffs. He left his rooms and strode down the hallway toward the front door, but as he passed the sitting room his child's voice caught his attention.

"That was too *short*," David wailed. "Tell us another."

"I have already told you two," Miss Winthrope's voice replied. "It is time for you and your sister to go to bed."

"No," the children protested, their cries echoed by older, but equally distressed, voices.

"You must tell us another," his grandmother's elegant voice stated.

"Just one more," chorused Amy's light, enthusiastic lilt. "Please, Prudence."

Silenced filled the room. Then Miss Winthrope gave a long, honeyed sigh. "All right. But this is the *last* one for tonight."

Edward paused by the door in the hallway shadows, out of sight. Telling himself he was merely curious he bent closer, listening.

"Someone must give me a starting sentence," she stated. "How about you, Sarah? I believe it is your turn."

Though he could not see her, Edward had no trouble picturing his daughter biting her lip in careful thought.

"I know. There was once a handsome knight, who was in love with a beautiful princess."

After a moment Prudence picked up the story. "But the knight could not speak of his love, for the princess was bound to an evil sorceress, who vowed that the day the princess found true love would be the day she died . . ."

Edward listened as she spun her tale, weaving words of fire and fancy into a magical tapestry. Her husky, passionate voice curled through him, drawing him deeper into the tale with every enchanting word. He stood in the shadows, savoring the rich tale of love and adventure like a schoolboy savoring his first stolen kiss, until the story reached its bittersweet end.

David piped up. "But why did the knight's squire have to die? Why couldn't the knight save him, too?"

"Because he could only save one of them, and the squire told him to save the princess." She paused a heartbeat before adding, "Not even the bravest knight can always save everyone he loves."

In the shadows, Edward felt an arrow pierce his heart. Blindly he sought and yanked open the front door, never stopping until he reached the edge of the sea. Below him plumes of dark water crashed up the cliffs into the moonlit night. But the violence of the ocean was nothing compared to the violence in his soul.

Years ago he'd believed in knights in shining armor, and princesses whose love was eternal and undying. He'd clung to those dreams as a boy, when an indifferent father and a self-absorbed mother had made a barren waste of his childhood. He'd followed his dreams and found his princess, and she'd filled his home with a love more wonderful than any of his imaginings. But her love had been neither eternal nor undying. And after she'd gone he'd cursed his dreams, and spent the next years proving to himself that there were no such things as love, or honor, or hope.

He'd given himself over to every kind of sin and debauchery, falling into a well so black and deep it had no bottom, going from woman to woman until Isabel's lovely, deceitful face was wiped from his mind. In the end, he'd crawled out of the hole enough to perform his business duties, and to see that his family was properly cared for. But his soul had never risen from that pit. In a way, he was still falling.

His duty to his family was the only decent thing left

in his life. He meant to protect them, from pain, from want—and from a silver-tongued charlatan who spun pretty tales of magic and passion. He would not let her build up their dreams, only to destroy them as Isabel had done. And he would not let her build up his own dreams, even if part of him wanted to believe again.

He fell to his knees and buried his face in his hands, exhausted in body and spirit. *Not even the bravest knight can always save everyone he loves.*

Hell, he couldn't even save himself.

Sabrina began to be quite pleased with herself for pulling off her daring bluff. Then, one evening at sunset, she looked out of an upstairs window, and saw the earl walking alone along the cliffs.

The ruddy twilight gloom wrapped his form in shadows. Unconsciously, Rina's hand tightened on the sill. She remembered the story of how Trevelyan's wife had deserted him and their children, and recalled the haunted look she'd seen in his eyes.

He was arrogant and cold, and she disliked him completely, but she couldn't deny the sorrow she'd seen beneath his harsh facade. Nor could she completely dismiss his kindness to Clara Hobbs. He was a complicated man. He had reason to distrust women, and the fact that she herself was even more of a cheat than his faithless wife brought an ache to her heart that she hadn't felt since her father died.

Sabrina was still watching Trevelyan when she heard a jaunty voice behind her. "We've struck it, Rina. The mother lode!"

Sabrina spun around and glanced worriedly down the corridor. Then she placed her hands on her hips, and gave the exuberant Quinn a censuring glare. "You used my true name. If someone had heard—"

"Now don't fuss. I'm not a grinagog, you know. I checked the hall proper before I came. The servants are having their meal and the swells are in the drawing room. There's not a Christian soul in earshot. And I've news, wondrous news!" He leaned closer. "One of the dowager's personal maids is cousin to the sweetheart of one of the stable hands. I overheard 'em talkin'. Seems the old woman is planning to have a ball at Ravenshold on Saturday next, to introduce you to the other swells in grand style."

Rina's eyes widened in alarm. "A *ball?* But I know nothing about balls. I don't know any dances save the steps Mother taught me, and that was almost ten years ago. I'd be laughed out of the county. Not to mention that I haven't a suitable gown—"

"The gown don't enter into it!" Quinn sighed, and stroked back what was left of his copper hair. "Lass, for all your wit, you're a mite bottle-headed. Whether you caper like a nob or step on every toe in the place, it don't matter. Balls mean finery, and finery means jewels. The dowager's giving the ball, so she's bound to be at it. And I'd wager my teeth that she'll be sporting the Dutchman."

The necklace. Unconsciously, Sabrina's hand rose to her throat, almost as if she had the diamonds on. She'd lost count of the times during her weeks of Quinn's coaching when she'd imagined lifting the diamonds from the dowager's dressing table. It had seemed so easy when Lady Penelope had been only a name to her, a caricature of the self-centered aristocrats she so despised. Now Rina knew the dowager to be a kind, caring woman who would be heartbroken when she learned that her "Prudence" was just another impostor.

Quinn's gaze narrowed. "What's the matter, gel? You look a mite green around the gills."

"I am fine. I just . . . I mean, 'tis just so sudden."

"Sudden! Lass, we've been waiting near a month for a chance like this. And don't act so hangdog. Spicing these swells should be a pleasure for ya, not a chore."

She and Quinn had been hoping for this opportunity ever since she'd agreed to his plan. She should have been as excited as he was. But all she could think about was how decent the dowager had been to her, and how Lady Amy had gone out of her way to be her friend. "I know it has got to be done. I just wish I didn't have to hurt them. They've been so kind to me."

"They've been kind to *Prudence*, not you." Quinn gripped her shoulders, and looked at her with a softness she'd never seen in his canny eyes. "These ain't your people, my girl. Now, I got eyes. I seen you getting all cozy with the nobs. And I know you got a soft heart, and that maybe you feel sorry for 'em. Well, *don't*. They'll sell you out in a second when they find out you're not one of them."

"I used to think that way, too. But now—"

"Now they've had two more weeks to look like fools when they find out the truth. Never feel sorry for the mark. It's easy to do, and many a good bloke's gone to the gallows for it. They seem all kindness, but their flowery talk won't mean nothing when they find out you've been putting 'em on. Keep your eye on the prize, my girl. Just like your da always did."

"Not always," she countered. "He left off cheating my grandfather when he fell in love with my mother."

Quinn's lips edged up in a slight smile. " 'Tis true enough. But your sainted ma were worth far more than the gold he would'a nipped from Lord Poole. A chance like that happens once in a lifetime—ten lifetimes.

Hearts are fickle as smoke in the wind. Count on gold and diamonds, Rina-lass, not true love. It don't happen often in this world—especially to the likes of us."

A look crept into his eyes—a sad, sweet gleam that made him look at once desperately young and impossibly old. Instinctively, Sabrina lifted her hand to his cheek. "Quinn? Have you . . . ever been in love?"

He shook off her touch and his expression at once. "Me? Moon around like a lovesick calf over some silly miss? I'd sooner be boiled in a Christmas pudding!"

"But for a moment I thought—"

"Well, you thought wrong, didn't ya?" He backed away and yanked down the hem of his yellow-striped waistcoat, his shrewd glance returning. "Gold and jewels is my love, girl, and I suggest you look to the same. Keep your eyes on the prize—and off of dangerous blokes like Lord Trevelyan."

He glanced past her shoulder at the window, the one she'd been gazing through when he approached. Apparently the sharp-eyed Quinn had seen the earl as well—and seen Rina looking at him. An embarrassed blush stained her cheeks. "I wasn't . . . it is not what you think."

Quinn rocked back on his heels. "And what is it I'm thinking? That you're falling under the Black Earl's spell like all the rest."

"I am not falling under anyone's spell, least of all his. Lord Trevelyan is the vilest, most ill-mannered brute I have ever had the displeasure to meet. I look forward to stealing the necklace because it means I can leave here and never lay eyes on him again."

For a long moment Quinn studied her face. Then he gave a sharp nod, apparently satisfied with her answer. "Sorry, my girl, but I had to be sure. The earl's known for his prowess with the fairer sex."

She turned to the window and stared out at the dying sun. "He has no *prowess* with me, I assure you."

"I can see that." Grinning, Quinn glanced down the hall. "I'd best be going. The servants will be about soon, and we'd have a devil of a time explaining what a stable hand is doing in the family corridor. I'll be leaving the stables tomorrow, just to put some distance between us. It'll be safer if we don't meet again until after the ball."

Rina's eyes widened in panic. "But, what if something goes wrong? How will I know what to do?"

Quinn smiled and chucked her chin. "It'll come to you, my girl. Now, the dowager's got a habit of leaving parties by ten—or so her maid told her beau. I'll be waiting with the horses at the main gate at straight up midnight. You nick the Dutchman, and we'll leave this place behind like a bad dream."

He started down the hall, but glanced back just before he turned the corner. "You're a queen, you are. My Queen of Diamonds. But the swells don't think anyone 'sides them is worth a damn. We're dirt to them, Rina-lass. Less than the dust on their boots."

He opened his mouth to say more, but at that moment Sabrina heard the sound of footsteps from the other end of the corridor. Turning, she saw Amy's slim, satined form running toward her down the hallway. "Oh, Prudence, I have been looking for you everywhere. For the first time in years Grandmother's opening Ravenshold for a ball. A ball in your honor, Cousin. Oh, it shall be so grand!"

Rina spared a quick glance down the hall, and was unsurprised to find that Quinn had vanished. She returned her gaze to Amy, and acted appropriately astonished and pleased about the ball. Within minutes she was swept up in a whirlwind of plans involving fans, flowers, gloves, dresses, and all the various and sundry articles that had to be procured to make them successes at the party.

On the outside Rina matched Amy smile for smile, but inside her heart had turned to stone. No matter how kind these people seemed, she could never let herself forget what they were, and what she was. They were gentry, rich and titled. And she was a fugitive from the law who was playing at a dangerous deception.

As they walked down the hall Sabrina stole a quick glance out the window. She needn't have troubled—Lord Trevelyan's figure had been obscured by the twilight mist rolling in from the sea. So much of what she'd believed had been swallowed up in mist. She could not allow herself to feel sympathy for him again—or for any of them. She'd let her fantasy of being a part of a family blind her to the facts. But, Quinn had spoken the truth—they'd hate her when they found out who she really was, and how completely she'd deceived them.

One hint of doubt, one single misstep, and she would land in a prison cell. Or be dancing from the business end of a rope.

Chapter Eleven

Amy's initial excitement quickly changed into a holy mission: to turn her "country cousin" into a lady of the first water overnight. She was aided in her endeavor by an equally enthusiastic Lady Penelope. Before Rina knew it, the dowager had engaged a modiste, who proceeded to poke and measure her until she felt like a giant pincushion. Amy deluged Rina with a flood of fashion books and magazines, discussing everything from balm of Mecca for the complexion, to the virtues of seemingly endless varieties of gloves, fans, and slippers, to the most advantageous man to be standing next to when the opening quadrille was announced. When Sabrina mentioned that she didn't need to worry about quadrille partners because she did not know the steps, a dance instructor appeared at Ravenshold within hours.

It was an exhausting, magical time for Sabrina, and she was human enough to enjoy the attention and gifts being showered on her. But she never forgot Quinn's warning. Every morning when she woke up, she glanced at the stuffed bear Ginger that sat on her trunk, and thought how easily she could have picked the wrong toy.

And every night when she went to bed she gripped the locket around her neck, and reminded herself over and over again that she was only playing a part.

On the Wednesday before the ball Sabrina and Amy traveled to the nearby port town of St. Petroc, to collect the gowns they'd been fitted for the week before. The port was busy and bustling with people, from merchants to sailors to soldiers on leave. Yet, despite the excitement, Amy was unusually quiet. It was not until they arrived at the dressmaker's that Rina discovered why.

At the modiste's shop, Amy burst out with the secret she'd been keeping for over a week. Her grandmother had quietly authorized the modiste to fashion not only a ball gown for her, but to use her measurements to create a dozen day and evening dresses as well. "She believed you needed a wardrobe that was, uhm, more suited to our plain country living," Amy confessed as the proprietress brought out a dozen new dresses. "We picked the patterns out together. I hope they meet with your approval."

The unexpected kindness overwhelmed Sabrina. She fingered the sleeve of a lovely robin's-egg blue morning dress, blinking back tears. Amy and her grandmother had obviously spent a great deal of time selecting outfits which would make the most of her limited attractiveness. It was the most generous gift she'd ever received—and the most undeserved one. On Saturday night she'd be leaving the country. And on Sunday morning Amy and the dowager would realize just how completely they'd been deceived—

"Do you not like them?" Amy asked, her gaze uncertain.

"Like them? I—" In answer, Sabrina enfolded the young woman in an extremely unladylike bear hug. The modiste gasped in alarm, but Rina didn't care. She closed her eyes and, for a moment, allowed herself to believe that this frivolous, dear girl really was her cousin.

As their purchases were brought to their carriage, Amy took Sabrina on a tour of the village. Like many of the towns in the Duchy of Cornwall, St. Petroc had a history that stretched back to Roman times, when the already prosperous mines were supplying the tin and copper to ports all over the Mediterranean.

"Tin has always been the lifeblood of Cornwall," Amy explained as they walked along the town's cobbled main street. "The stones on this road were laid by Roman centurions, so that the tin could be transported easily to the coast through the rough interior. Even the kings of England bowed to the Cornish tinners. In fact, it is said that King James the First was so impressed with Geoffrey, the first Earl of Trevelyan's, fortune that he offered him his cousin as a bride. But the earl did not accept. Instead, Geoffrey risked the king's ire, and married for love. It is a vastly romantic tale."

"Indeed," Sabrina acknowledged. "But I imagine that some of your relatives were less than pleased with your ancestor's choice. A royal connection would be a boon to Wheal Grace's profits. No doubt your brother thinks so. He seems to spend every waking moment at the mine."

Amy shook her head. " 'Twasn't always that way. Edward used to think of things besides business. Why, I can remember a time, when Isabel was alive . . . He's changed since then. Now he spends almost all his time either at our estates in the north, or in London, though I'm not entirely sure what he does there."

Rina recalled the beautiful opera dancers of Covent Garden, whose bejeweled fingers were always twined around the arm of some well-heeled gentry buck. She could easily imagine what Trevelyan was doing in London.

She looked down and brushed an imaginary piece of lint from her kid gloves, strangely unnerved by the thought. "Well, he seems to be spending a fair bit of time at Ravenshold now. I suspect he is keeping an eye on me."

Lady Amy's lip twitched up. "That is what Grandmother says. But she is glad you are here. So am I. And my brother will come around, you'll see. Even now I can see that he is softening toward you."

"Amy, I fear the excitement of the party has addled your wits. Your brother has made no secret of his profound dislike for me."

"Ah, do not be deceived by his rough manner. Remember, he risked his life to save you the day your bridle broke. And there are times when you are reading or looking into the fire in the evenings, that I catch him watching you. He shrugs and pretends it is nothing, but I have not seen that expression on his face in years, not since—oh, drat, the Larkin sisters are coming this way."

Rina wouldn't have cared if the devil himself were coming their way. She gripped Amy's arm. "His expression. You were going to tell me—"

"Yes, yes," Amy said, though her attention was clearly elsewhere.

Looking across the crowded street, Sabrina saw two middle-aged women perched on the curb, apparently searching for a break in the rumbling cart traffic. Their eager, almost hungry expressions reminded Rina of a pair of circling vultures. Amy leaned close and whispered furtively. "The Larkins are incorrigible gossips. If they catch wind of who you are, we'll never be rid of them."

Sabrina stiffened. Incorrigible gossips were not only unpleasant, they were dangerous. They asked questions—too many questions. Hastily Rina glanced around, her gaze lighting on the entrance to a narrow alley. "I can hide in there. Tell them I've gone down the lane to another shop or some such thing. You can fetch me after they've left."

Amy gave a quick nod of assent, and Rina slipped into the alley.

Stepping into the alley was like stepping into another world. The tall stone walls cut off most of the fresh air and all of the sunlight. The street sounds died too, muted by the thick, echoing walls. She wasn't one to jump at shadows, but this place unnerved her. The busy street was only a few yards behind her, yet she felt isolated and alone. Like entering a tomb.

She leaned against the cold wall and tried to set her mind on brighter imaginings. But no matter where she steered her thoughts, they kept returning to Amy's words about the earl. *I can see that he is softening . . . I catch him watching you.* But the girl was mistaken. If Trevelyan was watching her at all, it was only to catch her in a lie. He might have risked his life to save her that afternoon, but he'd never treated her with anything but cold disdain. Which made the quicksilver heat he stirred inside her all the more puzzling . . .

Muffled voices interrupted her thoughts. They came from the other end of the alley, from behind a crumbling brick wall where someone had tried to block off the narrow entrance. Rina moved toward the sound, grateful to have something to distract her troubled mind. She headed toward the alley's far end, only half listening to what the low voices were saying, until a single word caught her attention:

"Trevelyan."

She stole up to the wall, and pressed her ear close to the bricks.

"Cheatin', that's what I call it," said a sharp voice. "We did the deed and not a penny paid."

"But she ain't dead," answered another speaker,

whose voice was high and squeaky like a mouse. "The money for the corpse—that was the deal."

"Well, that ain't my fault. Wanted to stick her, didn't I? Wanted it quick and simple, like spittin' a Christmas turkey. But you, ya bleedin' sod—*you* wanted to make it look like an accident. So we used the horse."

The horse. *The runaway?* Rina pressed closer to the wall, holding her breath.

"It almost worked," squeaked the mouse.

"The boss don't pay for *almosts*. She's still breathin' and we're no richer. And if we don't snuff 'er soon, we'll—"

Sabrina's pressure on the wall dislodged a piece of the crumbling brick, sending it crashing to the ground. She heard a bawdy curse, followed by the sound of scrambling feet. Cursing herself, she dashed around the end of the wall, but she was too late. They were gone.

Her hands balled into tight fists, her Murphy blood boiling. She'd heard only bits of the conversation, but it was enough to convince her that her bridle ribbons had not snapped by accident. Some bastard wanted her dead. Some cowardly bastard who hired his assassins, who couldn't even face her like a man.

The scrape of boots on pavement made her turn her head. She caught sight of a tall man and his companion dashing away down the street. "Stop!" she yelled, charging after them. "Stop, or I'll see you hang!"

It wasn't a ladylike display, but at the moment she wasn't a lady. She was Sabrina Murphy, Daniel's Irish daughter, and she was mad as hell. The craven act of cutting the bridle had terrified her, and almost broken her neck. And almost broken the earl's too, which just made her angrier.

She ran as fast as she could, but it proved useless. Her long skirt and too-tight slippers were useless in a chase. The villains disappeared into the crowd before she even got another look at them. Cursing once more, she leaned against a shoulder-high crate, breathing in great gasps of air as her heart slowed.

She looked around, considering asking a passerby if they'd seen the villains. But the alley had led her onto the docks, a world of packing crates and barrels and rough men who were as transitory as their ship's cargo. She'd find no willing witnesses here.

Bending down, she rubbed one of her sore feet. If not for her stylish slippers she'd have caught them. The bastards. Sniveling bastards all of them, especially the man they worked for, this unknown boss. She'd find him out, just see if she didn't. They'd made a mistake trying to go after Daniel Murphy's daughter—

Rina stiffened. She wasn't a gambler's daughter here—she was Miss Prudence Winthrope, the long-lost cousin to the Trevelyan clan. Prudence had no enemies. Prudence wasn't even *real*. But real or not, she had apparently acquired an enemy—an enemy who wanted her dead. And if he was a danger to Prudence, he might just be a danger to the rest of the family as well. Amy, the children, *Edward*.

She remembered the evening when she'd watched the earl walk alone on the sea cliffs. The mist had been rising, obscuring his form and everything around him. It wasn't too difficult to imagine someone hiding, lying in wait for him. One little push, one well-timed shove, and . . .

"I must warn him." Rina pushed her way through the crowd, heading back toward the alley. Edward was arrogant and insufferable. And if he learned she wasn't Prudence, he'd have her in the bailey quicker than she could say Jack Robinson. But the thought of him in danger left her cold to the core . . . for the sake of his family, of course. It was simple Christian charity, something she'd have done no matter how much she despised him. And she *did* despise him, she assured herself as she approached the alley's entrance. Of that one fact she was absolutely certain—

"Not so fast, pretty Polly."

Sabrina halted, her way blocked by a substantial man in a frayed navy coat. His shirt was so badly stained that she could barely tell the striped pattern, and he stank of spoiled fish. She wrinkled her nose, recalling a saying she'd heard on the London docks. *Old sailors never die. They just smell like it.*

"You're mistaken, sir. My name is not Polly," she replied, trying to go around him.

He stepped sideways to cut her off. "I'll wager you can make it 'Polly.' If'n the coin is right."

He held out his beefy hand, revealing a tarnished half-crown. For a moment Rina didn't comprehend. Then she saw the lecherous gleam in his gaze as it raked over her gaudy gown. *Wonderful. I've been mistaken for a strumpet.*

Rina again told the sailor she wasn't what he was after and tried to push past him. She didn't get far. His ham-hock arm snaked out and gripped her hand so hard she winced.

"That coy act ain't bumping the price, lovey. I got an itch in my pants and you're the one to scratch it." He started to drag her over toward a stack of crates piled on the side of the dock.

Rina cried for help, but the only response to her plea was a chorus of cheerful, foul suggestions from a nearby group of dockhands. Panicked, her gaze went to the crowd on the street, but the few people who bothered to meet her eyes either sneered along with the dockhands, or shrugged their shoulders in disinterest.

The sailor gave her another bone-jarring yank, pulling her closer to the stacked crates. *This cannot be happening,* her mind reasoned. Memories of the night Albert tried to rape her rose in her mind. A scream lodged in her throat.

She cast her gaze around the dock in a desperate search for salvation. "Please," she cried, her voice weak with terror, "won't someone help—"

"Let her go."

The quiet, lethal command brought the hulking sailor to a halt. The speaker was hidden from Rina's view by the seaman's massive body, but it didn't matter. She knew the voice as well as she knew her own. Her heart soared at the thought that Trevelyan had come to her rescue.

And plummeted as she realized that the sailor outweighed the earl by six stone and topped him by a full head.

Chapter Twelve

Edward's visit to St. Petroc was supposed to be short and uneventful. He'd come to the port to discuss cargo charges for his tin with the local ships' merchants—an unscrupulous lot who would sell their own grandmothers if the price were right. Trevelyan knew how to deal with them, and the bargain he'd made was far more equitable then what they'd wanted. He should have felt triumphant when he left their offices on the waterfront. Instead, the only thing he wanted was to get away from the stinking, congested wharf and back to the wild cliffs of Ravenshold.

A commotion on the far end of the dock distracted his thoughts. A sailor and his strumpet were apparently having an assignation in broad daylight. Disgusted, the earl started to turn away. Then he heard the woman cry out.

Prudence?

Last evening, Amy had told him that she and Miss Winthrope were planning a trip to St. Petroc today, but they were visiting the dressmaker, not the docks. He shook his head, vexed anew with his counterfeit cousin.

He couldn't do anything about her voice and image invading his dreams, but he'd be damned if he'd let her commandeer his waking thoughts as well. Once again he started to turn away, casting a final, glaring glance at the hulking sailor and his doxie—

—and caught a glimpse of unmistakable auburn hair.

The sailor's back was to him, blocking the earl's view of the woman's upper body, but a quick glance at the skirt of the disastrously decorated gown told him all he needed to know. He pushed his way through the jeering crowd. "Let her go."

The sailor craned his thick neck around and shot a glare over his shoulder. "Get your own damn whore."

"You've made a mistake."

"I ain't the one makin' a mistake, mate," the big man sneered. "I've no quarrel with ya—yet. Piss off. You can have her when I'm done."

Fury rising, the earl grabbed the man's arm.

The sailor whirled back, his glare boiling to an open threat. He pushed aside his coat, revealing the bone handle of a knife stuck in his broad leather belt. "Leave off—or lose the hand."

The earl's jaw pulled taut. "If it's a fight you want, *mate*, I'll gladly—"

"Edward, do as he says."

Prudence's words silenced him. Beyond the sailor's shoulder, he caught sight of a pair of terrified emerald eyes. He stared back at her, completely flummoxed.

"You cannot win," she pleaded. "He's got a knife. And he's bigger than you are."

The sailor gave a barking laugh. "Right you are, darlin'. In more ways than one!" He gripped her hair and planted a slobbering kiss on her mouth.

Edward's blood turned to fire. With a feral growl he grabbed the sailor's shoulders and dragged him backward, shoving him against one of the wooden dock pilings. "Leave, Miss Winthrope," he commanded though his gaze never left the seaman. "As I said—if it's a fight you want, I'll gladly oblige."

Roaring a foul curse the sailor rammed into the earl. The knife flashed out, catching the sun as it slashed down. Edward twisted, feeling the rush of air as the blade sliced by his chest. The bastard was trying for his heart.

The big man stepped back and studied the earl, as if expecting to see a cringing fop scared out of his wits.

Edward stared back at him with all the lust and power that had been born into him. For years Edward had stifled his passions, fearing the return of the madness and grief that had almost destroyed him when Isabel deserted him. Now his rage coursed through him like fire—his blood sang with it. He saw the uncertainty in the sailor's eyes, the glint of fear. And he lunged on that fear like a wolf on its prey.

The knife came down again, this time rending his left sleeve. The near brush fueled Edward's bloodlust. With a battle yell, he drew back his arm and hit the sailor's jaw with a force that sent the big man staggering backward. The brute grabbed the piling, and his knife clattered to the wooden boards. The glint of fear in his eyes turned to cowardly panic.

"Look, mate, er, your lordship," he stammered. "I made a mistake—no sense two mates fightin' over a bit o' muslin."

"She's a *lady*!" Edward thundered. "You're a coward and a bully and someone ought to teach you a lesson. But I won't," he said, drawing in a deep breath. "I won't . . . the *hell* I won't."

Edward shoved the cringing sailor off balance, toppling him backward into the water. He stood on the dock's edge, watching the man flounder and sputter while the other dockhands reached out a pole to retrieve him. He doubted the dunking would make much of a difference in the man's behavior—but perhaps the brute would think twice before taking advantage of an unwilling lady.

He wiped his hand over his face, beginning to feel the exhaustion that came after a fine fight. Then he felt it, that strange awareness that had become as familiar as his own heartbeat. He turned to his left, knowing even before he saw her that she would be standing at his side.

Actually, Prudence was kneeling. She was tearing a strip of cloth from the hem of her hideous dress. She should have left, gotten to safety. If he'd lost the fight . . .

Her courage astonished him. Her lack of regard for her own safety infuriated him. He glared at her, using the same bellowing tone that had made the sailor cringe. "Just what do you think you are doing?"

"Your arm," she said, unimpressed by his fierce words.

He looked at his arm. The knife-gashed sleeve was damp with blood. Apparently the sailor's second blow hadn't missed after all. He'd been so caught up in the fight that he hadn't noticed. Now he felt the dull ache in his arm, the beginning fingers of pain. " 'Tis nothing."

Standing up, she gave him a scolding look, the kind his nanny used to give him when she caught him with his hand in the cookie jar. She started to dab the wound, appraising the cut with a sober frown and an experienced eye. "It is probably nothing more than a flesh wound, but it still needs tending. Even slight cuts can turn putrid without care. Hold still, my lord."

He could not have moved if he'd tried. Her touch was feather-light, and as capable as any doctor's. It had been a long time since Edward had felt such tenderness in a woman's touch, and it surprised him to realize how much he'd missed it. Her quiet ministrations filled up the cold places inside him like a gentle hearthfire on a winter night. Apparently pleased by his swiftness in following her orders, she glanced up at him and gave him one of her diamond-rare smiles.

Gentle flame roared to hellfire.

Desire flowed through him. They were standing on a fish-stinking pier in the middle of the day, surrounded by God only knew how many people. And he wanted her. Her smile, her scent, the competent grace of her slim hands mixed into an alchemy that turned his blood to raging fire. When he'd rescued her from the runaway horse he'd held her in his arms, but that was nothing compared to the raw need that thundered through him now. He licked his lips, his mouth suddenly gone dry. "Prudence."

She glanced up and met his gaze, and was caught fast in the same unholy fire that bound him up. Her hand stilled, her lower lip trembled. He stared down into her face, at the wise, strong features. How could he have thought them unbeautiful? She had courage and intelligence, and a sweetness that powder and rouge couldn't begin to counterfeit. His dark gaze caressed her porcelain skin, her courtesan's mouth, and her impossibly beautiful eyes. God, a man could drown in those eyes.

"Prudence," he repeated, his voice a husky whisper. The darkness that had surrounded his heart for years melted like a morning fog. He reached up and brushed a copper curl from her cheek, and felt her shiver. To hell with the dock, the crowd, the stink of fish. None of it mattered. Only her. Only him. He needed to kiss her, needed it like his next breath. He whispered her name a final time as he lowered his mouth toward hers—

"Edward!"

His sister's cry cut through the sensual haze. Startled, he jerked up and saw Amy marching through the crowd with several constables in tow. "I saw you fighting that brute, so I hurried back to the street and found these charming—Prudence, are you all right? Did that fiend hurt you? Did he—there he is!" She pointed to where the water-soaked sailor was climbing over the edge of the pier. "There's the brute who attacked her. Constable, do your dut—Edward, your arm!"

Amy continued talking at breakneck speed. She tsked and fussed over Edward's arm, talking all the while as one of the constables asked him what had happened. Edward barely listened to either one of them. Instead, he craned his neck and watched as two of the other constables escorted Miss Winthrope away from the crowd that had gathered around him. And as the curious onlookers crushed in on him, so did reality.

She was an impostor. The sweetness he'd seen in her eyes, the care he'd sensed in her touch, the innocence he'd felt in her trembling body—clever lies, all of them. She'd used her wiles to get to his decent and unsuspecting family.

Now, apparently, she'd found a way to get to him as well.

He caught a final glimpse of her as she disappeared into the alley. She paused and glanced back at him, and gave him one of her disarming, devastating smiles. The years fell away, and he remembered Isabel waving to him as he rode off on that final trip, smiling just as disarmingly as she threw him a kiss and bade him to hurry back.

And the ice that had left his heart closed around it once more.

"For a hero you are certainly in a foul mood," Dr. Williams commented as he studied the bandage wrapped around the earl's arm.

Edward grunted. He made a halfhearted attempt to tuck his shirt into his breeches, then turned back to his half-empty wineglass. "I'm no hero. And my mood is my own business. Yours is seeing to my arm."

"My *business* is patching my patient's wounds, whether they are in the body or the mind. The apothecary at Petroc did a commendable job with your wound. Your arm will be fine. But your mind . . ."

Charles pulled over a wooden chair and turned it backward. Sitting down, he rested his chin on the top of the chair back and studied the earl over the dark rim of his spectacles. "When I first met you I thought you were one of those foppish dandies, like Fitzroy. But during the past few weeks I've watched you work as hard as any of the miners at Wheal Grace—twice as hard in some cases. You're a good man, my lord. I've come to respect you. Which is why I think it only fit to tell you that you're heading for an early grave."

Edward hesitated, but only for a moment. He reached for the wine bottle and filled his glass to the rim. "This is a remarkable Bordeaux. Are you sure you won't have some?"

"Man, I am talking about your life! You cannot keep driving yourself like this. And for no reason. You have a loving family, wonderful children, and a fine home. Besides, if a lady looked at me the way Miss Winthrope looked at you—"

"That is *also* none of your affair." Edward's tone was low and lethal.

Dr. Williams's eyes narrowed shrewdly. "You do not trust her. Even after all these weeks, after all she has done for your grandmother and sister . . ."

"The only thing she has done is deceived them!" Trevelyan hurtled out of his chair. He stormed over to his desk and grabbed up a paper, and thrust it in front of the doctor's face. "This letter is from my solicitor, Mr. Cherry. I've instructed him to investigate Miss Winthrope's background. It has been a painstaking process—but in this letter he writes that he may have found something to challenge her story."

Charles studied the letter. He handed it back with a shrug. "He offers nothing here but vague speculation. *Thinking* he has found something and actually *finding* something are two very different things. As a man of science I rely on the evidence, and the evidence I see is that your cousin has brought a great deal of happiness to this household."

"You are just like my family. She has cast her spell over you, too, with her wide green eyes and her bewitching smile."

Charles stroked his chin. "She does have a fine smile. Nothing so enchanting as your sister's, of course, but a fine smile just the same. Still, it is not her smile that gives me a regard for Miss Winthrope. She is an intelligent and caring lady, remarkable in many ways, and I am proud to count her as my friend. Besides, if she were an impostor, would she not have shown it by now?"

Edward grimaced. He'd had much the same thought himself. For weeks he'd expected Miss Winthrope to show her true colors, to abscond with the family silver or a few priceless paintings. But she'd stolen nothing that he could discern, and he was running out of reasons not to trust her. She was either very clever, or completely honest.

He wasn't sure which prospect disturbed him more.

He picked up his wineglass and tossed down the remainder in a single draught. "Long-lost cousins do not appear from thin air, any more than pixies dance in the flower gardens. Her story is a sham—eventually Cherry will prove it. And when he does, it will break my grand-mother's and sister's hearts."

"Just theirs?"

Edward spun around, his eyes narrowing danger-ously. "Your services are no longer required, Doctor. You may go."

"Of course. Good night, my lord." Dr. Williams got up from his chair and collected his medical satchel, then headed for the door without a word. Edward watched him go, telling himself that he had nothing to feel guilty about, that the young man was a paid employee—a well-paid one, at that. Theirs was a business relationship. He owed the doctor nothing—not courtesy, not confidence, certainly not friendship—

"Doctor." He set his glass on the fireplace mantel and plowed his hand through his dark hair. "My friends, such as they are, call me Edward."

The young man's smile was hesitant, but sincere. "Mine call me Charles. Good night—Edward."

Left alone, the earl rested his head on the mantel and looked into the fire, his hand toying with the empty wineglass. He *did* have feelings for Miss Winthrope—he'd known by the blood lust that rose in him when he saw that bastard of a sailor kiss her. He didn't want to acknowledge it—hell, he'd have given just about any-thing not to acknowledge it—but the feelings were there just the same.

She wasn't his type. She was too thin—he liked his women buxom. She was too tall—he liked them petite and swathed in lace and frills. And she was too young—nearly a dozen years his junior, and while some men preferred schoolroom misses, he wasn't one of them. Logically, there was nothing about her that should have interested him in the least. Except her luminous eyes.

And her incredible smile. And her strange, uncommon grace that made his body ache when he imagined her with him, under him, around him . . .

He'd felt desire before, but nothing like this, nothing like this madness that pounded against his will. He wiped the back of his hand across his damp brow. Too thin. Too tall. Too young. Almost certainly a deceiver. *And he couldn't draw breath without wanting her.*

A knock on his door startled him out of his thoughts. *Hell.* No doubt the physician had returned, concerned about his state of mind—and his sobriety. The earl yanked the heavy door open. "Dammit, Charles, I don't need a bloody—"

Miss Winthrope stood on the threshold, her hand poised for another knock, standing as still as if she'd been carved in stone.

She was staring at his chest.

He was naked. Well, partly. His shirt was stuffed haphazardly into his breeches and open to the waist. The discreetly edited sketches of Grecian frescoes she'd seen in her mother's classical history books hadn't prepared her for the reality of the earl's naked chest, of the hot, heady scent of his skin, of the dusting of black, tightly curled hair that formed a dark V that tapered downward toward his—

Her chin shot up . . . and met a pair of eyes as cold and unforgiving as the rocks of hell.

"What do *you* want?"

Her gaze flickered once more over his state of undress. A dozen responses came to her mind, all of them shockingly inappropriate. "I . . . I wanted to thank you. For saving me. And also, I—"

"Fine. You've thanked me. Good-bye."

He started to shut the door. Sabrina stepped into the opening, blocking the door with her body. "Wait, there is more—"

"Well, I don't want to hear it," he snarled. "Get the hell out of my room."

She shook her head, unable to fathom his change of mood. He'd risked his life to save her from the sailor. And afterward, when she'd tended his arm, he'd been so gentle, so kind, so . . . She swallowed, and ignored the sharp pain that inexplicably pierced her heart. "I will not leave. Not until I've told you what I heard this afternoon."

For a moment she thought he might actually crush her in the door. Instead, he gave a raw curse and stalked away to his desk. Standing with his back to her and his legs braced in a fighting stance, he dumped the remains of a wine bottle into his empty glass. He grabbed it up, the dark wine sloshing over the glass's rim. "Well?"

She closed the door and leaned back against it. He was still facing away from her. She tried not to notice how his shirt stretched across his broad shoulders, and how his breeches stretched across his—

Rina wished quite sincerely that she had left when he'd asked her to. Still, she had a duty to tell him what she'd overheard in the alley. "Before the sailor accosted me I heard something, something I believe you need to know."

Without turning around, he shrugged. "Unfortunate that you didn't tell me this afternoon. Then you wouldn't be wasting my time now."

Rina's temper flared. "I cannot see what pressing matter I am keeping you from, my lord. Unless 'tis another drink."

The earl spun around, his gaze murderous. "These are *my* rooms, and in them I'll do as I please. If my drinking offends your delicate sensibilities, you are free to go."

"I intend to, but not before I've had my say." She tilted her chin defiantly. "When I was in the alley, I overheard two men. They mentioned the name Trevelyan, and spoke of an accident involving a horse. They talked of a deal—money for a corpse. *'She's still breathing and we're no richer'*—that's what they said."

Slowly, Edward set down his glass. "The runaway."

"I believe that is what they meant. The snapped bridle ribbons were no accident. And if they tried to hurt me, they might try to hurt other members of your family. You, the dowager, Lady Amy, or—"

"Or my children. By God, if anyone tries to harm so much as a hair on their heads, I'll—"

All at once he threw back his head and laughed. "Sweet Christ, what was I thinking?"

"Edward?"

"Taken in. Again! By God, I should have had Charles examine my head instead of my arm."

"But it's true!"

"No doubt. You just happened to be in the right place at the right time to hear this snippet of conversation. How do you explain that?"

"Luck?" she offered.

"More like guile." He tossed down the rest of the wine, then walked to the fireplace, still gripping the empty glass. He leaned against the mantel, his body a dark shadow against the bright, crackling fire. "Ply your lies elsewhere. I am not buying."

"But 'tis the truth. I swear it."

"Like you swear you are Prudence Winthrope?" He lifted his head, his expression holding both bitterness and regret. "If you are trying to gain my trust, you needn't bother. I have had some experience with deceitful women. You're a clever liar, *Cousin*, but a liar just the same. And I suspect there is nothing you would not do to further your own ends."

His words cut more deeply that she'd thought possible. She hoped—no, she'd *believed*—that after the way he'd come to her rescue he had some small regard for her. She saw now that that hope was in vain. No matter what she said or did, he would never see her as anything but a worthless liar.

She pressed her hand to her chest, trying to ease the fist of misery that had gathered around her heart. "If you believe all that of me, then why did you come to my rescue?"

His body went rigid. He stared at her, his eyes full of so much pain and anger that she felt it twist in her soul. She felt the battle raging inside him, saw it in the taut muscles, the subtle narrowing of his eyes. Every instinct told her to run, to get out before his fury turned deadly. But she couldn't run away from his pain. Underneath the rage was a man who had once loved a woman deeply, and had suffered for that love. She couldn't turn her back on him. Not when she felt . . . when she felt . . .

"Ah, *hell!*" Trevelyan hurled his wineglass into the fireplace, then stormed across the room. He took Rina's face between his hands, and covered her mouth in a devouring kiss.

Chapter Thirteen

Sabrina had been kissed by two men in her life, but when the earl's lips slanted over hers she realized she'd never been kissed at all. His mouth consumed her with devastating gentleness, moving across hers with a hot, moist, and very thorough caress. His tongue skimmed her lips, shattering her inexperienced senses like he'd shattered the wineglass. Tiny shocks of pleasure exploded through her body. Her knees faltered and she gripped his shirt for support. Her fingers brushed his warm chest. Tiny shocks turned to earthquakes.

Time stopped. Reason unraveled. She couldn't breathe, but suffocation seemed a small price to pay. She'd never imagined it could be like this—this fiery pleasure, this rough, sweet magic. She heard a feral growl, then realized it had come from her own throat. Once again her knees gave way, but this time it was Edward's arms that held her up, wrapping her in the velvet steel of a lover's embrace.

Ecstasy shuddered through her. She'd accepted her lot in life as a plain woman, destined to live without passion. But in this blinding instant she knew what it was to be wanted by a man—truly wanted—and the glory of it burned her alive. Moaning again she parted her lips, and offered herself to him with surprise, innocence, and joy.

He released her mouth. For an eternal moment he stared down at her, studying her with the same bewildered wonder that she felt. Then the wonder died, leaving the jaded wariness she'd seen in his eyes far too many times before.

"Well done, *Cousin*. You almost made a believer of me. But no blushing virgin ever kissed like that. Still, it seems a shame to waste such talent." He glanced toward a door on the other side of the room. "We could continue the rest of the show in my bedchamber. I might even be persuaded to stop digging into your past, if you—"

Her slap cut off the rest of his suggestion. She pushed herself out of his arms and bolted through the hallway door, desperate to get away before he saw the tears in her eyes. She hated him. She despised him. He'd seduced her, just as Quinn warned her he would. Just as he'd seduced so many other women . . .

She ran down the corridor, scrubbing away the feel of his kiss from her lips. But her skin still burned where he'd touched her, and the hot, tight wanting still ached inside her.

Sabrina stopped running. She leaned her head against the wall and took in deep gulps of air, trying to slow her pounding, shattered heart. The same feelings had coursed through her on the day the earl had rescued her from the runaway, only this was worse, far worse. Because this time she'd kissed him with all the need and longing in her soul. She hated and despised him, but she still wanted him to hold her, caress her, make love to her.

She'd thought that the humiliation she felt when Albert tried to rape her was the worst shame that a woman could feel. She'd been wrong.

• • •

The day of the ball arrived. Ravenshold was bustling with activity, from the frantic preparations in Mrs. Poldhu's kitchen to the tornado of dusting and cleaning that took place throughout the downstairs. The rugs were rolled up and stored away to allow for the evening's dancing. The ancestral banners were washed then unfurled in all their vibrant fighting colors, and the suits of armor were polished until they gleamed. Flowers filled every vase. Silver candelabras decorated every table. The whole house hummed with the brisk, happy momentum of a well-oiled machine.

By midmorning the cheerful industry was driving Rina insane.

Unnoticed, she headed for the cliffs, desperate for the solitude and the silence. It was a bright, blustery day and a fierce wind blew a chill from the northern sea. She stood near the edge of the cliff, so close that the toes of her shoes nearly touched the red markers that showed the safe boundary, but she barely noticed the precarious drop beneath her. Her thoughts were occupied elsewhere, just as they had been occupied all last night, and all of the day and night that had come before. *Edward.*

Try as she might, she could not blot out the memory of their last encounter. His kiss still burned her lips. Her fingertips still tingled from the feel of his warm, hard flesh. She wrapped her arms around her middle and drew the bracing air into her lungs, trying to calm the muddle of emotions inside her.

'Tis simply nerves, she assured herself. She'd been waiting for this night for so long. After the party she would steal the Dutchman's Necklace. Then, at the stroke of midnight, she'd meet Quinn at the gates of Ravenshold. They'd ride away before anyone was the wiser, off to a

grand future that did not include the arrogant Lord Trevelyan. She told herself she was glad of it, that she hated the earl with all the passion in her fiery Irish soul.

Unfortunately, that hatred didn't stop her from wanting to feel his arms around her just one more time.

A faint, high-pitched cry interrupted her thoughts.

"I am not a *baby*!"

"Are too," a slightly older voice replied. "Baby, baby, baby."

David and Sarah? Sabrina frowned. The children were supposed to be with their tutor, not capering along the tops of the cliffs. Rina hurried down the twisting path, past a large rock outcropping that stood in the middle of the rugged lane. David and Sarah were walking along the edge of the cliff, followed dutifully by their puppy Pendragon.

The dog was the first to notice her. He lifted his muzzle straight up, apparently sniffing the shifting wind. Then he turned completely around and launched his furry body straight into Sabrina's arms.

"Penny, stop . . . no, you can't lick my nose. You know I don't like . . . oh, stop wiggling, dear, or I might drop you!"

"Cousin Prudence?" Sarah stepped forward, looking at once contrite and contrary. She toyed nervously with the satin ribbon of her blue bonnet. "We weren't doing anything."

"Save walking along these cliffs by yourselves," Rina replied, looking as stern as she could with a frantic puppy in her arms. "You two are supposed to be in the school-room with your tutor, are you not?"

Tight-lipped, Sarah tilted her chin defiantly, but David pushed in front of her. "The downstairs maid asked him to help with the party. He kissed her when he thought I wasn't looking, so I guess he has to do what she says. So we 'scaped. Then Sarah went and called me a *baby*. You don't think I'm a baby, do you, Cous' Pru?"

Allowing Pendragon one last lick, Rina set the puppy at her feet. "Of course I do not think you're a baby, but neither you nor your sister should be walking these cliffs alone. They are very dangerous."

"Only to outsiders," Sarah answered sharply.

Instinctively Rina stiffened at the girl's tone. During the weeks she'd been at Ravenshold, Sarah had never warmed to her the way David had. At first Rina thought it was a mirror of the distrust her father showed. But lately Rina had seen her show the same coolness toward Amy and even toward Lady Penelope. It was as if the child had built a wall between herself and the rest of the world that kept anything from touching her.

Still, wall or not, the children could not be allowed to roam the cliffs alone. "Come, children. I want you to come home with me."

Immediately Sabrina realized her mistake. What had been a split defense suddenly became a united front against a common enemy—an adult. Lord David glanced up at his sister, arching his brow in a devilish expression that was the mirror of his father's. "We don't have to go back, do we, Saree?"

"Certainly not." Smiling, Sarah slipped her hand around her young brother's. Together they turned and started down the narrow path, their previous quarrel forgotten—along with any adult who sought to send them back to their lessons.

If Rina returned to Ravenshold for help, she'd have to leave them alone on these cliffs for another half hour or longer. She glanced at the cliff path, at the red markers that told clearer than words how treacherous the way could be for the careless. One false step, and . . .

Sabrina's jaw pulled taut. They wouldn't come with

her. And she wouldn't go back without them. "Wait! May I . . . join you?"

Sarah looked over her shoulder, and gave an indifferent shrug. "Please yourself," she said as she continued down the rocky path with her brother and Pendragon in tow. "But you'll have to keep pace with us. We'll not wait up for you."

Sarah and David scampered over the rocks and crevices of the narrow path with the skill of mountain goats. They rarely glanced Sabrina's way, apparently expecting her to fall behind quickly. But Rina had spent her early years chasing foals through summer pastures, and her later years nimbly avoiding carriages and carter wagons on crowded London streets.

She navigated the cliff-top path with as much skill as the children, and with a longer stride. She kept pace behind them with an ease that earned her a sour look from Sarah. David, however, dropped back to walk beside Rina, and smiled with surprise and open admiration. "You're good at climbing."

"Thank you, sir," Rina answered, a warmth spreading through her at the boy's heartfelt praise. She'd known him only a few weeks, but during that time the young master of Ravenshold had carved himself a permanent place in her soul. She was going to miss him dreadfully after she was gone. Him . . . and others.

Lady Sarah's command interrupted Rina's disquieting thoughts. "Hurry up, you two!" She crossed her arms and tapped her toe like a disgruntled schoolmarm. "Hurry, or we'll never make Wrecker's Point."

Sabrina frowned. "*What* point?"

"Wrecker's," David answered, his cheerful smile at odds with the frightening name. "People used to build fires at the top of the cliff. The ships thought it was the lighthouse down the coast. They'd turn into the rocks and get smashed to smithereens. Then the wreckers would murder the crew and steal their treasure and hide it in sea caves until they could sell it."

Sabrina fought to suppress a grin at David's enthusiastic retelling of the gruesome tale. "Well, that makes the wreckers very bad men, doesn't it?"

"I 'pose so," he sighed, though his tone was less than credible. He reached down and gave Pendragon a boost over one of the steeper rocks. Watching his unconscious kindness, Rina felt her heart constricting again. "They say that there's still treasure hidden in the caves—gold and diamonds and rubies as big as goose eggs. When I grow up, I'm going to search every cave until I find it."

" 'Twill be a long search," Sarah chided. "There are hundreds of caves all along this coast. And if the treasures really existed they would have been found long ago. Only a boodle-brain would think there really was a treasure."

"I'm not a boodle-brain. And there *is* treasure. Mama told me so."

Sarah went suddenly still. "That's not true. You don't even remember her. You were too little."

"I *do* remember her. She was warm and soft and she smelled like lavender. And when she tucked us in at night she'd tell us stories, just like Cousin Prudence does. Then she'd tell us she loved us—"

Sarah lashed out. "You're a liar! She never said any of those things."

"Sarah!" Rina stepped between the children, putting David behind her. "Your brother is not a liar. If he says he remembers, I'm sure it's true."

"It's not!" Sarah cried, her shout echoing through the cliffs. "She never told us stories, or tucked us in, or told us she loved us. She never loved us at all. And I don't care, because I hate her." Sarah's lower lip quivered and her eyes gleamed with tears.

Memories of Rina's own past came back to her—of running and running through the open fields, as if she could outdistance the pain that tore at her heart. Her mother had left for a different reason, but it still felt like desertion, was still a betrayal. And Rina knew that nothing could completely heal the wound.

"You do not hate her," Sabrina said quietly. "You're angry at her because she left you, but you don't hate her." She stepped forward, and reached out her hand. "Remember, I lost my mother, too. You mustn't hate her for what she did."

For a moment Sabrina saw the flash of doubt in the girl's gaze, and thought she might finally cross that cold, high wall that kept Sarah's heart hidden. But the moment passed and the chill aloofness returned to Sarah's expression. She turned her back on Sabrina, leaving the woman with a feeling that she'd watched something far more precious than the Dutchman's Necklace slip away. *After tonight I will never see this child again. Why does it matter so much to me that she's hurting inside?*

She watched Sarah skip away down the winding cliff path, scrambling over the boulders at a dangerous pace. She threw a taunting glance back at Rina. "Wrecker's Point is just ahead. See if you can catch me."

"Sarah, stop! You mustn't—no, David, you stay here. 'Tis not safe—"

"See if you can catch me," Sarah sang. She stood on the top of the boulder, waving down at them. "See if you can catch—"

Her song ended abruptly as the ground crumbled under her, and she slid over the edge of the cliff.

Chapter Fourteen

Rina raced to the cliff, nearly toppling over herself in her rush. She craned her neck, balancing precariously as she looked over the edge and caught sight of Sarah's blue dress on a rocky ledge a dozen feet below. Her heart started beating again. "Sarah, I see you. Are you all right?"

A thin wail assured Sabrina that Sarah was conscious, but possibly hurt and definitely scared out of her wits. *That makes two of us.*

"Is she going to die?"

David's hushed voice reminded Rina that she wasn't the only one who was frightened. She stepped away from the edge and gave the young viscount an encouraging hug. "Your sister is fine."

David glanced past her shoulder at the cliff edge, looking less than convinced. "I don't want her to die. I get mad at her sometimes, but I don't want her to die."

"She won't die. But we need your help. I want you to be brave, David. I need to climb down and see if your sister is all right. You'll have to stay up here—"

"But I want to help Saree!"

"I know you do, darling. But you can help her more by staying up here and keeping safe." She looked down, unwilling to let him see the fear in her eyes. "You have to stay here. Someone must look after Pendragon."

"That's right." David wrapped the puppy in his arms. "He's real little. He might fall off the cliff."

"Then you must see that he doesn't. If you keep away from the edge, he'll do the same." Rina gave the pup a pat, and rose to her feet. David could still make his way back to Ravenshold, even if something happened to her . . .

Steeling her mind against discouraging thoughts, Sabrina went to the cliff's edge. Sarah had fallen down the rock and rubble slope to a narrow ledge some twenty feet beneath the summit. Beyond that ledge was— nothing. Just a sheer drop to the churning sea far below. Rina stared out into the emptiness, feeling her own stomach begin to churn as she saw how close Sarah had come to that nothingness.

Well, Rina-lass, it's time to see if you've got your da's talent for risk, she told herself as she stripped off her kid gloves and knelt down. She gripped a rock and cautiously started to work her way down the steep, gravel-strewn incline. "Hang on, Sarah. I will be with you soon."

The slope was far more dangerous than she'd anticipated, with loose talus and treacherous rocks that appeared secure but broke away when she put her weight on them. Every handhold was an uncertainty, every footstep a gamble. She shifted her foot to a solid-looking rock, thinking that someone should have marked this slope with red markers. The thought ended in panic as the rock disintegrated under her.

She fell, sliding a full yard down the granite cliff face. Her hands flailed wildly for a handhold, heedless of the rough stone scraping her arms and tearing her dress.

She landed with a thud on the ledge as rocks and gravel fell into the abyss beneath her. Out of the corner of her eye she thought she saw something red further down on the slope, but she had no time to investigate.

"Cousin Prudence?"

Sabrina rushed over to the girl's side. Sarah was covered in dirt from head to toe. Her blue bonnet had been ripped away and her dress was in a shambles, but her eyes were clear of pain. She appeared shaken and bruised, but unharmed. Still, Rina felt her ribs and limbs for breaks. "Are you hurt?"

"I d-don't think so," she stuttered, clearly shaken by the fall. She started to push herself to a sitting position. "I feel—ooh, my ankle!"

The ankle didn't appear to be broken, but from Sarah's wince of pain when she touched it, Rina guessed it was badly sprained. She tried to sound cheerful. "I fear you will not be running any races on this leg for a while."

Sarah attempted a brave smile.

Rina gave the girl a smile of her own. Then she stood up and wiped her hands on her skirt, though whether that made them dirtier or cleaner was a questionable point. Sighing, Rina shielded her eyes and surveyed the cliff above them, trying to determine if she would be able to carry Sarah up. But the sheer rock and the loose gravel offered no safe way to the top. Indeed, she doubted if she could have made the climb even without the girl. She and Sarah were safe on the ledge, but they weren't going anywhere.

Sabrina cupped her hands around her mouth. "David? Can you hear me?"

David's head appeared over the summit. "I can hear you. Is Saree all right?"

"She is going to be fine, but she has twisted her ankle. You must go back to Ravenshold and get help."

David looked uneasily at the barren, windswept rocks. "I'm not 'lowed to walk on the cliffs by myself. Papa won't like it."

"Darling, this time is special. Your papa won't mind. Just keep away from the edge of the cliffs. You are the only one who can get to Ravenshold and bring back someone to rescue us."

David's voice brightened. "Rescue you? Like the knight in your story?"

Sabrina called back, "Yes, like the knight. But you must promise me to be very, very careful. Will you do that?"

Her only answer was the sound of a dog barking. Apparently David was already off and running before he heard her cautionary plea. She closed her eyes, and sent up a desperate prayer to whatever guardian angel might be listening. *I know I'm not in your good books right now, but please keep the boy safe. Please.*

"Prudence?"

Quickly, Rina scrubbed away the tears of despair that pricked her eyes. She wanted nothing more than to cry out her despair, but she couldn't afford to, not while Sarah needed her. She squared her shoulders and took Sarah's hand in hers. "There is nothing to fear. Your father will be here before you know it."

Sabrina expected her words to comfort the child. Instead, the girl's young face dissolved into anguish. "He won't come. Why should he? He knows it is all my fault."

Rina frowned. " 'Tis not your fault at all. This cliff path should have been marked as dangerous. You had no way of knowing that the ground would give way—"

"You don't understand." Sarah shook her head so violently that her red curls tumbled around her face. "Papa hates me. He knows it is my fault that Mama left."

Rina was momentarily too stunned to speak. "That isn't true. You mustn't say such a thing."

Once started, Sarah's confession poured out of her. "You were right. I did not hate Mama. I loved her. And I was so scared when she disappeared. Papa told me that she'd gone to visit an old friend, but I saw them dragging the bay. They thought she'd fallen in. I prayed to God that she'd be all right—I even dreamed that she was lost and in a dark place, calling my name . . ."

Gently, Rina smoothed the child's hair. "It's all right. You don't have to tell me the rest."

Sarah's mouth pulled into a hard line. "No, I want to talk about it, especially if we—" She glanced at the edge and the nothing beyond, not finishing the thought. "The dream about Mama scared me so much that I woke up. I went to Papa's room, so he could sing me to sleep—he used to do that when I was little. But Uncle Paris was there, and he was telling about a letter Mama had written Aunt Cassie. I watched through the door, and heard everything. He said she ran away to live with someone else. She wrote a letter that said she was tired of being a mother and being weighed down by children. I remember the words exactly—'being weighed down by children,' like we were stones around her neck. Then Uncle Paris told Papa that the ship Mama was sailing on had capsized, and that she had drowned—"

Sarah's voice broke. Tears streamed down her dirty cheeks. "It's my fault. David was too little to cause trouble. If I'd been better—if I hadn't been naughty and I'd eaten all my peas, she wouldn't have left and Papa wouldn't hate me for making her run away."

At last Rina understood why the child would never let anyone get close to her—Sarah was afraid her terrible secret would be found out. "My poor dear," Sabrina murmured as she pulled the quaking child against her. "Your father does not hate you. He loves you."

Sarah gave a watery snuffle. "B-but I made Mama run away."

"You did no such thing. I don't know why your mother left, but it had nothing to do with you. Your mother loved you, I'm sure of it."

"How?" Sarah whispered. "How can you be sure?"

"Because—" Rina stopped. She remembered Quinn's words, that she owed the Trevelyans nothing, that she was less to them than the dirt under their feet. Tomorrow she would be only a memory to Sarah—in a year the girl would probably forget her entirely. The only sensible thing to do was to keep her distance. But Rina had experienced too much pain in her own life to turn away from a hurting child. Especially a child who needed love as badly . . .

As badly as Sabrina needed to give it.

Rina hugged her. "I know your mother loved you because *I* love you. I never realized how much until this moment, when I thought I might lose you."

Sarah's hesitant, watery smile was the most precious gift Rina had ever received.

After that, the ledge did not seem so high, nor the wind so cold. The once taciturn Sarah chatted like a magpie, as if all the words she'd stored up for the past few years came tumbling out at once. She told Rina a hundred things. The amazing intelligence of her new pony. The flowers she'd planted by herself in a corner of the garden in Ravenshold. How she could tell the size of a fishermen's catch by how low his boat sat in the water. The way the clouds made shapes on summer days. She talked about everything and nothing, and Rina drank in every word. For this one moment she'd made this darling girl happy. And maybe Rina had helped to heal some of the pain Isabel had caused when she'd left, when she'd so callously delivered her grievances through an impersonal letter.

Sabrina frowned. She recalled what Cassie had told her about Isabel's letter, how it had told Cassie to bid good-bye to her "beloved children." Not weighty stones. Beloved. Why would Fitzroy make up something so cruel?

"Sarah, when you overheard your Uncle Paris talking about your mother—did he specifically say she wrote those things in the letter she sent to Aunt Cassie?"

Sarah shrugged. "Don't know. Maybe Uncle Paris didn't remember. I heard a story once of a man who forgot his own name. He was a fishmonger down in Penzance who got knocked in the head by a runaway milk cart and . . ."

Rina only half listened to Sarah's tale. During the years she'd lived with her father she'd developed a nose for dishonesty. This story carried the distinct odor of artifice. And there was something about it that sent a chill down Rina's spine, as if the ghost of Isabel had come beside her and laid a cold hand on her shoulder—

A call from above startled her. "Helloooo! Miss Winthrope! Lady Sarah!"

"We're here," Sabrina cried, leaping to her feet. She cupped her hands around her mouth, fighting to keep the wind from ripping away her words. "We are down *here*!"

There was a commotion overhead and stones and gravel started to shower down on them from above. Rina shielded Sarah from the cascade until a burly gent in a miner's jacket plopped down on the ledge beside them.

"Howd'ya do. Duffy's the name," the man said, politely touching the brim of his cap as if he'd met them on a country road instead of a precarious mountain ledge.

He gave the thick rope around his waist a solid yank, then lifted his voice heavenward in a lusty yell. "Aye! They're here and safe as houses. I'll bring the little miss up first."

"Please, Mr. Duffy, be careful," Rina said. "She has sprained her ankle."

"Not to worry, miss. I've got six of me own at home and there's not a day goes by what that one of 'em doesn't turn up with a bruise or bump. Drives my missus fair crazy it does, but I know how to deal with sprains. Now, you just wrap your arms around my neck, Lady Sarah, and nod when you're ready to go."

Duffy gave two yanks on the rope, and was hoisted skyward. Sabrina shielded her eyes and watched until they reached the summit. Rina let get of the breath she didn't even know she was holding.

A few minutes later Duffy returned to the ledge, and tied the rope around Sabrina's waist. For a few precarious seconds she dangled over the churning sea far below. Then the rope was pulled upward, and she scraped and scrambled her way to the top.

Once there, she was surrounded by a crowd of servants from Ravenshold, and a good portion of the villagers as well. Rina scanned the crowd, hoping for a glimpse of Sarah. Or her father.

What if he hadn't come? What if he'd just sent his servants to rescue Sarah? His daughter would see his absence as proof he didn't love her. *By God, has the man no heart at all? I thought even he would put his daughter's life above his business concerns.*

"Are you all right, miss?"

She spun around and found herself face to face with Toby, the lad who'd accompanied her on her ride with Amy on her first day at Ravenshold. Despite her heavy heart, she gave the boy a grateful smile. "I am fine,

Toby. But I'm concerned for Sarah. I cannot seem to find her."

"Her ladyship be over there," the youth said, pointing past Rina's shoulder.

She turned around and caught sight of a dark man holding a bright-haired child in his arms. Sarah's arms were wrapped around her father's neck as if she never meant to let go. And Edward's cheek was pressed against her hair, his ravaged expression wordlessly showing how much she meant to him.

Mesmerized, Sabrina watched the private, precious moment. She knew that Sarah would never again doubt her father's love for her. Blinking back tears of happiness Rina started to turn away. Then Edward raised his head, and his eyes found hers.

Raw, naked power ripped through her. His gaze poured into her, drowning her, filling her up with all the joy and pain and hunger in his soul. It was as if she stared directly into his heart, a heart so true and fine it made her gasp. The honor humbled her. The honesty devastated her. Though yards apart, they seemed connected in a way she'd never been with another living being.

The crowd closed around her, cutting off her view of the earl and their shocking intimacy. Rina stumbled back, grabbing Toby's arm for support. She dragged in a deep breath, struggling to regain her composure. But deep inside her something elemental had changed, something wonderful, frightening and unstoppable.

With a certainty that comes just once in a lifetime, Sabrina realized she'd fallen in love with the Earl of Trevelyan.

She's going to be all right, Edward repeated silently as he stroked his sleeping daughter's hair.

Edward wished he could be so sure about himself.

He bent down and kissed Sarah's forehead, then left the nursery bedroom. He didn't want to leave her, but Charles had said that she needed her sleep more than his hovering. He'd shooed the rest of the family out, but allowed Edward another quarter hour before he returned and "dragged him out by his ear." Much as the earl wanted to stay with his daughter, he knew the doctor was right. Sarah needed her sleep. And he needed time to make sense of what had happened.

Miss Winthrope, the woman he despised and distrusted with every fiber of his being, had risked her life to save his daughter. Such extraordinary bravery was out of keeping with the image of a self-seeking charlatan. He'd been wrong about that part of her character, mightily wrong. And if he was wrong about that, he might well be wrong about other things . . .

A faint knock on the door interrupted his thoughts. Edward grimaced. "For God's sake, Charles, I still have five—"

His ire fizzled as Prudence entered the room. She'd washed the dirt from her face and hair and replaced her ruined gown with a simple dress of cream muslin and a flowered cashmere shawl. But the bruises on her arms and the scratch across her cheek bore silent witness to her valorous deed. Edward stared at her, his feelings as hopelessly tangled as a skein of knitting yarn. "You . . . should be in bed."

"How is Sarah?"

"She's f-fine." Lord, what was wrong with him? He was stuttering like a green lad making his first assignation. Clearing his throat, he clasped his hands behind his back and stated in his most lordly tone, "Miss Winthrope, I have not properly thanked you for saving my daughter's life."

"But you have, my lord. I saw your face when you held her on the cliffs after she was rescued." She dipped her gaze, and finished in a voice almost too soft for him to hear. "The look in your eyes was thanks enough."

Edward remembered little of that moment. Since he'd learned of Sarah's accident he'd been like a man possessed. If two of the miners hadn't held him back, he'd have climbed down the cliff with his bare hands to save her. When Duffy had put his daughter in his arms, he'd held her as she hadn't let him hold her in years, ever since the pain of Isabel's desertion had wedged itself between both their souls. Against his ear she'd whispered brokenly, "I love you, Papa." The joy of it had nearly cracked his heart.

In the midst of that emotion he'd spied Prudence in the crowd. Her dress was in tatters and her hair was coated with dust and dirt. He'd never seen a more disheveled-looking individual, but it didn't matter. She'd saved his daughter, his precious, priceless Sarah. And when he looked at her, he thought her the most beautiful woman he'd ever seen.

Which only served to tie his emotions into tighter knots.

"Nevertheless, you deserve—something," he finished, his smooth words again deserting him. "Is there nothing that you want?"

Her chin shot up. For a moment he looked into her eyes, her breathless, drowning eyes, that had bewitched him with such tender sorcery the other night. He remembered holding her in his arms, feeling her heart beating against his chest, and losing himself in the innocent splendor of her eager kiss. Deep inside him something almost broke free. Almost. Then he cleared his throat again, pulled his cynical nature firmly back in place. "I ask again, Miss Winthrope. Is there nothing you want? If it is in my power to give, I shall grant it."

She glanced around the nursery. He knew what she was thinking, because he was thinking the same. This is where it had started. This is where she had picked out Ginger. This is where she'd begun her lies and deceptions. But it was also where she'd been accepted by his household—a household to which she'd brought only happiness, as Mr. Cherry had pointed out. She'd given his grandmother new spirit, and Amy a new friend. And now, she'd given his daughter her life.

"For heaven's sake ask *something* of me!" he demanded.

He half expected her to ask for him to acknowledge her. He wished she would. Blatantly asking for Prudence's birthright would go a long way to proving her the impostor he'd spent the last month believing her to be. But she didn't ask. Instead, she returned her gaze to him, a gaze as full of shadows and distrust as his own.

"Then I ask for your ear, my lord. Just for a moment. While I was on the ledge with your daughter she confided in me. On the night you found out that your wife had . . . gone, Sarah overheard you talking with Mr. Fitzroy. She heard him tell you that Isabel left because of her children. Since then, Sarah has believed that her mother left because of her . . . and that you blamed her for it."

"No. That cannot . . . oh, God." He collapsed onto a nearby chair and raked his hand through his hair. "I wondered why she would never let me comfort her after Isabel deserted us—why she pulled away from me as if my touch burned her. I thought it was because she blamed me for her mother's absence—and that she hated me for it. But to know she thought it was her fault . . .

that she's been carrying this monstrous guilt in her heart for so long . . ." He buried his face in his hands. "I should have been here to listen to her, to understand her. I should have *protected* her."

The pain of years past closed around Edward like a suffocating shroud. He was so caught up in it that he didn't know that Prudence had knelt down beside him until he heard her soft voice at his knee. "You couldn't know what Sarah was feeling inside. It is not your fault."

"The hell it isn't. Keeping my children and family safe is the only decent thing left in my life." He lifted his face from his hands and gave a short, cruel laugh. "Now I've failed at that, too."

At first she said nothing. Then her slim, sure fingers wrapped around his rough hand with the gentleness of a prayer. "I cannot pretend to know what you went through. But I do know that your daughter loves you. And so does your son, your grandmother, your sister, and . . . I'm sure many other people, as well. No man who has that many people who love him is a failure."

A hard, bitter lump rose in his throat. "I do not deserve their love."

Her fingers tightened around his. "My father—that is, a gambler who attended my father's mission, once told me that love was a lot like Lady Luck—a man who is fortunate enough to have it should not overmuch question his good fortune. Love isn't something one deserves. 'Tis a gift, freely given. Accept the love that your family offers. It is all that really matters."

Edward stared at her. *Charlatan*, his mind cried. *Impostor. Pretender. Liar.* Every word worked his insides into a more painful tangle. He could not understand why she was saying these things to him any more than he could understand why she'd saved his daughter, or why she'd brought such joy to his home, or why her kiss had filled him with such rare, sweet fire. None of it made sense, none of it. Unless . . .

"Edward! Miss Winthrope!" Charles entered the nursery and strode toward them, glancing at Sarah's closed bedroom door. "My lord, *you* promised me you would leave this room. And Miss Winthrope, *you* should be in bed. I want you to lie down for the entire afternoon, or there will be no ball for you tonight." He offered her his arm. "Come. I will escort you to your room."

Prudence gave Edward a final glance and accepted Charles's arm. The earl stood by the doorway, watching them disappear down the corridor. Then he leaned against the wall, rubbing his chin in deep, questioning thought.

There was only one possibility that explained Prudence's inexplicable behavior, one circumstance that laid out his tangled thoughts as straight as a plumb line. Like a rusty machine coming back to life, his mouth crept up in a smile that held no trace of cynicism.

Prudence Winthrope was telling the truth.

Chapter Fifteen

Sabrina laid her tortoiseshell comb down on the dressing table, and gave her image in the looking glass a frown. "It's no use, Amy. I might as well tie up my hair with seaweed for all the good I can do with it."

"Here, let me." Amy picked up the comb, and deftly began sculpting Rina's thick copper tresses into place. "It is not your fault. That lady's maid of yours is hopeless when it comes to any sort of style. And we must have you looking your best tonight. All eyes will want to have a look at the 'Angel of Wrecker's Point.' "

Rina winced at the name. The tale of her cliffside heroism had stampeded through the countryside, growing larger and grander with each wagging tongue. By the time the story made a full circle back to Ravenshold, Rina learned that she had been hanging from the cliff by one hand, and holding Lady Sarah with the other.

"*All eyes* will be sorely disappointed. My heroics have been monstrously overrated. If you had been there instead of visiting Clara you would have seen—"

"—I would have seen a woman risking her life to save my niece," Amy finished. "I know some of the details have been exaggerated, but the core remains. I shudder to think what would have happened to Sarah if you had not been there. She might have panicked, or even tried to climb back up if you had not gone down to her. Even Edward—who cannot string two nice words together to save his life—is praising you to the sky."

"He is . . . too kind." Even those few words were an effort for her. Just the mention of Edward spun her insides around. She'd come perilously close to confessing her love for him while they were in the nursery, but she'd caught herself just in time. He could never learn of her feelings for him, because of what he was, and what she was. By this time tomorrow he would be out of her life forever.

Amy's hands stilled. "Prudence, are you all right? You've suddenly gone so pale."

"I . . . I was wondering about Clara. How is she?"

"So many of her former friends have turned their backs on her. It is monstrous how everyone treats her—as if this whole business were her fault alone. Two weeks ago she was so unhappy that I began to worry about her baby, so I asked Dr. Williams to accompany me on a visit to her."

"You accompanied Dr. Williams? I thought you could not abide the man."

"Well, normally I would not tolerate him. But he has a way with Clara that gives her such comfort. And others, too. He shows great kindness to his patients, even the ones who can pay him nothing. The doctor who preceded him treated only the gentry, leaving the poor to the charlatans and gypsy witches. But Dr. Williams tends the poor with the same care and compassion that he shows to the wealthy. I knew that the first time I saw him with Clara. She's an outcast and she can't pay him a penny. But it doesn't matter to him. 'Tis so unexpected. He has always seemed so stuffy, so judgmental. But with Clara, he's—"

Amy stopped. She shook her head as if to clear it,

then renewed her efforts on Rina's hairstyle. "Enough about the vexatious Dr. Williams. And do not try to flummox me. I know there is more to your mood than concern for Clara. Truly, what is the matter?"

Sighing, Sabrina told her as much of the truth as she dared. "I have been to few parties in my life—now I am about to attend one being given in my honor. It is . . . unsettling to be the object of so much attention. I know I shall be found wanting."

"Stuff and bother," Amy replied as she artfully secured Rina's heavy auburn locks with a jeweled pin. "You shall be the most sought-after lady at the ball. Every gentleman there will fight to have the next dance with you—including my own Paris, were he not out of town."

"Mr. Fitzroy is out of town? He said nothing of it when he and his sister came for tea last Tuesday."

"It was sudden. Something to do with a distant relation, I believe. Both he and Cassie were called away, but they should be back within the week."

Sabrina pursed her lips, disappointed that she would not get the chance to see Lady Cassandra again. The thought of not seeing Mr. Fitzroy again was far less disagreeable to Rina. However, she would have liked to have talked with him once more, to settle her mind about how he'd come into possession of Isabel's confession about her children. Quinn would think her boodle-brained for wondering about it, yet her mind latched on to the curious puzzle. How had Paris known of Isabel's discontentment, when no one else seemed to have had so much as an inkling? And how—?

"Prudence!"

Amy's sharp word sliced through Rina's speculations. *Hang it all, Rina-lass, if you can't keep your wits about you before the party, how in heaven do you expect to keep them during it?* "Forgive me. I was . . . I was—"

"I know that you were imagining all the gentlemen who will be fighting over you for a dance tonight. I vow that by the end of the evening I shall be quite beside myself with jealousy."

Smiling warmly, Rina glanced up at Amy. Her golden curls fell in perfect ringlets around her face. She wore a white gown with silver trim that clung to her winsome form. She was as lovely as a storybook princess, and all the more beautiful because her goodness was more than skin deep.

Amy's physical beauty was as rare and precious as her heart and Rina admired her for both. Still, it was impossible not to contrast Amy's charming looks with her own plain countenance. "If the gentlemen quarrel over dances, they shall only do so out of charity. I am plain, Amy. That is the truth of it."

"The *truth* is that you have never given your looks enough credit. Perhaps when you first came here you were a bit pinched and peaked, but now . . ."

Amy set down the comb and grabbed Sabrina's hand, dragging the surprised Rina behind her. Pulling Sabrina forward, she stationed her in front of the full-length looking glass. "Take a look, Cousin. Tell me honestly what you see."

The sight of her reflection stopped Rina's breath. The woman in the reflection wore an elegant gown of bronze satin cut with panels of russet gold, its dipped neckline revealing creamy white shoulders. Her auburn hair was piled on her head like a crown, with jeweled pins winking like stars, and when she moved the candlelight danced across her as if she were made of fire.

But the most remarkable transformation of all was her face. Her once somber and despairing features had changed into a countenance of pride and assurance. Not beautiful, perhaps, but happiness and fulfillment shone from her eyes. Rina pressed her hands to her cheeks, her green eyes brilliant with tears as she recognized the ghost of her lovely mother. "This is never me," she whispered in wonder.

"It is," Amy assured her. "It always was."

Not always. Not when she was the unpaid drudge in the widow's house, with a hollow present and a hopeless future. Her unexpected beauty was a result of the kindness and friendship—and the love—she'd been shown by the people at Ravenshold. She spun around and gave Amy a hug. "I want you to know that no matter where I am, or what happens to me in the future, I shall always remember this moment, and the true kindness you've showed to me."

Amy returned her embrace, but when she pulled away her brow was furrowed in puzzlement. "You sound so strange, Cousin. Almost as if you meant to leave."

A knock on the door saved Sabrina from replying.

Amy glanced at the clock on the mantel. "He's right on time," she commented as she crossed to the door.

"Who?"

"My brother. He told me he would come at half past the hour to escort us to the ball."

Edward! Sabrina's recent confidence collapsed. She'd been steeling herself all evening for their inevitable meeting. Now that the moment had arrived, she realized she wasn't ready. In a hundred years she wouldn't be ready. "Please, do not open that door. I am not . . . finished with my hair."

"Nonsense, your hair looks lovely." Unconcerned, Amy opened the door—and met with a surprise of her own. Dr. Williams stood on the threshold, wearing his familiar brown topcoat and a plain white stock. His only concession to the festive occasion appeared to be hastily combed hair and a generally less rumpled appearance.

"Forgive the intrusion. Your brother asked me to escort you to the ball in his place. He—" As the doctor entered the room, he was able to catch his first full glimpse of Lady Amy in her ethereal white gown, with her blond tresses shining like silver in the firelight. Whatever else he'd intended to say died on his tongue. "You look . . . very nice."

Rina watched as a faint blush stained Amy's cheeks. She'd seen her receive bushelfuls of far more eloquent compliments with far less acknowledgment. She crossed over to the doctor, and placed a hand on his arm. "Dr. Williams, you mentioned Ed—my cousin. Has anything happened to him? Is he all right?"

Charles grinned, and patted her hand reassuringly. "Relieve your mind, Miss Winthrope. The earl simply had a prior engagement with another lovely lady—his daughter wished him to sing her to sleep. When I left them he was wrestling mightily with 'Three Blind Mice.' "

A lump rose in Sabrina's throat. She recalled Sarah's words about her father singing her to sleep, and knew that the long separation between them was coming to an end. In time Sarah would forget all but a shadow of her painful memories. She'd grow into a strong and beautiful young woman, secure in the knowledge of her father's love. *I wish I could be here to watch it happen. I wish it with all my heart.*

"Prudence, you are growing pale again," Amy cried in alarm. She turned to Dr. Williams. "I fear she is unwell."

"She does look a bit peaked," Charles agreed as he pressed his hand to Rina's forehead. "And you *are* unusually warm. After a day such as yours, I am hardly surprised that you should feel fatigued. Perhaps you should not attend the ball—"

"But I must attend!" Sabrina backed away from the two, away from their ministrations. Missing the ball meant missing her chance at the Dutchman. She could not bear to spend another day in this house, with its kind and loving occupants. She could not bear another day of being near *him*.

Sabrina lifted her chin, and attempted a lighthearted smile. "Surely you would not deny me my opportunity to be honored as the 'Angel of Wrecker's Point'?"

"Well, if you're sure you're all right," Amy mused, though she did not look entirely convinced.

Smiling broadly, Charles gallantly offered his arm to Sabrina. "I believe this is the first time that I have ever escorted a bona fide angel. Make that *two* bona fide angels," he added as he offered his other arm to a newly blushing Amy.

Rina returned his smile warmly, but a chill crept down her spine. Tonight she might be hailed as a heroine, but by this time tomorrow, Amy, Dr. Williams and everyone else in the county would most likely be calling her the *Devil* of Wrecker's Point.

The party was more magnificent than anything Sabrina had imagined. The great hall was illuminated by a thousand candles, making the grand old house shine and glitter like a palace. The ancestral banners hung down from the ceiling, displaying their stark, brilliant images of gold crowns, white crosses, and blood-red lions as they had on tournament days long past. Flowers in silver bowls decorated every table and alcove, and music from the quartet in the minstrel's gallery above flowed down on the guests. Couples swirled on the flagstone floor of the hall, their intricate moves reflected in the breast-plates of the polished suits of armor.

From the first moment Rina set foot in the hall she was the center of attention, far more so than even she had expected. Within minutes she was commandeered by a retired army colonel with a bushy white mustache and a talent for exaggeration. He told her the most outrageous tales of his campaign adventures as they danced the quadrille, and had her laughing until she cried. Before she'd had time to catch her breath she was inaugurated into the minuet by an elderly magistrate who danced with the exaggerated grandness of a self-important local official, and next by a brisk-stepping baron with a hearty laugh, who summarily introduced her to his two eligible sons with a decided gleam in his eye.

The regard of the well-meaning country gentry was both flattering and endearing, and the once-ostracized Sabrina was human enough to enjoy it. But all the while she kept an eye out for Lady Penelope, and was distressed when time after time her search proved unsuccessful. Thinking she might have more luck if she were not whirling around the dance floor, she cried fatigue to her next partner and took a seat on one of the brocade-and-gilt chairs that lined the hall. She lifted her fan, and peeked over the top of it as she surveyed the room for the absent dowager.

It was a beautiful sight, she thought as she watched the silks and satins swish and twirl across the floor. A strange sense of déjà vu settled around her shoulders, a memory she'd all but forgotten. Years ago her parents had taken her to a country dance in an old storehouse. She'd sat on the bales of sweet-smelling hay with the other children, clapping and laughing as the adults danced a merry jig. She could still remember the laughter, and the brightness in her parents' eyes that had outshone every candle in the room. Halfway through her father had pulled her from the loft and danced a round with her, uncaring that he had to nearly bend over double to do so.

A sharp, fierce love welled up in her heart for her

father, undiminished by time and the desolated wreck of the man he'd become. He'd been a good father once, and that was a treasure none could take away from her. *No matter what happens, I'll always have my memories of Da and Mum together. And I'll have my memories of this night, and all my days at Ravenshold, and of Edward on the cliff holding his precious daughter, with his hair blowing wild and his eyes burning with the fire of dark suns—*

"Bless me, Miss Winthrope, but don't you look sharp!"

Rina glanced up, her distress forgotten as she recognized the rotund figure of Trevelyan's lawyer. Her face blossomed into a smile. "Mr. Cherry, what a wonderful surprise. I did not know that you would be here."

"I would not have missed it. Or Mother either."

Rina's smile dimmed ever so slightly. "Your mother is here?"

"Most certainly. She is right over there."

He pointed to a semicircle of chairs at the far end of the room, where the stole-wrapped Mrs. Cherry sat, glaring with hard disapproval at the whirling dancers. Even in the midst of the brightness the woman seemed to have a dark cloud hovering above her. Rina chose her words carefully. "She looks . . . well."

"Oh, indeed, she has been quite well. But it is not my mother I wished to speak with you about." He settled his substantial bulk on the chair beside her, his beaming face growing pensive. "There is something I have been meaning to tell you . . . no, not just tell—explain. But it is not an explanation. It is more along the lines of a confession. Well, not precisely a confession. More like a—"

"Perhaps you should just say it outright," Sabrina suggested gently.

"Of course. You were ever the quick-witted one,

Miss Winthrope. But I must confess that on the day we arrived at Ravenshold—do you recall the day?"

Rina remembered every moment of that day. She remembered the tearing wind, the biting rain, the grand, desolate cliffs, the stab of lightning that had revealed her first glimpse of ancient Ravenshold. She remembered her first meeting with the proud dowager, and with Amy, whose beautiful, petulant exterior gave no hint of the generous heart beneath. But most of all she remembered Edward striding into the room with all the fury of the storm, smelling of rain and thunder, and burning with a raw energy that seemed to make every man she'd ever known seem pale and wan in comparison. He'd been terrifying, arrogant, impossible, and magnificent . . . and she'd started to lose her heart to him then and there, though she'd been too green to recognize it.

She laced her gloved fingers together tightly, as if doing so could help her keep an equally tight grip on her fragmented heart. "Yes, Mr. Cherry. I remember."

He nodded efficiently, but he fiddled nervously with the lace on his sleeve. "Yes, well, I must confess that even though I was completely convinced of your veracity, Lord Trevelyan was not. He instructed me to continue to verify your references, several times. I even traveled to Dublin to do so."

Rina's tight hands went limp. Quinn's documents of Prudence's false history were good, but they were still fabrications. Had Mr. Cherry found a hole in the story? Deliberately she lifted her fan, and made a show of nonchalantly toying with it. "La, business matters are so tedious. Tell me, what did you discover?"

"Well, in truth I could neither confirm or deny your testimony. But it matters little, especially after today. No one could doubt your true character after you risked your life to save Lady Sarah from certain death. I feel positively dreadful about continuing the investigation."

Sabrina laid a comforting hand over his nervous fingers. "Nonsense. I shall always be grateful for your kindness during those first few days. And in any case, you were only following the earl's instructions when you went to Ireland, were you not? I can hardly fault you for being a dutiful employee."

The lawyer's expression broke into a wide smile. "You are a remarkable lady, Miss Winthrope. And, as a dutiful employee of the earl's, I currently have a much more pleasant obligation to discharge." He leaned closer, his eyes as round and bright as his surname. "His lordship has instructed me to put a line of credit at your disposal, of a thousand pounds per annum."

Sabrina stared at the man as if he'd lost his mind. "A thousand . . . pounds?"

"Per annum," Mr. Cherry said, bobbing his head in acknowledgment. "The money is at your disposal immediately. The earl stipulated that it should be your money, free and clear, to be used for whatever purpose you wish. He said it was the least he could do after your heroic rescue of his daughter. Is that not generous?"

"Most generous," she repeated vaguely. Edward had paid her money for saving the life of his daughter. Paid her for rescuing a girl she could not have loved more if she'd been her own true child. Pain knifed through her, a pain that snapped almost at once to white-hot anger. It was base and demeaning—especially after the intimate feelings he'd shared with her in the nursery. But she'd been wrong to imagine his regard. He was the lord of the manor, and she was merely a vassal to be rewarded for her dutiful service. How could he think she would want money for saving Sarah's life? How could he dare to offer it?

Her fury rose like the tide. But angry as she was, she

had the sense to know that her passion had no place in this elegant gathering. Aristocratic Prudence would not be so bold, and if Rina wanted to convince the guests that she was Trevelyan's cousin, she would have to let her Murphy temper cool. She rose from her chair and turned to Mr. Cherry, using her fan to conceal her angry blush. "Forgive me, but I feel a bit fatigued. I believe a few minutes alone would do me a world of good."

A few minutes alone might have, but she wasn't to have them. As she got up from her chair she was surrounded by a sea of partners, all vying for her company during the next dance.

" 'Tis the waltz," a young man in a bottle green coat informed her. "And I am the finest waltzer in the county."

"Leave off," cried the son of the baron she'd danced with earlier. "You can't dance for toffee. Dance with him, Miss Winthrope, and you'll have no feet left."

"Dance with him, and you'll be black and blue from bumping into the other couples," another man offered. "Please, Miss Winthrope, dance with me."

The first bars of the waltz music shivered through the air. Rina glanced from face to face, confounded by their persistence. "Good sirs, you do me honor, but I—"

"But you will waltz with no one but *me*," a deep voice finished.

A strong arm reached out, capturing her waist. Between one heartbeat and the next she found herself swept into the powerful embrace of the Earl of Trevelyan.

Chapter Sixteen

Rina couldn't breathe. She'd been prepared to face the earl, and even to go so far as to let him take her out during an undemanding dance like the Sir Roger de Coverley. But to be swept into his arms, to feel the warmth of his hand holding her waist with an intimacy that was just shy of a lover's embrace—it overwhelmed her. Her breath came in short gasps. He held her as if she were made of the most fragile glass, and when they moved together the thrill made her tremble.

She was no more used to dancing than she was to being in love, and it took every last ounce of her self-discipline to keep her wits about her. With an effort that put her cliff-scaling feats to shame, she stiffened her back and kept her expression rigorously unemotional. She reminded herself that she was furious with him.

"How could you?"

Trevelyan arched a dark brow and looked down at her in puzzlement. "You mean you truly wanted to dance with one of those puppies?"

"No. I mean, I might have. That's not what I meant." She shook her head, trying to collect the thoughts that scattered like jackstraws whenever he looked at her. "Mr. Cherry told me about the thousand pounds. It was wrong of you, monstrously wrong. You should not have offered it to me."

He frowned, his confusion increasing. "You want more?"

"No! I don't want—" She dropped her voice, realizing that nearby couples were staring. Lord, the man was wood when it come to understanding. Glaring, she lowered her voice to a clandestine whisper. "I will not accept money for saving a child, especially a child who is as dear to me as Sarah. You were wrong to offer it, and I won't take it. And I don't give a fig for what you think."

The earl's lips edged up and his eyes sparked with a devilish gleam. "The only thing I think, Miss Winthrope, is that you blush quite charmingly whenever you're angry."

Sabrina's resolve melted. Looking up into the earl's consuming gaze and feeling his strong, gentle hands guide her body with a skill he'd never learned from dancing, Rina was struck by a sweet, terrifying confusion that coursed through her with every curve and dip of the waltz.

"Nevertheless, I cannot take your money," she said, trying not to sound as breathless as she felt. "I will not be paid for saving Sarah. I did nothing to deserve it. Anyone would have done the same in my place."

"Not anyone. Just an obstinate woman with far more courage than sense."

"I am *not* obstinate."

His rough, rumbling chuckle rolled through her like thunder. She nearly missed her step. "You *are* obstinate. And stubborn. And contrary—"

"We can end this dance anytime, my lord," she commented dryly.

With a slight turn of his hand he swept her into a dizzying turn, the smooth, silken move at odds with the raw hunger in his gaze. "Not until I have told you how much what you've done has meant to me—not just for Sarah, but for Grandmother, and Amy, and even for Ravenshold. You've brought life back into our home . . . and to me."

This time Rina did miss a step. His voice poured through her like warm, red wine, drowning her in hopeless dreams. "Thank you, my lord, but I believe you have mistaken gratitude for . . . for a much stronger emotion."

He said nothing, but his hand slipped down from her waist. In a moment his hold was demurely back in place—an observer would have barely noticed the swift, subtle movement.

It made Sabrina gasp aloud.

"I *am* grateful," he murmured. "But it is not gratitude I'm feeling now. It wasn't gratitude I felt in the nursery this afternoon, or the other night in my room, when we—"

"Ho, Trevelyan!"

Startled, Sabrina jerked back. Blushing with both embarrassment and arousal, she watched as a loud, large man partnered with an equally large lady in ostrich feathers sidled next to them.

"Trevelyan, heard about St. Petroc. Good show, old man!"

" 'Twas nothing, Fergus," Edward growled, trying to steer away from the couple.

"Nonsense. Talk of the town," Fergus replied, blithely following after the earl. "And I'll wager that this is the little lady who pulled your daughter from the jaws of death. Hildy, this is the girl they are all talking of."

"Pleased to meet you, dearie," the woman said, bobbing her head pleasantly. "You must come to tea."

"Not tea, Hildy. Supper! Next week. Both of ya."

"Fine. Anything. Good-bye." Taking a titan step, Edward swirled Rina away before Fergus and his wife knew what happened.

"Friends of yours?" Sabrina asked with an impish smile.

"Hardly. The only things Fergus speaks of are hounds and horses. But I'd have agreed to have dinner with the devil himself to get rid of him." He gazed down at Rina, his sensual mouth pulling up in a grin that turned her blood to hot honey. "Now, as I was saying—"

"Lord Trevelyan," a raucous voice intruded.

Edward cringed. "The devil with this," he growled. "We cannot talk with all these people around us. I must speak with you. Alone."

There were a hundred reasons why Sabrina shouldn't see the earl alone. At the moment, she couldn't think of a single one. "When?"

"When the guests go into supper, meet me in the garden. At midnight."

Midnight. At midnight Quinn would be waiting for her at the front gate with a pair of fast horses. She could not meet the earl in the garden even if she wanted to. And she admitted that a part of her wanted to very much. " 'Tis madness. We cannot meet. It would be . . . most improper."

The earl glanced down at her, his eyes shining with devilment. "Yes, it would be improper. But you've never struck me as the proper type." He leaned closer, his warm breath caressing her as he added, "Neither am I."

The warmth inside her blossomed to a raging furnace. He was right. Sabrina Murphy, gambler's daughter, was not a proper lady, and the more time she spent in his arms, the less proper she felt. But at the moment she wasn't Sabrina Murphy. She was Prudence Winthrope, a missionary-raised heiress, who would not think of making a midnight assignation with a man of the earl's reputation.

Sabrina had a role to play out, a job to accomplish. And loving the Earl of Trevelyan definitely wasn't part of it.

The music stopped. The other couples moved off the floor, but Edward made no move to release her. He stood in the middle of the dance floor, gazing down at her with the same intensity she'd felt on the cliffs. She saw the edge of doubt in his eyes, the vulnerability that drew her to him more than all his wealth and power. "Will you be there?"

Sabrina wanted to. Prudence didn't dare. The woman who was both of them opened her mouth to answer, unsure of what that answer would be. "I—"

"Edward! Would you monopolize the poor girl all evening?"

Only one person had a voice of such supreme authority. Sabrina spun around, and saw Lady Penelope striding toward them through the crowd, her silver-topped cane clicking against the flagstones. She wore a high-necked gown of cream lace, and her censuring expression made her look like an avenging angel. But it was neither her dress nor her expression that drew Rina's gaze. It was her necklace.

The Dutchman.

In Rina's wildest dreams she could never have imagined anything so beautiful. A waterfall of diamonds poured around the dowager's throat, each stone gleaming with its own fiery life. It was a masterpiece, something forged of dreams and fire, and Sabrina was enough of her father's daughter to want to make those dreams her own. For the first time she understood her father's fascination with gambling, his constant pursuit of the big score that would give him enough money to last a lifetime. She could almost imagine Daniel Murphy standing at her shoulder now, whispering in her ear. *Our ship's come in, Rina-lass. Finally, our ship's come in.*

The dowager laid a hand on Rina's arm, startling her out of her imaginings. "Come, my dear. I've a hundred guests to show you off to. You can converse with kin in the morning."

By morning she would be far from Ravenshold, with Quinn by her side and a stolen necklace in her saddlebag. She swallowed the lump in her throat, knowing that Lady Penelope's interruption was probably the luckiest thing that could have happened to her. There could be nothing between her and Edward. She was foolish to even entertain the thought. Sensibly squaring her shoulders, she turned back to the earl. "Thank you for the dance, my lord."

He said nothing, made no move toward her. Yet she could sense the emptiness inside him, the return of the hard remoteness that made him as unapproachable as the cliffs by the sea. In a way she couldn't explain, she could feel him closing himself off, hiding his heart behind the stern, forbidding facade. How long would it be before anyone took the trouble to look behind that facade, to see the special, caring man beneath? How many empty, loveless years stretched before him . . . and before her?

She looked up. The mouth that had grinned down at her so wickedly only minutes before was now set in a harsh, ruthless line. By morning he would despise her, along with everyone else in Ravenshold. But at least she could give him tonight.

She leaned closer, as if to thank him once again for

the dance, and whispered a single word before darting off to follow the dowager through the crowd.

"Midnight."

Sabrina quickly thought better of her decision to meet Edward in the garden. Before the next hour was out she'd sensibly surmised that it would be far better for everyone if she did not keep the appointment. She was, after all, planning to steal one of his family's most prized heirlooms. And even if she weren't, there was the little matter of Edward's "understanding" with Lady Rumley to contend with. It was ridiculous to even contemplate the idea of meeting him. And yet, as the hour approached, she found herself stealing away from the hall, and taking quick, urgent steps down the stone path that led to the Ravenshold gardens.

The blustery day had settled into a rare soft night. Clouds slid like silk across the moon, its fickle light silvering the vines and flowers like the paintbrush of a changeable fairy. The sweet, heavy fragrance of roses and hyacinths hung in the air, while a nearby fountain whispered like a magic spell in the silence. And running through it all was the low, distant thunder of waves washing against the stone cliffs, the never-ending pounding that had become as much a part of her as her own heartbeat.

She slowed and walked between the stone lions that guarded the entrance to the gardens. He had not yet arrived. Unnerved by the mysterious spell of the garden, she was tempted to return to the manor house and forget the whole business. But that would only make matters worse. She'd promised the earl she would be here—foolishly, perhaps, but there it was. If she didn't appear, he was likely to turn the whole household upside-down looking for her. *And that would make stealing up to Lady Penelope's bedchamber about as easy to conceal as week-old fish heads.*

Not an hour past, Sabrina had slipped two drops of laudanum into the dowager's punch—not enough to harm the older woman, but enough to ensure that she'd sleep like a babe when Rina crept into her room and nipped the necklace off the dressing table. It was a simple plan, and it was humming along like clockwork. All she had to do was keep her wits about her, and not let her feelings for Edward overwhelm her common sense.

A distant sound shook her from her disturbing thoughts. She looked up. "Edward?"

But it wasn't the earl. Indeed, she wasn't even sure if she'd heard anyone at all. The garden was full of rustling leaves and the scamperings of squirrels and rabbits. A cloud had drifted across the face of the moon, casting the hedges and vines into tortured shapes and shadows. She looked toward the far end of the garden, to where the well-tended plants left off and the wild edge of the sea began.

The mist was just beginning to rise, and in the fickle light the gossamer strands seemed to gather and curl into something like a shape. Sabrina told herself it was pure fancy, yet as she peered at the twisting, silver threads of mist she couldn't help remembering what Mrs. Cherry had told her during their trip to Ravenshold, about the ghost of the Countess of Trevelyan who walked the cliffs.

The ephemeral shape was already breaking apart. It was fancy, sure—still, Sabrina felt a heavy sadness weigh on her heart. *If her spirit does walk the cliffs, it must be so dreadfully lonely.* Almost unconsciously, she reached out toward the distant, dissolving shape. "Isabel?"

The sharp pounding of boots on stone jarred Rina back to reality. She whirled around toward the house and saw the dark but very real shadow of the Earl of Trevelyan heading into the garden. He stormed past the stone lions with all the bluster and rage of a Nor'easter. "Damn Fergus. Kept questioning me about horse liniment. Couldn't shake him until I promised to send over a while bloody barrel—"

Both his words and his steps came to an abrupt halt as he saw her. On the other side of the stone lion, he was a good two yards away. Yet his dark gaze caught and held her with a strength not even his arms could match, driving the thoughts from her mind, and the air from her lungs.

"God in heaven, you're even more beautiful in the moonlight."

His low, rough words turned her knees to water. She reached out, gripping the paw of the statue for support. "I . . . believe you are a bit drunk, my lord," she replied, fighting to keep her voice level. "I am not beautiful."

"I haven't had a drop, Miss Winthrope," he replied, flashing her his devilish grin. "And I can assure you from my vast and decidedly jaded past experience that you are one of the most beautiful women I've ever known."

Rina swallowed. His smile was a weapon, and he wielded it like a master. *I shouldn't have come. I was mad to think I could be near him and feel nothing.* "I . . . can't stay. You have guests. And . . . there's Lady Rumley to consider."

If Sabrina hoped the mention of Edward's fiancée would discourage him, she was sorely mistaken. He lifted his brow in an expression that looked more like confusion than guilt. "Cassie isn't here." He moved closer until he stood beside her, never taking his gaze from hers. "And my guests are currently gorging themselves on pheasant and sweetmeats. They won't notice we're gone for another quarter hour. That will be long enough."

He lifted his hand, and for a panicked instant Sabrina thought he was going to pull her into an embrace. Instead, he reached into his coat pocket, and set the contents on the back of the lion. The light was dim, but it was bright enough for Rina to make out the remains of one of the red cliff markers. She glanced up at the earl, her brow creased in puzzlement. "What are these?"

"One of my men found these hidden behind some rocks on Wrecker's Point. After you and the others left I searched further, and found the holes where these markers had originally been placed. They clearly marked off the ground at the head of the point, the ground where—"

"Where Sarah fell," Rina finished. She picked up one of the splinters of wood and turned it in her hand, feeling a little sick. "I think I saw another piece as I climbed down the cliff—at least, I saw a flash of red. Someone must have gone to considerable trouble to pull out the stakes and hide them. Who could do such a terrible thing?"

Edward's answer rang with barely harnessed rage. "Perhaps the same *someone* who cut your bridle ribbons."

Oh, God, someone meant to harm the children! Surely they could not be so vile. But as she remembered back to the conversation she'd overheard in the alley, she could easily imagine the two hired villains plotting against innocents. Anger and fear welled up inside her. She balled her hands into tight, fighting fists. "You must protect the children, Edward. Watch them every minute. Even send them away, if necessary. You cannot let anything happen to them."

"I won't let anything happen to them . . . or to you." Gently, he covered her fisted hand with his larger one. Even through their gloves Sabrina could feel his heat.

"I should have believed you when you told me what you'd overheard in the village. My pride kept me from trusting you, and my stubborn conviction that you could not be who you claimed. But you were telling me the truth. You have been, from the beginning. And today, for the first time since Isabel deserted us, my daughter told me she loved me. That would not have been possible . . . but for you."

He leaned closer, his expression softening with a tenderness that was far more destructive than his blustery anger. "Once I told you that I did not believe in miracles. I was mistaken. I know because that is what you are, Miss Winthrope—a miracle."

He believed she was Prudence Winthrope! The knowledge that she'd succeeded in her charade should have given Rina immense pleasure. Instead, she felt vaguely ill. She dropped her gaze, unable to continue to meet his eyes. She drowned in his words, dying a little with each syllable. He was wrong, so very wrong about her. Yet she'd have given the rest of her life to hear him say the words again. *A miracle.*

She closed her eyes, pressing the moment in her heart the way she'd press a rose in a book. Then, quietly and firmly, she withdrew her hand. "I really must go back inside."

"I know. 'Tis not *proper*," he said, the smile in his words sending thrills down her spine. "But I wanted to explain . . . to make you understand about the thousand pounds. I did not intend it as a reward for saving my daughter. It is yours by right as a Trevelyan. It is my way—a poor one, I'll grant you, but the best I could come up with—of putting all the doubts about you to rest. I wanted to show the whole countryside that you belong at Ravenshold, with your family."

Family. He couldn't know what that word meant to a woman who had been lonely for so many years. Even the value of the Dutchman paled by comparison. To have so much wealth within reach . . . but it was Prudence's wealth, not hers. Never hers. "I must—"

"Go back. I know. There is just one more thing. I . . . well, I . . . Damn!" He stroked back his hair, looking so endearingly frustrated that it ached Rina's heart. "It has been a long time since I have had dealings with . . . an honest woman. My behavior toward you has been unconscionable, and the fact that I was trying to protect my family does little to justify my actions. I cannot undo what I have done, but I can tell you that I regret it with all my heart. And I would be pleased . . . and honored . . . if you would accept my hand in friendship."

Sabrina stared at his offered hand, unable to move. His friendship. She could have accepted his smile, his belief, even his passion more easily. She blinked back tears, her young heart breaking for the life she wanted, but which she could never have. *He's an earl, rich as Midas, and pledged to another, better woman. There could never be anything between us. Never . . .*

"I see."

The two cold words sliced through her private sorrow. She looked up, and saw the bleak, hollow eyes of the man she'd met on her first day at Ravenshold. Too late she realized he'd taken her silence as a rejection. She shook her head. "No, you *do not* see. I—"

His roar cut her off. "For God's sake, don't be *kind*. It was foolish to think you could forgive me, that you could care, after I'd—" He took a deep breath, his words bleeding with a pain even his stone-hard expression couldn't hide. "Be assured I shall never foist my attentions on you again, Miss Winthrope. You may return to the ball. I will follow in a few minutes."

She knew this was the best way. She was a thief and an impostor. He was an aristocrat engaged to another aristocrat. She had nothing to give him, nothing at all. Mechanically, she forced her legs to move. He clasped his arms behind his back, standing still as the stone lion as she passed.

Slowly, she started up the steps that led to the house. It was the best way, the only way that made sense. What did it matter if her heart was breaking? She'd get over it. She'd survive, just as she'd survived all those years in her stepmother's house. And in the years to come, when she looked up at the moon, she would remember this night as a dim memory, without the aching sorrow, without the remembrance of the lost emptiness in his eyes, and without the knowledge that she'd walked away from the man she loved, letting him believe that she despised him. She'd—

"Oh, *hell!*" she cried as she whirled around and threw herself into his arms.

Chapter Seventeen

Edward had experienced many surprises in his life, but the shock of the reserved Miss Winthrope catapulting herself against him and showering sweet, urgent kisses on his face beat them all. He staggered back against the stone lion, unbalanced by both her weight and her sudden, inexplicable passion. For a heartbeat he thought he'd accidentally stumbled into one of the fairy rings that had plagued his Celtic ancestors and been sucked down into the madness of the Otherworld. Then her lips found his, and he was consumed by another kind of madness.

He was used to the practiced, calculating kisses of experienced courtesans, but her eager, untutored caresses drove him mindless. She was lush and wild and erotic in the way only a true innocent could be. He sank his fingers into the thick silk of her hair, guiding her head to a better angle. Then he fused his mouth with hers in a hard, desperate kiss.

She smelled like the night, like the dark earth of the garden and the salt wind from the sea. He pulled her hard against him, feeding on her sweetness, groaning as her lush, incredible mouth made silent promises. "Prudence," he growled against her lips. "Sweet, unpredictable, wonderful Prudence."

Her soft cry of pleasure exploded through him.

He was mad to touch her, to ravage her skin the way his tongue ravaged her mouth. He tore off his gloves and grasped her shoulders, caressing their silk softness with the rough pad of his thumbs. He whispered his touch along the elegant length of her neck, felt the hot pulse of desire throbbing at the base of her throat. His hands skimmed down her back, pressing her against him as he'd longed to do during their dance. Another tiny cry escaped her lips. He caught the sound in his throat, savoring her pleasure, her surprise, *her surrender*.

For years he'd lived without caring, seeing his life as something to be endured rather than lived. He'd accepted the fact that nothing would ever touch his heart again. But now the old parts of him creaked to rusty life, stoking a fire a hundred times hotter than the giant steam boiler at Wheal Grace. He bent back her head and slowly savaged her luxurious mouth. By the time he raised his head they were both trembling.

He wrapped her in his arms, finding another kind of pleasure in the simple joy of holding her. Sighing, he rubbed his cheek in the heavenly softness of her hair. "I thought you hated me."

"I tried," she murmured against his shirt front.

Her unflattering honesty made him laugh out loud. Lord, he couldn't remember the last time he'd felt this good. He lifted his head and breathed in the scent of the cool night air, wondering how the world could seem so much sweeter and richer with her in his arms. The tight, tortuous chains that bound his heart began to snap. He felt like a boy again, with all the wide world in front of him to discover.

She'd given him this, his hope, his belief. Everything

seemed new—the sights, the scents, the sounds of the night. He heard the call of a raven, the restless grumble of the sea . . . and the distant strains of a violin.

The ball. *Damn.*

Reluctantly, he pushed her out of his arms. "We must return to our guests. We've been gone longer than I intended. Your reputation—"

"Hang my reputation!"

She gripped the lapels of his coat, staring up at him with brilliant, desperate eyes. "Please, I cannot bear this to end. Not yet. I don't care about the guests, or the ball. Lord help me, I don't even care that you're going to marry Lady Rumley—"

"I'm *what?*"

His roar brought her tumble of words to a standstill. She let go of his coat and backed away. "You're to m-marry Lady Rumley. Amy told me so. And Cassie herself said that she and I were going to be related."

"And you will, when Paris marries my sister. Though it's doubtful whether the minx will live that long." He raked his fingers through his hair. "I do love Cassie, but as a *brother*. Lord, I've known her since she was twelve. Our feelings for each other have never passed beyond mutual regard. Amy might have bothered to ask one of us before jumping to absurd conclusions."

Her words came out as a strangled whisper. "Then . . . you are *not* intending to marry her?"

"No. I most assuredly am not." He put his hand under her chin. Gently, he lifted her gaze to meet his— and was surprised to find them bright with tears. "Why are you crying? I thought you would be pleased that I am not engaged."

"I am. And I'm not crying," she argued, though even as she said it she reached up to scrub away a tear. "I . . . caught a bit of dust in my eye. 'Tis nothing."

Like hell. Her small, brave face was tight with misery. She was breaking apart inside, and Edward hadn't the faintest idea why. Too late he remembered the high price of caring for someone, of feeling another's unhappiness twice as keenly as his own. He cupped her cheek and used his thumb to smooth away a tear, feeling awkward and helpless. *I failed so miserably before, so bloody miserably.* "Prudence . . . darling . . . if you're in some kind of trouble, let me help—"

Another note of the violin shivered through the air.

He cursed, dropping his hand. "We must go in. Even the kindest tongues turn cruel when it comes to gossip. But this conversation is far from over. We will continue it in the morning."

"In the morning," she repeated dully.

"Yes. A sunrise ride. We can watch the dawn break over the cliffs. Promise me you will not forget."

"Forget?" She lifted her hand, gazing at him with more tenderness than he'd thought could exist in this world. "I shall not forget a minute of this night, not a moment. But before I go—please, kiss me."

"That . . . would not be wise," he managed, gripping his hands behind his back.

"I *know* it would not be wise," she agreed, her lips turning up into one of her rare, hesitant smiles. "Yet I ask it all the same. Please, kiss me once more. Kiss me . . . as if you were doing it for the last time."

Edward had always thought of himself as a strong man—driven and determined, ruthless when necessary. But against her smile he was defenseless. He didn't understand her request any more than he understood her tears, but it didn't matter. At that moment he'd have climbed the sky and given her the moon if she'd asked for it.

He took her in his arms and held her against him,

wondering how someone so fragile had managed to break down all the high walls he'd ringed around his heart. Probably her courage. Certainly her honesty. *Not to mention her sweet body and her bloody marvelous mouth.* Nobility warred with lust inside him, and lust won handily. Groaning, he lowered his lips toward hers. "To hell with the guests. I want—"

The high-pitched scream split the night. She gasped and pulled out of his arms, looking toward the cliffs and the darkness beyond. "The ghost," she whispered.

"I wish to God it were," the earl answered, his voice as dry as dust. "It's Wheal Grace's siren. There's been a cave-in at the mine."

It was like standing at the gates of hell.

Sabrina leaned heavily against the door frame of the manager's office and watched as a line of sooty smoke cut across the rose-colored sky. The smoke billowed out of the whim engine like devil's breath, as it labored to bring the timbers, stones, and injured miners up from the collapsed passageways. So far two levels had been cleared and, though there were many injuries, no lives had been lost. Yet.

"Water."

Shaking off her apprehension, Rina turned toward the faint plea. She and a half dozen other women were doing what they could to tend the wounded in the makeshift infirmary, to treat their injuries and ease their minds. The second task was by far the most difficult. Pasting an encouraging smile on her face, Sabrina poured a measure of water into a tin cup, then knelt down beside the young man who'd called out.

Gently, Rina lifted his head to the cup, careful not to

jar the splints that Dr. Williams had wrapped around his broken arm and leg. "Easy, Tom. The doctor said to take the water in slow gulps. There's a good lad."

The boy took a final gulp, then lifted his gaze to Rina's. "Please," he whispered weakly. "Is there any word on my da?"

Tom's father had been on the lowest level when the cave-in occurred, along with a half dozen others. She stroked back the boy's dust-coated hair, wishing she had a better answer. "There's no word yet. But they're loading the whim lift with equipment now, and should be starting down within the quarter hour. I will let you know as soon as I hear. Now you try to get some rest."

She started to get up, but the boy caught her hand, holding it tight. "Bless you, miss," he breathed. Then, exhausted, he fell back to the pallet and into a fitful sleep.

Rising, Sabrina set the cup back on the table, then wiped her palms on the skirt of the serviceable cotton dress she'd changed into after the ball. She looked around at the room of broken and battered men, her heart aching. A few hours ago these men had been having supper with their families, or joking with their mates in the local pub, before going to work on the night shift. Now they were fortunate to be alive. Rina rubbed her arms, thinking how life could turn on a whisker. A person's whole world could be shattered by a bit of falling stone. *Or a single midnight kiss.*

She hadn't seen Edward since they'd left the garden, but she'd heard about him from the other men. Apparently he was coordinating the rescue effort, marshaling the men and machinery like a general. He'd put himself in the thick of danger, joining the rescue workers as they traveled time and time again down the mine shaft to free the trapped men.

The miners spoke of his courage and resourcefulness. The Cousin Jacks had even begun to make up verses about the "Black Lord with the heart o'gold." Rina tried to feel the same appreciation for the earl's courage, but all her emotions were blotted out by chilling fear. Not a second went by that her heart didn't pound at the thought of Edward in such terrible jeopardy. And as she heard the grating grind of the whim as it prepared to make another trip down the shaft, she pressed her fist to her lips, and prayed that the shored-up tunnels below would hold up just one more time—

A light hand on Rina's shoulder distracted her from her thoughts. "Cousin, you're looking pale again."

Sabrina turned, and gave Amy her best attempt at a smile. "I'm fine."

"Piffle. You are at the end of your tether, and the doctor says the same," she added, nodding toward the corner where Dr. Williams was binding up an arm wound. "Go back to Ravenshold and get some rest."

"Perhaps I do need rest. But they need me more," Rina replied, glancing around the crowded sickroom. "Be truthful—could you leave now, when so many people need your help?"

Amy glared at her, looking so like her older brother. "Honestly, you are the most stubborn person I have ever met, with the exception of Dr. Williams. Will you at least step outside for a few minutes and take some fresh air?"

It was easier to agree than argue. "All right, but just for a few minutes," she conceded, closing the office door behind her.

The "fresh air" outside proved to be anything but. Heavy with smoke and coal dust, it clogged Rina's throat and burned her eyes. She walked around the back of the building, away from the wind and smoke. She was blinking so hard against the sooty air that she ran straight into one of the miners. "Oh, forgive me. This dreadful smoke makes it difficult to see one's nose in front of them."

"Even when one's nose be a tremendous hooter like mine?"

Sabrina's eyes shot open. She found herself looking into a familiar pair of lively blue eyes.

"Quinn!" Forgetting her weariness, Rina wrapped him in an impulsive hug. " 'Tis so wonderful to see you. I've missed you so terribly."

"Well, you'll miss me more if'n you squeeze the life out of me. Lord love you, gel, what if someone sees us?"

"Oh, you're right," she said, pulling away. She glanced from side to side, but luckily the yard behind the building was blessedly deserted. "You must go. You shouldn't be here."

"*I* shouldn't be here?" He crossed his arms across his chest, his eyes snapping fire. "And who was it who left myself and the two fastest steppers in the county cooling our hooves and heels by the Ravenshold gate?"

Rina stared as if he'd lost his mind. "But I was needed here. The nursing skills Mother taught me have helped save a half dozen lives tonight."

"And what about *our* lives? You've missed a prime chance at the Dutchman, and might just have queered everything we've worked for."

"I know, but I had no choice. These people needed my help."

"*These people* would turn you in quicker than you can spit if they knew you were only a gambler's daughter." He rubbed his chin, his eyes narrowing. "And I'm thinking maybe *you've* forgotten who you really are."

Sabrina looked past Quinn's shoulder, to where the dying moon hung low and heavy in the western sky. She could still feel the searing heat of Edward's mouth on hers, could still hear the deep baritone that turned her blood to fire. Could still hear the name on his lips that was not her own. "No, Quinn. I have not forgotten."

Her answer seemed to satisfy her partner, for his mouth softened a tick and his eyes lost their angry glare. "I suppose I couldn't have expected Katie Poole's daughter to turn her back on folks in trouble," he sighed. "We'll just have to make another go at the sparklers. And we'll have to look sharp about it. My mates in Ireland tell me there was a bloke sniffin' around for news of your past."

Sabrina nodded. "I know. It was Lord Trevelyan's solicitor, Mr. Cherry."

"Cherry," Quinn mused as he scratched his temple. "I don't rightly recollect that being the name."

"Then it must have been someone who worked for him. But whoever it was, they didn't find out anything. They all believe beyond a shadow of a doubt that I am Prudence Winthrope. In fact, the earl has given me a thousand pounds."

Quinn sucked in his breath. "A thousand pounds! Well, that's a horse of a different color and no mistake. Seems as if you've done fine at foxing the swells, my girl. Your da would be proud of ya."

Sabrina looked down and started to twine her apron tie around her finger. A week ago she might have felt some satisfaction at the praise, perhaps even a day ago. But not after this night. Not after Edward had offered her his hand in honest friendship, then kissed her the way no man ever had before or would again. Guilt and passion crashed inside her, tearing her apart.

Now Quinn wanted her to make another try at the necklace. That meant being near Edward. Needing him. Wanting him. Knowing everything they had together was a lie.

"Quinn, we don't need the necklace. We've a thousand pounds that's mine for the asking. I know it is not the grand future we hoped for, but 'tis a fine start. We can still go abroad, maybe buy a boardinghouse in the colonies. We can go tomorrow—"

"No," he replied, his voice bitter. "It ain't enough. Whether it's a thousand pounds or a thousand thousand, it ain't enough. I mean to make him bleed. It'll make him the laughingstock of his class, to know a mere girl hoodwinked him out of a fortune. It'll wound his bloody Trevelyan pride, which is worse than killing 'im. And even that ain't enough."

"But why? What has the earl done that makes you hate him so?"

Quinn lifted his gaze to hers, his eyes full of the aching sorrow she'd seen in them just once before. "Because—"

"Prudence!"

Rina spun around, and saw Amy coming around the edge of the building. Panicked, she turned back to her partner. She saw him press against the side of the building, the shadow from the drainpipe barely shielding him from Amy's sight. Barely.

Thinking quickly, Rina hurried to meet the girl, steering her away from her partner. Quinn had cut it close. *Too close.* "Amy, you look distraught. I daresay I should have insisted that you take a few minutes of fresh air t—"

"P . . . Pru," Amy interrupted, laboring to catch her breath. "Come quick. You must help."

"What's wrong? Is one of the patients—"

"Not the patients." Amy headed away from the manager's shed, dragging Rina after her. " 'Tis Edward. He's trapped in the mine. And Charles is going after him!"

Chapter Eighteen

By the time they reached the shaft, Sabrina was able to piece together most of what had happened from Amy's frantic sentences. The last of the miners had been freed from the lowest level, but the lift bringing them up was dangerously overloaded. The earl had remained behind with the equipment while the rest of the men headed for the surface. They were almost to the top when they felt the shudder, and heard the sickening sound of the tunnel collapsing.

"No one is sure how damaging the cave-in was," Amy said. "But I overheard one of the miners say that he'd called down the shaft, and that Edward didn't answer."

Dr. Williams was already at the whim's lift when they arrived, loading up the last of his medical supplies. His rolled-up sleeves and soot-streaked face were a stark contrast to his usually reserved appearance. He looked up briefly as the women approached, then bent down and picked up a case of medicinal alcohol and bandages. "You two should be in the infirmary."

Sabrina brushed the comment aside. "The infirmary can get by without us. We have come to help."

"I have help," the doctor replied, nodding to the two hulking miners who were already in the lift.

"I mean medical help." Rina stepped between the doctor and the lift. "You know that if Edward is hurt, he will have a better chance with both of us there."

"And he will have my *head* if anything happens to you. I cannot take you."

He hoisted the last crate of supplies and started to brush past her. She reached out and gripped his arm, compelling him to face her. "Please, let me come. I cannot just wait here, doing nothing. I cannot stand by while he is in danger. I must go to him. I *must*."

For a long moment the doctor stared at her, reading the emotions she was far too distraught to hide. His resolute expression softened, and his mouth turned up in a resigned smile. "I understand more than you think, Miss Winthrope. And you are right about the earl having a better chance with the two of us. Besides . . . given a choice, I think I should rather face Edward's wrath than yours." He nodded toward the lift. "Get in."

Impulsively, Sabrina gave him a swift kiss on the cheek. Hoisting her skirt above her ankles she stepped onto the lift, a wooden platform surrounded by a low metal cage and suspended from the whim by four stout chains. She had little time to notice much else, however, before a yelp behind her made her turn around.

Dr. Williams had the elegant Lady Amy by the scruff of the neck. "I said she could join us, not *you*. You are not coming, and that is *final*."

Amy struggled out of his grip and spun around, her eyes spitting fire. "Edward is my brother. I have a duty to help him."

"Then stop making a nuisance of yourself. Get back to the infirmary, where your incompetence is not so apparent."

Amy's bold expression crumbled. "My *incompetence*? But . . . when we were with Clara you said I was a help to you. You said—"

"I said exactly what a lord's sister wanted to hear," he replied stiffly. "But this is dangerous work, and I do not have time to play nursemaid."

"Why, you ungracious, ill-mannered . . ." Amy's words choked to mortified silence and Rina could see that she was on the verge of tears. Nevertheless, she raised her chin proudly. "Be assured, Doctor, that you shall never be subjected to my incompetency again."

Amy flounced off toward the infirmary without a backward glance. Rina watched her go, confused and amazed by the doctor's behavior. Amy might have been inexperienced, but she had a good heart and was a quick learner. "You were beastly to her," she accused Charles as he joined them on the lift. "And she has been a help to you—genuinely. Why did you deny it? You've broken her heart."

"Better her heart than her head," he answered quietly, his inexplicable anger just as inexplicably gone from his voice. "I do not want her with us. I could not bear it if anything happened to her."

The whim started and the lift lurched beneath them. Rina's stomach turned a queasy somersault. Thoughts of Amy, Charles, and everything else left her mind as she realized that there was nothing beneath her but a few wooden planks and hundreds of feet of empty air. *Lord, this is worse than the cliff ledge.*

The descent was slow and jerky—which only added to Sabrina's already squeamish disposition. She clung to the chain and watched as the circle of dawn light above them was quickly swallowed up by the devouring darkness. Only the faint illumination of the safety lantern and the miner's Davy lamp helmets held the blackness at bay. Sabrina had never considered herself a fearful person, and had never before grasped why some people experienced great anxiety in close places. But as the jagged walls of the mine slid by, plunging them deeper into the tomb of the earth, she suddenly sympathized with their fear.

"Hold there, miss. If ya grip that chain any tighter you'll squeeze it in two."

Startled, Rina looked at the miner who'd spoken. His helmet was pulled low on his face, and the mesh-covered candle provided little light. But she recognized the voice instantly. "Mr. Duffy?"

"Howd'ya do," he intoned, touching his helmet's brim with the same pleasant politeness he'd shown when he'd rescued Sarah and her from the cliff ledge. "Appears like we've both been doin' our share of rescuing."

"Appears so," she agreed, smiling warmly. Just the sight of him cheered her. Cautiously, she loosened her grip on the chain and turned toward the other miner.

"This here's my oldest boy, Harry," Duffy offered. "Well, don't stand there gaping like a toad."

The lad shifted from foot to foot. "Er, p-pleased to make your 'quaintance."

Duffy shook his head. "You'll have to excuse him, miss. Harry's not used to mixin' with gentry, 'specially womenfolk."

"No apologies necessary," Rina said, giving the young man a sincere smile. "Harry, I want to thank both you and your father for volunteering to help the earl."

Harry shrugged. "Well, o' course. The earl's a mate, ain't he?"

The whim continued on its lurching, laborious way. Sabrina tried to keep her thoughts on the mission ahead, and off her nauseous stomach. But she would have suffered ten times the queasiness if it could have rid her of the cold terror that gripped her heart. *He must be all right. He simply must be.*

Her troubled thoughts jarred to an end as the lift thumped against the bottom of the shaft. The rough-hewn rock walls had an eerie way of echoing and swallowing sound at the same time. Dark water dripped down from the ceiling, reminding Rina that they were now well below sea level.

Taking a fortifying breath she held her lantern high and followed Dr. Williams, forcing her mind to hopeful thoughts. But as they threaded their way through the rubble-strewn corridors, and stepped over a series of fallen timbers, she began to despair that anyone could survive in this unnatural place. *He cannot be dead. I would know it. Somehow, I would know it—*

"I've got 'im!"

Duffy's yell sent her scrambling over the piles of debris, heedless of the sharp stones and choking dust. Posts and rubble obscured her view, but she could see the glow of Dr. Williams's lantern. And as she clawed her way over the final hill of rubble she saw that the doctor hunkered down beside a fallen timber. Then she saw a lean, dark form pinned beneath the timber—a lean, dark *unmoving* form. "Edward!"

The earl's eyes flickered open. His gaze focused poorly, clouded by the delirium of pain. "An angel," he muttered groggily. "Look, Charles. Is 'san angel, and she's almost as pretty as . . . Prudence." His words died as he lost consciousness.

"He's lost a lot of blood," Charles said as Rina dropped to her knees beside them. "I've given him something for the pain, but 'tis no cure. There may be other injuries. I must get him out of here as quickly as possible. Can you stop his bleeding while I help the men clear the beam off him?"

"I can try," Sabrina said as she pressed a cloth firmly against the gash in the earl's forehead. A crimson stain bloomed like a deadly flower across the cloth. Fighting down panic she applied a new cloth, and another. Memories of her father's last days came back to her, when the life had slipped out of his body like a shadow slipping across a midnight room.

"It *is* you."

The rusty whisper rolled through her like thunder. She looked down and saw Edward gazing up at her, his eyes clear and lucid, but his jaw still taut with pain. She inched closer, cradling his head against her chest. "You need to save your strength. Don't speak—"

"Like hell." He cast his gaze around the tunnel. "Christ, this whole place could come down in a heartbeat. I want you out of here. Now."

She smoothed back his hair, and calmly applied another cloth to his wound. "My lord, you are in no position to order anyone anywhere."

"Dammit, you are the most contrary of females, worse than . . . than . . ." His words trailed off as the pain medicine Charles had given him began to take effect. "Trusted her . . . believed in her. But she left."

He was talking about Isabel, crawling back into the horror of that time. Sabrina took his hand, bringing it to her lips. " 'Tis long past, Edward. She can't hurt you anymore. I'm here now. I . . . won't leave you."

She'd wanted to calm him. Instead, her answer made him more agitated. He thrashed his head from side to side, muttering parts of sentences. "Can't let it happen again . . . dream of her on cliffs, walking . . . so lost . . . maybe if I'd . . . but I didn't. All my fault."

The earl's head lolled to the side as he slipped back into unconsciousness. Rina clutched his limp hand, confused by his disjointed words. It might have been the laudanum talking, but she knew the difference between fact and fancy. And Edward's words, however jumbled, had the ring of truth. What was his fault? What was it that he could not let happen again?

"Heave to!"

Rina saw the three men struggle to lift the heavy log. For the space of several heartbeats she held her breath, unsure if they would have the strength to move the beam. The timber moved an inch, and then another. She watched as a finger of lantern light appeared between the bottom of the timber and the earl's chest. "Dear God, you've done it!" she cried as tears streamed down her face.

The earl was still unconscious as they pulled him from under the beam. Duffy and Dr. Williams lifted him between them, and carried him down the passageway. Rina started after them, but hesitated as she realized that Duffy's son had stayed behind. Turning around, she saw that he'd knelt down beside the fallen timber. He'd taken out his knife, and was working a piece from the wooden surface. "Harry, this is no time to take souvenirs."

"I weren't, miss. I just wanted to show it to my da. I can't be sure, but . . . well, it 'pears this post's gone slack."

Rina cast a suspicious glance at the precarious ceiling overhead, then stepped closer to the young man. "Slack?"

"Weak as six-water grog," he explained as he stuck the knife in his pocket and rose to his feet.

He held out the piece of wood in his beefy hand, turning it over so Sabrina could get a good look at it. Even by the faint light of his Davy lamp she could see that it was molded and rotted through. "Yes, 'tis in terrible condition, but that's bound to happen in this damp place over time."

"Over time, sure. But this here's the new tunnel, and these beams weren't laid but a month past." He looked at her, his broad face puzzled and worried. "Seems to me that someone's made a fair go at scuppering the Grace."

Chapter Nineteen

Dr. Williams determined that none of the earl's bones were broken, but his numerous injuries, the great loss of blood, and the threat of infection made him fearful that Trevelyan might not recover. Rina spent hours ministering to the earl's cuts and bruises. She spent long nights sitting by his bedside, applying cool towels to his burning brow until the fever that accompanied his wounds had broken. She spent every waking moment praying for his recovery. And in the end, those prayers were answered.

On the evening of the third day Charles officially pronounced Edward out of danger—and promptly ordered Rina to her room to get a good night's sleep. She fell into her bed fully clothed, too exhausted to undress, too happy to dream. She slept like the dead, and woke to the new day refreshed and filled with hope—until she caught sight of the stuffed bear Ginger sitting on her mantelpiece, a reminder of her deception. Too late, she realized that helping Edward battle for his life had only strengthened her love for him. She'd helped to save Edward's life, but the deed might very well have cost her her heart.

Edward recovered rapidly, and the rest of the household began to recover as well. Lady Penelope stopped hovering around the earl's rooms and began to preside over afternoon tea like the grande dame she was. The children's laughter could be heard once again in the halls. Even stiff-backed Merriman lost his anxious pallor and went back to his usual grumbling. All the inhabitants at Ravenshold began to return to normal—with the singular exception of Lady Amy.

The girl remained oddly cool to both Rina and Dr. Williams, avoiding them both at every turn. Rina put it down to Amy's continued concern for her brother, but there was no denying that she was stung by her cool indifference. Rina had gotten used to having a friend.

Edward's recovery continued with astonishing speed. By the end of the week he was going stir-crazy in his room, and Charles—more out of self-preservation than medical judgment—gave leave for the earl to be taken out in the garden to enjoy some late spring sunshine. Toby had wheeled Lord Trevelyan out in the dowager's chair, but the boy hadn't been gone fifteen minutes before he came rushing back into the main hall, where Sabrina was arranging sprigs of lilacs in a Venetian glass vase. "Earl's gone, miss."

Rina stared at the agitated boy. "What do you mean, gone? Lord Trevelyan promised he wouldn't leave the chair."

"Can't say what he did or didn't promise. Alls I know is that he told me to check out a sound he heard behind the hedge. 'Maybe a poacher,' his lordship said. I rounded the hedge but couldn't find nothin'. When I got back he was vanished, right like that bird in the magician's act."

"He will wish he *was* a bird by the time I get through with him," Rina muttered as she grabbed her shawl and headed for the door. "Toby, tell Merriman what has happened, and to send out the footmen and stablehands as quickly as he can. We must find the earl before he endangers his recovery." *Or meets with one of the "accidents" that have plagued the estate.*

Sabrina had no trouble finding the empty wheelchair—the trouble came when she looked around, and saw that Edward could have chosen half a dozen paths to make his escape. Breathing an oath no lady would have uttered, she put her hands on her hips and swiveled around, searching for some clue to the earl's whereabouts.

Then she heart it. The far-off hush of the sea.

Sabrina found Lord Trevelyan leaning against a cairn of stones, staring out at the sea. The afternoon wind was brisk and strong, and had blown his dark hair into a wild tangle. Nevertheless he watched the churning water below with the intensity that marked his nature, standing so still that it seemed as if he were made of the same melancholy stone as the cliffs. He looked like a dark angel, magnificent and terrible, isolated from the men he walked among and the heaven he'd once called his home.

Unconsciously, Rina pulled her shawl closer to her throat to fight the chilling emptiness she felt in him. Her heart constricted as she realized how desperately she wanted to end his loneliness . . . then she caught sight of the sling on his left arm. Her fanciful thoughts came thudding back to earth. Angels did not suffer from sprained wrists, or have their bruised ribs trussed up in bandages, or have a vicious gash on their forehead that had nearly cost them their lives. Magnificent or not, he was still recovering from a dangerously close brush with death. Rina hoisted her skirt and scrambled up the rocks, determined to shepherd the very mortal earl back to bed where he belonged.

He did not turn around as she approached, but he must have heard her. Still staring at the ocean, he spoke. "I knew you would find me. I just did not expect you to find me so quickly."

After a week of tending to him as a bedridden patient, she'd forgotten how the sound of his voice could make her heart beat faster. "I should not have had to find you at all. You promised Dr. Williams that you would not leave the wheelchair."

His mouth edged up. "Charles is an old woman. Besides, if I had stayed in the chair, I would have lost an opportunity to make you angry. And you are quite beautiful when you are angry."

His slow, devilish glance slid across her skin like a caress. Her heart thundered against her ribs with such force that she was amazed he could not hear it. "Do not try to flummox me, my lord. You are not well enough for so much activity. And even if you were, you should not be out here alone, so close to the cliff's edge. The villain who sabotaged your mine is still very much at large. And we already know from Sarah's accident that he has moved at least some of the red markers—"

"I need no markers to tell my way." He waved his hand as if to claim the vast landscape of emerald sea, melancholy cliffs, and endless sky for his own. "These are Trevelyan cliffs. *My* cliffs. I learned them before I learned my ABC's, and I can assure you that the rocks beneath our feet will be standing sure and strong long after I am gone to dust. And as for climbing up here . . . I have done a deal of thinking this last week, and I promised myself that the moment I rose from my sickbed, I would come to this spot."

"Coming to this spot will surely put you right back *into* your sickbed," she replied tartly. "Why do such a thing?"

"To visit ghosts."

Even in the afternoon sun his chill words sent a midnight shiver down her spine. "There are no such things as ghosts. The climb has overtaxed you. We should return to the house."

She stepped away, but he made no move to either answer or follow her. Instead, he turned his gaze once more to the sea. The only sounds were the low howl of the wind, and the eerie cries of the wheeling gulls. In that moment Rina could almost believe in ghosts. But no ghost could be more alone than the man who stood with his back to the cliffs, staring out at the empty sea.

He was shutting her out—she could see it in the hard line of his jaw and the coldness of his gaze. Whatever he was going through, he seemed determined to go through it alone. He hid so much behind his rugged face, so much loneliness, so much pain. She remembered what he'd told her in the nursery—that he did not deserve the love of his family. He'd warned her once that if she dug too deeply into his past, she might not like what she found. But if there was a way to ease his pain, she needed to find it. She had so little time left with him.

"Edward. Please, do not shut me out."

For the space of several heartbeats he said nothing. Then, as suddenly as a tern diving into the waves, he asked, "Did your parents love each other?"

The question surprised her so much that she answered with the truth. "Deeply. Papa said my mother meant everything to him, and I know she felt the same. They were each other's lives."

Once again his mouth edged up in a smile, but this time there was no warmth in it. "Then you were fortunate. My father loved wealth and power above all things, and my mother reserved her affection for fashionable gowns and equally fashionable friends. If they held any regard for each other, or for me or my sister, I never witnessed it. I grew up believing that love was something which existed only in fairy tales and flowery poetry. Until I met Isabel."

Oddly she felt no jealousy at his statement, just sadness for a love gone tragically wrong. She stood facing him with her hands clasped tightly in front of her, and prayed that she would be wise enough not to betray his trust. "I have heard she was very beautiful."

His harsh smile softened at the memory. "That she was. But there was more to her than mere beauty. She had a light about her, a brilliance and generosity that drew people to her. I met her at Almack's in London. I'd gone to the city for business and was browbeaten by an old friend of Grandmother's to attend the assembly. I had no time for parties—my father had died only a few months before and I was still learning how to manage all his holdings. I was not planning to fall in love, but when I saw her standing at the edge of the crowd, as delicate and golden as a storybook princess . . . well, I was but one-and-twenty, and had spent most of my life among the gray moors of Cornwall. Isabel, and London, seemed as distant from the world I knew as the dust of the earth from the stars."

Rina glanced at the landscape around them. She had learned to love the bleak, wild magnificence of the land, but she could easily imagine a serious young Edward being seduced by the glitter and pageantry of London. "You cannot blame yourself for falling in love with a beautiful young girl. Whatever happened is in the past. The wrong she did to you is over."

"And what of the wrong I did to her?" he asked

softly. "What about the fact that, more than anyone else, I am responsible for her death."

His words were as quiet as a prayer, but they shook Sabrina with the force of an earthquake. "I . . . I do not believe it. Even if you were to swear to me it was true, I would not believe it."

He lifted his hand and brushed his fingers against her cheek. "No, you would not. If you believed in someone, I suspect you'd argue with Saint Peter himself over their salvation. You are stubborn like that—infuriatingly, maddeningly, wonderfully stubborn. But Isabel wasn't. She was delicate and kind, but she was not strong. And this land requires strength to survive."

He lifted his gaze, staring past her shoulder to the sea. "We were happy for many years. Then, shortly after David's birth, she began to accuse me of losing interest in her. At first her fears were small and I was easily able to convince her that they were groundless. But as the months passed, and my business concerns required me to spend more time away from Ravenshold, she became more and more obsessed with my absences. She became convinced that I was having an affair."

"Could you not have taken her with you?" Rina asked.

A flicker of warmth sparked in the earl's eyes, but it was gone in an instant. "A sensible solution, Miss Winthrope. I suggested it to Isabel, to show her that her fears were groundless. But David was too young to travel and she would not leave him. She was a wonderful mother to both David and Sarah, and I loved her all the more for it. Yet with each passing day her belief in my infidelity grew stronger. Nothing I said made any difference. Her constant accusations made our life together intolerable. In the end I began to seek out business affairs that would take me away from her for weeks at a time. I put gold in the place of my lost love, and sought wealth with the passion my wife no longer wanted. I was one of the most successful men in England—and I felt every bit as alone as I had when I was a boy growing up on the moors. Then, when I was in York—"

All at once Edward winced, and pressed his hand to his ribs. *Damn*, Rina thought, inwardly cursing herself for getting so wrapped up in his story that she'd forgotten that he was just out of the sickbed. "My lord, you should not be standing, much less climbing down these rocks. The men should be nearby. I'll get help—"

"No!" The earl's arm lashed out, capturing her wrist with a strength that belied his pale countenance. "Let me finish. Let there finally be an end to it."

Sighing, he leaned back against the rock wall, as if some part of him could draw on the strength of the stones. "I was in Yorkshire when I received a letter from Isabel. She said that she had discovered that she'd been wrong about my infidelities, and said that she had a secret to share with me. She said . . . she said that she loved me—that she had never stopped loving me, even when she believed I was unfaithful. I felt as if I'd sprouted wings. I finished up my business in record time and started for home before the week was out. But when I arrived home I found . . . well, you know what I found. Isabel's letter had been a sham. My wife had left me. My preoccupation with business had driven her into the arms of another man, and ultimately to her death."

Rina shook her head. "It was not your fault."

"It was no one else's," he fired back. "Her final letter to me might have been a lie, but my neglect of her wasn't. I should have stayed at Ravenshold, should have tried harder to convince her of my faithfulness. I should have moved heaven and earth to prove my love, instead of running off like some callow lad to nurse my wounded pride. She deserted me, but I deserted her first. God, it must have killed her to leave the children, but she did it to escape me. I did not think she could hate me that much, not when she'd once loved me so dearly.

"After she left, everything fell apart. I didn't give a damn about my business. I could not stay at Ravenshold, which had been our home. I avoided my children because I saw her in them, accusing me through their eyes. God, some of the locals even claimed they saw her ghost walking these cliffs. I had to get away—as far away from the life I'd known as possible. I sank myself in senseless pleasures and debaucheries. I sought out women who asked nothing of me but my coin. I'm not proud of what I did, but I thought I had nothing left inside me, nothing left to give to anyone. Sometimes I felt as if I were the one who had died, not Isabel. Sometimes, God help me, I wished that I had."

Rina knew that emptiness. She'd seen it in her father's eyes after her mother died, a hollow, direction-less emotion. Grief over her mother's untimely death had eaten Daniel Murphy alive. Both men had felt they'd betrayed women who'd loved them. Edward was younger than her father, and had a strength of character the gambler had never possessed. But if guilt over Isabel continued to eat at Edward's soul, he would end up just as lost and wasted as her father.

She reached out and curled her fingers around his. "I cannot know what was in Isabel's mind and heart. No one can. But I do know that, whether she walks on these cliffs or in the hills in heaven, she knows the truth. She knows you were not unfaithful to her. She knows that you loved her. And the woman you loved would not want you to waste your life, or your children's lives, grieving for a mistake she'd made."

At first she didn't know if her words had reached

him. Then she saw a spark flare in his gaze, the beginning of the healing she had never seen in her father's eyes. With his loving family to support him, Rina knew that eventually his heart would heal.

A lump rose in her throat. By the time it did, she'd be nothing more than a distasteful memory to him of a clever, conniving thief. If he thought of her at all, it would be with disgust and revulsion. *His heart will heal, but what about mine?*

"Prudence, are you crying?"

" 'Tis the wind. It blew something in my eye," she temporized as she brushed away a hopeless tear. *Foolish, Rina-lass. Wanting cards that haven't been dealt to you.* She pasted a bright smile on her face. "You've been out and about long enough, my lord. You should return to bed."

"Not just yet."

She heard the rough edge in his voice, but by then it was too late. With a single move he shrugged off his sling and tugged her into his arms, wrapping her in an embrace so intimate it made her gasp. "Edward, your wounds!"

"Hang my wounds. I'm strong enough for this. God knows I've been dreaming about it long enough." And without another word he lowered his mouth to hers.

The cliffs and sea faded to nothing as she tumbled into the fiery magic that he spun inside her. She reached up and buried her hands in his hair, pulling him closer, losing herself in sweet passions that bubbled through her like fine champagne.

"Christ, what you do to me," he groaned against her mouth. "Ever since that first day, when I found a red-haired vixen sprawled on Grandmother's drawing room floor."

"I was not sprawled," she murmured.

He laughed, and started to feather swift, searing

kisses along her throat. "Sprawled or not, you were a picture. I wanted you from the first, but I did not know then that I'd want even more. So much more."

He took her face between his hands and stared down at her with a tenderness that shattered and remade her with every heartbeat. "I knew you were brave when you rescued Sarah. Yet when you risked your life to come down in the mine for my sake, I knew I'd found a treasure beyond price. I loved Isabel—I want you to understand that. But it was a boy's love. Not once, not even in those first heady days of our courtship, did I experience even a portion of what I feel for you."

He lifted his glance to the cliffs and the sea. "I know this isn't the way a woman imagines it. There should be moonlight, and roses. You should be wearing a white dress, and I should be gallantly going down on one knee. But moonlight is hours away, and my ribs ache like the devil. I could not bend over, much less kneel. I can offer you none of the appropriate trappings, but I can offer you this."

Gently, he took her hand, and placed it over his heart. Then he straightened his shoulders, looking every inch the stern, commanding lord as he said, "Prudence, would you do me the honor . . . the very great honor—"

"Aye, I've found 'em!"

Duffy's cry shattered the tender moment. A minute later Sabrina and the earl were overrun by a swarm of well-meaning servants, stablehands, and laborers, all determined to assist Lord Trevelyan back to the manor house, whether he wanted to go or not. In the end Edward gave up gracefully, casting just one exasperated look at the woman beside him before he allowed the men carry him down the slope to the wheelchair waiting below.

Sabrina did not follow. She lingered at the cliff's edge and stared out at the distant horizon, her heart too full for tears. What had started out as a simple masquerade had spun far out of control. She'd fallen in love with a strong, good man, a man whose love ran as deep and wide as the ocean beneath her. How could she face him now, knowing how much he'd lost when Isabel had left him, and how much it took for him to risk loving anyone again?

How could she face him, knowing that the woman he believed he'd fallen in love with had been dead for over a decade?

Chapter Twenty

Lady Rumley set down her teacup with a decisive clink. "Prudence, I do not believe you have heard a word that I've said."

Sabrina lifted her gaze from the Persian rug she had been staring at and smiled apologetically at her guest. "Forgive me, Cassie. I was wool-gathering."

"Well, it must have been a prodigious sheep," the lady remarked good-naturedly as she poured herself another cup of tea. "Perhaps you should have a lie-down like your grandmother."

"No. I am fine." *Liar.*

Cassie smiled and picked up a finger sandwich with her elegant, black-gloved fingers. "Well, I cannot fault you for your distraction. With the unpleasantness at Wheal Grace and a saboteur running loose in the county, I am amazed that any of you at Ravenshold have a wit left in your head. And I am sure your thoughts are still much occupied with Lord Trevelyan."

Sabrina took a quick, self-conscious gulp of her tea. Cassie's innocent comment had hit the mark far closer than the lady imagined. It had been six days since Rina had stood with Edward on the cliffs and he had all but asked her to marry him—six days of quick thinking and improvising ways not to be alone with him. So far the earl was largely confined to his rooms, and between visitors, servants, and the watchdog eye of Dr. Williams, she'd managed to avoid a private conversation. But that situation was about to come to an end.

Charles had told Rina that he was officially releasing Edward from his care this evening. The doctor was going to Truro for a few days to purchase medical supplies, and he'd planned to remove the two burly miners he'd enlisted to watch Edward's door before he went. Tomorrow the earl would be free to seek her out. And sidestepping the advances of a weakened patient trussed up in bandages was an altogether different matter from discouraging a determined, powerful lord who she just happened to be in love with.

"Prudence, you are doing it again!"

Rina searched her mind for a plausible lie to explain her absent-mindedness, but before she could think of one, Cassie interrupted.

"My dear, this will not do. I cannot bear to see you so distressed. We must endeavor to take your mind off your troubles." She lifted a gloved finger to her cheek and slowly tapped it, apparently in deep thought. Then her eyes lit up. "I have it. The very thing. We shall tell each other a secret. The one who reveals the best secret wins."

Rina took another gulp of her tea. "Oh, I do not think that is a good idea at all."

"Nonsense. You know it will do you good. Besides, I have a tremendous secret that I am simply dying to tell." With pantomime furtiveness Cassie glanced to the left and to the right. Then she nodded toward the open door of the drawing room, where Amy and Mr. Fitzroy conversed on the sun-washed garden terrace. "As we were riding over this afternoon, my brother confessed to me that today is the day."

"What day?"

"*The* day. The day he means to ask Lady Amy to accept his proposal of marriage. There has been an understanding between them for some time, but today they will set the date."

Sabrina glanced at the couple on the terrace, biting her tongue. Amy wore a simple dress of white muslin, looking as fresh as a spring flower. Paris, on the other hand, sported an elaborate coat of blue striped satin that seemed overdone and ostentatious in the simplicity of the country afternoon. Though Amy had been cold to her of late, Rina couldn't help feeling a quick regret stroke through her as she thought of the sweet, fine-hearted girl spending her life with such a preening dandy.

Still, it was none of her affair. This was Trevelyan business, and she was not a Trevelyan. And the more she pretended in her heart that she was, the more she risked forgetting her true identity—Sabrina Murphy, fugitive, impostor, diamond thief. She gripped the handle of her teacup until her knuckles turned white.

Seeing Paris also made Sabrina remember something else, a question she'd all but forgotten in the excitement of the mine cave-in and Edward's recovery. "Cassie, when I was on the cliff with Sarah, she mentioned that Paris claimed that Isabel's letter had talked of escaping from her children as well as her husband. Paris said she wrote that they 'weighed her down.' But you said that Isabel wrote of her children as 'beloved' in the letter. Why would Paris make up something like that?"

Cassie poured herself a new cup of tea, and uncharacteristically spilled a portion onto the saucer. "I can't think why. I'm sure she was mistaken. Paris is not prone to fabrication. He is nothing at all like—"

Abruptly she stopped and shook her head, almost as if she were waking from an unpleasant dream. "Heavens, now *I* am the one who is wool-gathering. Come. Now it is your turn to tell me a secret."

Sabrina swallowed. Unconsciously she reached up and touched the locket lying between her breasts. "Uhm, I cannot rightly think of any. Truly, I cannot."

"Now, play fair," Cassie admonished as she wagged her finger at her reluctant friend. "Every woman has at least one secret."

One? Rina was busting with secrets. She raised her cup for another sip of tea, only to discover that the cup was dry—like her usually resourceful mind. "Truly, I have nothing to tell. No secrets at all. Truly."

"You said that. Several times." Cassie's eyes narrowed perceptively. Setting aside her teacup, she reached out and took Rina's hand in hers. "My dear, I did not mean this to be a trial for you. You know that you are under no obligation to say anything. But I cannot help marking your agitation. Something is clearly weighing on your mind. And it has been my experience that, when a woman vehemently denies having a secret, the secret that she denies having usually involves a suitor."

Sabrina blushed. "Why, that is . . . I mean, it is preposterous to think . . . that is, I couldn't possibly." She shut off the tumble of excuses, feeling gauche under Cassie's stare. There was no point in denying a truth that was so plainly written on her face. She bowed her head and whispered, "Is it so very obvious, then?"

Lady Rumley gave her fingers a warm squeeze. "Not to everyone, my dear. Just to me and to Lady Amy, who confessed similar suspicions to me when we were out riding the other day. But why are you seeking to disguise your emotions? There is no reason to be ashamed of your feelings—especially when they are fixed on such a fine gentleman as the one you've chosen."

"You *know* who he is?"

Cassie gave her a knowing smile. "I cannot be sure, but I believe I can venture an educated guess—especially since Amy's thoughts marched with mine on the matter. You have not exactly been discreet. By all accounts you have spent most of the days and nights of the last fortnight in his company."

"But, I had no choice. He needed my help."

"Calm yourself. I was not meaning to imply anything untoward. He *did* need your help, and your courage and charity does you credit. Without your assistance I doubt the earl's illness would have had such a happy outcome. And if you love the man as I am sure he loves you—"

"I love him," Rina confessed. "Oh, Cassie, I love him more than my life."

For a moment Rina caught the hint of a shadow in Cassie's eyes, but it was gone in an instant. "I am sure everything shall turn out to everyone's satisfaction. He is a sober and prudent individual. Amy has nothing but praise for him, and I am sure the rest of your family will also welcome the match."

Sabrina had no doubt that Lady Penelope and the children would—until they learned the truth about her. And when Edward himself found out . . .

Rina closed her eyes, misery aching her soul. She knew Cassie was trying to help, but every encouraging word drilled into her heart like a coffin nail. " 'Tis impossible. Hopeless. We come from different worlds. I might as well wish for the moon."

"Nonsense, you have a great deal in common. You

have a sympathetic spirit and a fine mind. What you do not know about comforting the afflicted, I am sure you will learn. The doctor will no doubt find your future assistance in his work invaluable."

The doctor? Sabrina frowned, wondering what Charles had to do with anything. Then she recalled Cassie's recent words, about spending days and nights in her lover's company, and how he was a sober and prudent individual. Edward had many virtues—but being sober and prudent were not among them. Belatedly, Sabrina realized that Cassie had come to an entirely false conclusion.

"You think I am in love with . . . *Dr. Williams?*"

"Well, of course. 'Tis obvious."

" 'Tis no such thing! I am fond of the doctor to be sure, but I am certainly not in love with him."

Cassie set down her cup and gave Rina a puzzled, look. "Well, if you are not in love with Charles, then who are you in love with?"

Blast! It was one thing agreeing with Cassie when she'd thought she had no other choice—it was quite another admitting to a love that could only end in heartbreak and disaster. She took a deep breath, and set up a desperate prayer for a miracle. *Lady Luck, I need an ace smart quick—*

For once, Lady Luck was listening. At that moment Mr. Fitzroy came charging into the drawing room, his usually languid face crimson with rage. "The chit. The bloody, simpering chit!"

Cassie leapt to her feet and hurried to her brother's side. "Paris, what has happened?"

"She refused me. Me!" He grabbed up the brandy decanter and sloshed a drink into a glass. "After all I have done for her. All I have endured. I am heartsick."

Sabrina watched Fitzroy toss back his drink, then

adjust his lace cravat. She was glad for his fortunate interruption, but she couldn't marshal much sympathy for him. To her mind the dandy looked a great deal more disturbed by the disarray of his shirt than his recent romantic rejection. His sister's face, however, was a study in desolation.

"Surely it cannot be so," Lady Rumley cried. "You have devoted yourself to Lady Amy."

"Demmed if I didn't. Bent over backward to please the silly baggage. Put up with her schoolgirl foolishness— even said she could keep up her charity work until the wedding. 'Tis then that she refused me. Said she did not love me. As if the chit knew anything about love."

"She knows enough about it to want it," Rina stated quietly.

Fitzroy swiveled to face her. His gaze drilled into her, and for the first time Rina saw the sharp edge of cunning beneath his foppishness.

"*You* are to blame for this—you and that bleeding-heart doctor. Before you came the girl was manageable. Then you showed up, with your sanctimonious ways and oh-so-noble ideals. You've ruined her. And I'll pay you back for it. I swear I will."

He stormed out of the room, leaving a distressed Cassie behind. "Please," she cried, gripping Rina's hand. "Do not attend him. He is distraught. I pray you will not tell Edward what he said. He did not mean it."

Sabrina would have bet the price of the Dutchman that Fitzroy meant every word, but she was too fond of Lady Rumley to upset her further. "I . . . believe I should attend to Amy. No doubt she is distraught as well."

"Yes, I am sure she is. And I must talk with Paris," Cassie agreed as she moved to accompany Sabrina to the terrace door. "Please persuade Amy to reconsider. Make her see that she is committing a grave error. It is imperative that Amy marry my brother. Everything depends on this. *Everything!*"

And with that she turned and followed her brother from the room, leaving Rina to wonder exactly what "everything" meant.

Sabrina found Amy on a bench under the rose arbor in the garden, sitting so still that she seemed to be painted in place. Her lovely face betrayed no trace of emotion, but the rose clutched in her hand had been shredded past all recognition. Rina settled on the bench beside her, her heart going out to the girl she'd come to love as dearly as a sister. She searched her mind for something to say that would overcome the strange barrier that had grown between them during the past weeks, but Amy spoke first.

"I was going to accept him. I really was. We have been betrothed practically since the cradle. And, save my brother, he is the finest catch in the county. He would have given me anything I asked for without a second thought. It would have been such a little thing to say 'yes'—and yet I could not say it." She swallowed, blinking back tears. "Edward and Grandmother will be so disappointed in me. They will think me bottle-witted."

"Not bottle-witted. Brave," Rina corrected gently. "You do not love Fitzroy. I suspect your grandmother and brother will be proud that you did not accept a loveless bargain, just as I am. And someday soon I am sure you will meet a man worthy of you, one that you can truly love with all your heart."

Rina had expected her words to comfort Amy. Instead, they had the opposite effect. Amy plucked another flower from the arbor and began stripping off the petals. "I have no wish to meet anyone. I intend to die a spinster."

"Darling, you are not going to wither on the shelf. Dozens of young men will be lining up to court you."

"Dozens, but not—oh, I cannot bear it!" Amy dropped the crushed rose to the flagstone, her composure crumbling into heart-raking tears. "I love him so terribly!"

Sabrina blinked in confusion. "But you just said that you did not love Mr. Fitzroy."

"Oh, not Paris. I don't love him a wit, and I don't believe that he truly loves me. I am speaking of—oh, I cannot tell you. It is *too* dreadful."

Gently, Rina pushed a strand of hair from Amy's damp cheek. "I am quite sure that no one you love could be dreadful."

"He isn't," the girl sobbed. "Charles is won—wonderful."

"Charles? *Dr. Williams?* But I thought you loathed him."

"I did. At first. I mean, he was terribly rude—always saying what he thought, no matter who it offended. But gradually I realized he was not being rude—he was being honest. He cares about people, not titles or money. He's the most selfless man I've ever known. I wanted him to be proud of me. I wanted to prove to him that I wasn't the spoiled, silly debutante everyone thought I was—that *I* thought I was, until I met him. But I did not realize that I loved him until the night of the cave-in. That's when I found out he lov . . . loves *you*."

"But Charles does not—" Sabrina's words ended in stunned silence as the puzzle pieces clicked together in her mind. Cassie's belief in her "secret" love for Dr. Williams. The lady's admission that Amy believed the same. Amy's inexplicable coolness toward Rina these last weeks. Suddenly all of it made sense—preposterous, foolish, tilt-the-world-on-its-ear sense. She could almost hear her father laughing at the brilliant absurdity of the mix-up. "Amy, Charles is my friend, but I assure you that he does not love me."

For an instant, doubt overpowered despair in Amy's gaze. Then her eyes pooled for another bout of tears. "You are just saying that to make me fe—feel better. But 'tisn't true. I knew that he loved you when he chose you to help rescue Edward instead of me. He swatted me away like a bothersome bug. Said I was incomp . . . incomp . . . *oh*."

Another sob racked her body. Rina held the quaking girl, smoothing her hair. "Amy, listen to me. Charles does not think you are incompetent. He only said so to drive you away, to keep you out of danger. He told me that he could not have borne it if anything had happened to you."

Amy lifted her head. "T-truly?"

"His very words. He said it to me as we were traveling down the shaft."

Amy's watery eyes brimmed with hope instead of tears, but her voice was still edged with distress. "But what of you? You love him, too. I cannot steal your intended."

Honestly, 'tis like beating one's head against a stone wall! "For the last time, I do not love Charles."

"But Cassie tumbled to it as well as I, and we could not both be mistaken. I saw it in your eyes—when you watched Charles bend over my brother in his sickbed."

Rina didn't doubt that Amy had seen love in her eyes, but that emotion had been for the earl. Lord, this ball of twine was getting more tangled by the minute. "I cannot speak to what you saw," she said carefully, "but I promise you on my dear mother's grave that I never cared for Charles as anything more than a friend. And I am equally certain that he has never loved me."

For a long moment Amy sat absolutely still. Then, in a kaleidoscope of motion, she bounced up, sat down, bounced up again, gave Rina a tremendous hug, then twirled around like a top. "Oh, this is wonderful! Wonder—no, this is disastrous," she exclaimed, coming to a sudden stop. "Because of my misery I have been horrible to both him and you these past few days. How can he ever forgive me?"

"I know he will, because *I* have forgiven you. I am sure Charles will understand completely when you tell him how you feel."

"But how can I tell him? What should I say? I do not even know if he loves me," Amy cried as she dropped to the bench. "Cousin, you must help me think of a ploy—something to test his heart. My happiness depends on it."

Rina had already decided not to get involved in any more of the family's personal affairs. The risk to her safety was too high. But the desperate look in Amy's eyes broke her heart. And Rina knew all too well what it meant to suffer from a hopeless, helpless love.

"All right," she sighed. "Here is what you must do. First, get a good night's sleep, to remove the tired shadows from under your eyes. Now, it is my understanding that Dr. Williams will be away until Monday purchasing medical supplies in Truro. But the moment he returns you must go to his infirmary and tell him exactly how you feel."

Amy blanched. "You mean, just tell him? But I cannot. What if he does not return my feelings? I would die, simply die."

"Better to die than to live not knowing the truth.

You will not have to endure a life of wondering if he cares for you, aching to know his heart, torturing yourself over whether he can love you in spite of all the terrible things you have done—" Rina stopped abruptly, and cleared her throat. "Yes, well, you see the way of it. You must tell him the truth, or you shall never know the truth yourself. And, when you do tell him, know that all my prayers and hopes go with you."

"Yes, you are right," Amy acknowledged. " 'Tis the only way. I must tell him the truth. And I must wear my prettiest dress. And ribbons—my periwinkle grosgrain, I think. And my ivory combs—he told me once that he admired them. And my—"

Rina laughed. She almost felt sorry for the straitlaced doctor—Wellington himself would not have stood a chance against this beautiful dynamo. "I do not think Charles will care if you wear sackcloth and ashes. Ivory combs and ribbons are not what makes a man fall in love."

"No, but if he isn't *quite* in love with me, it will not hurt to give him some encouragement." She gave Rina a tremendous bear hug. "When I was younger, I used to wish that God had given me a sister. If he had given me one, you are exactly the person I would have wished for."

"And I you," murmured Sabrina as she watched Amy dance off to plot her campaign. She loved her with all her heart, and hoped Charles would have the sense to see that Amy was the best thing that had ever happened to him. It would be nice to know that some romances could end happily ever after.

Wearily, Sabrina rose to her feet. It had been quite an afternoon. In the space of a few hours she had managed to lie to Cassie, make an enemy of Fitzroy, and advise Amy to follow the bold course of her heart. And laced through it all was her love for Edward—the strange, invisible bond they shared that grew stronger with every heartbeat, but which would sever the instant he learned the truth about her.

"Quite an afternoon," she muttered as she walked through the arbor toward the steps that led up to the terrace. "Well, at least there is one certainty. Things cannot possibly get any more complicated than they already—"

Her words faltered as her gaze fell on a slip of paper that was stuck in the lattice of the arbor. She glanced around, but no one was in sight, save two laborers who had just come out to wash the windows. They tipped their caps to her and she waved back, grateful that they were too far away to see her anxiety.

With a shaking hand she extracted the note from the arbor. It was not signed, but she recognized the hand instantly. Quinn's.

Midnight. The stables.

She'd been wrong. Suddenly things had become a good deal more complicated.

Chapter Twenty-one

The heavy stable door swung open with a faint creak of protest. Sabrina cast a swift look behind her, then pushed back her unbound hair and pulled her cloak closer around her night-shift.

The place seemed deserted. Her bare feet made hardly a whisper on the floor. The air was filled with the smells of damp hay and warm horses, and the sounds of soft whinnies and restless hooves pawing straw. A sharp jangle drew her gaze to a large nearby stall, where the earl's black stallion Brutus shook his head, demanding attention. Grinning, she walked over to the big horse and patted his velvet nose. "There, there," she cooed softly. "You're as proud as your master—and just as handsome."

Childhood memories flooded back to her, of a night when her father had taken her with him to his stables to tend a sick horse. She could still remember the soft nickers of pleasure when she scratched the mare's ears, and the huge, brown eyes that looked up at her with such faith and trust. Her father had marveled at the way she gentled the nervous creatures with a single touch. *You've a bonny gift for healing, Rina-lass,* he'd told her. *And I'm that proud of you for it.*

"It took ya long enough," a voice behind her quipped.

She spun around. Quinn sat astride an old saddle that had been thrown over a sawhorse, with his back leaning against the iron stall railing behind it, a shaft of moonlight knifing across him.

Rina hurried toward her friend. "I came as soon as I could. I had to wait until everyone was asleep."

"Aye, and it's the second time you've left me cooling me heels for the better part of an hour."

Without waiting for a response he slid off the saddle and lit a single tallow candle. The flame flickered in a faint draft, throwing eerie shadows on the walls. "Well, at least you're here now. I—mercy, gel, are you wearing your night-shift?"

Sabrina blushed as she glanced down at the fringe of linen that peeped out from under the hem of her cloak. "I did not want to risk a maidservant coming by my room and finding me dressed. 'Twould have looked suspicious."

Quinn rubbed his chin. "That it would. That's quick thinkin', lass. You may have a future in larceny after all."

Rina profoundly hoped not, but she kept the thought to herself. "I found your note. Quinn, you took a terrible risk leaving it in such a public place."

"I slipped it in just before you started talkin' with that chatterbox girl. 'Twas risky, I know, but it was a chance I had to take. You had to know: Your cover's been queered."

Sabrina went numb. She'd known this had to happen someday. Quinn's background story of Prudence's former life was never intended to last forever. But there was a part of her that had hoped, that had dreamed, that this day would never come.

Quinn saw her distress, and apparently misread it.

He took her hand and patted it gently. "Now, don't blame yourself. It weren't you—just some clerk in Dublin let out more than he should in his cups. I knew I should'a paid for his boss. Well, it's all water under the bridge and that's a fact. We've got ten days before the tale unravels—a fortnight if we're lucky. So we've got to pinch the Dutchman before the week's out."

"But how? The dowager keeps it locked in a safe hidden in her rooms. Even her maids do not know its whereabouts. Unless Lady Penelope takes the necklace out herself and hands it to me, I cannot get at it."

"Darlin', that's why they call me the Jack o' Diamonds," he bragged. "Trevelyan's men ain't the only ones who can buy a pint to loosen a tongue. This past week I hunted down a former footman from Ravenshold. Heard he might know somethin' to our advantage—and that he had no love for the Trevelyans. Well, I pulled an ace from the deck to be sure. Seems they offed him sudden-like for weeing in the prize roses, even though it probably did 'em good. Anyway, the bloke can't hold his liquor worth a damn so I got 'im talking. And what he told me was worth every drop I bought 'im."

"He told you where the safe is?"

"Better'n that. He told me the bleedin' combination! Once he helped her nibs open the safe when the door got stuck, and read the numbers over her shoulder. Not that the secret did him much good—the dowager's rooms got more maids hovering around them than a hive has bees. Anyone who isn't supposed to be there would be spotted in a snap. That's where you come in, lass. You can slip into her rooms while the lady's at supper—say you come up to get her some do-da or such she forgot. Then you could nick the sparklers and be out the door before a bloke can say 'jacks over kings.' "

Quinn took a slip of paper from his waistcoat and slipped it into her cloak pocket. "Here's the combination. It'll work, by glory. I can feel it in my bones!"

It *would* work. Rina's instincts told her the scheme was a winner. But she didn't share her partner's enthusiasm. The thought of betraying the people she loved brought a lump to her throat. Unfortunately, she didn't have a choice.

She picked up a bit of brittle straw and twirled it between her fingers. "So when do I steal it?"

"Saturday. I know that's cuttin' things a might fine since it's only a few days away, but it's the day when most of the servants is off. Ravenshold will be as deserted as it's ever going to get. We'll make our move then. A red queen to trump a bloody black king."

Sabrina had never heard him sound so cold, so completely soulless. Suddenly she realized how very little she really knew about her father's old mate. "Quinn, I know you want the necklace for its price, but there is more to it than that. You want revenge. Why do you hate the earl so much?"

At first she wasn't sure if he'd heard her. He stared at the candle, his expression so icy that the reflection of the flickering light in his eyes seemed to be the only warmth in him. "Because there's blood on his family's hands, my girl. *Her* blood. The Black Earl of Trevelyan caused the death of the only woman I ever loved."

For a long moment Sabrina could only stare, too stunned to move, almost too stunned to breathe. Edward, a murderer? And the victim Quinn's love? She shook her head in confusion, trying to take in both pieces of information. "I know what it is to lose someone you love, and I know there's no clean healing for it. But you're wrong to blame the earl. He could not kill anyone—"

"His blood caused her death as surely as he'd stuck

the blade through her heart with his own hands. My sweet, shy, trusting Lottie—" He fell silent as the crushing wave of loss washed over him. "I should have told you from the first. I meant to. But I was afeared you wouldn't play your part so well if ya knew. Lottie—her full name were Charlotte Winthrope. She's mother to the bairn whose place you took."

Rina clutched the locket she always wore around her neck. She'd always wondered how Quinn had come by the locket, and how he knew so many of the details of Prudence's early life. Still, she'd never suspected that he actually knew the girl—or that he'd been part of the story rather than just a man who'd stumbled upon a tragic tale and turned it to his advantage. "But Prudence and her parents died when their house caught fire. You told me so yourself."

"That were a lie, girl. Jesus, I've told so many of 'em, it's hard to ken the truth anymore. But I *did* love Lottie, and the Trevelyans *did* cause her death." He suddenly looked much older than his forty-odd years. "I expect I'd better start at the beginning."

The tale spooled out, slow and sad as an Irish ballad. After Quinn had split with Rina's father he'd kicked around the continent for a few years, running games when he could and doing odd jobs when he couldn't. He had ended up in Venice, as a valet for a gentleman in the diplomatic service, Sir Anthony Winthrope. His employer proved to be a vulgar brute, given to lewd acts and drunken fits. "He valued no one and nothing save his own sordid pleasures," Quinn bit out, his voice carrying a disgust that the years had not diminished. "I would have left the sod a dozen times over. But I couldn't. See, sometimes in his cups he'd take out his rages on his young wife, and I was the only one who dared get between 'em."

Sabrina knew what some men were capable of, and her heart went out to the poor young woman who had been married to one of them. "Why didn't Charlotte leave him?"

"She was afeared to. For all his vices her husband was a powerful man, and he'd threatened to keep the child if she left him. She had no friends in the foreign town, and no blood kin save the Trevelyans, what she hadn't seen in years. She was that alone in the world until I showed up. I never touched her, and nothin' passed between us that we couldn't stand before the Almighty and confess with a clear conscience. But I loved that sweet girl with everything in me. And I could no more watch him squeeze the life out of her gentle, decent soul than I could sprout wings and fly.

"It were risky for both of us—her husband had eyes everywhere. But we made our plans, and one night I spirited her and her daughter away and put 'em on a ship bound for England. On the dock, she gave me the locket with Pru's picture, as a keepsake, like. Then she kissed me bold as brass, and said that when all this was past, she meant for us to wed. I told her she was daft—I was a gambler and no bloody good." A sweet, crooked smile crossed his face as he recalled the memory. "But my Lottie, she said I were the bravest man she'd ever known. Me—a no-account con with half a crown in me pocket. As the ship cast off she and Pru stood on the deck, smiling and waving, and here was me standin' on the docks blubberin' like a moon calf. It was the grandest moment of my life."

Rina reached out and gave his hand a quick squeeze. "She loved you, Quinn."

"That she did, for all the good it did her. Cer'ain, it would've been better if I'd tied a millstone round her neck and tossed her down a well than put her on that ship. Gave us hope, it did. We didn't know the game was already lost."

He leaned against the saddle he'd been sitting on, his shoulders bent as if under an immeasurable weight. "You know most of the rest. She stayed at Ravenshold some six weeks. I worked the coast towns, making scratch fast as I could, so's I could make a home for her and Prudence when the time came. She wrote me regular, telling me about the kindness of her cousins and grandmother, and especially the earl—the da of the one you know. I thought the dice was finally rolling our way. Then her letters stopped. I knew she wouldn't 'a quit on her own, so I hightailed it back to Venice. Got there at midnight and stormed into Sir Anthony's house, but I was too bloody late."

"I am so sorry, Quinn. You don't have to go on."

"I do. For her . . . and for you. He'd gone after both of them in a drunken rage, but my brave girl had used the last of her strength to shove a blade through his evil heart. The little girl was gone, but Lottie had a flicker of life left in her. I held her close, and with her last breath she told me how the old earl had betrayed her to her husband. She'd told him she meant to marry a commoner. Made him furious. Said he wouldn't let her disgrace the *noble* Trevelyan name, as if her pig of a husband weren't a far worse disgrace. After she was gone I set a torch to the house, so that her sweet name wouldn't be fouled by scandal. I could give her that, at least."

Quinn's tale was at an end, but in Rina's heart she knew that the story would never truly be over for him. Or for her. Stepping into Prudence's life had given her a strange kinship to the long-dead girl, and to find out that she'd died so suddenly, and so very tragically—well, in an odd way Rina almost felt as if a part of herself had died. "You gave her more than you know, Quinn. You loved her, and that is the greatest gift any man can give to a woman. You can cherish that memory forever."

"I don't want a memory. I want *her*. I want her sittin' by the fire mending socks, and me smoking a pipe, and young Prudence playing with her dolls on the hearthrug. I want all the days of all the years that her bastard husband and the bloody earl robbed from us. And I mean to take every minute of those years out of Trevelyan's hide!"

Sabrina understood his anger. She also saw that it was misplaced. "You are right to hate Sir Anthony, and the Trevelyan earl who betrayed your Charlotte. 'Tis monstrous what they did. But the current lord is nothing like his father."

Quinn cut her a sharp look. "Don't be daft, girl. They're aristos, all of 'em cut from the same cloth. They care for nothin' but their own soddin' kind."

Rina shook her head. "The Trevelyans are not like that. The earl is a good and honorable man."

"Good and honorable." Quinn spit out the words as if they left a foul taste in his mouth. "Well, my gel, if'n he's so *good* and *honorable*, then tell me how it comes that the sharps in the village pub are layin' odds that Clara Hobbs's bastard babe is gonna be born with Lord Trevelyan's dark hair?"

The soft nickers of the nearby horses seemed a million miles away to Sabrina. Quinn had left the stables over a quarter of an hour before, but she remained behind. She stood with her back leaning against the old saddle, stared into the candle flame . . . and wondered how she was going to keep her heart from breaking in two.

She remembered the time that Amy had confided to her that she believed Clara's lover was a man of the gentry class. And she recalled the day she'd found the earl writing instructions that provided for the young woman's care and comfort. She'd thought he was simply being kind. But what if it wasn't generosity she'd witnessed? What if it was guilt—guilt over using an innocent girl for his pleasure, then tossing her out as soon as she became an inconvenience? Rina had seen it happen before—but Edward wasn't like that. He *couldn't* be like that.

Clara's babe . . . Trevelyan's dark hair . . . Trevelyan's bastard.

"Stop it!" Rina pressed her fists against her throbbing temples. It was hearsay, nothing more. Clara's unfaithful lover could be the greengrocer for all Rina knew. But even if she found out that the earl was the father of Clara's child, it wouldn't make a jot of difference. In less than a week she would be out of Edward's life forever. *I will never see him again. 'Tis not as if we ever had a future together.*

She heard the faint creak of the stable door opening behind her, the same door that Quinn had left by a few minutes before. Apparently her partner had returned to give her more instructions for the robbery, or more reasons why she should hate Edward and his family. She wasn't up for either. Sighing wearily, she turned around to face him. "Quinn, I love you dearly, but I'm just not up to—"

A man strode out of the shadows, his boots striking the stone floor like hammer blows, his furious gaze piercing her like a sword driven straight through her heart.

"Who is *Quinn*?" the Earl of Trevelyan demanded.

Chapter Twenty-two

Edward had been walking on the cliffs, as he'd done nearly every night since the day he'd been dragged back from the rock outcropping. Charles had forbidden him from leaving his rooms until he was entirely well, but Edward needed the sea like he needed air. So he slipped out every night and walked the cliff's edge, where the thundering waves and cold salt wind poured more healing through his veins than a chemist's shop of curative tonics. He was on his way back when he noticed the light in the stables. Making a mental note to ask the stable master about it in the morning he started to pass by, but froze as he heard a familiar voice cry out.

He shoved open the door, ready to defend the woman he loved to the death. But she didn't need defending. She stood calm as a glassy sea, wearing little more than her night-shift, with her unbound hair tumbling wild over her shoulders . . . and another man's name on her lips.

"Who is *Quinn*?"

"No—no one," she stuttered. "My lord, you should be in bed."

"To hell with bed. *Who is Quinn?*"

She dropped her gaze and toyed with the material of her clock. "No one. There is no one here. You . . . must have misheard me."

Like hell. She was lying—he could see it in the slump of her shoulders, the way her gaze slid away from his whenever their eyes met. And every nuance of her duplicity felt like a strip of skin being flayed from his body. The same pain he felt two years ago began to twist inside him. He spoke, his words low and lethal. "I trusted you."

"And I you." She lifted her chin and met his gaze with defiance. "I do not have to explain my actions to you. After all, *you* have secrets, too."

Aye, he had secrets. Secrets of broken hearts and misery and a pain that went on and on without hope or reason. It had taken him years to climb out of the darkness and let himself believe in someone enough to trust again, to love again. And to be betrayed again. The sickening darkness washed over him and he turned away, afraid of what he might do. "At least Isabel had the decency to leave Ravenshold when she took a lover."

Prudence's defiance shattered. She ran around in front of him, blocking his way out of the stable. " 'Tis not like that, not at all. You must believe me."

He *had* believed her. All the time he'd been stuck in his bedchamber he'd trusted her to be faithful. In her eyes he'd seen the man he wanted to be, the man he knew he could be with her love. But that love had been a lie, like her goodness, her decency, and everything else about her. While he'd been trussed up like a Sunday chicken, she'd been secretly giving herself to a lover. The bitterness of her betrayal rose in his throat, nearly choking him. She'd played him like a pennywhistle, and he'd fallen for every honeyed lie she'd told him. Christ, he'd even asked her to marry him!

He'd trusted her. And as he looked down into her glorious eyes, and stroked his gaze over the ripe lips and the sweet body that he'd fought to keep his hands off of, he realized he still wanted to trust her. He wanted desperately to cling to his belief in her—just as he'd clung to his belief in Isabel, until the truth of her betrayal destroyed him bit by bit until nothing was left of him but a hollow, bleeding husk—

"No!" he roared. He stripped off her cloak and gripped her shoulders, forcing himself to look at her thin night-shift, her bare feet, her cascade of sunset hair that begged for a lover's caress. That begged for *his* caress. God help him, he still ached for her sweet innocence with every fiber of his being, even though the evidence of his eyes proved that she was neither sweet nor innocent. She'd given herself to another man, this *Quinn*—and perhaps to others. Perhaps she'd talked about him as she'd lain in their arms, laughing at the foolish, lovelorn earl who'd been so completely and thoroughly deceived.

He took a deep breath, barely containing his rage. "You will leave Ravenshold. You will be provided for as is your right, but I'll be damned if I'm going to let another shameless trollop make a cuckold of me."

A deep blush spread across her throat and cheeks. "I haven't. I've done nothing wrong. You must believe me. I am not like Isabel. I have not betrayed you."

Damn, she was good. Her beautiful eyes were all innocence, her blush a study in naiveté. Under other circumstances he might have appreciated her skill at deception.

His mouth pulled into a slow, dangerous smile. "You say you are innocent. Very well, then. Tell me you have not been with a lover."

Her blush deepened, but she answered boldly. "I have not been with a lover."

His smile hardened. "Tell me you are untouched."

Her gaze slanted down with just the right touch of maidenly modesty. "I am . . . untouched."

His hold on her shoulders tightened to a punishing grip. "Now tell me that you love me."

She lifted her head, her lovely eyes shining with tears as she whispered, "I love you."

Innocent. Beautiful. False as dust. The madness of his past raged up inside him, blocking out everything but his pain, his anger, his hollowness. He pulled her against him, ignoring her struggling protests. "You love me, little maiden? Then prove it."

He curled his fingers in the hair at the back of her neck, and brought her mouth to his in a merciless kiss.

Edward had kissed her before, but there had always been a gentleness in him, the restraint of a gentleman. This kiss was savage and carnal, cutting through her senses like a scythe through hay. She staggered under the assault. She gasped at the violence. Then she groaned and locked her arms around his neck, knowing this was what she'd hungered for since the moment she'd met him.

His tongue and teeth ravaged her mouth, thrusting into her with an almost brutal force. His hands stroked her shoulders and back through the thin material of her shift, running his palms against the sides of her breasts. Deep, coiling heat pulsed in her core, then spilled out through her arms and legs. He laved hot kisses along the column of her throat, rubbing his rough cheek against the softness of her skin. She bent back to give him greater access, wanting both the pleasure and the pain. Wanting him.

She knew he was seducing her body only, without

tenderness and without love. He was using her the way he thought she'd used him. And she could no more fight it than she could stop the waves crashing in from the sea.

Still locked in his embrace she helped him shrug off his coat and his shirt, frantic to explore his body. She ran her hands over the hard planes of his shoulders, the powerful expanse of his back, the coiled power of his muscular forearms. He smelled of the sea and tasted of the wind. She felt his mouth curve into a smile against her throat.

"God, you're a witch," he growled. "Your hands alone could drive a saint straight to hell. No wonder your lover Quinn risked trespassing to have you."

"He isn't my—" Her sentence died in a shocked gasp as he covered her breast. Slowly, ruthlessly, he began to knead her through her shift, rubbing his thumb across her taut nipple. A sweet, desperate pressure began to throb inside her. She arched eagerly against his hand, knowing she was behaving like the wanton he believed her to be. It didn't matter. Nothing mattered except the beautiful, aching magic that he was creating inside her. That *they* were creating together.

Words she couldn't deny welled up inside her. "I love you," she cried softly.

He froze. He stared down at her, his expression as pitiless as the granite cliffs. "I don't *want* your love."

She winced as if he'd struck her. Her love was the only gift she had to give him, the only truth in her whole charade. And he didn't want it. "Then what *do* you want?"

He didn't answer, but his gaze held a hunger that drove the air from her lungs. The Edward she knew had become a dark stranger—merciless, cold, without an ounce of conscience. Rina realized she was looking into the face of the madman he'd become after Isabel's desertion. Instinctively she stepped back, and found her way blocked. She glanced over her shoulder, and saw that he'd backed her into the old saddle.

Squaring her shoulders, she gathered her wits about her. "Edward, I think we should consider what we are doing. We need to sit down and discuss this like—"

Her words disintegrated as he circled her waist and lifted her, plopping her unceremoniously astride the saddle. She gasped at the shock of the hard leather against her naked womanly center, then struggled to pull her shift down over her exposed calves and ankles. "This is *not* what I had in mind when I said we should sit down."

The earl's hard mouth ticked up a notch. "You asked me what I wanted."

Embarrassment turned to indignation. "You wanted to see me in a ridiculous pose?"

"Not quite. *This* is how I want to see you." He gripped the neckline of her shift. With a single stroke he ripped the thin material open to her waist.

Edward had thought that his ample experience with consorts and courtesans over the past years had jaded him to any surprises. He'd been wrong. Under her demure night-shift, Prudence Winthrope had the most stunningly beautiful body he'd ever laid eyes on. Her sweet figure narrowed to a waist that he could circle with both hands, then flared to hips that seemed impossibly voluptuous in such a slim frame. Her pale breasts were high and full, and peaked with nipples so erotically dark that they made his mouth water. He watched them rise and fall as she breathed, and felt his own body swell and harden with each soft, shallow breath.

He wanted her. He *ached* for her. His hungry gaze swept over her, gorging on the sheer, breathtaking glory of her naked skin. He wouldn't be her first, but by God he'd be the one she remembered. He stepped into the V of her legs, intending to take her hard, quick, and any other way his body demanded. Without ceremony he started to shuck his breeches.

Her faint gasp drew his gaze upward.

Her hair fell in a wild tumble across her face, adding to the erotic picture she presented. But behind the curtain of hair he caught a glimpse of her green eyes, and what he saw in them riveted him. Desire. Need. And fear. Her glorious hair and goddess figure belonged to a woman, but her uncertain expression belonged to the innocent he'd fallen in love with. The woman who didn't exist.

It was a trick. It had to be. He'd heard the evidence of her deceit on her lips. She didn't need gentleness, and he was in no mood to give it. His body screamed for a hard, hot coupling—hell, she owed him that much for the dance she'd led him on. She didn't deserve the gentle wooing he would have given the Prudence he'd cared about. She didn't deserve—

"Ah, *hell*," he muttered as he took her mouth in a tender, thorough caress.

Chapter
Twenty-three

Rina had resigned herself to the fact that Edward no longer loved her. She'd accepted that he would use her, then cast her aside when he was finished. Since he'd rejected her love, her body was the only thing she had to give him, and she was prepared for it.

What she wasn't prepared for was being drawn down into a slow, smoldering, achingly gentle kiss.

His mouth devoured her with lavish hunger, melting her uncertainty like wax in a furnace. His tongue filled her mouth, stroking and exploring her softness with a boldness and intimacy that left her weak. She placed her hands on his shoulders, partly for balance, but mostly for the feel of his naked flesh. His skin was unexpectedly smooth, like velvet stretched over steel. She reveled in his strength, the barely contained power that radiated from him. She could feel the tightness in his muscles, the bowstring tautness of a powerful man holding himself in check. She didn't understand the change in him, but asking would have meant ending his intoxicating kiss, and she could no more do that than she could stop loving him.

His kiss went on and on, changing and deepening with every heartbeat. A slow, deep thrum started in her, like a distant drum growing louder and more insistent. She wanted his kiss to go on forever, and gave a small mew of disappointment when he broke it off. Her disappointment disintegrated, along with conscious thought, as he lowered his head and brushed his lips against her nipple.

Lightning shuddered through her, radiating to every nerve in her body. She'd thought nothing could be more shockingly intimate than the feel of his hand on her breasts. She'd been wrong. He ran his tongue over her, suckling her with the same thorough skill he'd used to seduce her mouth. She buried her hands in his hair, guiding his glorious, wicked mouth from one breast to the other. She was being shameless, but she couldn't help it. Her body seemed to have a will of its own. Her aching center began to throb with an almost unbearable tightness. Whimpering, she writhed against the hard leather.

His low, feral chuckle was as erotic as his kiss. "This pleases you?"

She bit her lip, stifling a moan that would have told him just how much it pleased her. She had some pride left—not much, but some. She cleared her throat, and tried to sound worldly and nonchalant as she commented, "I thought that a gentleman was only supposed to kiss a lady on her lips."

He shot her a look rife with disbelief and humor. "Then your education is sorely lacking. Your Quinn could use a few lessons."

"I told you before, he's not—" Her protest ended in a strangled gasp as he pressed his hand into the V of her legs.

Her thin shift was no barrier to his demanding fingers. He stroked her with ruthless gentleness, pressing the soft material against the swollen and aching folds of her sex. Time seemed to stretch and contract with each exquisite stroke. Her breath came out in tight, short gasps. Her head fell back and she groaned, seduced by the erotic caress. She felt as if she were two people: the staid, sensible Rina who kept her feelings locked tightly inside her, and a new woman, shameless and wild, who gloried in every stroke of the earl's wicked fingers.

"Look at me."

Like a sleepwalker in a dream she obeyed his command. His gaze smoldered with fire, the same fire that burned in her. A faint sheen of sweat gleamed on his body. She could smell his heat, and the rich, masculine scent of him. She saw the tautness in his jaw, could feel the strain in every muscle in his powerful frame. She knew that he was fighting for control.

"Move back," he ordered roughly.

Still wrapped in the sweet lethargy of passion she slid back against the edge of the saddle until she was pressed against the iron railing behind it. Edward climbed up on the saddle and straddled her across his legs. Her night-shift pooled around her hips and thighs, but underneath she was spread open and totally exposed, and only inches away from his half-undone breeches, and the bulging evidence of his own desire.

Rina's knowledge of lovemaking was limited at best, but she was fairly certain it involved the woman on her back, with the man properly on top. She'd never imagined anything as shocking as this, where his hands cupped her naked backside, and his bare chest brushed the straining peaks of her sensitive breasts. She'd never imagined the most private and secret part of her being so open to a man, so completely vulnerable to whatever he chose to do. She swallowed. "Edward, shouldn't we . . . lie down?"

His smile flashed like a knife in the darkness. "I want you to see me," he said roughly. "I want you to see everything I do to you. And when I take you, I want you to know it's me who's doing it. *Me.*"

His final word shattered through her, breaking the last of their control. The passion they'd both been holding back roared out in a mighty torrent. His mouth and hands were everywhere, stroking, sucking, gentling, and caressing her body into a shuddering frenzy. She arched against him, discovering him with greedy fingers and ravenous kisses, gorging on the taste and smell and feel of him. Her breath came in ragged bursts. Her flesh burned from the inside out. Arms and limbs tangled until she could no longer tell where his body ended and hers began. And still he fondled her, caressed her, and claimed her in every place except the exposed aching part of her that wanted him the most.

She fell against his chest, gripping his shoulders, weak with desire and unsated need. "Please," she cried softly. "Please."

His guttural words were barely human. "Look at me."

This time she couldn't obey his command. Her head felt heavy as lead and she had no strength to raise it. Aching, she breathed a soft, tortured mew against his chest and moved her bottom, pressing herself fully against his hard, hot sex.

His shudder rocked her like an earthquake. "Damn it, look at me!"

With the last of her strength she lifted her head. His dark, feral eyes penetrated her, reaching into the deepest, most secret part of her. Long ago she'd built this place inside her as a sanctuary, a safe haven she could run to when the world became too cruel. But it was safe and secret no longer. Edward had claimed it, just as he'd claimed every other part of her. There was no where to run from his savage gaze. No where to hide.

"Say my name," he growled.

She licked her dry lips. "Edward."

He moved their hips, starting a rhythm. "Say it again."

"Edward," she repeated as they rocked again. "Edward, Edward, Edward . . ."

She breathed his name over and over, as he increased the rhythm. She writhed and bucked, bound to him by his iron hands on her hips, and his dark, devouring gaze. Her body grew painfully tight and her voice disintegrated. Nothing existed but his eyes and his hands and her burning need to be whatever he wanted, whatever he asked. Her love for him burst forth like a star, driving her past physical hunger to the edge of madness. She wrapped her arms around his shoulders and gazed fully into his eyes, letting him see what she felt for him, all of it. "Edward, I love you, I love—"

With an animal growl he thrust into her with one smooth, hard stroke. Pain and pleasure tore through her. Her fingers raked his shoulders and she cried out. He covered the scream with his lips, plunging into her mouth the way he was plunging into her body. Past and present burned away in the glory of his claiming. He braced his hands against the railing behind her, and drove into her again and again, possessing her more deeply with every stroke. He took and she gave with a white-hot hunger, until somehow her giving became taking and his taking, giving.

They moved together as one, finding a wholeness in each other that they'd never found alone. They lived and died in each other's arms, burning as one, crying out with one voice, one breath, one heartbeat. And when they thought they could burn no more, they shattered in an oblivion of ecstasy, destroyed and remade by the wonder and power of their love.

Sabrina stretched languidly in the pile of straw. She looked up at the stable rafters, listened to the muffled whinnies of the horses, smelled the coolness of the night air that was just beginning to hint at dawn. It was the same stable she'd visited a dozen times before. But now she looked at everything with new eyes, seeing the old stable as a richer, sweeter, more precious place than she'd ever imagined. Nothing about it was the same. Because nothing about *her* was the same.

She stretched again, smiling deliciously. She was completely naked. Somewhere along the way Edward had striped off her tattered night-shift, probably when he'd lifted her off the saddle and laid her in the straw, then proceeded to take her a second time. He'd done it the proper way, with her beneath him and him on top. But there'd been nothing "proper" about the way he'd driven into her, thrusting so deeply that she could feel him touching the gate of her womb. The heated memory made her shift wantonly. The brittle straw pressed against her, making her aware of the tender ache between her legs. She'd probably be sore as blazes in the morning, but she didn't care.

She glanced over at the man who lay a few feet away from her, lying on his side with his back to her. She ran her gaze over the length of his frame, from the layered muscles of his shoulders to the taut planes of his buttocks, to the strong columns of his legs. Her breath quickened as she remembered that body inside her, impossibly hard, impossibly deep.

His breeches were pushed to his knees and he still wore his boots, but that only added to her pleasure. He'd been so mad for her that he hadn't even stopped to take off his clothes. She loved that his need for her had stripped him of the social niceties. She loved what he'd made her discover about herself, the fire and savageness she'd never dreamed existed. She loved what they'd become together, pledging themselves to one another in ways that could never be expressed in words.

She loved *him*.

She raised herself on her elbow and reached out, needing to touch him. But as she brushed his shoulder he jerked away. With his back still to her he rose to his feet. Without a word he reached down and began to fasten his pants.

She frowned, confused by his distance and his silence. "Edward? What is wrong?"

"Wrong? Nothing is wrong. You gave me a damn good ride."

"But it wasn't just a . . ." She swallowed, unable to speak the coarse word. Her words came out in a hushed whisper. "We made love."

He glanced over his shoulder, his smile a sneer. "We made *sex*, my sweet. Good sex. But that is all it was."

How could he be saying this, after all they'd done, all she'd felt? "That's not all and you know it. Why are you trying to deny what we feel for each other?"

"Lord, you *are* an innocent." He scooped up his shirt, and pulled it over his head. "You're a pleasing tumble. But the things a man does in passion don't equate to love. A seasoned bit of muslin should know that. A few more lovers and you'll catch on."

She pressed her hand to her stomach, feeling betrayed, embarrassed, and lost, so very lost. She'd given herself to him shamelessly. She'd welcomed him into the most intimate places of her body and heart. She'd let herself fall into a well of love so deep that it had no bottom. But he didn't love her. She was falling on her own, into aching, empty, endless nothing.

Somehow she found the strength to stand. Pausing just long enough to retrieve her cloak, she walked out of the stable and didn't look back. She wrapped the material around her, tying the strap securely around her throat, pulling the hood up to protect her from the night wind. And wondered how she was going to find the strength to live through the rest of the hour, the rest of the night, the rest of her lifetime without him.

She was gone. Edward heard it in silence, and saw it in the unshadowed candlelight that flickered on the wall in front of him. Most of all, he felt it in the emptiness inside him, in the hollow place where his heart used to be. She was gone because he'd driven her away. And the fact that he'd had no choice didn't make it any easier to bear.

Edward, I love you. Her husky promise echoed in his mind. Nothing in his life had prepared him for what he'd found in her arms. Nothing even came close. No woman had ever given herself to him that freely, with such ardent pleasure, such eager, unbridled passion. She'd taken everything he'd given her, accepting him more completely than any other woman. And when he'd been inside her, feeling her young, tight body draw him in deeper and deeper, he felt his loneliness burn away and found a wholeness he'd never known, a pure, sweet love that belonged only to him . . . until he came back to his senses, and remembered that her *pure, sweet love* belonged to another.

"Damn her!" He slammed his fist against a stall, hitting it so hard that his knuckles bled. He didn't care. The pain was nothing compared to what she'd done to him, how she'd stripped him of his pride and dignity in his need to have her. He'd known she was faithless, but he'd taken her anyway. Twice. And if she'd stayed any longer, with her glorious hair mussed and tangled from his loving, and her luminous body gleaming in the candle-light, he'd have taken her a third time.

He groaned, his traitorous body aching for her. She'd betrayed him as completely as Isabel. He'd heard the evidence with his own ears—words of love and another man's name on her lips. He knew she was false, that she'd dishonored him with another, that she didn't have a truthful bone in her body. He knew all of it. And if she'd stayed, he'd have *still* taken her again.

He had to get out of this place. It was too full of the heat and smell of their loving. Haphazardly he stuffed his shirt in his breeches and strode over to his coat. He bent down, but paused as he caught sight of a patch of white out of the corner of his eye, on the ground beside the old saddle. Turning his head, he saw it was the night-shift he'd stripped from her during their lovemaking.

Pride and reason told him to retrieve his coat, gut the candle, and leave. Still, he found himself reaching out, and picking up the shift instead. He held the fabric in both hands, handling it as gently as if it were a holy relic. He swallowed, telling himself that the tightness in his throat was only a bit of hay dust. Then he lifted the ruined garment to his face, and breathed in her ripe, intoxicating scent. *I love her. God help me, I still love her.*

He felt something sticky on his palm. He lowered the garment, thinking that he'd injured his knuckles worse than he'd thought. But the stickiness was on his left hand, not the one he'd used to hit the stall door. He frowned, turning the material over for a better look, wondering how he'd managed to stain it with the wrong hand . . .

His eyes widened. He grabbed up the candle and

raised it over the saddle. In the light he saw what he'd missed in the darkness, the dark discoloration just visible on the leather. He ran his hand across the smudge then raised it to his face, staring in disbelief at the stain on his fingertips.

Blood.

Chapter Twenty-four

"Prudence, you look dreadful this morning."

Sabrina set down the fork she'd been using to push her eggs around her breakfast plate. "I . . . did not sleep well last night."

The dowager raised her quizzing glass to her eye, and observed Rina with canny scrutiny. "Humph. You look as though you have not slept in a week. Are you ill?"

Rina was worse than ill. She was heartsick. After she'd returned to her room, she'd drifted into a kind of slumber, but had awoken only a few hours later feeling more exhausted than before. Her spirit was shattered, her soul was miserable. And her body ached like the very devil.

Still, as unhappy as she was, she dared not show it to Lady Penelope. Rina had only a few days left in her masquerade as Prudence. It was important that she spend those days as if nothing were out of the ordinary. She straightened her shoulders and hid her anguish behind her well-practiced wall of unconcern. "I vow 'tis the weather. They say that there is a storm brewing."

The dowager slowly lowered her glass. "This is

Ravenshold. There is *always* a storm brewing. However, I suppose inclement weather might explain your weariness—and why Edward seemed to be suffering from the selfsame lack of sleep when I saw him earlier."

Sabrina's eyes widened. "He was?"

"Indeed. I came downstairs for breakfast just before he left for the Wheal." Lady Penelope narrowed her eyes, and tapped her index finger against pursed lips. "Is there any other reason why he might look so . . . fatigued?"

Rina raised her napkin to her face, making a pretense of dabbing her mouth as she covered her sudden blush. "I can think of no reason whatsoever."

Lady Penelope sniffed, and waved over the footman for another cup of tea. "Well, I suppose it is all one. The whole house seems to be acting a bit peculiar, with Edward dashing off for the Wheal when he is just out of his sickbed, and with Amy dashing off to her room to lay out every dress she owns. Do you think the agitation has something to do with this saboteur unpleasantness?"

"Perhaps," Rina said woodenly. She set down her napkin, and pushed her chair away from the table. "Please, if you will be so kind to excuse me, I have matters to attend to."

"Yes, yes," Lady Penelope said absently as she stirred sugar into her tea. "Why should you not dash off like the rest? Be off with you."

Rina walked down the hall, trying to organize her thoughts for the day ahead. There was correspondence to return, menus to review, two candidates for kitchen maid to interview, and a score of other responsibilities. She had a host of obligations, but her mind could not fix on any one of them. No matter where she looked, she saw Edward's face. She felt his arms around her, holding her, loving her, completing her . . . then discarding her like a soiled rag. He'd cast her off, believing that she'd betrayed him. But Edward had betrayed her, too—with his passion, his gentleness, and with the terrible, wonderful wholeness she'd felt when they had became one. *But it had meant nothing to him. Nothing.*

The sound of laughter startled her. She glanced through a nearby window, and saw Sarah and David chasing their puppy across the lawn, with their distraught tutor running after them. Despite her gloom, the charming scene made her smile. She lifted her hand to wave at them, but stopped when she felt a strange tug at her heart. It was a curious feeling, as if somewhere deep inside her a cord had pulled taut—

She whirled around. Edward stood in the shadows of a nearby doorway, watching her.

She was frozen in place, but whether from fear or longing she couldn't tell. He wore mud-spattered boots and his worn riding gloves, as if he'd just ridden hell-for-leather from the mine. His black hair was tousled from the sea wind, just as it had been last night.

He walked toward her, seemingly far more concerned with adjusting his gloves than with her. He cleared his throat. "Prudence, I must speak with you."

He was every inch the lord of the manor—commanding, remote, with his emotions in complete control. Rina was not so fortunate. Her body and heart still ached from the damage he'd done to both last night. He'd taken her to heaven, then rejected her love in the coarsest terms possible. She wasn't about to let him do so again.

She lifted her chin and pronounced icily, "I would rather speak with the *devil*."

She was magnificent when she was angry, Edward thought as he watched her turn her back to him and walk coolly away down the hallway. Magnificent—and stubborn as *two* mules. She had no intention of listening to a thing

he had to say. Unfortunately, the speech he'd been prac-
ticing since dawn required that she stand still for at least
five minutes.

In three strides he was in front of her, blocking her
way. "I desire you to listen—"

"Your *desires* are no concern of mine." She tried to
push past him, using both hands to shove him aside. He
didn't budge. Undaunted, she turned on her heel and
marched off in the other direction.

"Oh, for Lord's sake!" Edward reached out and
gripped her wrist with his gloved hand. "Will you be
still?"

She twisted against his hold. "Why? So you can
insult me again as you did last night?"

He winced. "Of course not. Just hear me out." He
paused a heartbeat. "Please."

Her struggling lessened, but the defiant set of her
jaw warned him the calm would not last long. Seizing
the moment he took a deep breath and began his carefully rehearsed speech. "Prudence, last night I made a
grievous error—"

"Last night I was a *bit of muslin*. This morning I am
an *error*. If you sought not to insult me, my lord, you
chose a poor way of doing it!"

Well, his speech was out. And if she continued to
fight so vehemently against his hold, he would have to let
her go before she hurt herself. He had to make her listen
and he didn't have much time, so he cut straight to the
heart of the matter. "I found your night-shift."

"What of it? 'Tis no use to me and none to you—
unless you wish to hang it on your wall as a trophy."

God's teeth, but the woman tried his patience! He
yanked her against him, bringing her eyes level with his.
"*Listen* to me. I found your night-shift. It was stained
with blood."

"I do not care if you found a—"

Her sentence disintegrated. The angry brilliance in her eyes died, replaced by a stark, achingly young vulnerability. For an instant Edward caught a glimpse of the uncertain, fragile girl beneath the furious exterior.

"Oh," she said.

Just *Oh*. Edward had hoped for something more. Such as, *I was not meeting a man last night, but this is why I was alone in the stables half-dressed.* Or, *I was meeting a man, but there is a perfectly innocent explanation as to why.* Or, *I understand why you thought the worst of me, but I still love you . . .*

Her silence dragged on. It appeared he was not going to get any explanation from her—or one jot of forgiveness. Until this moment he hadn't realized how much he'd hoped for it. But, with or without her forgiveness, his course was set.

"My behavior was unconscionable," he continued, ignoring the ache in his heart. "I cannot change what has happened, but I can make some measure of amends. This Sunday, I will instruct the vicar to read the banns. The marriage will take place within the fortnight."

"M—marriage?!" She pulled out of his arms and stared at him in shock. "You cannot be serious."

Her disbelief rankled his already sourly tested ego. He crossed his arms over his chest, and glared at her with every ounce of his Trevelyan pride. "I can assure you that I am *most* serious. I have no intention of dismissing my responsibility to you. I have wronged you. Marriage is the only honorable course of action."

Sabrina felt as if her heart were being cut into a hundred pieces. Honor. Responsibility. But not one word of love. She recalled the near-proposal Edward had made to her as they stood on the cliffs, seven days and a lifetime ago. He'd spoken of finding a treasure beyond price, of loving her more than anyone, even Isabel. Now she was merely damaged goods, a blot on the noble escutcheon of his family name. She'd thought he couldn't hurt her any more than he had last night.

Rina breathed the only word her anguished soul could utter. "No."

His eyes widened in surprise, then narrowed to gleaming slits. "Don't be a fool. I am offering you the protection of my name. You deserve that. If nothing else, you saved my daughter's life."

"If *nothing* else," Rina cried, her voice choked with unshed tears. " 'Tis nice to know you value my virtue so highly."

"That's not what I—oh, for God's sake! We must wed, and soon. You have no choice. I might . . . I might have gotten you with child."

A child! Instinctively, her heart leapt at the thought of his seed growing inside her. But the joy died almost as soon as it was born. He'd have no more love for a child made between them than he had for her. He would see the babe as another responsibility. Another *grievous error*.

She would not let him hurt the child that might be inside her. She would not let him hurt her any more than he already had. "Your concern for your possible off-spring is touching, my lord, but a bit surprising. It is common knowledge that you did not show the same consideration to Clara Hobbs, when you got a child on her."

He went still, his jaw pulled so tight that she thought it might crack from the strain. When he spoke, his voice was so bitterly harsh that she could barely recognize it as his.

"You are right. It is *common* knowledge that the Hobbs girl's child is mine. And no self-respecting woman should marry a man she believes has done such a dishonorable thing. I shall bother you no further with my proposals."

He let go of her and strode past her out of the hall, but just as he was about to turn the corner he glanced back. His look lasted only a few seconds, but it was long enough for her to see the hollow, haunted sorrow in his eyes.

"I thought you were different from my wife. But if you can believe such things about me, then you are very like Isabel indeed."

Sabrina waited until the thundering sound of his boots had disappeared. Then she collapsed into a nearby chair, put her face in her hands, and gave herself up to an abyss of grief too vast for even tears to heal.

Thursday afternoon Lady Amy stormed into Sabrina's bedchamber. "He is a booby! A thickheaded, blue-footed booby!"

Rina glanced up from the window seat, where she had been attending to an exhaustive inventory Mrs. Poldhu had made of the pantry. "Come again?"

Amy plopped down on the cushion beside her, her blue eyes blazing with a passion Rina had never seen in them before. The girl gripped her periwinkle ribbon sash, winding it over and over around her hand. "The king of lummoxes, that's what Charles is."

"You saw him? But I thought he was in Truro."

"As did I, but when I visited Clara today she told me that he had returned. Apparently, he found the supplies he needed in St. Petroc. So I did as you suggested. I put on my prettiest dress, and went to see him. I tried to find you before I went, but you were not in your room."

"I was on a picnic with the children. I wish I had been here. I would have gone with you."

"Perhaps it is best you didn't, since the man is such a lummox."

Sabrina's heart fell. She had been so sure of the doctor's affection, so hopeful that Amy would have the love she longed for. *Honestly, I could strangle Charles.* "Oh, my dearest, I am so sorry. If the man had an ounce of sense he would be madly in love with you."

Amy's gaze dropped to her lap, and the hand winding the ribbon stilled. Her voice was soft as rose petals as she answered. "Actually, he *is* madly in love with me."

Rina shook her head. "But, if he loves you, then why is he a lummox?"

"Because he is so misguidedly honorable," Amy cried, rolling her eyes heavenward. "You would not believe what I had to go through to get him to reveal his true feelings."

Sabrina took a thorough look at her friend, noticing subtleties that she'd missed before. Amy's usually immaculate hair had been hastily pinned up by her ivory combs. Her porcelain complexion was heightened by a decidedly ruddy glow, and there was a tiny bruise at the corner of her mouth that could have been caused by a man's ardent kiss. A few days ago she might have missed the telltale signs. But those few days had given her a lifetime's worth of experience—in love, and in loss.

Protectively, she circled Amy's shoulders, all too aware of the part she'd played in this. "Darling, did you . . . I mean, did he—?"

"No, he did not," Amy interrupted, her dejected look showing that the retention of her virtue was clearly not her decision. "But he kissed me. And he—oh, Pru," she cried, hugging her arms tightly around her waist. "You cannot imagine what it feels like to have someone you love, and who loves you, hold you in his arms."

I believed I did. Since their meeting in the hall

Edward had spent almost all his waking hours at Wheal Grace. She'd caught barely a glimpse of him, and when she had his expression had been harsh and distant, without a trace of emotion. She should have been grateful that he was avoiding her. Instead, she felt more wretched and lost than ever.

There's no sense crying over a poor hand, Rina-lass. You play the cards that are dealt to ya.

The memory of Daniel Murphy's words sobered Sabrina. Good or bad, she'd been dealt her cards, and there was no sense wishing for anything different. She stuffed down the unhappiness inside her, and turned to Amy. "I am glad things have worked out for you and Charles."

"But they haven't. He will not have me. He told me that I was meant for better things than to be the wife of a poor country doctor. He says I should marry a man who can give me a life of wealth and ease. But I don't want a life of wealth and ease. I want *him*."

Tears pooled in Amy's eyes and the anguish in her expression nearly broke Rina's heart. Sighing, she drew the girl against her chest, and began smoothing her mussed, golden locks. "Don't cry, darling. Charles may be a lummox, but he is an intelligent lummox. I'm sure that eventually he will realize that you would make a fine doctor's wife. It just might take a little time."

"I do not *have* time. Charles is going away. He said that he could not bear to be near me, knowing that we can never be together. He has already applied for a position at a Welsh mine, and plans to leave the beginning of next month." She lifted her tragic gaze to Rina. "Prudence, what shall I do? I love him more than my life."

Rina shut her eyes, remembering that she had spoken the same words to Cassie when she'd "confessed" her love for Edward. His indifference to her had not changed that feeling a whit. She understood what a fragile and break-able thing the human heart was, because hers had been broken into a million pieces. She could not stand idly by and watch the same thing happen to Amy's.

"Don't worry, my dear. I will talk with Charles. He values my opinion. Tomorrow I shall call on him and tell him that I believe you will make an exemplary doctor's wife. Everything will work out, you will see."

It was a lie, of course. In a couple of days Rina's opinion would matter less than dust. But she could give Amy those days, those few precious hours of hope.

She thought back to the night she'd spent with Edward. Sometimes a few hours of hope was all that heaven allowed.

Rina made good on her promise. The next morning she had her horse saddled and rode over to the infirmary. But Charles was not there. A note posted on the door indicated that he was out seeing to a burn at the mine, and would return by the afternoon. Disappointed, she turned to young Toby, who had ridden with her. "It looks as if I have made a wasted trip."

"Not 'tirely," the lad supplied. "Mrs. Poldhu writ down some recipes for Miss Clara's mum. Wouldn't let me leave the kitchen without promising to deliver 'em personal."

Considering how jealously Mrs. Poldhu guarded her recipes, Rina was surprised she hadn't sent along an armed guard with the young man. "Well, then, you must deliver them at once," she said as she remounted her mare. "I would not like to think what Mrs. Poldhu would do if her recipes fell into the wrong hands. I will meet you on the road back to Ravenshold."

"Don't ya want to come with me, miss?"

Rina worried her lip. She cared for Clara, and knew the girl would welcome a visit. But after the accusation Rina had made to Edward—an accusation which the earl did not deny—well, facing the mother of Edward's child exceeded even Rina's courage. She shook her head and turned her mount in the opposite direction of the Hobbs's cottage. "I must return to Ravenshold. But be certain to tell Clara that I hope she is well, and that my good wishes go out to her . . . and the babe."

She started across the field beyond the village. It was a fine summer day with a cool west wind to stir the air. A rabbit sprinted into her path, and stared at her for a moment before darting back into the underbrush. Birds of all size and voice chorused in the nearby woods. The whole world brimmed with peace and contentment— except for Rina's heart. Tomorrow evening she and Quinn would be miles away with the Dutchman in her saddlebag. Her charade would end, and she would no longer have to care about what happened to Amy, Clara, or Clara's baby. And yet, Rina would care—deeply, and for the rest of her life. She could shed Prudence's name but she could not shed her love for the inhabitants of Ravenshold. *Even if one of them no longer loves me.*

"Prudence!"

The call shook Rina out of her musings. She glanced up and caught sight of Lady Rumley riding toward her out of the woods. Rina clicked to her mount and turned the reins in the lady's direction. "Cassie, 'tis good to— but what is wrong?"

"No—nothing."

Underneath her elegant sable riding hat Cassie's face was as drawn and pale as a ghost's. Concerned, Rina sidled her horse closer. "I am your friend, Cassie. If something is wrong, please tell me."

"You know me too well," the lady replied with a

tremulous smile. "Oh, my dear, the most dreadful thing has occurred. I was on my way over to Ravenshold to tell Lord Trevelyan, but I fear I lacked the courage and turned back. You see . . . Paris and I are leaving Fitzroy Hall."

Rina owned that it was an unexpected piece of news, but it hardly seemed like a confidence that Cassie would need courage to divulge—or that would engender such devastation in her countenance. "I know everyone at Ravenshold will be sorry for your absence. I hope you will not be gone too long."

"That is just it—we are not coming back. You see, I believe that my beloved brother is . . . the saboteur."

"Paris?" Rina stared at Lady Rumley in shock. She had no love for Fitzroy, but the thought of the pompous dandy as a cold-blooded assassin was ridiculous. "That is impossible. He has known Edward since he was a child. He almost married Amy. You must be mistaken."

"I only wish I were. But after Amy rejected him and we left Ravenshold, Paris began saying things in his anger—coarse and dreadful things that raised terrible suspicions in my mind. Last night I screwed up my courage and rifled through his private papers. I found . . ." She swallowed, and twisted the reins torturously in her gloved hands. "I found proof that he had been dealing with a pair of villains in St. Petroc, and that they had conspired to seed the Wheal with rotted timbers, and to cause certain accidents to occur to the inhabitants of Ravenshold . . . including cutting your horse's bridle."

A cold chill squeezed Rina's heart. Cassie's words matched the discussion she'd heard between the two ruffians in the alley of St. Petroc. The evidence pointed to Paris. And yet . . . "Cassie, I cannot believe that your brother would do such a heinous thing. Besides, the incident with my bridle happened almost two months ago, well before Amy had rejected him. He had no reason to wish ill to the Trevelyans."

"He has a great many reasons. My father spent his life traveling the globe to find a cure for our afflicted mother. In doing so he depleted much of his fortune, and ended up borrowing heavily from Edward's father. The former earl was . . . well, he was not known for his charity. He called in many of the debts suddenly and took most of my father's lands and estates. My father died a few months later, a bitter, broken man."

Rina recalled Quinn telling her the story of Charlotte's betrayal at the former Lord Trevelyan's hands. If the earl had so ill-used one of his own, she could easily imagine him taking advantage of Cassie's father, whose only crime was loving his wife. "But Paris was to wed Amy, at least until a few days ago. Her dowry would have returned much of what your family had lost. Only a madman would jeopardize a family he wishes to marry into."

Cassie went still. When she spoke, her voice was so cold that it brought winter to the sunny afternoon. "You know that my mother was ill, but I never told you the nature of her illness. Soon after my birth she was diagnosed with advanced melancholia, which grew worse as the years passed. For over a decade she has been sequestered in an institution—hopelessly insane."

"Oh, my Lord," Rina breathed. As a girl on the London streets she'd seen a woman who was carted off to Bedlam. She was tied up to prevent her from scratching her own eyes out, and she was screaming at the top of her lungs. The horrible sight had haunted Rina's dreams for months. "You poor darling. What you must have gone through to keep this secret. But you did not have to go through it alone. I'm sure if the earl knew, he would help."

"As his father helped us?" For an instant Cassie's usually serene eyes flashed fire, but the ire died in an instant. "Forgive me. Edward has shown nothing but kindness to Paris and myself, which makes my brother's actions all the more despicable. That is why I am taking him away from here—to distance him from the people he sought to harm."

"But what of his crimes?" Rina cried, her own ire rising. "His actions almost cost Edward his life—and the lives of Sarah and David, too. I cannot let him walk away, Cassie. Paris must pay for his crimes."

"You are right. But I thought if I could take him away from this place—perhaps find some treatment for his disease—he might escape my mother's fate . . . but that is not to be." She lifted her chin, and looked at Rina with serenely tragic eyes. "I suppose that is why I told you, when I could tell no one else. I knew you would help convince me to do the honorable thing, because you yourself are so honorable, and have no secrets shadowing your life."

Rina had secrets, all right—secrets so dark and devious that they made Cassie's lies shine like the sun. Murderer. Fugitive. And, by tomorrow, thief as well. She had no right to pass judgment, on Paris, or on anyone. *As long as Edward and the children are safe, that's all that really matters.* "You will . . . take him far away from here?"

Cassie pressed her fist against her lips, stifling a sob of joy. "Oh, yes, I shall," she promised tearfully. "And if he ever so much as looks in the direction of Cornwall, I will contact the authorities immediately. Paris will understand that. In time, I believe he will thank me for it. And you, too, my dear friend, Prudence."

Lady Rumley wheeled her mount toward Fitzroy Hall, but before she clicked to her horse she stopped, and pulled back on the reins. She glanced around to Rina and paused, seeming to think twice about what she was to say. "I suppose this is none of my concern, especially since I am leaving today. But I must know. The other day in the sitting room, when we were trading secrets . . . 'Tis Edward you love, isn't it?"

Rina swallowed, then gave a quick nod. It would have done no good to deny it. Cassie would have seen the truth in her eyes anyway.

Cassie's face brightened into an angelic, portrait-perfect smile. "Then I wish you all the happiness that I wished for Isabel, on the day when that sweet lady graced our shore."

In her mind's eye Rina caught a glimpse of a wedding party, with her in a dress of white satin that sparkled in the late summer sunlight. Edward stood at her side in his finest black coat, his demeanor stern and lordly, but his harsh countenance softened by a smile so loving it stopped her breath. The vision was so clear that it brought a bittersweet lump to her throat. But such a future was not to be.

She turned her mare toward the road that led to Ravenshold, but she hadn't gone a quarter mile before she heard the pounding of hooves behind her. Toby was riding toward her, kicking poor old Socrates into a full gallop. "Miss, miss, come quick!"

Rina sighed, out of patience with the young man's crises. "Toby, I have had my fill of surprises for one day. This one will just have to wait."

"But it *can't* wait," the breathless lad cried. "Miss Clara's 'avin' her baby. And there's not a soul in the village who'll help her!"

Chapter Twenty-five

Rina soaked a cloth in cool water, and started to bathe Clara's forehead. "Only a little while longer, dear."

The girl attempted to give her a wavering smile, but the expression ended in a sharp wince as the pain knotted through her. Rina took Clara's hand, trying not to wince herself as the girl squeezed it to the bone. Rina glanced around the small bedroom, willing the door to open and help to step through. It remained resolutely shut. Swallowing panic, Rina reminded herself that it had been only a little over an hour since she'd sent Toby to fetch Dr. Williams. But it felt like ten hours. Ten *years*.

Clara started to thrash her head against the pillows, her eyes glazed in pain-induced confusion. "Momma? Where's Momma?"

Rina smoothed Clara's damp hair, and spoke with a calm she did not feel. "You remember, Clara. You told me yourself. Your mother went to visit your aunt in St. Petroc." And is not due to be back until late this evening, she added silently. *Where the blazes is Charles?*

Clara thrashed again. "And my love? Where is my love?"

Her cry broke Rina's heart. Clara was still in love with her baby's father, even though the man had cast her aside to bear their child in shame. It wasn't right that Clara should still care for the blackguard, but Rina had learned that right and wrong didn't matter much when it came to love. She still loved Edward, even after what he'd done to her. Even after what he had done to this poor girl . . .

The door opened.

"Charles, thank heaven! I was beginning to despair—" Rina's relief died as Amy stepped into the room. "Where is Charles?"

"I do not know," Amy said as she stripped off her gloves and deposited them along with her reticule on the bedside table. "I met Toby on the south road, and came at once. How is she?"

"She is—" Rina bit her tongue, realizing that her true opinion of Clara's condition was the last thing the suffering girl needed to hear. "She's doing just fine," she stated, so that Clara could hear her. Then she stood up and nodded her head toward the door. "Amy, we need more cloths and hot water from the kitchen . . ."

Once out of earshot, Rina gave Amy a true picture of the young girl's condition. She told Amy about the painful contractions, and the fading in and out of Clara's reason. "But 'tis more than just the physical pain. Clara's spirit is disheartened. Her mother is away, her neighbors will not lift a hand to help her, and the villain who did this to her has washed his hands of her. She feels as if she hasn't a friend in the world."

"Well, she is wrong in that. She has us," Lady Amy stated as she efficiently started to roll up her sleeves. "I hope that young Toby finds Charles in time, but if he does not, we shall have to attend to this ourselves."

Rina did not share her friend's confidence. "Amy, have you ever been present at a birthing?"

Amy's confidence faltered momentarily. "Well, not precisely. But I assisted in a number of foalings and calvings over the years—at least, until my pompous governess deemed such behavior unseemly for a lady. As if *anything* to do with Ravenshold could be unseemly to a Trevelyan. In any event, I assume the birth of a baby is much the same as that of a cow or horse. But what about you, Prudence? Have you attended a birthing?"

"N—no," Rina answered hesitantly. It was not entirely a lie. She had not actually witnessed her brother's birth. It was only afterward that she'd peeked into the room and seen her mother's motionless body, and spied the pitifully small bundle of the child who'd been born too soon. She'd heard the choking sounds of her father weeping, smelled the viscous odors of blood, terror, and death, felt the numbing despair that would warp her dreams into nightmares for years to come.

Rina reminded herself that her mother had been older and weakened by influenza, and that Clara was a healthy young girl. Still, such assurances could not stop the memories that filled her with the fear, the despair, and the paralyzing thoughts of a helpless child who'd watched her safe, happy world crumble to dust.

Rina and Amy gathered the cloths and water and returned to the bedroom. Another hour passed without the doctor. Then another. Afternoon shadows stretched and lengthened across the wooden floor like gaunt, spindly spiders. Clara faded in and out of lucidity as her pains grew sharper and more frequent. Rina and Amy took turns mopping the girl's brow and holding her hand, but as the final hour ticked by Amy pulled Rina aside.

"I fear we cannot wait any longer for Charles. Her time is almost here. We will have to bring this babe into the world by ourselves." Amy glanced back at Clara, who looked pitifully fragile and as pale as the sheets she lay against. "The child is coming. We must do what we can to help."

"I . . . don't know if I can," Rina whispered brokenly. "Amy, I lied to you before. Years ago I saw a birth, and it went terribly wrong. The mother and the baby both . . . well, I do not think I can face that again."

Amy gripped her hand almost as tightly as Clara had. "Pru, you *must*. I cannot do this alone. I can tend her body and deliver the babe, but you must tend her spirit and keep her calm. You must try. For Clara's sake. For my sake. And maybe for the sake of that poor woman you saw die all those years ago—"

Clara's scream swallowed her words.

Amy rushed back to the bed, casting a final pleading look at Rina. In that instant Rina realized that Amy was almost as distressed as she was. But Amy valiantly hid that fear as she arranged the bedclothes for the birth. She worked with the single-minded diligence that marked the Trevelyan breed, and Rina felt a new respect for her friend. But that respect was tempered by a soul-deep fear.

The birth was not going well. Clara's eyes were ringed white with pain and panic, and her strength was spent from months of disdain and abandonment. Her breath was shallow, her brow clammy, and the fear in her eyes grew with every contraction. The girl might die. The baby might die. *Edward's baby* . . .

Clara screamed again.

"Push, Clara," Amy cried. "Pru, tell her to push!"

For a moment Rina could say nothing. The smell of blood and the cries of terror were her childhood nightmares come to life. But she was no longer a child. She wasn't the lost little girl who'd stood helplessly by as her mother's life ebbed away. She was a strong and capable woman, tempered to steel by the trials of life, who had a family who loved her, and a man she loved. She was no longer helpless, lost, or alone.

She leaned over Clara, planting her arms for the girl to grip on to. "Listen to me, Clara. You are going to be all right. Your baby is going to be all right. You are not alone, not anymore. Now *push!*"

From that moment on the three girls struggled as one to bring the baby into the world. Clara's cries, Amy's commands, and Rina's encouragement blended together into one fighting voice. And just when they thought the babe would never come, she slipped out with ease and into Amy's waiting arms.

An hour later Charles barged into the room, his hat missing and his glasses askew from his ride across the moors. The fear in his eyes changed to relief as he saw Clara sleeping peacefully in her bed. His relief turned to wonder as he caught sight of Amy asleep in the rocking chair by the brazier, with a tiny, contented baby in her arms. "What the—?"

Rina lifted a cautioning finger to her lips. She got up from beside Clara's bed where she'd been holding her hand, and shepherded the amazed doctor out the door. "They all need their rest. 'Twas a difficult birth."

Charles rubbed his chin. "I feared as much. If I had suspected the child would come so soon, I would never have left the village today. I'm grateful you were here to help her. Quite possibly, you saved her life."

"No. You are wrong to give me the credit. If I had been here alone, Clara and her baby would have surely died. Amy is the one who deserves your praise." Rina gave him a brief description of Amy's courage and coolheadedness during the dangerous birth. When she had finished, she crossed her arms and gave the doctor a meaningful glance. "Amy told me what happened between you two yesterday. After what I witnessed this afternoon, I can promise you that she would make an exemplary doctor's wife."

Charles swallowed, his usually sober eyes raw with very unsober emotion. "I . . . know that. I knew it yesterday. But I cannot condemn her to my austere life. No matter how hard I work, I will never be a rich man. I can never give her the things she has grown up with, the things she deserves—"

"She deserves to be *loved*. She does not want an empty life of wealth. If she did, she would have accepted Fitzroy's proposal. But I will own that you are probably right—if you go away, she will eventually marry someone who can give her all the things you believe she needs. She will be wealthy, but she will never be truly happy. Her brave spirit will suffocate under silks and satins, her heart will grow cold and hard without love. Is that what you want for her?"

"Of course not!" He stroked back his hair with both hands, his voice tortured with frustration. "But do you not see it is impossible for us? I have nothing to offer her. Nothing!"

Rina's expression softened as she looked up at the earnest face of the man she'd come to care for as a brother. "You are wrong. You can offer her a life filled with purpose and meaning. You can offer her your faith that you trust her enough to share that life with you. But, most of all, you can offer her your heart. That is all the wealth she needs. Indeed, 'tis the only wealth worth having." She reached out and wrapped her hands around his. "What Amy *needs* is a husband who can love her with all his heart. She needs you, Charles. And unless you are the world's biggest fool, you will see that you need her just as much."

For a long moment Charles remained silent, his

head bent in thought. Rina held her breath, hoping that some of her words had gotten through. More than anyone, she knew how rare and precious real love was. And how empty life was without it.

Charles cleared his throat. "I believe—" he began, then stopped to clear his throat again. "I believe I should discuss this with Lady Amy. A frank and sober examination of the future is not out of order."

Rina's mouth ticked up. The doctor's sensible words could not mask the hope in his voice. "A wise choice," she offered as she gave his hands an encouraging squeeze. "Wait here. I will send Amy out to you."

"But I should see to Clara and the baby—"

"They can wait a few more minutes. I cannot say the same for you." She opened the door and slipped through.

A minute later Sabrina stood beside the closed bedroom door with the baby in her arms, listening to the muffled sound of voices on the other side. She could not make out their words, but she noted when those words ended abruptly, the sudden silence marked only by hushed murmurs and soft sighs. Sighing herself, Rina stepped away from the door, and smiled down at the tiny, gurgling baby. "Well, young lady, it appears as if those two will live happily ever after. Perhaps you and I should hang out a shingle as matchmakers?"

The baby stared up at Sabrina with serious blue eyes under a shock of chestnut hair. *Blue eyes*, Rina thought as she smoothed her finger against the baby's cheek. She knew that all newborns had blue eyes, but there was something about their color that stirred her memory. *I suppose 'tis because I recognize Edward in her. But I expected her eyes to be darker, like Sarah's and David's . . .*

A soft cry from the bed shook Sabrina from her thoughts. "Miss Prudence? My baby, is she—?"

"She is fine," Rina said as she hurried to Clara, and laid the child in her mother's arms. "She is the healthiest baby I have ever seen. And the most beautiful."

"She is, isn't she?" Clara whispered, her voice weak with happiness and exhaustion. She cuddled her daughter, staring at her with love and awe. "You're the prettiest baby in the whole world, you are. And lucky, too. Got his blue eyes. And his 'andsome chestnut hair."

Rina froze. "*Chestnut* hair?"

"Aye," Clara murmured as she slipped back toward unconsciousness. "Chestnut hair, groomed perfect fine. So handsome, my gentleman. So lovely elegant . . ."

The girl drifted back to sleep without finishing her sentence. True to the man she still loved, Clara had not revealed her sweetheart's name. But is hardly mattered. The baby's hair color, coupled with Clara's muddled words, revealed the father's name as clearly as if it were written in the family Bible. Rina stared down at the girl, her heart hammering so hard that she could barely breathe.

"Paris," she muttered.

Thunder rolled through the halls of Ravenshold as the clock chimed eleven.

The two sounds echoed through the vast, empty corridors before fading to lonely silence. Grimacing, Sabrina shifted uneasily in the gilt and velvet chair stationed across from Edward's rooms. The ornate antique dated to the reign of France's Sun King and had clearly been built more for beauty than comfort—and she'd been sitting in the blasted thing over an hour. Still, the discomfort in her body was nothing compared to the discomfort in her mind. Even her pleasure over Amy's soon-to-be-announced engagement did not lessen her disquiet. She had an apology to deliver. A huge one. And she had to deliver it tonight. In the morning there would be no chance to see him alone before he left for the mine. And in the evening, she would be gone.

She bit her lip, fighting against the quicksand of anguish that lay just beneath her discomfort. The apology wasn't the only reason she was here. She wanted to see him. *Had* to see him, even though she knew it was foolish beyond measure. He didn't love her, didn't want her, and—after tomorrow—would speak her name in the same betraying breath as his wife's. Seeing him tonight would accomplish nothing. Except that she could apologize for thinking the worst of him. Except that she could tell him that she believed in him, even if that belief meant nothing.

Except that she could see his face and hear his voice one last time.

A flicker of candlelight caught her eye. Rina watched as the Earl of Trevelyan trudged down the empty hall holding a single taper. She started to rise, but her legs wouldn't move. Frozen in place, she drank in the sight of the man she loved beyond reason, cherishing the confidence of his step and taut power of his body that was evident despite his weariness. His greatcoat was soaked through from the storm, and his dark hair was plastered against his forehead. *Someone should make him take better care of himself,* she thought automatically. A sharp pain stroked through her as she remembered that that someone would not be her. "Edward?"

Quick as a cat he whirled around, holding his candle high. His dark eyes widened slightly when he caught sight of her, but that was the only sign of emotion in his face. "You should be asleep."

"I know, but I—" Her carefully planned words vanished like smoke under his intense gaze. "Edward, I wanted—"

He held up his palm, silencing her. His stern gaze glared past her down the hallway. "Is there something you wanted, Mary Rose?"

Surprised, Rina looked around and saw the maid detach herself from the shadows she'd been half hiding in. "Uhm, no, my lord. That is, Cook was wondering if you'd be wanting some supper."

The earl's mouth twitched up with the barest hint of humor. "Tell *Cook* that I am not hungry. You may go."

The maid's glance flickered between Prudence and the earl. Then she bobbed a curtsey, and scurried off into the darkness. Edward watched her go, his mouth settling back in its cold, harsh lines. "Unless you wish your words discussed openly in the servants' hall, Miss Winthrope, I suggest we continue this in my rooms."

He pushed open his door. Rina hesitated an instant, then stepped into the room, feeling oddly unnerved as he shut the door behind them. She drew her cashmere shawl around her, shivering. *'Tis like being sealed in a tomb.*

He must have noticed her shiver because he walked over to the hearth, and set a pair of heavy logs on the banked fire. He picked up the poker, and began to coax the embers into a hearty blaze. Without looking up he asked, "What was it you wanted to say to me?"

She rubbed her arms, wishing she couldn't so clearly remember the feel of his coaxing hands on her body. "I wanted to . . . that is . . . well . . ."

He glanced back at her and arched a sarcastic brow. "Fascinating. Is this sparkling narrative to end soon, or should I put another log on the fire?"

Honestly, he was the *rudest* of men. "Another log shall not be necessary, my lord. I simply wanted to tell you that Clara Hobbs had her baby, and—"

"And you wanted to inform me of the birth of my child," he finished coldly. He turned back to the fire and stabbed the logs with a vengeance. "You are *too* kind, Miss Winthrope. Now if you don't mind, I'd like some peace. I've had a hell of a day."

"So have I," she replied, her temper quickening. "It was a difficult birth, though both mother and baby are fine. You do not have to be so surly."

"*Surly?*" With the poker still clutched in his hand he crossed the room like an angry god, with his eyes blazing lightning and his voice booming thunder. "You'd be surly too, if you narrowly averted an explosion in Wheal Grace's outdated steam boiler, nearly broke your back helping to carry ore to the stripping washes when the tram rail buckled, and listened while some superstitious idiot spread rumors of a Tommy knocker on the mine's lowest level. I reached the end of my rope hours ago, so you'll forgive me if I don't leap for joy when a self-righteous female accuses me of fathering a son on a girl I barely know."

"I'm not self-righteous," Rina fired back. "Besides, Clara had a daughter. And I know she isn't yours!"

Edward's poker thumped to the carpet. "You . . . know?"

Rina drew as shaky breath, and nodded. "I . . . I should have believed you from the first. 'Tis unconscionable that I believed the worst of you without proof. Absolutely—"

"Prudence," he said quietly.

"Absolutely unconscionable," she continued, her words flooding out in a deluge of remorse. "You were right to compare me to Isabel. Except that my crime is far worse than hers, because she wasn't with you all the time and I was, and I should have known that you could never do such an ungallant thing to a poor—"

"Prudence."

"—girl like Clara. You would never misuse your authority in such a reprehensible way, never. In my heart I knew that you could not—'twas only my foolish head that told me otherwise. And because of that I hurt you and I'm sorry because I'd rather died than—"

"Prudence!"

His roar silenced her. She looked into his eyes—eyes as unreadable as the sea. He smelled of the storm. Raindrops glittered in his dark hair like an ancient crown. She licked her lips that had suddenly gone dry. "I'm sorry, Edward," she whispered. "I should not have doubted you."

"You had ample cause," he said, as he reached up and brushed away tears she didn't even realize she was crying. "You are the most *confounding* of women."

She blinked, and gave a slightly inelegant sniff. "I do not mean to be."

His stormy gaze softened. "I know. And that is the most confounding thing of all."

Absently, he traced his rough thumb across her cheekbone. Too late, she realized that she'd wanted more from their last meeting together than to see his face and hear his voice. She wanted him to kiss her. It didn't matter that he didn't love her. It didn't matter that he thought of her as a grievous error. She was nothing to him, but that did not matter either. She needed to feel his mouth on hers one last time. Swallowing, she tilted her lips toward his, and—

He stepped away.

Clamping his hands behind him, the earl went to the fire. With his back still to her, he continued. "Tomorrow

I will be leaving for Truro on business. When I am finished I . . . will not be returning to Ravenshold."

Sabrina blinked in surprise. "You cannot leave Ravenshold. It is your home."

"It was once. But now . . ." He rubbed his eyes. "Everyone at Ravenshold will be better off without me."

"That is not true," she stated, moving to stand beside him at the hearth. He looked so lost—just as he had on the afternoon she'd spoken with him in the nursery. Her heart somersaulted in her chest. "Edward, you cannot leave Ravenshold. Your grandmother and your sister love you. Your children—"

"—will be better off without me," he finished grimly. "It seems to be my lot in life to damage that which I hold most dear. My wife. My children. You."

Rina gripped the mantel. Had he called her *dear*? But she must have misheard him over the crackle of the flames. She was merely a responsibility to him—an error. "I know that you feel an obligation toward me, but—"

His bitter laugh cut her off. "I fell a *profound* obligation toward you, Miss Winthrope. But that obligation does not extend to seeing you day in and day out, treating you with polite courtesy as if we were little more than strangers, watching you live your life—a life that I will never be a part of. And in the end, watching you share that life with another, better man."

He stroked back his damp hair with both hands, and breathed a soul-deep sigh. "I understand why you turned down my proposal. I wronged you beyond all forgiveness. But I cannot endure the farce that my life would become if I stayed here with you. The world is a wide place—wide enough for a man to get lost in. If I look hard enough, I might find a place where I can find some measure of peace, and forget that I love you."

Rina struggled for breath, finally managing a strangled, "You . . . love me?"

"I never stopped. But I know that you do not feel the same, and I would not try to change—"

His words ended abruptly as she threw her arms around his neck and stopped his mouth with a kiss.

Chapter Twenty-six

'Tis a dream, Edward thought. Dreams of her had tortured him since their night in the stable. In a moment he'd wake up, stiff as a pike and aching for the burning heaven he'd found in her arms. But the hot, honeyed mouth fused with his tasted real. The lush curves under his questing hands felt real. And the carnal lust that speared through him made him feel alive for the first time since their night together. Groaning, he plundered her mouth, losing himself in the sweet madness of her caress. *Dear Lord, if this is a dream, do not ever let me wake up.*

But when the dream struggled to unfasten his greatcoat and breathed an unladylike oath when she couldn't, he realized this was no dream. This was the woman he'd dishonored, the woman he loved. He would not shame her again. Gritting his teeth, he forced himself to hold her at arm's length. "You can't . . . want this. I deflowered you. You do not love me. I know and accept that."

Her mouth curved into her bewitching smile. "But I do love you. I have always loved you. Even when I thought you'd fathered Clara's child. Even when you said my love meant nothing—"

"It meant everything," he confessed roughly. "But I was afraid to believe it. And because I was afraid, I hurt you." He reached up and tenderly brushed his fingers across her cheek. "I can still see that hurt in your eyes."

"Then take it away," she breathed, her eyes shining with new tears. "Only you can, Edward. Only you—"

Her words stopped as he captured her mouth in a devouring kiss.

They burned together like holy fire, knowing the glory that lay ahead and fighting toward it with every ounce of their strength. They struggled out of their clothing, laughing when he ripped the sleeve of her dress, and again when she fell on her backside removing one of his boots. He realized they'd never laughed with each other, and the pleasure of it was every bit as erotic as her adventurous hands and her lush, sweet mouth. They laughed and struggled and caressed until they were both naked and he had her beneath him on the carpet in front of the hearth, with her glorious hair pooled around her.

Her beauty stole his breath. The firelight licked her curves and hollows like a lover's caress. His hungry gaze roamed over her body as he gorged himself on her sweet breasts, her wanton hips, and the soft dusting of auburn hair that nestled at the apex of her thighs. Her throaty moan drew his gaze to her face, and he saw that she was studying him, too. Her widened eyes had boldly fastened on the part of him that most plainly showed his desire.

She whispered brokenly, "In the stable . . . the darkness . . . I didn't know you were so . . . substantial."

Edward grinned like a schoolboy, knowing she didn't realize what a remark like that did to his ego. "Glad you approve," he chuckled. "And fortunate, since this is the only *substantial* man you're going to see."

He expected her to share the joke. Instead, she turned her head to the side. She was quick, but not quick enough for him to miss the flash of shame in her eyes, and the gleam of remembered terror that said far more than words ever could. A wave of nausea washed over him. *Christ, not to her.* He gripped her chin and brought her back to face him. "Who was he?"

"It doesn't matter. He didn't . . ."

"He tried," Edward growled. "And it matters like hell. Some bastard tried to force himself on you. I want his name."

"Albert," she whispered. "He's . . . dead."

He's lucky, Edward thought. Any death would have been more pleasant than the one the earl would have given the foul cur. Questions crowded his mind. How did it happen? When did it happen? And where had the bastard touched her? He wanted to know everything, but this wasn't the time. She needed to forget what happened, to remember the cherishing love and honor that a man's touch could yield. *His* touch.

He lowered his mouth to her breast, and suckled her with slow, searing kisses. She gasped and buried her fingers in his hair, her eyes glittering with the passion of her present, not the shadows of her past. She arched against him and breathed a guttural moan. Smiling, he continued his tender assault, devouring her sensitive waist and belly with wet, wicked caresses until he claimed her swollen center with a delving intimacy that left them both gasping. She gripped the carpet, writhing with aching need. "Now, Edward. I need you."

Blood thundered through his veins. He was as hot and wanting as she was, but he held back. He positioned himself over her, staring into her eyes. "I need *you*," he breathed, his words coming out in tight rasps. "Touch me. God, I need you to touch me."

A flicker of uncertainty crossed her eyes. He bent down and took her mouth in a deep, carnal caress. A deep moan echoed from one throat, but he couldn't tell if it was his or hers. They were still kissing when she took him in her hand. The glory of it shuddered through him. Raising her hips, she spread her legs and guided him to her yearning core, welcoming him with every part of her body and soul. They moved as one, joining together in the same blinding magic that had consumed them in the stable. He drove into her, wedding his strength to her softness until he could no longer tell where his soul ended and hers began. And when the madness shattered them, he fell to the carpet beside her and pulled her close and, with the last of his strength, pressed a final, cherishing kiss against her brow.

Sabrina woke in Edward's bed, lying against his warm chest, with his arm curled possessively around her shoulders. Sometime during the night he'd carried her to his bedchamber, saying it was high time she became acquainted with it. Her lips curved into a secret smile as she recalled exactly what that *acquaintance* had entailed.

Sighing contentedly, she snuggled closer to his chest, lulled by the gentle rise and fall of his breathing, feeling completely safe and protected for the first time in her life. *And loved*. She opened her eyes, and gazed up into the sleeping face of the man who'd given her more love in one night than she'd had in a lifetime. His face was turned to the side and his other arm was bent behind his head on the pillow. His dark hair was ragged and wild from their passion, and a shock of it had fallen across his forehead. He looked achingly young. Unable to resist, she reached up to smooth his hair, but her hand stilled when she realized that the soft light coming through the window was the first questing fingers of dawn.

Dawn. The servants. She imagined the maid coming

into her room to deliver the morning chocolate. Speculation would ensue. Tongues would wag. Before long Mary Rose would add the tidbit that she'd seen Miss Winthrope and the earl together last night. . . .

She had to return to her room at once. Casting a final look at her lover she started to gently pull herself out of his embrace.

The arm around her shoulder didn't budge.

She glanced back at his face, and saw his eyes watching her with intense pleasure. His mouth pulled up in a wicked grin. "And where do you think you're going?"

His rough growl melted her bones like beeswax. She swallowed, barely hanging on to her good sense. "I must return to my room. 'Tis nearly dawn, and you know what will happen if the servants find out that we . . . well, if the servants find out."

Edward settled deeper into the pillows. "Hmm. Yes, I see. The news will spread through the county like wildfire. You'll be scandalized. I'll be beyond redemption. We'll have to marry immediately." He closed his eyes and gave a sleepy yawn. "I do not see the problem."

She breathed a frustrated sigh. "My lord, you are—"

He opened one eye. "Substantial?"

"Incorrigible," she finished, blushing furiously. "You cannot be drawn into a scandal. Think of your grandmother. Think of your children."

His hand skimmed down her arm and circled her waist, pulling her against the powerful length of his naked body. "I *am* thinking of my children. Yours and mine."

Every ounce of air left Rina's lungs. The thought of marrying him and bearing his children filled her with a happiness she could barely contain—and an agony so profound she could barely conceal it. Edward's loving her didn't change the fact that she'd lied to him and his family—or that she was a murderer.

She turned away, keeping her eyes from his as she answered. "Sir, if you think to rob me of a proper proposal—with flowers and music and you down on one knee—you are sadly mistaken. Now, I really must return to my rooms."

She twisted agilely and pulled out of his arms. He made no move to hold her. Believing he was finally agreeing with her, she pushed back the covers and started to slip out of the bed.

The next heartbeat she was spread-eagle on the sheets, pinned under Edward's body. Grinning, he leaned down and whispered against her ear. "And if you think I'm going to let you out of here without an answer, *you* are the one who is sadly mistaken."

He nuzzled her neck, scorching her flesh with moist, unhurried caresses. Rina bit back a gasp. The man was a complete scoundrel when it came to getting his way. Her eyes drifted shut and the sweet ache built inside her. "My lord . . . you are not . . . playing fair."

"I play to win, my darling. And I mean to win you. But for now I will settle for a 'Yes.' We can discuss the particulars when I return."

Her eyes flew open. "You are leaving?"

"I still have business in Truro to attend to." He took her face between his hands, and placed a gentle kiss on the tip of her nose. "Don't look so bereft. I will only be gone a few days. Now nothing could keep me from returning to Ravenshold . . . and you."

By the time Edward returned she and Quinn would be long gone, and Edward would be cursing her name. She closed her eyes, concealing a despair that she could never let him see. "I love you."

Sighing, he leaned his forehead against hers. "I know you do, sweetheart. But I also know that your clever little mind has more twists and turns than a rabbit warren. I want a straight answer before I leave." He lifted his head, and stared down at her with an intense gaze. "Will you marry me?"

She saw the uncertainty in his eyes, the edge of the despair that had almost destroyed him after his wife left. He needed her as much as she needed him. Rina swallowed. He loved her. He might even love her enough to forgive her deception and marry her. But she was still a murderer. She could not have him tying his heart to a criminal. Even if they tried to keep it a secret, the truth would eventually come out. And the scandal would destroy him and everyone else at Ravenshold.

She looked up into his rugged face, studying every cherished line and beloved hollow, branding the memory on her heart. Then she gave him the only promise she could. "I shall never marry anyone but you."

His smile lit the room like the sun.

She wove her fingers through his hair, pulling him down against her open mouth in a fierce, desperate caress. Her sudden passion surprised him, but his startled exclamation changed instantly into a growl of pure lust. They rolled on the sheets, their limbs and hearts tangled together in a love so hot that it nearly melted their souls. She gave herself to him completely, loving him with her body the way she could not with her words. In strokes and groans and fiery kisses she recited her silent marriage vows. And afterward, when he'd drifted into an exhausted and blissful sleep, she brushed a cherishing kiss across his lips, and slipped out of his arms forever.

"If you please, Miss Winthrope. The dowager would like to see you in her rooms."

Sabrina glanced up from her needlework at the politely bobbing maid. It was a welcome interruption—

the poor cherub she'd been attempting to stitch all morning looked more like an overgrown melon. She'd only undertaken the activity to try to take her mind off Edward. As if anything could erase the memory of their passionate night together . . .

"Miss?"

"Oh, y-yes," Rina stammered. "Thank you, Violet. I'll attend Grandmother directly." *And I'd best have a few more of my wits about me when I do.*

The dowager's apartment was decorated all in blue, with a view of the sun-dappled sea through her windows. When Rina entered, the glass panes were thrown open, letting in the salt breeze and the low thunder of the distant surf.

"Prudence."

Rina whirled around, surprised by the weariness in Lady Penelope's voice. That surprise turned to alarm when she saw that the dowager was lying in bed, pale against the azure pillows. She ran to the bedside. "Grandmother, you're ill!"

"I'm old," Lady Penelope corrected as she pushed herself to a sitting position. "There is no cure for that. Now, do not fuss. I get these spells every so often. They pass with rest."

"Then I will come back later when you are stronger."

"Later will not do. I've an important matter to discuss with you, my dear."

"Surely it can wait until you are feeling stronger."

"It most certainly cannot. I told you once that little happens in this house without my knowledge." Her weariness dropped away as she squared her shoulders. "You spent last night in my grandson's rooms, and I want to know what you mean to do about it."

Chapter Twenty-seven

This time it was Sabrina who turned pale. "I . . . I believe you are mistaken. I *did* speak with the earl in his rooms last night, but I left—"

"At five in the morning. In a torn dress. With your hair in a tangle. My source was very thorough. I am old, my dear, but not so old that I cannot recall what a woman looks like when she's just been made love to."

Rina bent her head, a fierce blush creeping up her throat. "I suppose 'twould be useless to deny it."

"A prudent observation," Lady Penelope proclaimed. A touch of scandal definitely brought the roses back to her cheeks. She leaned over and patted the bed beside her, urging Sabrina to sit down. "Now, I ask you again. What do you intend to do about it?"

I mean to steal your necklace and break all your hearts, Rina thought bleakly. "Perhaps you should ask Edward when he returns."

The dowager hurumphed. "That boy has been angry as a bee-stung bear ever since you arrived. Any fool with eyes could have seen he was mad for you. The fact he took you into his bed proves it—Edward would not have done such a thing unless he intends to make you his bride. But, while I have always been certain of my grandson's heart, I am not so sure of yours."

She leaned forward, her proud countenance revealing an uncharacteristic vulnerability. "Edward's father, my son, was a disappointment to me. He cared for nothing save money and power. But Edward has his grandfather's spirit. Every time I look at him, I see the image of my own dear Henry . . ." She paused, and wiped a tear from her eye. "Edward has a bold and generous heart, but Isabel nearly destroyed it. Another false love might finish the job. So I need to know—do you or do you not love my grandson?"

Sabrina turned her gaze to the window. For a moment she watched the seagulls wheel and dip over the open water, and listened to their lost, plaintive cries. "I love him," she confessed hesitantly. Then the sob that had been building in her throat broke free, and she threw herself into the dowager's arms. "Oh, Grandmother, I love him *dreadfully*."

She cried against Lady Penelope's shoulder, weeping out her anguish in raking sobs. The old woman stroked her hair, cradling the girl in her arms in a way no one had done since Rina's mother died. "Honestly, you children—always weathering some crisis or another. I've no doubt you and Edward will have your share of stormy seas, but if you love one another everything will come out right in the end. Now, you dry your eyes. I have something I want to give you."

Rina loved the old woman dearly, but her staunch belief that she and Edward would find happiness was like a knife in her heart. Scrubbing away the last of her tears, she slipped off the satin bedcover. "I appreciate your advice, Grandmother. But I assure you, I want nothing from—"

Her words died as Lady Penelope placed the Dutchman's Necklace into her hands.

Rina stared at the diamonds, pouring their glittering beauty over and over again between her fingers. Somewhere, as if over a vast distance, she heard the dowager's voice.

". . . given to me by my husband on our wedding night. I always intended to pass it on to Isabel, but something held me back. I think now it must have been because, as much as I cared for the girl, she was not the right woman for my grandson. She did not love Ravenshold as Edward did—as a Trevelyan must. But you have always loved this land—I saw it in your eyes the day you arrived at Ravenshold. You can share that part of my grandson's soul that he could never share with his first wife."

She reached up and brushed Rina's cheek. "I used to fear what would happen to my dear boy and my family after I am gone. I fear it no longer. You have brought love and laughter back to this household, back to all of us. Take the Dutchman, my dear. Wear it proudly. It is your birthright, for you are one of us. You are, in every way that matters, a true Trevelyan."

The Dutchman's Necklace was the reason she had come to this place, the fortune she had been risking her neck for all these months. She didn't have to sneak into the dowager's rooms. She didn't have to break into the safe. All she had to do was slip the gems into her pocket, and leave them there until she met Quinn later on this evening. She could almost hear Daniel Murphy's voice whispering in her ear. *Your ship's come in, Rina-lass. I always told you it would.*

All she had to do was to lie to an old woman one last time. What was one more lie on top of the hundreds she had already told? The family would find out the truth about her in a few days anyway. Lady Luck had dumped a fortune into her hands—she would be England's biggest fool not to take it.

She lifted her gaze, prepared to falsely reassure the dowager that the necklace, and her grandson's heart, would be safe in her care. She met Lady Penelope's eyes—eyes that gleamed brighter than any gemstone. Edward's eyes. *You are, in every way that matters, a true Trevelyan.*

Make that the *world's* biggest fool, Sabrina thought as she handed the necklace back to the dowager.

"Take a deep breath, Quinn," Rina said as she pounded him on the back. "Yes, that's it. You will be all right in a minute."

"The *hell* I will! You gave it back. You had the Dutchman in your hand, yours for the takin', and you gave it ba—"

He gripped his chest, seized by another fit of sputtering coughing. Rina made him sit down on the stone fence that ran beside the little-used back road Quinn had chosen for their evening rendezvous. "You must try to relax. Otherwise you might injure your health."

"That's rich. You throw away the only chance we 'ad for a future, and you're worried about my health." He glared at her, stroking back his copper fringe so hard she thought he might pull out what was left of his hair. "God's teeth, lass, whatever possessed you to do something so bottle-witted?"

Grazing nearby she saw the pair of horses Quinn had procured for their getaway, a getaway she was not going to be a part of. "I could not take the necklace. Quinn—I'm going to stay."

"You're *what*?!" He jumped to his feet, his words

tumbling out all at once. "You can't mean . . . bloody crazy thing to . . . you don't know what you're . . . are you *mad*?"

"No. But I cannot hurt anyone in this family, especially Edward. He—he asked me to marry him."

"Oh, lass. You can't think that he'll wed you. Not after he learns the truth."

"Nor would I accept him, even if he still wanted to. But I must tell him the truth about who I am—with my own lips. Otherwise, I will not be able to—" She dragged in a breath, barely holding back the tears. "I'm sorry, Quinn. You have done so much for me, and I know 'tis not the way you wanted this to end."

"No, it ain't. Not by a bleedin' long shot." He went to the stile and angrily scooped up his hat. "I won't tell you you're being a fool—you already know that. But I'll be jiggered if'n I'll be a fool with you."

He glanced down the deserted lane, nodding toward the horses. "You can come with me or no. 'Tis your choice. But if you choose the Black Earl, that's an end between us. My neck's the only thing I got left, and I ain't gonna risk it on pure folly, even for Daniel Murphy's daughter. So what's it to be, lass?"

Sabrina pressed her fist to her heart. She knew Quinn was right. It was lunacy to risk telling Edward the truth about her deception. At best he would cast her off. At worst he would call the magistrate, and have her dragged back to London to stand trial for Albert's murder. And even if, by some miracle, he still wanted to marry her, she would have to deny both their hearts. She loved him too much to let him destroy his family honor by marrying a murderer. No matter what she did, she would end up heartbroken. And yet . . .

"Quinn, I cannot let him think I have betrayed him

without remorse, as his first wife did. Even if it means my death, I cannot."

For a long moment Quinn stared at her. Then without a word he stomped off toward the horses. A sharp pain creased Rina's heart. She loved Quinn and it hurt her to have him walk away from her without so much as a good-bye. She watched as he grabbed the bridle of one horse and mounted the other, then rode off with both of them into the gathering darkness.

The fog was beginning to roll in from the sea. Rina pulled her mist-damp cloak around her and headed back toward Ravenshold. She hadn't gone a dozen steps before she heard the sound of hooves behind her. For a moment she nourished the crazy hope that Quinn had returned to say good-bye. But the figure that emerged from the swirling mist rode a high-stepping thorough-bred, and wore a black mourning dress. "Cassie?"

"Thank *God*," the distraught lady cried as she pulled her horse to a halt. "I was coming to Ravenshold to see you. Paris left for London this morning, but I stayed behind to deliver some last-minute instructions to the staff. I was planning to join him this evening, but when I found—" She dropped the reins and buried her face in her hands. "Oh, Prudence, you must come with me to Fitzroy Hall at once. I know what happened to Isabel."

Lady Rumley held the lantern close to the ornate paneling. "The switch is here somewhere. I just have to—ah, this is it." She pressed a small carved rose. With a hushed click, a portion of the wall swung noiselessly open. "Come, Prudence. I've found the smugglers' door."

Sabrina looked with concern over the lady's shoulder at the dank, cobweb-covered stone stairway beyond.

Cassie had explained that her brother had stumbled onto a secret door in Fitzroy Hall, and discovered that it led to a network of caves that had been used by smugglers to store their illicit goods. Still, the connection eluded Rina. "What has Paris's discovery of this secret passage got to do with Edward's first wife?"

"I'll show you. Follow me."

Before Rina could stop her, Cassie disappeared around the first bend in the descending stairway. She had no choice but to follow.

The place smelled like a dungeon. Mold and foul water pooled in the low spots of the rough-hewn passage, and the ceiling was sometimes so low Rina had to bend to pass by. Every so often her lantern would illuminate a rotting, cobweb-covered pile of what had once been the smugglers' ill-gotten gain. Beyond the lantern's glow, Rina could hear the telltale rustle of scampering rats. She shivered, unnerved by the unwholesome place.

" 'Tis not much further," Cassie called from up ahead.

As she hurried to catch up to her friend, Rina saw that Cassie was standing on the stone-lined edge of what appeared to be a well.

"The smugglers used this well to store their kegs of brandy," Cassie explained. "The steep walls prevented the occasional tippler from sampling the inventory."

History lessons were the last thing Rina wanted at the moment. "But what has any of this got to do with Isabel?"

"The smugglers and wreckers used these passages for almost a hundred years," Cassie intoned, apparently determined to continue her lesson. "But some fifty years ago, the secret to the caves was lost. The saboteur stumbled on it years ago, and determined that the passages could be used to some advantage—but only if they were kept a secret. That is why Wheal Grace's new tunnel had to be destroyed. If the miners had kept digging, they would have found these caves."

Rina's jaw tightened. "So Paris thought he could accomplish two goals at once—destroy the tunnel and kill Edward."

"No!" Cassie's sharp protest rang through the passageways. "Edward was never supposed to be hurt. The goal was only to keep this place a secret."

"But what is so blasted special about these caves?"

Cassie raised her lantern high, and pointed down into the well.

Wonderful. Another history lesson, Rina thought in frustration as she turned her gaze into the well. The smooth-walled opening was twice as deep as a man's height, and empty of the brandy kegs it had once guarded. In fact, there didn't seem to be anything at all in the well, save for a small bundle of rags in the corner. It was hard to make out details in the shadows, but the rags seemed to be made of bright and unusually fine material, not the sort of thing a smuggler might wear. Frowning, Rina leaned further over the edge for a closer look. It was definitely a dress. Unusually well preserved for being half a century old. And as her gaze traced the elegant line of the well-cut sleeve, she saw the faint, dull ivory gleam of a bone.

Sabrina jerked back and stared at Cassie with horrified eyes. "It isn't—please tell me it's not—"

"It is Isabel," Cassie said sadly. "That is why the saboteur could not risk these caves being found. If they found the caves, they would find her."

Rina looked back at the poor little skeleton, the horror of what Paris had done growing with each heartbeat. "Cassie, I know you love your brother, but you cannot deny his madness any longer. We must tell the authorities. Paris is not just a prankster, he is a cold-blooded murderer."

Cassie's answer was strangely calm. "Not Paris. The saboteur killed Isabel."

"Paris *is* the saboteur!"

Cassie placed an elegant, gloved hand on Rina's arm, and gave her a sympathetic smile. "I am afraid you have it wrong, my dear. *I* am the saboteur."

Still smiling, she shoved Rina over the edge of the well.

Chapter Twenty-eight

The first thing Sabrina was aware of was the pain in her side. The next was the warm stickiness of blood running down the side of her face. The last thing was that she was lying at the bottom of the smugglers' well, where she'd been pushed by a woman she'd believed to be her friend.

The lantern's glow appeared over the lip of the well. Looking up, Rina saw Lady Rumley staring down at her, still wearing her concerned smile.

"You're alive," she said, her pleasant voice stirring with a touch of disappointment. "Isabel survived the fall also, which was too bad. I was tolerably fond of Isabel."

"Fond? You killed her!" Rina struggled to her feet, and felt a knife of pain stab through her ankle. She leaned against the wall, balancing her weight on her good leg, and glared up at Cassie. "For God's sake, *why?*"

"Because it's mine. Ravenshold is mine. I knew that from the first moment I set eyes on it. That is why I didn't mind it when Father kept selling our lands to the earl. I knew that one day I would have it all back. It is my destiny to be the Countess of Trevelyan."

Rina recalled Cassie telling her that she'd fallen in

love with the land of the estate at first sight. The once innocent words took on a sinister meaning. Sabrina had been so convinced that Paris was the saboteur that she'd forgotten the fact that Cassie shared the same heritage of madness as her brother. "You will never get away with this. Edward will find you out."

"As he found out about Isabel?" Cassie indifferently flicked a bit of dust from her sleeve. "For years I waited for him to grow tired of his bride. I even encouraged Paris to form an attachment for Edward's simpering sister—which gave me ample opportunity to visit Ravenshold. But the earl proved resolutely attached to the little chit. So I started to foster her distrust. I filled her mind with tales of Edward's infidelity. It was ridiculously easy—Isabel believed every word I said. But I miscalculated—just as I miscalculated with you, when I stopped my efforts to be rid of you after I saw your face. It never occurred to me that Edward would fall in love with such a plain woman. But in the end my oversight did not matter, any more than it mattered with Isabel. One day she confessed to me that she was going to have another child. For the sake of her growing family, she told me that she was going to confront Edward with the 'dalliances' I'd told her of, and to tell him that she was willing to give him a second chance because she still loved him with all her heart. It was quite touching, really. But of course I could not allow it. If Edward had found out that I'd been telling lies to his gullible wife, he'd have lost all regard for me. So I took Isabel to see the smugglers' caves that I'd stumbled on as a child. That, too, was ridiculously easy."

"There was never a lover, was there? You made it up to make Edward believe that Isabel had deserted him."

"Very perceptive. I saw the story of the shipwreck in the *Times*, and used it to my advantage. There was no old governess, but since Isabel's relatives were all dead there was no one to contradict me. It offered a nice touch of authenticity, did it not? Finally, I penned a letter— Isabel's *confession.* Cyril and Paris both saw me receive it, though I made certain they never got a good look at the contents or the postmark. I'll own I underestimated you again, my dear, when I told you of Isabel's love for her children—forgetting that I'd told Paris that she spoke ill of them in the letter. After a few years one forgets, you must understand. In any event, Cyril tossed the letter in the fire when he saw how deeply it affected me, as I knew he would. Dear Cyril. He would have done anything for me. But with Isabel gone, he was no longer necessary to my plans. He was already quite ill. It was a very little thing to increase his laudanum dose to a fatal amount."

Rina listened in horror as Cassie calmly told of not one murder, but two. Three, counting Isabel's unborn child. *And now she means to make it four.* Rina chose her next words as if she were walking on eggshells. "Cassie, you are ill. Do not add another crime to the ones you've already committed. Help me out of here. There are people who can help you. Doctors—"

"*Doctors,*" Cassie snarled, and for an instant the depth of her madness gleamed in her eyes. "I saw what they did to my mother. But she was weak—afraid to do what was needed to claim her destiny. But I am not weak and I will not fail. I *will* be Countess of Trevelyan."

"No, you will not," Rina stated quietly. "Edward will never marry you. He loves me."

Cassie's mouth curved into a satisfied smile. "My dear, you put too much stock in men's fickle nature. When he learns you have deserted him, his love will vanish like dross in the wind."

"Edward will *never* believe I deserted him."

"Until a few days ago, I might have agreed with you. But that was before I learned you are *not* Prudence Winthrope."

Rina's whole body went numb. "Th . . . that's preposterous."

"Please, do not waste my time. My father made many friends during his foreign travels, and I contacted several of them to check out your story. Three days ago I learned the truth. I considered telling Edward, but I was uncertain whether the truth would entirely dispel his infatuation for you. You see, I understand him, far better than either you or Isabel. I will tell him that I confronted you with the truth, and that you left rather than face the consequences of your actions. I will say that you laughed about his besotted love for you. And when he sees that you never loved him he will turn to me, just as he did after Isabel died."

Helplessly, Sabrina realized that Cassie might be right. She would spin lies about Rina's duplicity, seeding just enough damning truth to give the story credence. Edward would believe that Rina never loved him, that the wonderful wholeness they'd found in each other's arms was a lie. It would destroy him, but that would not matter to Cassie. Brokenhearted, he would marry her, believing she was the only woman he could trust. He would enter a loveless bargain, his heart growing more tarnished and jaded with each passing year.

"Please," she breathed desperately. "Please, do not do this to him."

"You are hardly in a position to dictate," Cassie noted as she got up from the ledge. "Now I really must be going, lest the few servants remaining in this house note my absence. But if it eases your mind, I promise you that I shall make Edward a good wife. I will give him sons—two, I think. They will be a great consolation to him after his eldest son meets with an unexpected accident. After all, it must be my blood that continues the Trevelyan line."

"No!" Rina's scream rang through the caves. She clawed at the wall until her palms bled, trying to climb up the rough rocks. But it did no good. Helplessly she watched the light from Cassie's lantern fade, knowing that it was her deception that had given the evil woman the means to spin a credible story of her betrayal. The only chance Edward and David had was if she escaped from this dungeon. She tried again to climb the rocks, knowing she had to find a way out, she had to. . . .

Despair was a place. Rina found it in the darkness, lived it in a way that had no time, no hope of release. For a while the passage of hours was marked by hunger, and thirst, but even those faded into the consuming nothingness of despair. Her hands were caked with blood. Her ankle was swollen and useless. She had failed in her escape. Cassie had won. Again.

Sleep and waking became one. The air was thick with the smell of decay and old death. She glanced at the corner of the well that contained Isabel's remains. How long had the poor woman lived in the darkness after Cassie had left her?

How long would *she* live?

She fell asleep and dreamed that she was on the cliffs of Ravenshold, walking arm in arm with Isabel. Through the swirling mists ahead she caught sight of Edward. She cried out to him, warning him about Cassie's evil plan. But he looked through her as if she didn't exist. Isabel smiled sadly. *You are dead, just like me. He will never hear you, no matter how much you cry out, no matter how much you want to warn him. He will never know the truth.*

She woke screaming.

She continued to try to escape until she became too weak to continue. She must have fainted, because when she came to she was delirious. She heard a voice babbling that she could only vaguely recognize as her own. Memories of her life became jumbled, disjointed. Sometimes she thought of herself as Sabrina, sometimes as Prudence, and sometimes as Isabel. "Funny," she muttered with a giddy laugh. "So funny. Borrowed Prudence's life. Borrowed Isabel's death. S'funny, don't you see . . ."

She fell into a heap on the opposite side of the well from Isabel—she would not pollute the lady's honest bones with her own tainted ones. Rina was a liar and a murderer. She deserved everything she got. But Isabel had been innocent; her only crime was loving her husband enough to believe in him. Edward would never know that. He would continue to believe that Isabel's love was false, just as he would believe that Sabrina's love was part of her deception. "I'm sorry, Isabel, so desperately sorry. I should have tried harder to find out how you died. I should not have trusted Cassie. I should not have stolen Prudence's life. But I do love Edward—that much was real. Forgive me, Isabel. No one else will."

She imagined she saw the darkness brighten with the faint gleam of a heavenly light. She felt the soft brush of fresh air curling against her cheek. "Isabel," she breathed, knowing the sweet lady had touched her with her ghostly hand, forgiving her. Sighing, Sabrina closed her eyes for the last time. She knew death would come soon, for in the distance she heard the sound of the heavenly choirs.

But as the darkness swallowed her, she wondered why the angels' voices sounded so much like Pendragon's bark.

• • •

". . . waking up. Hand me the cup."

Sabrina's eyelids fluttered open, then closed again against the bright sunlight flooding in through her bedroom window. Her bedroom? But she'd died, hadn't she? She had a distinct memory of dying, and a series of vaguer memories involving water soothing her parched throat, warm broth stilling the ache in her empty stomach, and sweet-scented bathwater cleansing the dirt from her exhausted body. She'd thought she was in heaven.

Rina changed that opinion when a cup of noxious-tasting liquid was pressed to her lips. She spat out the drink and a curse. "What the—?"

A silvery laugh interrupted her. Rina opened her eyes, and stared up into the face of an angel who looked remarkably like Amy.

"I think she's feeing better, Charles," Amy said as she handed the cup back to the doctor. "Welcome back, darling. We feared we'd lost you."

You did, Rina thought. The memories flooded back to her: the darkness, the terror, Cassie's madness. Rina gripped Amy's arm. "Cassie. You mustn't trust . . . she's—"

"We know," Amy said quietly as she smoothed Rina's hair. "She left you in that terrible place to die. It very nearly worked. We all believed you'd gone away, just as Cassie said you had. If it had not been for Pendragon, we'd never have found you."

"And Mrs. Poldhu's been feeding him steak ever since," Charles added with a grin. "Not that the hound doesn't deserve it. We knew you were somewhere in Fitzroy Hall, but we had no idea where to look. Pendragon led us to the secret panel, and through the tunnels to the well."

Sabrina stared up at Amy, not quite believing that

she was really alive. "But how did you know I was in Fitzroy Hall? If Cassie told you that I had left, and you believed her, how did you—?"

"Hello, Rina-lass." Quinn stepped forward to Rina's bedside.

It took Rina a moment to gather enough breath to speak. "Quinn. Oh, Quinn." Her eyes brimmed with tears at the sight of her friend. "But you told me you were leaving."

The sunlight glanced off his yellow waistcoat, making it shine like a golden breastplate. Yet his wide smile outshone it. "I did leave, darling. Miles away by sunset, I was, and glad to see the back of the place. But something nagged at me—kept me from moving on. I boarded overnight at an inn not twenty miles from here. Stayed there the whole of the next day, though devil take me as to why. Then that night in the pub, I heard a bloke going on about a gentry miss who'd pretended to be an heiress and absconded without so much as a by your leave. Well, I knew that weren't the way of it—if leaving was on your mind, you'da hightailed it with me. So I headed back to Ravenshold as fast as my horse could take me. Thought I'd 'ave to fight my way in the door, but his lordship was quick to see me when he heard my name."

Rina recalled the night in the stables, when Edward had heard her mention Quinn's name. She didn't doubt that he'd have wanted to see the "Quinn" he'd once thought she was in love with. "But you put yourself in great danger. You were free."

He chucked her chin with his fist. "And what would freedom be worth if I turned my back on a mate? 'Sides, weren't much danger to it—not after I told the great bleedin' sod that you'd stayed behind because you were in love with 'im."

Amy laughed. "He used those very words, too. You

should have seen my brother's face. He looked as if he had been hit by a runaway carriage!"

Sabrina didn't share Amy's smile. She was beginning to grasp all that had happened while she was trapped in the well, and all that it implied. They all knew the truth about her now, about her terrible deception. "Amy, Charles, I wish . . . I wanted . . . Oh, I'm so dreadfully ashamed."

Amy pressed a finger to Rina's lips, silencing her. She exchanged a loving glance with Charles before continuing. "Hush. We'll sort it all out later. Meanwhile, you need your rest. You—"

A commotion in the hall outside the bedchamber interrupted Amy. Rina froze. She knew the voice of the man arguing with Duffy for entrance to her room as well as she knew her own heartbeat. She glanced from Amy, to Charles, to Quinn. "I cannot see him now. Please don't let—"

Edward stormed into the room. His hair was ragged, his cravat was hastily tied, and his beard looked as if it hadn't seen a razor in a week. Charles moved to intercept him, but the earl looked through him as if he were made of glass. He had eyes for only one person in the room.

"Out," he commanded.

To Rina's distress, the others obeyed. She clutched at Amy's hand, but the girl smiled and pulled gently away. "It will be all right," she whispered as she gave Rina an encouraging wink. Then she took Charles's arm and followed Quinn out of the room.

If Sabrina had had an ounce of strength, she'd have jumped from the bed and run after them.

She turned her head away, part of her wishing that she was still trapped in the smugglers' well. She squeezed her eyes shut and gritted her teeth against the shame welling up inside her.

He said nothing. The room was so silent that for a moment she imagined that Edward had left with his sister. But that hope died when she heard his heavy-booted tread, and felt the mattress sink under his weight as he sat beside her. Strong, warm hands enveloped her icy ones.

"Look at me."

The tenderness of his voice only deepened her shame. "I cannot. I cannot ever look at you again."

"As you wish. But I fear that will make it difficult to recite your wedding vows."

Her eyes snapped open, but she could not turn to face him. "Edward, we cannot wed. Everything you believed about me is true. I am a thief and a liar. The only reason I came to Ravenshold was to steal the Dutchman. Quinn must have told you."

"What Quinn told me is that you gave the necklace *back* to Grandmother, and she confirmed his story. You may have come here to steal the Dutchman, but you could not go through with it. You are not a thief. And as for being a liar . . . well, I told you my fair share of them. There is only one thing I must know. Were you telling the truth when you said that you loved me?"

The uncertainty in his voice drew her like a magnet. Unable to resist, she turned back to him, and stared up into the face of the man she loved more than her own life. She saw the echo of fear in his expression, and the shadow of despair that still lingered in his eyes. She knew exactly what that despair felt like—she'd experienced the same feeling when she'd been trapped in the smugglers' well, thinking that she would never be able to tell him the truth. *But now I can tell him the truth. I must—even though it means we can never be together.*

She reached up and traced the lines that had been

etched into the edges of his mouth, and into his soul. "It makes no difference. I cannot marry you. Ever. There is something in my past, something terrible that happened before I met you. I am much worse than a liar. I am a mur . . . a mur—"

"A murderer," Edward finished with a shrug. "Yes, I know."

"You *know?*" Shocked, she started to rise from the bed.

Edward held her down. "Lie still, darling."

She shook her head from side to side, struggling with her limited strength against his hold. "Do *not* call me that. You mustn't. I cannot marry you. I will not let you link your proud family to my name."

Impossibly, Edward's mouth began to edge up in a smile. "Yes, I thought your stubborn mind might come up with something like that. So as soon as Quinn told me of your past, I sent Mr. Cherry to London to find out how things stood. I received his post last evening. He was able to confirm much of your story, and from a rather unique source—the murder victim himself."

Rina stopped struggling. "*Albert?*"

Edward's smile turned to an outright grin. "Tremaine did not die. In fact, he was lustily downing a large plate of braised beef when Cherry came upon him. Seems he and his mother exaggerated his injuries in order to force you to marry him. My solicitor 'encouraged' him to sign a statement absolving you of any blame in the attack—though not before he'd seen to it that the villain had a few less teeth with which to finish his dinner. A bit out of character for Cherry, but he's quite fond of you in his own blustering way. Still, the thrashing he gave your stepbrother was better than he deserved."

The earl's smile vanished, and his eyes grew dark

and lethal. "If I'd found Tremaine rather than Cherry, there *would* have been a murder to prosecute. He was the Albert who tried to rape you, wasn't he?"

She nodded shakily.

His eyes still held murder, but he traced her jaw with a tender touch. "God, what you must have gone through. And then, to get trapped in that hellhole . . . in my heart, I knew you hadn't left me, even before Quinn appeared. I was looking for you from the start. But I feared we'd never find you. The cliffs have guarded their smugglers' secrets for hundreds of years, and I held out little hope after Cassie—"

His words stopped abruptly and he looked away. Rina swallowed. "What happened to Cassie?"

"When she learned what Quinn had told us, and that we had proof of her deceit, she . . . she leapt from the cliffs."

Rina turned her face to the pillow, shutting her eyes in pain. Cassie had betrayed her and tried to kill her, but Rina hadn't wanted her death. There'd been too much of it already. " 'Tis my fault," she whispered brokenly. "If I had not come to Ravenshold—"

Edward gripped her hand as if he were holding onto a lifeline. "If you had not come, Cassie would have succeeded. Because of you, we discovered her plot before it was too late. If you had not come—if you had not risked your freedom to stay behind and face what you had done—I would never have found out the truth about the saboteur, or about the danger to my children, or about . . . Isabel."

In her distress, Rina had forgotten that Edward was still dealing with the horror of his first wife's murder. She reached up to brush his cheek. "You must not blame yourself for what happened to her. There is nothing you could have done."

"Perhaps. But I will never stop wondering—if I had trusted her more, or trusted Cassie less . . . We have a choice, both of us. We can bury ourselves in the mistakes of our past, or we can put those mistakes behind us and look to the future. So I ask you again, Pru—" He arched a dark brow. "Hmm. I cannot call you Miss Winthrope any longer. And Quinn speaks of you as Murphy's girl, Rina-lass, and occasionally the Red Queen. The whole thing has me blasted foxed. What exactly is your name?"

"Sabrina," she said softly.

"Sabrina," he mused with a slight grin. "Well, it fits you a great deal better than 'Prudence.' Caution was never your strong suit. But in spite of that, my family has formed quite an attachment for you. Amy is planning a double wedding. Grandmother is deciding on the names of our children. And Sarah and David are pestering me to know when they can start calling you 'Mama.' I shall not have any peace until we walk down the aisle. So, my beautiful, brave, *uncautious* Sabrina, I ask you again—were you telling the truth when you said that you loved me?"

His strong fingers laced protectively and possessively through hers, and she felt the shadows of her past melt away under his warm, treasuring love. What had started out as a deception had become a reality. By playing Prudence Winthrope, Quinn's Queen of Diamonds, Rina had found a home she had longed for, a family she could cherish, and a strong, good man who needed her love as much as she needed his. *'Twasn't the Queen of Diamonds I was playing, but the Queen of Hearts.*

Edward was right. They had a choice, and in that moment she made hers. No more lies. No more deceptions. She looked up, with her love for him shining in her eyes like the sun, and whispered, "Yes."

Epilogue

"Cor, Aggie, will ya look at that!"

Agnes Peak stopped walking down the Cheapside street and peered through the iron bars of the fence that ringed the old church graveyard. "Can't see much through this snow. What is it?"

"Have you no eyes?" Livy demanded. Once more she stabbed her bony finger in the direction of the churchyard. "Look over there. Near the Murphy grave."

Dutifully, Aggie pulled her shawl closer against the March wind and obeyed her friend. This time she saw the couple standing next to the Murphy grave—a dark, distinguished-looking lord and an elegant young lady. The fact that they were visiting that fallen soul was strange enough. The fact that they looked as if they'd both stepped out of Mayfair was even stranger. "Well, I'll be jiggered. What's quality like that doing at Murphy's grave?"

Livy squinted through the bars and licked her lips, as if she could almost taste the juicy morsel of gossip. "Will you look at his cloak? That's made by a Par-ree tailor or my name ain't Sneed. And that muff of hers—"

"Livy—"

"That muff is ermine. Not the tricked-up kind, mind you, but the real article. Oh, I'd give my Joe's wages for a month to know what—"

"Livy, it's—"

"—they're up to. Nothing good, I'm sure. Of course, I'm not the kind to think the worst of anyone, but if I were, I'd—"

"Livy! It's her!"

Annoyed, Lavinia glanced at Aggie. She wasn't used to being interrupted. "What are you on about?"

"It's her. His daughter. That lady is Murphy's daughter!"

Livy gave the shorter woman a patronizing pat. "Now, now, Aggie. Murphy's daughter disappeared well neigh a year ago, and good riddance. She was a brazen strumpet to be sure, and though I've never wished ill on a single soul, I'm sure that chit got her just comeuppan—"

Her words died as the aristocratic lady turned to the side, revealing a stunning fall of unmistakable auburn hair. Livy's jaw dropped. "Jesus, Joseph, and Mary. It *is* her."

"Sure as frost," Aggie commented. She turned her gaze back to the churchyard, nearly as stunned as Livy at the transformation in the woman. A year ago Sabrina Murphy had been a plain, pitiful waif without a friend in the world. Now she was an elegant lady, as polished as any of the gentry who passed this way in their fine carriages. The images were as different as day and night, yet they both had one thing in common. The grief Aggie'd seen on the girl's face a year past was the same as the grief she now saw on the woman's.

Sabrina knelt down and laid a bouquet of flowers on her father's grave—a grave his widow had never graced with so much as a nosegay. It did not seem to be the act of a brazen strumpet. Aggie continued to watch as the lady carefully wiped the snow from the headstone's letters, then rose into the embrace of the man at her side. The look that passed between them warmed Aggie's heart despite the cold wind. *That's just how Tommy looked at me when we was courtin'*, she thought as a soft smile creased her lips. "I'm glad the poor waif's found someone to love."

"Humph," Livy commented, her speech returning with a vengeance. "And how did she find him, I ask you? By no honest means, I'll vow."

"Oh, what does it matter? Isn't it enough that she's found some happiness?"

"For now, maybe. But it will never last. Daniel Murphy was a no-good scoundrel and his daughter's the same. She's a black-hearted gambler's daughter, and she'll come to a bad end, you mark my words."

Aggie watched as the couple walked arm in arm out of the churchyard, disappearing into the curtain of swirling snow. She looked at the beautiful bouquet on the grave, and recalled the memory of the gentleman's loving smile. Perhaps Daniel Murphy had been black-hearted—she really hadn't known the man well enough to judge. But black-hearted or not, his daughter had loved him, and found love herself. "I don't think she'll come to a bad end. I think she'll live happily ever after."

"Shows what you know. She's as wicked as sin, she is. Just like her da. Blood will tell, Aggie. Blood will—"

"Livy."

"Yes."

"Do shut up." Whistling jauntily, Aggie turned away and started down the street, leaving the speechless Livy behind.

About the Author

RUTH OWEN is the author of many highly praised Loveswepts, including the Maggie Award-winning *Taming the Pirate*. She has been writing ever since she could pick up a pen. Though she loves writing contemporaries, a secret part of her is living out adventures in Regency England. This is her first historical, and she hopes that you enjoy reading it as much as she enjoyed writing it.

Ms. Owen loves to hear from her fans. Write her at P.O. Box 432, Winter Park, Florida 32790–0432, or e-mail her at rmowen@mindspring.com.

*Turn the page for a
sneak peek at Ruth Owen's
next historical romance*

Scandal's Mistress

*coming in spring 2000
from Bantam Books*

January 1, 1808
London

Juliana Dare sat in a wing chair in her father's study and watched her world come to an end. Her father, Frederick Dare, the Marquis of Albany, stood behind his desk, his shoulders bent in despair. And in front of the desk, with his back to her, stood the tall, rigid figure of Connor Reed.

"I want the truth, boy. By God, you owe me that much." The marquis leaned forward, his face as pale and drawn as a death mask. "Connor, why? Why did you take the money?"

Juliana gripped the chair arm, feeling the pain in her father's voice stab through her. Eight years ago he had pulled Connor from the filth and squalor of the London docks. He'd raised the boy as his own, and no father could have loved his son more. Connor had become a part of Juliana's family and had been her protector and companion during their seafaring adventures. She'd lost count of the number of times he'd saved her from the occasionally life-threatening situations her curious nature got her into. He was her hero—

"Why, damn you?!"

Her father slammed his fist on his desk, sending quills and papers flying and teetering the single candle that provided the room's only light. For an instant the erratic light shimmered through Connor's dark blond hair, turning it into an angel's halo. Connor bent his head and clasped his hands tightly behind him, as if the iron manacles were already on his wrists. "You have my confession, my lord. Why should my reasons matter?"

"Why *indeed*." The thin, dark form of Mr. Rollo Grenville, Juliana's second cousin, stepped into the small circle of light. At twenty-six, he was only five years older than Connor, but his elegant coat of plum-colored superfine and his polished manners made him seem like another breed entirely. "He has admitted to taking the five hundred pounds from your strongbox. 'Tis more than enough to send him to Newgate. I say we send for the magistrate and be done with the cur."

Rollo's words dripped with disdain. Juliana watched as Connor's hidden hands balled into hard fists, and felt the ghost of a smile flicker across her lips. There had never been any love lost between Connor and her pompous cousin—Lord knows there had been times when *she'd* longed to pommel Grenville for the insults he'd directed at Connor. But her father's old first mate Tommy Blue had told her to pay the dandy no mind. *It's deeds what makes the man, not words spoke by some silly popinjay.*

Of course, Tommy's words lost much of their comfort when she recalled that Connor's most recent deed was stealing five hundred pounds.

"I'll not send for the magistrate."

Lord Albany's pronouncement brought shocked gasps from Grenville, Connor, and Juliana. She pressed her hand to her heart. Connor wasn't going to prison. Her father had seen that somehow this was all a terrible misunderstanding—

"I'll not send for the magistrate if you resign your commission and are out of London by tomorrow's dawn and out of England by week's end."

Juliana's relief shattered. In exchange for his freedom her father was stripping Connor of everything he possessed—his career, his shipmates, the country he loved . . . and her.

"Well, boy, do you agree?"

No! Juliana's heart screamed. *Do not agree. Say you didn't steal the money. Say that you never saw it. Say anything, just don't leave me—*

"I agree."

Like a man who'd just been handed a gallows sentence, Connor backed away from the desk and gave a nod of respect to the Marquis, then a swift, unreadable glance at the smirking Grenville. As he turned toward the door, Juliana finally glimpsed his eyes, his brilliant, sky-blue eyes that had always gleamed with easy laughter. The laughter had died. In its place was the lost, hopeless expression that Juliana had seen only once before, on the long ago day when she'd first seen him on the London docks—a filthy, starving beggar boy who'd been too proud to accept her coin. With a soft cry she reached out to comfort him. His mouth hardened at the sound, but he passed her by without a word. He slipped out of the room, leaving behind a whisper too soft for anyone else to hear. "I'm sorry, princess."

The sob that had been building inside her finally broke free. Eight years ago he'd saved her from an icy grave in the Thames, showing more courage than any man on the docks, including her cousin Grenville. In the years that followed he'd saved her from the loneliness of her mother's death, and they'd become the best of friends. When Connor had left three years ago to join the Royal Navy, he'd taken a piece of her heart with him, but even distance couldn't break the bond between them. He had remained her trusted confidant and her hero. Until last night, on the eve of the new year, when he'd become so much more. *In a few years they say I'll be promoted to commander. After that 'tis only a short jump to captain, and a man can support a wife on a captain's pay. . . .*

"You should have listened to me," Grenville purred as he loomed over her, wrenching her thoughts back to the present. "I have always said that wharf rat would show his true colors one day." He took her chin in his manicured fingers, holding it in a tight, almost painful grip. "Perhaps next time, my dear, you will not be so foolish as to entertain the attentions of a man so far beneath you. No doubt he found it quite amusing. Why, he probably laughed about your *tender feelings* with a woman of his low and vile class—"

"That's not true!" Juliana wrenched free of his grip and bolted from the chair, leaving the room before he could see the hot blush of shame stain her cheeks. Rollo was wrong. Connor loved her. Whatever else he had done, he loved her.

By the time she reached her bedchamber she had a plan. The Marquis of Albany was a man of passion and daring, and his daughter was cut of the same cloth. She opened her wardrobe and shoved aside the beautiful gowns that her doting father had lavished on her, and pulled out a sturdy oilskin from her seafaring days. She shrugged on the old coat and twisted her hair into a serviceable bun easily concealed beneath the hood. Efficiently masked, she opened her jewel box, removing the emerald necklace and earrings that she'd inherited from her mother. She breathed a silent prayer to the long-dead Anna Dare, asking for her forgiveness. *I know you wanted me to pass these on to my children, Mama, but Connor will need the money the gems will bring until he gets back on his feet.*

She penned a quick note to her father, telling him not to worry and promising to write soon. More than that she dared not say, not until Connor and she were safely wed. Then, without so much as a twinge of regret, she turned her back on her world of wealth and privilege and slipped down the back stairway.

It was a foul evening, with a cold, dank drizzle dripping down from the starless sky. Yet to Juliana it was like walking through heaven. She was on her way to join the man she loved, the man she believed in with all her heart. Together they would put right this dreadful mess. He needed her love and support now more than ever. And he would have her . . . *for richer and for poorer, in sickness and in health . . .*

Married. She raised her hand to her lips, recalling the soft kiss Connor had brushed across her lips to seal their engagement. It was the first time she'd ever been kissed— his mouth had been warm and gentle as a South Seas trade wind. Just thinking about it started a sensation like a whole flock of butterflies fluttering in her stomach. In that single instant she had felt a whole new life open up to her, a life that was as full of possibilities as the exotic cities she'd visited as a child—enchanting, mysterious, and more than a little frightening.

. . . laughed about your tender feelings with the woman of his low and vile class . . .

Juliana tried to tell herself that Rollo's words meant nothing, but the truth was, she was less than confident about Connor's romantic feelings for her. Too tall, too thin, and with a bothersome spray of freckles across her nose, she could hardly be considered a beauty. Besides, she was sixteen and barely out of the schoolroom, while Connor Reed was a man of twenty-one who had spent almost three years sailing under the king's flag from one port to the next. She'd spent enough of her childhood visiting such ports to know that far more went on in such places than young ladies were supposed to know about. Far more than, at the moment, she *wished* to know.

She had loved Connor for longer than she could remember. She had no doubt that he loved her—as a friend. But until last night he had never touched her in anything except a brotherly fashion. And the possibility that he might have touched other women differently filled her with a chilling ache that had nothing to do with the January wind.

She turned under a stone arch to the courtyard of the building that housed Connor's second-story rooms. Looking up, she could see his window, brightly lit and covered with the rose-embroidered curtains she'd made for him during her finishing school needlework lessons. The uncertainty left her when she recalled how he'd handled the amateur efforts as if they were the finest silks, vowing that he would treasure them always because *she* had made them. She remembered the look in his eyes—sure, strong, and so full of love it made her heart skip a beat.

She lifted her skirts and dashed across the courtyard. Grenville was wrong. Connor had not been unfaithful to her. Even if the whole world turned against Connor, she would still believe in him. And no matter what, she would never stop loving him.

Shadows crossed the window. Against the backlit screen of her lovingly embroidered curtains Juliana saw the broad-shouldered silhouette of Connor Reed wrap his arms around another woman.

January 1, 1812

"I am out of patience with heroes," Lady Juliana Dare declared as she rose from the cream-colored settee in the Earl of Morrow's side parlor. She unfurled her pearl and ivory fan and fluttered it eloquently beneath her chin. "The rest of the city might stand on their heads for this Archangel fellow, but not I."

A chorus arose from the group surrounding her, momentarily drowning out the music from the nearby ballroom. Lady Juliana had been the toast of London for the last two seasons, and it was anticipated that she would be just as popular when the next official season began in March. Beautiful, accomplished, and arguably one of the wealthiest heiresses in the country, her style and wit set the bar by which all the other ladies of the *ton* were measured. But her harsh comments about the heroic and mysterious privateer known as the Archangel, who was to make his first public appearance at Morrow House later that evening, were without precedent.

"But how can you say such a thing?" Miss Millicent Peak uttered. "The Archangel and his ship have run the French blockades dozens of times, bringing badly needed supplies to our soldiers in the Peninsula."

"For a pretty price," Lady Juliana replied.

Mr. Hamilton shook his head so firmly that his new wig slipped askew. "Well paid or not, you must own that the man showed uncommon courage. True, he sails under a letter of marque and gains a share of the cargo he captures in the prize court, but that is hardly the point. Three times he has put his bannerless ship between Boney's cannons and our innocent merchant vessels."

"More likely 'twas just an ill-timed shift of the wind," Juliana drawled as she smoothed the gold net skirt of her lace and satin evening gown.

"Extweemly well spoken," Lord Renquist exclaimed in his fashionable lisp. "I agwee with Lady Juliana."

"You *always* agree with Lady Juliana," Hamilton muttered.

"Well, I still think the Archangel is splendidly heroic," wide-eyed Millicent offered. "There was an account of his foiling of the French attack on our troops on Portobello island. It seems he brilliantly anticipated the enemy's every move—"

"There was nothing brilliant about it," Juliana interrupted. "The French had only one choice. The channel currents run strong and deep in that part of the Mediterranean. Any tar worth his barnacles knows that the only way a ship can approach Portobello harbor is from the leeward si—"

Juliana's words dwindled to silence as she realized the others were staring at her. *Drat!* Her seafaring past crept out at the most inauspicious times. She raised her fan, fluttering it coquettishly in front of her reddening cheeks as she added, "Or so I have heard my father say. Not that I understand a word of it."

The censoring frowns turned to wry chuckles. Mr. Hamilton patted her arm. "Of course you don't, my dear. Such talk is for men of business, not young ladies like you. I'd forgotten that the Marquis of Albany had a ship."

"*Fifty* ships," Juliana murmured. "My father owns the Marquis Line, a shipping concern second only to the East India Company in trade routes."

Lord Renquist reached into the pocket of his plum-colored waistcoat and pulled out an elaborately decorated silver snuffbox. "Yes, I'd heard he dabbled in *twade*. An eccentric pursuit, to be sure, but such failings may be forgiven in so distingwished a gentleman—especially one with such a lovely and remawkable daughter."

Julian barely stifled the urge to ask him how he could look down on trade when the merchant captains risked their lives to supply the spices for his food, the tea for his breakfast—indeed, the snuff for his snuffbox. But such a social breach would have made her a pariah in the *ton*. She could not afford such censure, for her father's sake. Only last week she had received a letter from him in the Caribbean, saying how proud he was of the accomplished lady she had become, and how much she reminded him of her beautiful, well-loved mother.

Gritting her teeth, she returned Lord Renquist's obsequious smile. "La, sir, you make my head light with such compliments. A poor creature such as I cannot bear the weight of such acclaim."

Renquist leaned closer and dropped his voice to a fervent whisper. "That is not all I wish you to bear, deawr lady," he hissed as his moist, slightly stale breath assaulted her ear. "Have you given more thought to our pwior conversation, when I asked you to be my w—?"

"The minuet!" Juliana exclaimed. She flashed a brilliant, apologetic smile. "Heavens, I promised this dance to Commodore Jolly and he will be absolutely *devastated* if I do not seek him out. If you will excuse me . . ."

She slipped out of the parlor before anyone could protest.

Once she was out of their sight, she slowed her pace, lingering in the nearly deserted corner of the ballroom, her thoughts distracted. Her dance with Jolly had merely been an excuse to leave the parlor and Renquist's proposal behind. She had few qualms about deserting him so abruptly—despite his lofty title the man was a pig, and she had little doubt that his *tendresse* for her was based solely on the fact that he owed a small fortune in gambling debts. Besides, she had received three other offers of marriage this month alone, one of them from a viscount who she felt had true affection for her. But when she had opened her mouth to accept him, the words had stopped in her throat. *What is the matter with me? I am past twenty—nearly on the shelf. Yet when a fine man offers me marriage, I turn him away.*

"Farthing for your thoughts?"

Juliana's worried frown smoothed into a sincere smile. "Meg, you minx. How could you leave me alone with the likes of Lord Renquist?"

Margaret Evangeline Evans's usually sober expression turned to one of pure mischief and the eyes behind her spectacles gleamed. "My attendance would have made scant difference—the man treats me with all the regard of furniture. But I paid for my desertion. For the past quarter hour I have been fending off the attentions of the Very Reverend William Hardy, who has informed me that God has called me to join him in his work among the heathens in India." She winced, pushing back the tight brunette curls that never seemed to stay in place. "Honestly, Julie, just because I am as poor and plain as a missionary's wife does not mean I want to be one."

"You are not plain," Juliana stated. Dark and petite as her Welsh ancestors, Meg Evans may not have had the cream complexion and statuesque beauty that were the rage of the London set, but her heart was as true as a champion-aimed arrow. "And as for not being wealthy . . . I daresay there are plenty of men who would jump at the chance to marry a lady of rare intelligence and fine spirit, even without a fortune."

Meg gave her a smile that did not quite reach her eyes. "I fear you are beginning to believe those 'penny dreadfuls' we used to purchase in the bazaar when the commodore wasn't looking. But I can assure you, if I ever do marry, it will be to a staid, stuffy, and boring businessman who will set me up in a cozy little parlor and keep me warm and safe."

Meg's fine voice was as lyrical as a Welsh song, yet Juliana picked out the wispy thread of bitterness weaving through the bright tones. Meg's father, an itinerant actor, had dragged the girl and her gently bred mother through nearly every rural town in England in his quest for fame. The gypsy lifestyle had been hard on his daughter and devastating on his wife, who died of consumption when Meg was barely thirteen. Griffin Evans had carted his daughter along with him for a few more years, but his interest in the girl lessened as his disappointment in his flagging career grew. In the end he deposited her on the doorstep of Commodore Horatio Jolly, an old friend of his dead wife's family who also had charge of the daughter of the seafaring Marquis of Albany. Despite their closeness, Meg had never spoken of the years she spent alone with her father. Yet Juliana had her suspicions about those years. Meg had been half-starved when she was abandoned, and a year later, when Evans was killed in a drunken carriage accident, Meg had not shed a single tear. Juliana, whose unusual upbringing had given her a very ungenteel knowledge of just how cruel the world could be to young women, surmised that the girl had lived through hell.

"You *will* marry," Juliana promised. "And he shall be the finest, bravest, and most handsome gentleman in the land. I will see to it."

Meg's smile deepened. "Well, if anyone can arrange such an impossibility, you can. But I doubt he shall be the finest and bravest gentleman. After all, *you* have already set your cap for the Archangel."

Startled, Juliana unfurled her fan and began to wave it under her chin with little of the grace she had shown before. "Heavens, where did you procure such an absurd notion? Half the ladies in London have made a proper cake of themselves fawning over the man. But I am not so easily enamored. He is a sailor like my father. I am curious about him in an entirely detached sort of way—like a museum botanist studying a rare kind of insect. Nothing more."

Meg's grin turned sly. "Like an insect, you say. Then why have you pored over the news accounts of his exploits like they were holy writ? Why did you practically swoon at Almack's last month when we heard the rumor that he might have been killed while taking Portobello? And why did you practically browbeat dear Jolly into procuring an invitation to the Morrows' party tonight, when you know you can barely stand the haughty earl and his equally insufferable friends?"

"All right!" Juliana snapped her fan shut and glared at her friend, dropping her voice to a clandestine whisper. "Perhaps I have followed the man's adventures a bit closer than I choose to admit, but 'tis because I admire his courage and nautical prowess, not because I am enamored of him."

"Perhaps you should be. I have heard he is handsome as the devil."

Juliana had heard much the same, but she had assured herself that it didn't matter. "He could have one eye and a wooden leg for all I care. It is his skill I admire, not his appearance. I know the waters he sails—I traveled to many of those same harbors in my youth. They are some of the roughest, most treacherous seas in the world, yet he navigates them with a master's skill, a skill I have not seen since—"

Juliana bit her tongue. She'd shared much of her past with Meg, but not all of it. No, definitely not all of it.

After that fateful night, Connor Reed's name had never been spoken in her house or on her father's ships. Her father had forbidden it, and the one servant who had thoughtlessly misspoken had been sacked on the spot. The few officers who had been friends with Connor seemed just as anxious to forget the man's existence as her father was. As for Juliana, she'd thought she would die of the pain of Connor's betrayal. She'd prayed to die. But her young, healthy body betrayed her as surely as Connor had. Instead of wasting away she grew stronger. Life went on. She went back to finishing school. She made new friends. She grew into an admired and accomplished young lady. She even fell in love a few times, just to prove that she could. In time the memory of the boy who had broken her heart faded, until the only time she remembered him at all was in dreams of the carefree days of their youth, when they would outrun thieves in the backstreets of Madagascar, or climb like monkeys through the rigging of her father's ship, or play with the other children on the beaches of Tahiti. . . .

"Julie?"

The concern in Meg's voice snapped Juliana back to the present. She looked around at the swirling dancers, the laughing guests, the blazing chandeliers, the musicians. There was no room in her life for ghosts. "I admire the man," she repeated as she glanced down the lushly appointed ballroom to the velvet-curtained entryway where the Archangel was to make his appearance. "I admire anyone who makes the seas safer for my father and other captains. But the Archangel is still a privateer. He sails for money, not honor. And I learned long ago not to put much faith in heroes."

"What?" a nearby voice demanded. "What's all this about 'haste in heroes'?"

A large man with a wide smile loped toward them through the crowd. With his graying temples, commanding figure, and liberally decorated naval uniform, he looked the picture of uncompromising authority, but there was a pleasant befuddlement in his grin which suggested otherwise, as if the world were a chess game where he was always one move behind.

"Not *haste* in heroes, Jolly dear," Meg explained as she stepped forward and gently twined her hand through her guardian's arm. "*Faith* in heroes. Juliana has her doubts about the Archangel. Have you met him yet?"

"Me? Odds fish, no. Dunno a thing about the blighter, save that he's quite a devil with the rapier. Like me in my younger days, what?"

Meg and Juliana glanced at each other and shared an indulgent smile. Commodore Jolly might have had the size and strength to be an accomplished swordsman, but his kind heart would have made him useless in a fight. Though he made friends easily and had moved steadily up the ranks of the Admiralty, there was little evidence that he had ever been in a battle. Currently he worked at Whitehall in an office with a large window and a small desk, where he did, in the words of Juliana's father, "as little as humanly possible."

But while some may have disputed Commodore Jolly's wit, there was no one in the Upper Ten Thousand who doubted his heart. The Marquis of Albany had chosen the aging bachelor and his elderly, bedridden mother to care for his beloved daughter while he was away at sea. And when all the world turned their backs on the penniless, orphaned Miss Evans, Jolly took on the responsibility to make her his legal ward and heir. What he lacked in cleverness he made up for in compassion, and as Juliana watched, he gave Meg's hand a fatherly pat. She thought how lucky they both were to have such a kindhearted guardian.

A commotion at the far end of the room caught her attention. The music died and the dancers stopped midstep, looking perplexed until they saw the velvet curtain begin to part. The Archangel had arrived! As curious as the rest, Commodore Jolly and the two girls stepped toward the curtain along with the other guests. The crowd pressed around them, pushing and jostling the trio with an almost stifling closeness. Everyone wanted to be the first to see the notorious privateer who had won such acclaim. Jolly tried to squire his charges through the throng of people, but when he tried to clear a path the crowd closed around him and cut him off. Meg and Juliana pushed after him, but a tipsy, rotund gentleman stumbled and knocked Meg forward so violently that her spectacles fell off and clattered to the floor.

"No!" the girls cried in unison, for Juliana knew how much her friend depended on her glasses. Meg could not see a foot in front of her without them. Juliana glanced around for Jolly—indeed, for any face she recognized—but she saw only patched and powdered strangers in various stages of dissolution who dismissed her entreaties with an irritated shrug as they hurried toward the parting curtain.

Breathing a sailor's curse, Juliana urged Meg to stand still, and knelt down, prepared to brave the crush of boot heels to retrieve her friend's precious spectacles. But before her knee touched the floor she felt a firm hand grip her arm and draw her back to her feet. "Leave me be. I must—"

Her protests died as a figure dove down and scooped up the spectacles. As he straightened, Juliana got her first good look at the fellow. He appeared to be somewhere in his late twenties and wore the gaudy gold livery and stark white wig of the earl's footmen. But while Morrow's servants were generally clean-shaven, as polite society prescribed, this man sported a bushy, black, and exceptionally well groomed mustache. The comical image of the dark mustache contrasting with the snow-white wig brought a smile to Juliana's lips, but the smile changed to a surprised frown as she watched him lift Meg's hand with a very unservant-like familiarity, and tenderly place the glasses on her open palm.

Meg gave a delighted cry. "Oh, thank you."

The footman held her hand a moment longer than was necessary, then stepped back and gave a smart bow. "*Je vous en prie*, my lady," he replied, then disappeared into the crowd.

Meg put on her spectacles and searched for a glimpse of her savior. "Julie, did you hear? He was French."

"Yes, and too forward by half."

"I am hardly ruined," Meg replied dryly. "The man did me a kindness. Honestly, sometimes I think you are growing as stuffy as old Mrs. Jolly."

The commodore's bedridden mother had once been a high stickler of the first stare. Iron was less rigid than her opinions on class and social custom. Juliana had originally scoffed at her absurdly proper notions of how a lady did and did not behave, but she had to own that it was largely Mrs. Jolly's tutelage that had made her the darling of the *haute ton*. By following the older woman's instructions to the letter, Juliana had gained a place in the politest of polite circles, a position of prominence that had made her father proud. But in her heart Juliana knew that no matter how hard she tried to become the poised and elegant creature whom so many admired, there was a part of her that longed to strip off her expensive silks and satins and run barefoot on a stretch of sun-washed beach. Sometimes she felt as if two entirely different people lived inside her, each pulling in an opposite direction.

"Look, there he is!" Meg gasped.

Two men had stepped out from behind the curtain—the portly Earl of Morrow and a taller, younger man. He wore a dark coat and a plain white shirt bereft of the lace and jewels that normally accented a gentleman's clothing. Yet, despite the omission, he seemed more suited to the role of command than any at the privileged gathering. He stood with his feet apart and his hands clasped behind him, his lean, powerful form as out of place in this fashionable assembly as a fox in a henhouse. No wig adorned his sun-bleached hair, and no powder disguised the long scar that scored his cheek. He made no attempt to hide what he was, no attempt to apologize for his ruthless appearance. He surveyed the crowd with the disdain of a king for his lesser vassals, and his pale blue eyes were as cold and pitiless as the northern sea.

Meg gave Juliana a nudge. "No eye patch. And there is not a peg leg in sight. I daresay he is one of the handsomest gentlemen I have ever seen. It appears you were quite wrong about his looks, my dear."

Juliana could hardly breathe. She had been wrong about the Archangel's appearance, but far more wrong than even Meg imagined. Years had passed, but there was still no mistaking the tall form, the bright hair, and the deep-set eyes that had once looked into hers with so much love. There was no mistaking the face that had turned her dreams to nightmares.

Connor Reed.